A Place to Die

A Place to Die

An Inspector Georg Büchner Mystery

Dorothy James

Library of Congress Control Number:		2010905139
ISBN:	Hardcover	978-1-4500-8270-9
	Softcover	978-1-4500-8269-3
	Ebook	978-1-4500-8271-6

This book was printed in the United States of America.

To order additional copies of this book, contact:
Xlibris Corporation
1-888-795-4274
www.Xlibris.com
Orders@Xlibris.com
72941

For Marjorie
in memory of our father
John Ivor James
1905-2003
and
for Marianne
in memory of her mother
Annelies Meyer Ritter
1908-2002

Oh as I was young and easy in the mercy of his means,
Time held me green and dying
Though I sang in my chains like the sea.

—Dylan Thomas, *Fern Hill*

Chapter 1

Four people had died in the month of December in the Haus im Wald. This was not a surprising number because people came to this house, deep in the Vienna Woods, expecting to die there. At all events, they came not expecting to live anywhere else ever again. The youngest came into the wing called Melanchthon, where there were apartments of various sizes in which they could install their own furniture and their own carpets. They were generally in their seventies or even younger. The oldest were in their nineties. They could bring a few pieces of furniture into their single bedrooms in the Martin Luther wing, but no carpets. They had spent their lives walking through carpeted rooms—the Haus im Wald did not cater to the poor and the indigent—but they would now live and die in rooms where no carpets were allowed. Three of the four who died in December breathed their last in such rooms, but the fourth was found on the morning after Christmas Day, lying on his own thick Persian carpet. He was found by his son, who came to pay his Christmas visit late on that Sunday morning. And late it certainly was. Too late.

1

At five o'clock in the afternoon of the day that she still thought of as Boxing Day, even after years of living in New York City, Eleanor was sitting in the café on the ground floor of the Haus im Wald. It was then that the news of Hans Graf's death began to spread through the community. She was drinking tea and eating chocolate cake and thinking how very civilized it was of the Haus im Wald to run this café every afternoon for its inmates and visitors. Inmates, she had thought, as if they were in prison. Well, in a way they were, especially the ones in the carpetless rooms, who were confined to their one-room spaces by illness, infirmity, and in some cases, a rather dramatic loss of bladder control. This was, she had finally realized, largely what deprived them of their right to have carpets. "Carpets just make our work more difficult," Frau Huber, the housekeeper, had explained when they first brought Franz's mother in. How selfish, Eleanor had thought, until they arrived on Christmas Eve to find Franz's mother sitting in her chair by the window, an unhappy expression on her face and a spreading pool of urine under her chair. "I rang and rang," she said helplessly, adding with a touch of vindictiveness, "but nobody came."

What a relief to escape for an hour from the room with the bare linoleum-covered floor, where the little old woman with gaping mouth and wild gray hair sat, panting after every small exertion; how good to sit now in the warm carpeted café, with the muted radio in the background, the clatter of cups, and the sound of quiet voices. The normality of it all, she was thinking, just like a real café, when the phone rang suddenly behind the counter. The young man who answered it seemed disturbed at what he was hearing. The elegant older lady at the next table had been looking nervously at her watch for a while and now looked questioningly at the young man. When he hung up, she went over and asked him if he would call up to apartment 32 in Melanchthon to see whether Herr Graf was there. At that instant, all the cozy normality faded away. "Oh, Frau Hagen," said the young man. "Herr Graf has . . . passed away."

Eleanor watched as incomprehension gave way to disbelief on Frau Hagen's lined but lovely face.

"It's not possible," she said, and she held on to the counter's edge. "He always comes for coffee in the afternoon."

Well, yes, thought Eleanor, suppressing an inappropriate desire to laugh, but not if he's dead. Guiltily standing up, as if her thought had been spoken aloud, she put out a hand to Frau Hagen. "Can I help you?" she said.

"Do I know you?" asked Frau Hagen in a distracted way, pushing strands of her pale, platinum blond hair from her forehead, but politely giving her hand to Eleanor, as years of obeying the conventions no doubt dictated.

"Eleanor Fabian," she said. "From New York. I'm only visiting—my mother-in-law just moved in—but I've seen you several afternoons this week in the café with . . ." She paused, realizing that the gentleman companion whom she had indeed seen several times must have been Herr Graf. But he had looked so fit, elderly, yes, but spruced up in jacket and tie, white hair neatly combed, quite suave in fact, and drinking a schnapps, she remembered. Most of the tables were occupied by ladies, alone or in twos, with the inevitable, unkempt gray hair—none pretty, a few reading, very few looking cheerful, some staring into space. These two had stood out: they had talked so animatedly, looking at each other with a still-in-the-world self-possession. Eleanor had somehow thought he was there as a visitor, not out of duty, but because he really wanted to see this lady. So he hadn't been a visitor after all; he was an inmate too, and now he was dead.

The shock of his being dead penetrated Eleanor's mind as she pictured him, dapper and alive, the way he was in the café on the afternoon of Christmas Eve, just two days ago. Frau Hagen too seemed to be beginning to absorb the fact, as she turned shakily back to her table, white-faced. The coffee she had ordered was already there, and Eleanor said, "Can you take some coffee?"

"No, no, I must go to my apartment."

"I'll come with you," said Eleanor, thinking, Heavens, what am I doing? I'd better tell somebody about this. But whom? Frau Hagen actually took her arm, seeming grateful for the support, and the two made their way out of the café, through the entrance hall to the right, and to the elevator that served the two floors of apartments in which people had their own carpets.

2

In the carpetless room, Franz was sitting alone with his mother. He was trying to think of something to say to this desperate little woman, who had moved in only a week ago. His wife, Eleanor, had left them half an hour before, saying that she was still English enough to want her afternoon tea and, in any case, they needed a chance to talk to each other. He knew perfectly well that what she really wanted was her own solitary hour in the café. She knew he never really talked to his mother, hadn't done so in the twenty-five years of their marriage. In fact he hadn't done so in all of his own sixty-plus years. So it wasn't terribly likely that he would start at this point, particularly since his mother was now very deaf and had for years refused to wear hearing aids, so that all conversations had to be carried on at foghorn pitch. Franz was a quiet speaker, and Eleanor had often accused him of being so to the point of hostility, since people with perfectly good hearing frequently had to ask him to repeat what he had just said. He would do so, but he was aware that he always spoke at exactly the same volume as the first time so that if indeed they managed to hear him the second time, it would seem that they were in the wrong, as if they hadn't paid proper attention the first time. And in fact, they usually did hear the second time, proving to him that he was right. This tactic had clearly annoyed his mother when she was younger and had realized that he was upstaging her. Now she was past provoking such behavior from him. He had to shout like everybody else if he wanted to get anything across to her.

But what was there to get across any more? thought Franz glumly as they sat opposite each other at the small wooden table by the window on two armchairs brought last week from Mother's apartment to make this room look like home. His cousin Ingrid had organized the move to the Haus im Wald just in time for their arrival from New York for the Christmas holiday. "Oh yes," Ingrid had said complacently, "we brought her television set from home, her wall unit, the armchairs, you see? Quite like home! And look at the view!" He had looked. "Yes, very nice," he had said, his heart sinking at the sight of the snow, cold on the branches of the trees, cold on the field beyond, cold on the benches, "where they can sit in the summer," as Ingrid had said. Her exaggerated enthusiasm still sounded in his head. Of course she was enthusiastic, he thought. Family members were probably always enthusiastic about the Haus im Wald, if the elderly relative could afford to pay for it. They were finally able to off-load the guilt of picturing a solitary old person, likely to fall, to die alone in a house, a seeming victim of family neglect. Well, he thought, I couldn't have her live with me, could I? Not only because I have made my life in a New York apartment. More to the point, I simply can't stand her and never could. I must, however, try to talk to her.

"Since you didn't want the little corner cupboard in the apartment," he said, "Ulrich is going to take it."

"Can't hear you!" shouted his mother.

"You said you didn't want the little corner cupboard," he repeated, and this time he really tried to shout, "though it would have fitted in quite well here. So Ulrich is going to come and get it tomorrow. He and Ingrid would like to have it."

"Ulrich?" his mother shouted, and a change came over her face. "No no no! I promised it to Frau Hartmann." She was enraged. And she could still shock and frighten him with her anger. Her dentures moved up and down as her mouth worked angrily. "I'm not dead yet. You have no right to make decisions. Ulrich must not get the little cupboard. He never did anything for me. Frau Hartmann was always good to me."

A terrible weariness came over Franz. Frau Hartmann had been his mother's cleaning lady for years, and of course, it was reasonable to give her something. But Ulrich, Ingrid's husband, had been helping him clear out the apartment and had obviously coveted the corner cupboard, a pretty little antique piece. It would have been easy and pleasant to give it to him. How he disliked this angry little woman who could still impose her will on him, incapacitate him, treat him like a child. It was the lifelong tussle that often took place now in reverse. "Don't treat me like a child!" she would say when he tried to make some mild suggestion about what she ought to do.

"Do what you like with the damned cupboard," he muttered ungraciously and then shouted, "All right, all right!" He stood up. Had it been long enough? Could he now decently go and fetch Eleanor from the café?

3

Eleanor got out of the elevator on the second floor of Melanchthon with Frau Hagen leaning quite heavily on her arm.

She did not feel she could say that her arm was actually hurting quite badly. She had wrenched her shoulder moving furniture in Mother's apartment, but this seemed a trivial complaint in the present circumstances. She was supposed to be young and able-bodied—sixty-three was pretty young in this setting. Ahead of them, carefully wheeling a walker along the corridor, with all her accoutrements attached to it—walking stick, purse, glasses case—was a lady with a thick waistline and wide hips under a shapeless beige cardigan, white ankle socks over thick stockings, and a tweed skirt with a wavy hemline. Just looking at her back made Eleanor feel quite young, though she could pass for a resident herself, she supposed, as she walked slowly behind her, supporting Frau Hagen.

"Ah, Frau Hagen," said the large lady, turning awkwardly as she heard them. "Have you heard about poor Herr Graf?"

"Yes," said Frau Hagen shortly, stopping at door 21. She fumbled for her keys in her little handbag. "Yes, yes," she said again without looking around. She opened her door and slipped inside without another word to Eleanor who was left openmouthed outside.

"Well, who are you?" said the lady with the walker.

"Oh, nobody," said Eleanor. "Well, that is, I'm a visitor. I happened to be in the café when Frau Hagen heard the news. She seemed a little shaky, so I came upstairs with her. Do you think she'll be all right?"

"Oh, she'll be all right," was the reply. "She's always all right. It's poor Graf I feel sorry for."

Well, yes, thought Eleanor again, he's dead. One might well feel sorry for him. Not that it would help much. Why do I keep having this absurd desire to laugh? To curb the impulse, she held out her hand and said, "Eleanor Fabian." She allowed herself a smile—this was, after all, a polite introduction.

"Ritter," responded the lady, giving her hand without a smile.

The door of the next apartment opened, and a small man—dapper, you might say, though with a little belly visible through his open jacket—smiled at Eleanor. "Are you new here?" he asked, looking pleased at the idea.

"Frau Fabian is a visitor. This is my husband. We live next door to Frau Hagen." Eleanor shook his hand.

"Come in and have a cup of coffee," said Herr Ritter. Eleanor, who had left her own tea to get cold on the table in the café and felt like sitting down for a minute, was also curious to see what the grown-up quarters were like. Inside, she looked around and found herself in quite a spacious room with a rich brown rug on the floor and some good Biedermeier furniture. "What a nice room!" she said. The apartment was in the front of the house, and from where she stood, she could see through the big window to the garden; the driveway curved down to the road through the woods that gave the house its name.

"Do you like it?" he asked. "Well, we've done our best with it—not much scope, you know. Do sit down, Frau Fabian. We used to have a splendid house in Döbling. And now just these two rooms."

"Two rooms are all I can manage now," said Frau Ritter, who had made her way slowly to the armchair by the window. "We are fortunate to be here."

"Yes, fortunate," he sighed. "That's what Hans thought, and now . . . Did you find out any more?" he asked his wife.

Frau Ritter hesitated. "Frau Fabian is a friend of Frau Hagen."

"No, no," said Eleanor, "I tried to explain. I only ran into her by chance in the café and then the dreadful news—I walked up with her, that's all. Shouldn't somebody check on her? She seemed dreadfully upset."

"I'll go at once," said Herr Ritter, jumping to his feet.

"I thought you offered us coffee," said his wife with a deliberate tone that seemed to force him slowly back into his chair.

"Well, yes, I'll make the coffee then . . ." his voice trailed off, and he hopped into the kitchen. Like a little bird, thought Eleanor. How does he come to have this ponderous person for a wife?

"And who are you visiting?"

"My mother-in-law has just moved in. My husband is with her now. I'll have to go back soon or else they'll wonder where I am."

"In the rooms or in the apartments?" asked Frau Ritter.

"The rooms," said Eleanor, with a quick, guilty vision of carpetless rooms, the bleak view from the back windows of the house.

"Oh well," said Frau Ritter without interest. "We don't have much to do with them." How strange, thought Eleanor. Here they are living almost normal lives—big rooms, carpets, kitchens, bathrooms. Wouldn't you think they could visit the room-people? Have them over once in a while, in a wheelchair perhaps, to remind the poor things of what the outside world was like? But perhaps the room-people don't want to be reminded.

"We know," Frau Ritter explained, with a sudden glint in her eye, "that we will be over there ourselves soon enough. We don't want to think about it." So they were the ones who didn't want to be reminded. A mutual ignoring, forgetting, and not remembering.

Eleanor felt her own gray hair being scrutinized, the lines on her face, her own—God help us—thickening waistline. How much time did she have left herself? She was glad to focus instead on the gold-rimmed cups and the silver sugar tongs on the small tea trolley being pushed in by the smiling little Herr Ritter. There was also a bottle of peppermint schnapps and several glasses. "Not for me, thank you," said Eleanor when he raised the bottle.

He poured a glassful for himself under the baleful glare of his wife and said to her, "So, my dear, what is the word on poor Hans?"

4

"A sad day for the Haus im Wald," the tall white-haired woman was saying to her companion as they rode down in the elevator with Franz on his way to find Eleanor. Franz was not a tall man, and this woman was decidedly taller than he was, much more stately than most of the women here, who tended to shuffle through the corridors with bent shoulders. She had a calm, smiling face and thick hair pulled back in a bun, one might almost say a chignon, he thought, since it had an elegant rather than a schoolmarmish look. Must tell Eleanor that. Short haircuts on women seemed to turn into scrubby, wispy things with increasing age. In fact Eleanor herself sometimes had that unkempt, scrubby, aging look about the head these days. "Better not say anything." Had he thought that, or had he said it aloud? Someone had certainly said it as he stepped out of the elevator. He realized that it had been the voice of the tall woman's companion, a smaller version of herself, and also dressed in gray, but a short chubby person, her hair in a bun that did not remotely convey a sense of elegance. "Better not say anything, Sister," she had said with a nervous look in his direction. Sister? Were they sisters? Nurses? Or retired deaconesses of the Protestant church, moved into the establishment for their old age? This was, after all, a Protestant foundation. A sad day for the Haus im Wald? Why? he wondered as he walked along the corridor to the café. There seemed to be a lot of people about. It was the Christmas holiday, lots of visitors, he supposed. He looked out of the windows on the left at the parkway. There were two police cars parked outside the main entrance. Well, policemen have elderly relatives too. And now here was the café that Eleanor was so enthusiastic about. But she wasn't there.

The two sisters had gone into the café ahead of him. He sat down at the only other empty table and wondered where Eleanor could be. If she were only in the ladies' room, she would be back shortly. He might as well have a cup of coffee. But the young man behind the counter was talking to one of the uniformed occupants of the cars that he had just seen. Here visiting, in uniform? thought Franz. The policeman moved on to talk to the people at one of the tables, and the young man came out from behind the counter. Addressing the tall sister, he said, "What can I get for you, Sister Agatha? We'll be closing shortly." A handsome tall dark-haired young man. What was he doing here? A creature from another world, striding about in a polo-necked black sweater and black trousers. He came from behind the counter where the cakes had been sitting all afternoon. There were still a few pieces left—black forest cherry cake, nut cake, streusel cake. This young man works here? A real man in this world of sagging gray wool and wispy hair, humming along with the radio and tapping his foot as the sisters looked at the depleted cake display and ordered coffee. He came to Franz's table. "Last orders for today, sir, we close in half an hour. You moving in with us, sir?"

"No," said Franz shortly. "A cup of coffee please." Moving in? Did he really look that old? Looking at his own reflection in the dark glass dividing the café from the corridor—he was wearing as usual a well-cut suit intended to disguise his slight tendency to a paunch—he hoped he might be taken for a distinguished-looking midfifties type. But of course, for this young man, they were all the same. Gray hair and wrinkles.

He became aware that a policeman was coming toward him. "May I ask you a few questions, sir?"

"Well, yes, I suppose so, why not? What about?"

"Did you know Hans Graf, sir?"

"Never heard of him," said Franz crossly. "What's all this about?"

"There seems to have been a murder, sir," said the policeman mildly, "and we're just checking."

"A murder here? Good God."

"Quite so, sir. Were you here yesterday evening?"

"No, yes, well, only until about six o'clock. I'm just a visitor, you see."

"Ah yes, well, perhaps you could give me your name and phone number where you can be reached in the next few days."

"Well, of course." Where the hell was Eleanor? Did she know what was going on? He would have to get back soon to his mother, but murder or not, he would drink his coffee first. The two sisters had now sat down at the next table. He inadvertently caught the eye of the tall deaconess—he had decided that was what she was.

She inclined her head graciously toward him and said, "Good afternoon. What a pity such unpleasantness should greet you. Are you thinking of moving in with us?"

Oh God, he thought, not again. "No, no, my mother has just moved in."

"Your *mother*?" The raised eyebrow and tone of surprise were hardly flattering.

"She's ninety-four," he said, wondering why he felt obliged to explain.

"Ah, well then, perhaps you won't have to bother her with all this. They live pretty much in their own world, don't they?"

"Do they?" he said. Was he irritated by the lady's calm assumption that he knew all about it or by her relegating his mother automatically to the non compos mentis crowd? She smiled charitably back at him. He wanted to ask her what was going on but, as usual, balked at giving his conversational partner the satisfaction of thinking he actually wanted to talk. He turned rather pointedly to the business of putting sugar in his coffee and then drank it quickly. The young man was clattering away cheerfully behind the counter, washing cups and saucers, cleaning the coffee machine, and humming along with a silly American song now playing just audibly on the radio:

I want to be forgiven

I want to hold you in my arms again.

What rubbish, thought Franz. In a place like this, why couldn't they play real music? But it was pleasant to look at the lithe young man. Once I was young too, he thought, and now I pass easily as a candidate for this place. "I want to be forgiven," sang the young man sotto voce. You're far too young to have done anything really bad, thought Franz nonsensically. Am I losing my mind? Time to get moving. He stood up and said, "Auf Wiedersehen," with the small polite bow that still came naturally to him even after forty years in America, and left the café.

5

Eleanor was sipping her coffee, knowing she should leave, but curious despite herself about poor Hans.

"I didn't really find out anything," said Frau Ritter. "I went down to the porter's desk and asked Gruber what he knew. He said"—she paused for maximum effect—"he now had permission to tell people that Herr Graf had died a violent death and the police were investigating the possibility of murder and would be asking people questions."

"Murder?" said Eleanor and Herr Ritter simultaneously, and Herr Ritter stood up, glass in hand, and walked to the window.

Finally, with a tremor in his voice, he said, "I thought when I saw the police cars this morning that something was wrong. But how? When? Why?"

"I haven't the faintest idea," his wife replied crossly. "You'll have to do your own detective work. I'm not up to it anymore."

"Oh, Hildegard," he said, still staring out of the window. "Hold off a bit, couldn't you? Hans has gone, and in some terrible way. No, I can't take it in . . ." His voice trailed off.

Eleanor stood up. "I must go. I'm sorry. I shouldn't be bothering you at a time like this."

"No bother, my dear," he turned and held out his hand to her. It was small and cold now and fluttered in her hand, and there were tears in his eyes. "Come again," he said. "It's nice to see someone new."

A little snort from his wife was followed by a gruff "Auf Wiedersehen." She did not try to get up. Herr Ritter tiptoed across the floor, as if afraid to make a sound, and opened the door for her. A sense of sadness at leaving this little bird here with such a companion accompanied her past Frau Hagen's door—how was *she?*—to the staircase. The elevator stopped at that moment, so she stepped inside.

"Grüß Gott," said a short and uniformed lady, who was standing in the elevator, carrying an armful of sheets. "I'm afraid it's going up. I'm going up to the storage room on the third floor." She held out her hand to Eleanor and, with a very firm handshake, said, "Huber. I am the housekeeper of the Haus im Wald. I don't think we have met."

Eleanor remembered having met her when they brought in Franz's mother. "Only briefly," she said. "My husband and I are visitors here. Fabian is our name. My mother-in-law has recently moved in.

"Oh, of course," said Frau Huber. "We shall no doubt meet again. Please let me know if you need anything. I am in charge of all household affairs here."

She said this with a self-important air that struck Eleanor as somewhat absurd.

"You have some rather difficult household affairs to deal with at the moment then," she said incautiously and immediately regretted it as Frau Huber flushed an angry red.

"Auf Wiedersehen, Frau Fabian," she said and stalked out onto the third floor, unlocking an unnumbered room on the right. The elevator doors stood open for what seemed like a long time—they were all timed to be slow in this house. She stood inside, looking out at the third floor corridor. On the left were apartments 31 and 32, immediately above the ones she had just left. Number 32 had a cord tied across the doorway with a police sign attached: "Entry prohibited by law to all but authorized personnel." Probably where Herr Graf had lived—and died, she thought, pressing repeatedly on the Close button. Any unseemly urge to laugh had disappeared.

Chapter 2

*There were forty-two residents in the Haus im Wald, or rather forty-one after the sudden departure of Hans Graf. Twenty-six of them lived in the Martin Luther wing in single bedrooms. These were called bed-sitting rooms, and they had chairs to sit on, some small tables, even bookcases, but the focus of each room remained the hospital bed in the corner, a bed which had various contraptions to move it up and down and movable railings on either side. Hanging over the bed within reach of the patient—*patient *was surely the word that came first to mind in this setting—was what in the language of the country was actually called a gallows. It was a triangular eyesore in the room and tended to bob about and draw all eyes to it, but it was a crucial piece of equipment for the weaker patients who still wanted to retain some sense of independence; they could hold on to it and pull themselves up off the pillow, also lower themselves carefully down on to the pillow. Such specially equipped beds were not provided for the Melanchthon inmates, who lived without the more crass reminders of mortality that adorned the Martin Luther wing.*

1

Chefinspektor Georg Büchner looked around at the living room of the three-room apartment in the Melanchthon wing, erstwhile home of Hans Graf. The carpet was thick and beautifully patterned, one of those expensive handwoven carpets, he thought, on which the poor, the needy, and quite likely the underaged had sweated for long hours in a third world country so that rich Europeans could walk through their homes in luxury. He looked at the place where the spread-eagled body of the wealthy Herr Graf had been marked in chalk on the patterns woven by the poor. The rich colors of the carpet were darkened beyond the edges of the chalk with the rich man's blood. The inspector sensed a certain grim satisfaction in himself at this thought. There is perhaps some justice in the world, though not the kind that he had hoped for when young, not a righting of the scales, a giving back to the poor, only retribution, a vicious striking back at the rich. Steady on, Georg, he said to himself, you have absolutely no idea whether Graf was struck by a poor or a rich man. He gathered his thoughts to tackle the problem at hand. It must be the atmosphere of privilege in this refuge for the elderly rich that was bringing out the simpleminded prejudices of his youth. Time he retired. But right now, he had a job to do. The murderer was still walking around, after all, and these old people here would be nervous when word got out. It was already out, probably, since he had begun to deploy his men around the place to check out who was there and what they had been doing around the time of the crime. He had been in the Haus im Wald only an hour, brought in from downtown Vienna to take charge of the case. He needed to cast aside old prejudices against what the Viennese called the "noble" sections of town and quickly get a feeling for this Haus im Wald as it really was.

Just look at the facts of the case, he told himself. He had examined the body in the police morgue on the way here. An obvious assault, a blow to the left temple must have knocked the man to the floor, where he had lain on his back. The first police doctor had put the time of death at anywhere between seven and nine the previous evening, Christmas Day itself, but the detailed report from the autopsy lab would not be back till tomorrow, slowed up by the holiday. There was no sign of a weapon. The face of the victim was still distinguished in death, an aquiline nose, white hair falling over the high forehead with its ugly wound, blue eyes uncannily wide open, a mouth clamped open in rigor mortis and the shock of his own passing. Passing? thought Büchner. Passing where? He had long since lost the comfortable hope that the end of life would lead, as his grandfather used to say, to another shore. Graf had gone, poor old sod, period. And gone in a horrible way that suited neither the man nor the setting. Hold on, thought Büchner, a horrible death suits no one. He was letting himself be influenced already by the atmosphere in this place to think that a pleasant place to live out your years in peace and die in peace was what these people deserved just because they could pay for it. Either everybody deserved a peaceful death or nobody did.

"The younger Herr Graf is back," announced a young officer from the local constabulary. "He went home after finding the body and is here now to talk to you."

The son of the dead man came in and recoiled at the sight of the chalk marks.

Büchner introduced himself, "Chefinspektor Büchner, Kripo Wien. My sympathy."

Graf uttered a small nervous laugh. "Yes, yes, thank you. Yes. It's terrible. He didn't deserve this."

"No, quite," said Büchner, not thinking this the moment to give a lecture on the deserving poor. "Would you like some time alone, or could I ask you a few questions?"

"No, I don't need to be alone. But I would like to get out of here." He gestured vaguely at the chalk silhouette.

"Of course. They've put an office downstairs at my disposal. We can go there if you like. You will want to deal with the rooms later, but for the moment, they are cordoned off while my men check for fingerprints and so on. Later you can help us, perhaps, with a sense of whether anything was stolen."

"I doubt if I can be of much use. I was not privy to his personal belongings or where he kept them."

"Ah, well, let's go downstairs then."

Moving the cord from the doorway and passing the notice prohibiting entry to all but authorized personnel, they walked downstairs to the lobby.

2

Eleanor made her way through the lobby of the Haus im Wald, past the front desk where the porter sat, several elderly ladies trying to engage him in conversation—no doubt on the same grizzly topic, she thought—past the little shop that she had never seen open. It seemed like a good idea to have such a place; all kinds of things could be seen on display through the big glass windows, from shampoo to magazines, chocolates, and artificial flowers. She lingered at the window as she had done several times, held there by the appeal of the real world; she was dreading the return to the little old woman with her gaping mouth and wild gray hair in the carpetless room with the "gallows" hanging over the bed. Eleanor shivered. Somehow typical that the local inhabitants called it a gallows. The American word, she knew from visiting friends in New York who were struggling to haul themselves around in hospital beds, was a *trapeze bar*—a much more athletic sound to that. There was something to be said for the relentlessly positive veneer of the American health profession, she thought.

"What in the world are you doing hanging around here?"

Hanging? Oh dear. Still looking in the glass, she was not pleased to see the familiar tubby silhouette of her husband appear behind her own. "Well, I could ask the same of you," she replied, addressing the reflection in the glass. "Couldn't you even stick it out for an hour with your mother?" She felt an instant flinching in the figure behind her, turned quickly, and said, "I'm sorry, Franz. I didn't mean to start getting at you."

"That's OK," he said. "Where have you been? Do you know what's going on?"

"What do you mean *going on*?"

"Well," he said, "I gather there's been . . . a death."

"A murder is what I heard," she said.

"Oh, so you do know what's going on. Where have you been all this time?"

"There was a lady in the café who was upset. I went upstairs with her."

"Ah, well," he said as they began to walk toward the Martin Luther wing, "I have already been interrogated by the police."

"You?" she laughed. "Why you?"

"Routine stuff," he said, slightly irritated in tone. "They'll probably want to see you too. We were both here when the crime was committed."

"We were? Do they know?"

"Well, I don't know, roughly, I suppose. The cop asked me if I was here yesterday."

Passing the café door, Franz nodded at the young man who was just locking up.

"Have a nice evening, sir," said the young man cheerfully.

"Thank you," said Franz, slightly embarrassed. "And you too."

"Well, you are certainly in with the local populace," said Eleanor. "Don't tell me you've been in the café chatting up waiters instead of sitting with your Mama." Again the flinch on Franz's part, and the instant pang of regret on hers. "Oh God, I'm sorry. I'm just a bit upset by all this." They walked on past Director Schramm's office with its carefully printed nameplate: Dr. J. Schramm, Office Hours, Monday–Saturday, 10-12. Two doors down was another door where a piece of paper had been stuck over the printed nameplate. Typed neatly on it was Chefinspektor G. Büchner, Kriminalpolizei Wien.

"Well," said Franz, "our chief inspector from the Viennese police has a literary name."

"He can't be Georg," said Eleanor. "No one here called Büchner would call his son Georg."

"What makes you think that all the Viennese have heard of Georg Büchner? Even in the old days, only the educated bourgeoisie knew the names of nineteenth century German dramatists."

"But Büchner was an icon of the revolutionary Left."

"To whom?" Franz laughed scornfully. "Only to people above a certain educational level. You live in a middle-class world."

"So do you," replied Eleanor automatically. "In any case, what class do police detectives belong to nowadays?"

As they began to go upstairs, they heard footsteps and, turning, saw two men go into the door marked Büchner. One was a very tall thin man with a circle of dark, graying hair around a bald pate, rimless glasses, slightly stooped, a dark gray suit that hung loosely on him, the other shorter and fatter, short-cropped hair, a round face, a not-quite-clean blazer over rumpled trousers.

"And which is our detective?" said Franz.

"Neither of them looks the part," said Eleanor. "Did one of them interrogate you?"

"Heavens, no, I'm small-fry around here."

And most other places too, came into Eleanor's head, but she didn't say it. What's the matter with me? Why am I feeling so hostile to him? He has enough to contend with right now.

They were on the second floor of Martin Luther at the door of room 12. "You go in first," said Franz. "You know, in case."

"Why me?"

"You're a woman."

"And you're her son."

While they were shilly-shallying, a young uniformed policeman appeared, accompanied by Sister Dolores, the kindly woman in charge of the floor. "I'm sorry, Herr Professor, but Wachtmeister Schmidt has to take a look at each room and have just a word with the residents."

"We have already met," said Franz, recognizing the young cop from the café. Sister Dolores went in first and introduced him to the senior Frau Fabian.

"Good evening, ma'am, just doing a routine check-up." Bewilderment on Mother's face.

"Have to speak louder," said Sister Dolores.

"Just a routine checkup," he shouted, looking around and noting down the number of the room. "You were here yesterday?" he said to Eleanor.

"Yes, up to about six in the evening," she said.

"Same address and telephone number, I take it?"

"Yes," said Franz. "This is my wife."

"Good evening to you," said the young man, saluted politely and left.

"They surely can't imagine," said Eleanor, "that the murderer lives here."

"Murderer?" shrieked Mother.

"Oh, for heaven's sake," muttered Franz. "Did you have to get into it with her?"

"How could I know she would hear?" said Eleanor sotto voce. But in any case, the die was cast. "Mother," she said calmly and loudly, "someone has died, and they are afraid it might be a murder."

3

"I suppose," the younger Herr Graf said, "there is no doubt that it was . . ."—he hesitated—"a murder."

"I'm afraid not," said Büchner. "Severe frontal blow to the head, left temple, hardly self-inflicted or accidental."

A sharp intake of breath suggested that Erich Graf had choked back his usual little laugh. He smiled, though, nervously. "Oh yes, well . . ." His voice trailed away.

"Can you tell me anything about your father, if it's not too painful for you at the moment?"

"Painful?" he hesitated. "No, no, not really. Herr Inspektor, I might as well tell you, my father and I were not close. I had not seen him in a couple of months."

"So you didn't visit him on Christmas Day itself?"

"No, I did not. Since my mother died two years ago this November, we have ignored Christmas, well, in the sense of a family holiday."

"I see. Were you closer to your mother?"

"Yes," said Erich shortly, fiddling with the fabric on the arms of the chair. "Look, I suppose you couldn't rustle up a cup of coffee or something, I don't feel so great at the moment."

"I don't know my way around here very well yet, I'm sorry," said Büchner. "But I keep my own little supply of whiskey, if you'd like a shot of that."

"Normally that would put me under the table, but under the circumstances . . ." Büchner poured two small shots of whiskey. If he could only put this funny little man at his ease, maybe he could actually get some useful facts out of him.

"Thanks." Erich swallowed, coughed like a man who never drank whiskey, and gave his little laugh.

"Your father was an investment banker, I gather, and a very successful one."

"Oh yes," Erich took another swallow. "Success was the name of his game. He didn't have a failure in his life—well, except me, of course. From his point of view, I was a pretty big failure."

"And from yours?"

"I haven't made money. I have in fact lost quite a lot. I am a teacher by profession, if you can call it a profession. He didn't. He thought it was an admission of failure."

"And you?"

"Well, I like to teach. I teach history. I like to stand in front of a class and talk about the past. The problem is that no one really wants a teacher to teach nowadays. You're supposed to organize projects, get pupils to think for themselves. How on earth can they think for themselves about history when they don't know anything?" He had got up nervously during this speech and stood now in front of Büchner, shifting his weight from one foot to the other. He was sweating slightly. Büchner had a picture of him in the classroom with bored adolescents looking at his unprepossessing personage and thinking, What does this guy know about life?

He did a quick change of subject. "We shall, of course, obtain all this information from your father's attorney, but may I ask, do you expect to inherit from your father?"

"Haven't got the foggiest," said Erich. "I always thought he would live forever. He was far better preserved at his age than I am at mine, and I thought he would outlive me."

"You are an only son?"

"Yes."

"Did he have friends? Enemies?"

There was a pause, then he answered slowly, "There was a time—it is in the public record, so you can read all about it—when my father was attacked in the press for having inherited a fortune made from . . . well . . . artworks acquired in the thirties and forties, you know." He stopped and picked at the arms of the chair with nervous fingers.

"Ah," said Büchner, and waited.

"To give him his due, he has since made massive contributions to restitution funds. Probably one reason for his extreme financial caution in recent years."

"Could all this, in your opinion, have been a reason for anyone to harbor a grudge against your father?" Perhaps retribution, after all, he thought.

"Herr Inspektor, I haven't had much to do with my father lately. When my mother died, he had just retired, and they hadn't been living together for ten years. He is . . . was . . . seventy-six years old, you know. About three years ago, he decided it was more economical and less trouble to move in here than to keep up the house and pay for help—he had a cook and various personnel before he gave it all up. He always had an eye on the bank balance. I imagine he had enough money to live here in comfort for years."

"Thus diminishing his assets steadily?" said Büchner.

"Well, yes."

"And now I have to ask you this. Where were you on Christmas Day after about five in the evening?"

"I was alone in my apartment. I kept to myself for the day. No desire to go out pretending to be jolly with a bunch of people eating and drinking too much."

"Any visitors? Any phone calls?"

"No, I turn off my phone in the evenings. No desire to be bothered by the phone."

"So no one can actually corroborate your story?"

"Story?" He finished his whiskey. "Are you saying that I need an alibi?"

"We have to ask everybody these questions."

"Yes, but here I sit, a poor schoolteacher with a motive and no alibi." He laughed. "He was always good at putting me in impossible positions, and he's done it again."

"And what brought you to the Haus im Wald this morning?"

"This will sound strange, but after I turned the phone back on, it rang three times in succession. Each time I picked it up, there was no one there, just a silence, then the caller hung up. I had an odd feeling that something might be wrong here—call it intuition—and I had thought to look in on my father at some point over the holiday, so I just got dressed and came out here."

"What time was that?"

"About eleven, I'd say. They were having their service in the chapel. I went past the porter's desk and up to my father's apartment. He didn't answer the door, so I tried the door handle and walked in."

"The door was open?"

"Yes. I believe people here often don't bother to lock their doors. As you get older, you know, there's more danger in being locked in than in leaving your doors open. Not in this case, obviously." He laughed nervously. "Well, I went in, and there he was on the carpet. I saw the blood on his face and just ran down to Gruber, the porter, who called for help and went to get Sister Agatha out of the church service. Schramm was out of town, apparently. She came up with me, looked at my father, and said, 'I'm afraid he's dead.'"

"Did she turn the body over?"

"Oh no, she just felt for the pulse in his neck. She stayed there, and I just ran out."

There was a knock at the door, and Wachtmeister Schmidt came in carrying his notebook. "Oh, sorry, sir, I didn't realize you were busy." He began to retreat.

"No, no, Schmidt, that's OK. We're pretty much through for the moment. Is there someone who could drive Herr Graf home? He's had a big shock."

"Thanks, but there's a bus that passes the door every couple of hours—it takes me to the U-Bahn. I can get the next one if I hurry. I'm used to public transport, and I could do with walking a bit. I'd like to get out of here. No offense meant. Thanks for the whiskey." He was already at the door, shifting his weight from one foot to the other.

"You'll be at this phone number for the next few days if we need to talk to you again?"

"Yes, yes. Good night, Herr Inspektor, Herr Wachtmeister." Bowing slightly to each of them, he left.

"Schmidt," said Büchner, sitting back and stretching his long legs, "that's a funny duck."

"Is he, sir? Well, I've been round most of the residents. Here's the list, who was here last evening, whether they had visitors, names, phone numbers, etc."

"Excellent." Büchner took the papers but closed his eyes. "I need to think a bit. Do you want to go home now, Schmidt? Can't do much more tonight. Get back by 8:30 a.m. though. I can bunk down here for the night, they said. They'll give me one of the visitors' rooms in Martin Luther. Get the feel of the place. At my age, I'll fit right in." He chuckled. No contradiction from Schmidt, oh well. "Good night then."

"Night, sir."

As Schmidt opened the door to leave, a very tall and stately lady in gray almost stumbled in. "I was about to knock to see if you needed anything, Herr Inspektor. You are spending the night with us, I gather. I'm Sister Agatha, a resident here, but I also help out as an unofficial matron in the Martin Luther wing, especially in the evenings when the day staff has gone. When would you like to see your room? I'll come and get you."

"Right now would be just perfect," said Büchner, gathering up his notes and feeling suddenly hilarious. "Let's be off on the wing to the Martin Luther wing!"

Sister Agatha looked sharply at him. Her glance also took in the two glasses on the table. "We are all very upset about this," she said. "It's a sad day for the Haus im Wald."

"Yes, of course," said Büchner, chastened. This lady reminded him of his Sunday school teachers. "A sad day indeed."

4

Eleanor tried not to look at the way Mother's jaw worked up and down as she absorbed the information that the Haus im Wald had had a murder. They had both often wished that she would get new dentures fitted. Why do we have to be treated to the spectacle of her gums every time she gets excited about anything? Just like the hearing aids. She won't do anything that might make life easier for anybody else. But that was nothing new.

"Mother, pay no attention," Franz said loudly. "It has nothing to do with us. It was in the other wing."

"Other wing? What other wing?" She was shaken and agitated.

"You know," said Eleanor, trying her best to sound calm and reassuring while shouting at the top of her voice, "the wing on the other side where people live in apartments."

"Where I wanted to go, I wanted an apartment, not this room . . . with a gallows," she said, shaking her fist in the direction of the bed. Eleanor contemplated and quickly rejected the idea of giving a brisk pep talk about trapeze bars.

"Here we go again," muttered Franz. "If you had decided to move in ten years ago," he said in his most pedantic way, "then you could have had such an apartment."

"Oh, for heaven's sake," muttered Eleanor, who had long since decided that if-then sentences, complete with could-haves and would-haves, were a complete waste of time with Mother.

"So that somebody could murder me too?" asked Mother angrily. Latching on to a point regardless of logic was not a phenomenon of her old age. She had always specialized in this, and Franz could never just let it go by.

"Not so that you could be murdered, Mother, so that you could have had the kind of apartment you wanted." She stared uncomprehendingly at him.

Eleanor said quietly, "Let it go, Franz," then more loudly, "we'll have to go soon, Mother. We have to get back to the Zehenthofgasse. There's a lot to do there, and it's almost the end of the month. You don't want to go on paying rent there while you are also paying rent here, do you?"

"No, I don't. I don't. Well, you go then. But this murder, who is it? What is it?"

"We have no idea," shouted Franz, already getting into his coat. "Don't even think about it."

"We really don't know anything," said Eleanor. "We'll try to find out by tomorrow. Have a good night's sleep, Mother. Sister Dolores will be in to see you shortly. We'll be back tomorrow afternoon."

"Yes, yes," said the old lady, turning her face to the darkened window. She did not look around again though Eleanor made a pass at kissing her good-bye.

They said nothing to each other as they walked down the one flight of stairs to the lobby. Passing them on their way up, a tall lady in gray and an even taller thin man in a dark suit were also walking in silence—it was the man they had seen before, going into the detective's office.

"Good evening," said the lady, looking at Franz. "I hope your mother is well."

"Why, thank you, yes, she is," said Franz uneasily, touching by instinct the brim of his nonexistent hat. "Good night, Sister."

"Good heavens," said Eleanor, "you seem to know everybody. I thought you didn't like talking to strangers."

"I don't. And I didn't talk to her. She talked to me."

Eleanor decided against pursuing this point any further; she was tired and just wanted to go home. Home? Mother's first floor apartment in the Zehenthofgasse, though denuded of much of its furniture, was at least warm, very warm. She hadn't much liked this when Mother was still there, the smell of the old, of urine, and of stale hot air mixed—was there any way of avoiding this when one got old oneself? Probably not.

The front door of the Haus im Wald was locked. "Odd, I thought it was always open," said Franz.

"We're later tonight. See, there's no porter anymore."

"How the hell," said Franz crossly, "are we supposed to get out?"

"Maybe," said Eleanor, 'we're not supposed to be still here."

"Well, that sure as hell doesn't mean we have to spend the night here." They looked around them uncertainly.

"Can I help you?" A pleasant-faced woman, small and round, with neatly permed hair, came toward them, stopped in her tracks, and said, "Eleanor? Aren't you Eleanor?"

"Well, yes, I am. Do we know each other? Good God, Christa! Christa, what are you doing here?"

"I'm afraid I live here," said Christa apologetically. "More to the point, what are you doing here?"

"Oh, I'm sorry," Eleanor was flustered. Christa was an old friend from her student days. She'd stopped writing to her years ago, though at one time in the past she used to see her every time she came to Austria. She felt guilty about this and had always been a bit afraid of running into her again when she came to Vienna with Franz in recent years. But now? Here? It would never have occurred to her. "I'm sorry, Christa. This is my husband, Franz. I don't think you've ever met."

Christa shook him by the hand. "No, well, Eleanor and I haven't seen each other for years and years." Her forgiving smile held a touch of a reproach.

"You live here, Christa? But you're too . . ." her voice trailed off.

"Too young?" Christa smiled. "I'm two years older than you are. Not all that young. And for someone like me . . ."

"Someone like you?" Eleanor interrupted, feeling Franz's impatience; he wanted to get going. So did she. But still, Christa! She couldn't be rude to her after all this time. "We'll be back tomorrow," she said. "Isn't there somewhere you and I could have breakfast? Remember how we always used to have wonderful breakfasts in that café opposite your place in the Josefstadt?"

"That would be wonderful." Christa still had that look of eager gratitude for attention paid that Eleanor had found endearing when they were both young.

"Shall I pick you up in your room, or shall we meet in a café?" Christa had always lived in an awful mess—seemed to have no idea of housekeeping.

"In a café," said Christa, flushing slightly. "There's one called the Goldene Glocke in Feldberg—I can get an early bus there from just outside. I do have an apartment here, of course." She gestured toward the Melanchthon wing. "Apartment 35, on the third floor."

"Heavens, Christa, very close to . . ."

"So you've heard about it then? I can't bear to think about it."

"Of course not, and we have to go. I'll call you first thing in the morning to find out when you want to meet."

"Yes, call the house number, then extension 35, my room number."

Franz was standing impatiently by the closed door. "Perhaps," he said with ironic emphasis, "your friend could tell us how to get out of here." How rude he was.

"Oh yes," said Christa eagerly. "After six o'clock, you have to leave through a side entrance. I'll take you." They walked back the way they had come, and there, at the end of the lobby beyond the staircase, was a door. "It has a bar on it that you push to get out. Nobody can get in through this door. If you wanted to change your mind and come back in, you would have to ring the front doorbell."

"No chance of that," said Franz firmly, "but thanks anyway for going out of your way."

"Oh, I didn't," she said. "I'm on my way upstairs in the Martin Luther wing to visit someone. She's quite old and doesn't get out much in the evenings. Until tomorrow then."

So, thought Eleanor, at least one person from the grown-up quarters goes to see the children. And they went out into the snow.

5

"Visitors?" asked Büchner as he and Sister Agatha made their way up the second staircase in the Martin Luther wing.

"I believe so," said Sister Agatha. "I happened to meet the gentleman in the café just after the news had broken. His mother moved in only last week. What a welcome."

"Indeed," said Büchner. "Did you know the deceased?"

"I prefer not to discuss it in the corridors," said Sister Agatha, looking reprovingly at him, sideways over the top of her steel-rimmed glasses.

"Quite so, but in your position in the Haus im Wald, you must know a lot of people, and perhaps you could help us."

"I am not a gossip," said the sister.

She was beginning to annoy Büchner, who decided it was time to assert his authority. He pulled out his list and said coldly, "I trust you will be coming to my office on the ground floor tomorrow morning at nine thirty. I shall be officially interviewing all residents in turn."

"Very well," she said, taken aback, but still haughty. They stopped outside the second door on the corridor of the third floor. "These two rooms are reserved for visitors, one single room, one double, each with bathroom and toilet, like the residents' rooms. They are usually occupied over Christmas, but this year, one person cancelled because his mother died here two weeks before."

"A natural death?" asked Büchner, intending to provoke.

"What do you think we are, Herr Inspektor? This is a place where old people come for their last stop on the road to a better world. It is a place to die with dignity."

"Or without it, as the case may be." He could not resist this, but regretted it immediately. The lady had no sense of humor, and at the moment, she held his well-being in her hands—along with a large bunch of keys, which clattered loudly as she looked for the right one and thrust it rather violently into the lock of the first guest room.

The room looked bare and cold to him. It *was* cold. "What is the heat situation?" he asked, wishing he had been a bit more tactful.

"You can turn on your own radiator," she said. "No one has been in here for days, so the room is chilly at the moment."

Freezing is more like it, he thought. It was now eight o'clock in the evening, and since his midday meal at the station, he had only eaten a sandwich brought in by Schmidt. But he wasn't inclined to ask this chilly lady for advice.

"How long are you proposing to occupy the room?" she asked icily. "It seems a little unusual."

"The Haus im Wald, Sister, is certainly an unusual setting for me. I propose to immerse myself in the atmosphere, shall we say, as long as is necessary."

For the first time, Sister Agatha looked uneasy, but drew herself up to her full height in a way that was beginning to look familiar to Büchner. "Can I do any more for you?" she asked, implying that she had already done quite enough.

"No, thank you, I can manage. I look forward to our conversation tomorrow. I might take a bit of a stroll round the corridors this evening, just to get the feel of the place. I hope that won't bother anybody."

"Most of our people in this wing are in bed and asleep by nine o'clock," she said. "Their evening meal is served at six. You won't see much. But I'll tell the two night sisters on these two floors. Strange men wandering the corridors could give them a bit of a fright under the circumstances."

"Rest assured, I will quickly introduce myself." He bowed politely. "Good night, Sister." He'd had enough of her Sunday school presence by now and wanted to be alone and turn on his radiator.

"Good night."

Alone, he tackled the radiator and felt immediately a touch of warmth in the pipes. Thank God, he thought and took his whiskey bottle out of his overnight bag. A quick shot for warmth, then I'll go for a walk as soon as she is out of the way. By the time I come back, the room may be warm enough to sit and read in it. He wanted to look at his own notes and Schmidt's lists.

The light outside his door was dim, but he could see that the end of the corridor was much lighter. Because of the moonlight? he wondered. Yes, he decided as he walked the length of the corridor into the lighter part. He looked through the uncurtained windows at the end. He felt a lift of the heart at the sight of a cold full moon riding the moving clouds of the winter sky. If he'd been a real poet instead of a policeman who wrote poems for fun . . . He heard a door open and a little shriek from somewhere back along the corridor. A short plump woman was standing in the shadows, her hand over her mouth, staring at him with—he saw as he came quickly toward her—fear in her eyes. "Don't worry!" he said loudly and cheerfully. "Inspektor Büchner, Kripo Wien. I'm only a policeman, here to keep an eye on things."

He took his identity card out of his pocket, but she immediately relaxed and started to apologize. "Oh, I'm so sorry. It's just that, at the moment—"

"No, I'm sorry," he said. "I quite understand. Do you usually wander the halls at night?"

"Well, I did hesitate tonight, as a matter of fact, but I said to myself, don't be silly. I often come over of an evening to make a cup of cocoa in the communal kitchen"—she gestured toward a door on the right—"for Frau Winkler, such a nice lady, and I knew she would be upset tonight about . . . what happened, so I came anyway. But then it turned out she was already asleep."

"Are the doors in the wing open, then?"

"Oh yes, the sisters come and go, of course, some of the people couldn't possibly be locked in alone. It's perfectly safe . . . well . . ." She peered nervously in the direction of the stairs. "We always thought it was perfectly safe."

"I'm sure it is, but would you like me to walk back with you to your room? I'm just getting the lay of the land here, and it would be another look at the territory for me." This lady looks a bit on the young side for the Haus im Wald, he thought as she smiled gratefully at him.

"Oh yes, that would be wonderful. I must admit I feel a bit different here tonight. Thank you. You don't seem at all like a policeman, you know."

"Well, I can assure you, I am, and have been for thirty years," he said. "More than my tour of duty."

"Oh, of course, I didn't mean that I didn't believe you!" she said, flustered. "It's just that you're, well, so . . ."—she was looking for a word—"kind."

"Thank you," said Büchner drily. "I try. Georg Büchner is my name." He gave her his hand with a little bow as they reached the bottom of the two flights of stairs.

She smiled. "Quite a name to live up to. Mine is more mundane. Beck. Christa Beck. I live there." She gestured toward the Melanchthon wing as they traversed the main lobby. "Are you as revolutionary as your namesake?" she asked.

"I was a street fighter in my day." Büchner laughed. "A long time ago. The sixties generation, you know, Joschka Fischer and people like that—not that I made it into the corridors of power as he has. Nor have I written a couple of world-shattering plays like my namesake. I'm just an ordinary policeman. I have, of course, lived a lot longer than he did—what would he have become if he had not died at the age of twenty-three? Not a policeman!" He laughed again. "But most of us outlive our rebellious youth."

"I never really had one," said Frau Beck. They got into the elevator and rode to the third floor.

"Beck," he said, running his mind over his list. "You must live right opposite Herr Graf's apartment."

"Yes, I'm afraid I do."

"Then my young colleague will have asked you to come and see me tomorrow. I am talking to people who might have seen anything unusual."

"Yes, I'm so glad I met you first. Now I won't be so nervous."

"No need to be nervous. Well, here we are."

As they stepped into the corridor on the top floor of Melanchthon, a tall gray-clad lady slipped into a door ahead of them at the end, near the window. "That's Sister Agatha," said Frau Beck with a sigh. "She's always snooping about the place. Well, I shouldn't say snooping. She keeps an eye on all us old folks, you know." She laughed self-deprecatingly. "She lives there in the nicest apartment on the floor, the end one with windows on two sides. Her friend lives there too. Sister Barbara. They are retired deaconesses of the Protestant church, you know."

"Yes," said Büchner. "I have met Sister Agatha. She does seem to be pretty ubiquitous."

"Yes, she visited Herr Graf on Christmas Day."

"Did she now?" said Büchner. "Well, you can tell me all that tomorrow. Better get a good night's sleep. Good night, Frau Beck. See you tomorrow."

"Good night, Herr Büchner. Thank you."

He walked at a brisk pace back to Martin Luther and up the stairs, seeing nobody. He was glad to find his room much warmer. He looked over the lists of names and locations that Schmidt had gathered and made a small floor plan of the ground floor and the upper two floors of the two wings. All the offices, the café, shop, dining room, and so on were located on the ground floor; and in both wings, the second and third floors were home to the residents. He meant to read through the notes he had made so far, but after an indeterminate length of time, he woke up to find his head resting on the table. He couldn't seem to do any serious thinking in the evenings these days. And of course, there was the whiskey. Might as well go to bed and get up early. He opened his curtains looking for the moon, but it wasn't visible yet from here. He got into his bed thinking that he would lie awake until the moon came round to his side of the building, but before it cast its silver light on his pillow, he was fast asleep.

Chapter 3

The residents of the Haus im Wald, the ones who could still hear, were usually awakened in the morning by the big black birds that flew around the house, perching in the bare branches of the trees, sometimes digging with their big yellow beaks in the flowerpots on the little balconies outside the rooms of the Martin Luther wing. Not too many of the residents had flowerpots. The little concrete balconies in the back of the house looked shabby and desolate now in winter. Once in a while, a family member would still bring a potted plant, which would be put outside by the staff, and the big black birds would investigate if the earth was not frozen solid. Subzero temperatures discouraged the digging but not the cawing. Louder than any alarm clock, their raucous cries would penetrate the light sleep of the old, merging with bad dreams at first light and forcing a return to the consciousness of where they were living now and would be living till they died. For some, waking was still a shock: so I have come to this. For others, it was a moment of immense relief: I am no longer alone. For a few, there was no consciousness at all, just the vaguely frightening loud cawing that tugged at what remained of their awareness. Happy in this, at least, were the totally deaf, who awoke in their own time, not jarred into consciousness by the big black birds of the Haus im Wald.

1

So rooks have their purposes. Büchner needed to get up early. He stretched now and saw through his window that it must be after six. The light was breaking, and the rooks had been on the wing for the last half hour, urging him to get up and get on with it. He'd recently heard a nature broadcast on the Österreich Eins radio station telling him that the rooks who migrated to the vineyard area around the city were not the villainous birds that most people thought they were. They were often hunted down, their nests in the high trees destroyed. The birds might look ugly, large, and threatening, but apparently they were really very playful creatures who dug up bulbs from the earth and threw them to one another in play. He had himself seen from his office window, which looked out on a park, how they dug up those awful ornamental cabbages that are planted nowadays for flower decorations in the winter. He had never liked these and had been heartily amused to see a pair of rooks tackling one, digging it out, and then tossing it about in their beaks. That was probably why the broadcast had caught his attention. He remembered the sportive pair in the park. And they were lifelong mates, apparently, faithful unto death. More than I have ever managed, he thought again now. That night, after the broadcast, lying in the single bed that he loved and had never wanted to exchange for the marriage bed, he'd half-composed a piece of verse in his head; he scribbled it down the following morning. It often came back to him:

Like rooks who stay together all their lives
And do not ever tire of their wives
Or if they do, they still prefer to stay
Partners in crime or, as some say, in play,
I know that playing and marauding too
Is much more fun
When it's not done
By only one
And yet I cannot give my life to you.

He laughed to himself. He was no poet, but he liked this verse. No, even at his age, a life partnership was something he just didn't want. He ran the verse through his head now to the background cawing of the birds, who sounded more ominous than playful. And it was hardly going to be a playful day at the Haus im Wald. The night had been quiet; he'd slept like a log—he had the gift of sleep, no matter what—but he'd better get going, find somewhere to have a good cup of coffee and a decent breakfast, look at his notes, and be in the office downstairs by eight before Schmidt arrived.

A quick shower and a shave, a clean shirt and underwear, he felt like a new man and would have gone whistling out of his door if it hadn't seemed indelicate under the circumstances. This was the moment in a case that he liked best, when the cast of characters was beginning to assemble and everything was wide open. Everything—he discovered when he got downstairs—except the front door. Still locked? How did people get in and out? Well, it was only six forty-five. One wouldn't expect the porter to be on the job yet. Why hadn't he thought to ask for some keys? A very young man hove into view, seeming to come from Melanchthon. Who's this? wondered Büchner. The young man stopped short at the sight of the inspector, momentarily flustered, and both men said simultaneously, "What are you doing here?"

They laughed, and Büchner took his identification card out of his pocket. "Chefinspektor Büchner," he said. "Kripo Wien."

"Neumann, Michael Neumann," said the young man. "Everybody here calls me Michael. I work here. Sort of handyman cum gardener cum waiter. I do all sorts of stuff."

He smiled charmingly. A good-looking fellow, thought Büchner. How did he come to be working in a place like this? "Well, you're up and about early. Can you tell me how to get out of the building when the front door is locked?"

"Yes, I can. There's a side door back there that opens onto the garden from the inside. But I can let you out here too. I have a master key. That's a bit of a secret in this place, but I can't have secrets from the police, can I?"

"Better not. Well, perhaps you can tell me where I can get some breakfast in the vicinity."

"Not much open at this hour in the village," he said with his ready smile, "but I'll get you some if you like. I'm just going to the café to make some coffee for myself."

"Well, thanks a lot," said Büchner, and they walked back together through the lobby to the café.

Michael opened the door, locked it behind them, and they went behind the little counter into the kitchen. "Have a seat, Herr Inspektor. I won't be a minute." He bustled around, turning on the coffee machine, getting out the rolls, putting them into the oven to warm. "Like an egg, sir? Or even a weißwurst?"

"Weißwurst sounds good. I didn't have much to eat last night. Sister Agatha showed me to my room, and that was it."

Michael laughed. "Yes, you wouldn't get much more out of Sister Agatha. Not exactly your warm and fuzzy type."

"Indeed not. Do you live here too?"

"No, I just come in to work."

"Oh, you seemed to be coming from Melanchthon this morning, I thought."

"I got in early today," said Michael, busying himself with the coffee machine. "I thought with everything going on, perhaps I could be useful."

"And so you are," said Büchner. "Excellent coffee." He drank a few sips in silence. "Did you know the unfortunate Herr Graf?"

"Oh yes, everybody knew him here. I used to see him in the café most afternoons around four. He'd have coffee or schnapps with Frau Hagen."

"Frau Hagen?"

"Yes—she's our star, you know. Ursula Hagen, prima donna in the Vienna State Opera in her day. Don't you know her? Most people of your generation do." What, Büchner wondered, does he think my generation is? "The two of them, she and Herr Graf, were very close, I believe. She must be taking it very hard. She almost passed out in the café when she heard he had died."

"And you, Herr Neumann, how did you take the news?"

"I was shocked, of course. Herr Graf was always good to me." He paused, as if uncertain what to say next, then added, "Well, I don't want to sound heartless, but people here quite often die, you know."

"Yes, a bit of an odd setting for young fellow like you, isn't it?"

"A job's a job. Not so easy to come by nowadays. And in any case, I like old people. I was brought up by my grandparents. I'm used to being around people three times my age."

"And where are they now?"

"*Opa* died a couple of years ago. *Oma* was home with me until I couldn't look after her any longer."

"Oh, does she live here now?"

"Come now, Herr Inspektor, do you really think so? She's in a Caritas home on the other side of town, a very different kettle of fish." A bitter note had entered his voice. "I half-hoped I might be able to work a special deal and get her in here. Maybe Direktor Schramm would have done it, but Sister Agatha wields a lot of influence around here, and she's got it in for me."

"Does she?" Büchner had seen the inside of the "homes" that catered to the poorer elements of society, and he sympathized with Michael. "Well, thanks a lot, young man," he said. "I enjoyed the breakfast."

"Sir, I'd appreciate it if you didn't mention to Sister Agatha that"—he paused—"that I was here so early."

"My job consists of keeping my mouth shut while others open theirs," said Büchner. Michael flushed. "Wachtmeister Schmidt will set up a time for you to come and see me, and we'll talk again." He gathered up his papers and made for the office.

2

The alarm went off at 7:30 a.m. in the half-empty room in the Zehenthofgasse where Eleanor was sleeping on her mother-in-law's couch. Franz was still asleep in what had been his own little room there. Neither of them had even thought of sleeping in the double bed, which had been Mother's solitary sleeping place since the death of Franz's father some ten years earlier. The bed was stripped, and she and Franz, by tacit consent, had turned off the radiator in that room and closed the door.

Eleanor went into the kitchen and made herself a cup of tea. She liked to have a quiet half hour to herself in the mornings and was always annoyed if Franz woke up and started making his coffee before she had managed to drink her tea. It was quite easy not to wake him at home since they had been sleeping in separate rooms for years. I wonder how different it all might have been, she wondered, if we had put more effort into being together. Hell, there he was now, going to the bathroom. She waited for the inevitable loud fart. Maybe, she thought, if you'd kept up the closeness, that kind of thing wouldn't bother you. She sighed, taking a sip of her tea.

"Good morning," he said, coming into the kitchen and blowing his nose loudly. He suffered badly from blocked sinuses.

"Good morning," she said. "I've put your coffee on. How's your head?"

"The usual." He sat down heavily.

Of course, she thought, what else? "How shall we handle the day?" she asked, putting some stale rolls into the oven to warm them up for him. Soon she would have fresh ones with Christa.

"Well, you complicated things by arranging that breakfast with your friend—what's her name?"

"Christa," said Eleanor. Franz always pretended he couldn't remember the names of her friends. His mother had done the same thing to him. For years she had called Eleanor Ellen, though she knew perfectly well what her name was. "Christa Beck. Look, Franz, I have a bad conscience about her. I haven't written to her for years though I knew that her mother had died and she would be having a hard time, and now suddenly, to run into her like this—of all places in an old folks' home—I just felt so bad."

"You're always feeling bad about your girlfriends," said Franz. "Why don't you think of your own convenience once in a while?"

And of course, yours, thought Eleanor. The fact was, she really wanted to have breakfast with Christa. She remembered how, when she had stayed with her in the apartment in Josefstadt after Christa's mother had gone into a home, they had had some very happy hours talking to each other over breakfast in the nearby café, away from the dirty dishes, the mess and confusion in the apartment—so odd that a grown woman like Christa had never figured out how to cook and wash up and keep an apartment clean. Her mother's old cleaning lady had still come in a few days a week just to wash up. Maybe she'd died too and that's why Christa had moved into the Haus im Wald. "Well, anyway," she said, "it's too late to cancel now, and don't you see, she'll be able to keep an eye on your mother for us. She has quite a thing about old people."

"She must," said Franz, "moving in there like that at her age."

"Our age," said Eleanor. "How about it, Franz? Fancy moving into an old folks' home?"

He gave her a withering look. "Well, anyway, what'll we do today? You'll need the car to go out there this morning. I can't face my mother before the afternoon. You'll have to come back and fetch me."

"OK, fine. We could try rolling the carpets now, that's what we intended to do."

His mother wanted Franz to have her good carpets. She claimed to have hidden seven hundred euros for him to get them sent to the U.S. So far they hadn't found the money, and this had been another cause of several shouting scenes at the Haus im Wald.

"Forget the carpets for now," Franz said. "When you've gone, I'll hunt again for the seven hundred euros."

"Funny business that murder," said Eleanor, who hadn't quite got it out of her mind all night. "Makes you think, doesn't it? You go to an old folks' home to be safe, and then you get murdered."

"*You* don't," said Franz. "*He* did. It's an isolated event with its own logic or lack of it, about neither of which we have to bother our heads."

"Well, let's hope it's an isolated event. Maybe they'll all start dropping like flies out there."

"Sure, that'll be a nice topic of conversation for you girls over breakfast. Speculation is not my bag. I wish we had a newspaper."

Eleanor stood up and rather noisily washed her cup and saucer in the sink. There was a time when such a remark would have had her rushing out to try and buy him a newspaper. Forget it. Breakfast with the girls was just what she felt like. The phone rang. "That'll be Christa," she said.

"Ja, hallo, Fabian residence."

"Hallo, Eleanor," Christa's voice sounded distinctly upset. "Could you be at the Goldene Glocke in about half an hour, do you think?"

"Yes, if I hurry. Is something wrong?"

"Yes, things are terrible here. You see, Frau Winkler, my friend"—Christa's voice quavered—"she died in the night."

"Oh, Christa, I'm so sorry. Well, are you sure you want me to come?"

"Yes, I do, please, I'd like to talk to you. And I have to see the inspector at ten. I can get the early bus from here."

"OK, I'll leave here in about a quarter of an hour. See you soon."

"You see?" she turned to Franz. "They're dropping like flies. Frau Winkler is dead. Died in the night."

"Who the hell is Frau Winkler?"

"You know, the old lady she was going to see last night. Lives in the same wing as your mother. We don't know her."

"We don't know any of them, thank God, nor do we want to. My mother is quite enough."

That was true, Eleanor thought, as she rushed into the shower. His mother is more than enough. Still and all, her curiosity was certainly aroused about what was going on at the Haus im Wald. Had she seen Frau Winkler, she wondered, in her days of visiting the place? Christa would be able to tell her. She had sounded quite upset on the phone, and she surely wouldn't relish being interviewed by the inspector. She ran a comb through her damp hair and dressed quickly. No time for beautifying this morning. "See you later, Franz," she called as she ran out of the door.

3

Büchner sat in the office, looked through the data gathered by Schmidt and his colleagues along with the interview list, and filled in names and ages in his own floor plan. Graf's apartment was on the third floor of Melanchthon. There were six apartments on that floor, the three bigger ones in the front, on the left side of the corridor walking from the head of the stairs, and the three smaller ones looking out on the woods in the back with two end storage rooms. Graf's apartment was the middle one of the three front apartments. Next door on one side were Sisters Agatha (73) and Barbara (66), deaconesses; in the apartment nearest the staircase on the other side of Graf lived a Dr. Lessing (75), retired psychiatrist. He would be seeing him this morning. A resident shrink, eh? Couldn't hurt. The end apartment facing the back was empty at the moment; its occupant, Kecht (78), widow, was away for Christmas. In the middle was Beck (66), retired schoolteacher, the lady he had encountered last night; and the one next to her housed a Reverend Pokorny (93), retired Baptist minister—ninety-three and still in his own apartment? Immediately below Graf, there was a couple called Ritter (81), retired art dealer, and his wife (83); on the one side of them, Ursula Hagen (73), retired opera singer; and on the other side, a Dr. Zimmermann (80), retired tax accountant, and Frau Zimmermann (75), still a tax accountant. He would see all these people first, as they would all have been within view or earshot of the Graf apartment on Christmas Day. Were any of them murderers? These septua-octogenarians? With enough strength to knock down a still relatively strong man? Unlikely, but he'd need to see them anyway.

There was a knock at the door, and hardly waiting for an answer, in strode a tall well-dressed man. "Schramm, Direktor. You must be Chefinspektor Büchner. I came back as soon as I could. Cut short my trip. Told them to give you this office and do all they could. Have you got everything you need?"

"Why yes, I've been here since yesterday, and I'm very glad to meet you, Herr Direktor. Do you have a moment to talk to me?"

"Well, yes. Just for a moment. I have to get over to Martin Luther. I'm afraid one of our older residents passed away in the night."

"Another?" said Büchner, raising an eyebrow. "From what I hear, that makes five in December, including Herr Graf."

"This was a very old lady in Martin Luther, Herr Inspektor. Quite a different situation. December and January, you know, are months when people tend to die—the short dark days of winter," he said airily, "memories of Christmases past—and all that. We do our best here, you know, but the midwinter is a hard nut to crack."

The harsh words of the Christmas carol raced through Büchner's head along with its sweet cadences:

In the bleak midwinter
Frosty wind made moan
Earth stood hard as iron
Water like a stone.

"Yes," he said, "a hard nut to crack. But who is the latest to succumb?"

"A ninety-three-year-old, Frau Winkler."

"Winkler?" said Büchner, shocked in spite of himself. "Martin Luther, room 24?"

"Well, you are certainly on top of our circumstances."

"I was sleeping not far away myself last night."

"In the midst of life, we are in death," said Schramm unctuously.

"Are we not? Perhaps I had better just come with you and see what's going on in the midst of the third floor of Martin Luther."

"No need for that, surely."

"Maybe not, but I'll come anyway. My first appointment here is not till eight thirty."

Schramm bowed to the inevitable, and the two men left the office.

He has a regal way of surveying the territory, thought Büchner, as he stepped out briskly to keep up with Schramm, whose head was swaying around constantly, checking the door of the café as they walked past to be sure it was locked, booming a *good morning* to anyone who was about, and smiling benignly at the "Good morning, Herr Direktor" that came quickly echoing back to him. Yes, he's the king, all right, in this place. He smiled to himself, quickly suppressing a smile as he saw Schramm compose his features into a look of sadness and concern on stepping into the third floor of Martin Luther. The door to the nurses' room at the end of the corridor was open, and with a knock, Schramm strode in. “Ah, Sister Maria, sad news, sad news.”

A pretty dark-haired nurse was gathering up sheets in a bundle. She had obviously been crying. “Frau Winkler was a sweet lady. Such a sweet lady. And yesterday she was fine. She was upset at what had happened in the other wing, but she had her dinner here in the common room and seemed quite well.”

“Common room?”

“Yes,” said Schramm. “Each floor in Martin Luther has one room set up with tables and chairs and a little kitchen, where the residents who are still mobile are encouraged to come and eat their meals together. Good for them, you know, not to eat alone.” And to Schwester Maria, “Has all the family been informed?”

“There was no family, sir.”

“No, indeed, I had forgotten for a moment,” Schramm looked embarrassed. “She lost her husband, you see, in the war.”

“I called over to Frau Beck in the other building, sir. She often visited her. She’ll make arrangements for the funeral service.”

“And the doctor?”

Sister Maria held out the death certificate. “Cause of death, heart failure.”

“Did she have heart trouble?” asked Büchner.

“Oh, come now, Herr Inspektor, she was over ninety years old.”

“The doctor said she must have gone peacefully in her sleep,” said Sister Maria.

“A consummation,” said Schramm, “devoutly to be wished.”

“Could I perhaps see the death certificates of the other residents who have recently departed this life?”

“Well, of course,” said Schramm. “All perfectly natural deaths, you know.”

“That,” said Büchner, “is indeed devoutly to be wished. Where is the most recent corpse? Sorry, Sister,” he said to Maria, who had flinched at this word.

“They have already taken Frau Winkler to the funeral home in the village,” Schramm said. “She will be cremated later this week. There will be a small service in the chapel here.”

"Ah, yes, I suppose you have a pretty brisk routine for this sort of thing here."

"That's not how I would describe it," said Schramm coldly. "But yes, we try not to linger over such things. It isn't good for the residents. They have enough to contend with."

"Yes," said Büchner. "Earth as hard as iron, water like a stone."

"What?"

"Never mind. I'd better get back to my first interviews. See you later, I hope."

Büchner took his leave. A cold fish, he thought. Perhaps you had to be pretty hardened to life's sorrows to do a job like this. But wouldn't it be nicer to have a warm, round, comfortable woman in the job? Or a warm, round, comfortable man, of course. Well, warm, round, and comfortable, Schramm certainly was not. But he probably ran a competent show. Still, four deaths, now five in December, and one of them a murder—frosty wind made moan, indeed. As he let himself back into his office, a big black bird flew past his window. Büchner shivered and notched up the radiator.

4

The early-morning traffic was heavy on the short stretch of the expressway along the Danube that Eleanor had to traverse to get back out to the Haus im Wald. The rush hour ought to have been winding down by nine o'clock. However, she felt cheerful as she sat, slowly inching the little rented Volkswagen forward. Really a stroke of luck running into a bit of her own past life in this unlikely place. She had known it was going to be a terrible Christmas, not just having to come and spend it with Franz's mother, but also to deal with the whole traumatic business of settling her in the home and sorting out the apartment. Just to spend an hour now away from that whole range of problems was bliss. And she did like Christa a lot. Why had she stopped writing to her? Well, life in New York had been pretty exhausting in the early years, trying to make a living as a freelance editor and a part-time teacher, riding the subway constantly, just coping with the New York scene, and then later trying to deal with all the unfinished business in her life—why she had no children, why she stayed married to Franz, why she was what she was. Oh, what the hell. She'd just been too self-absorbed, that was the point. But now, at this moment, she was very happy that it was Christa she was going to have breakfast with.

She swung off the expressway and took the small hilly road through the frozen vineyards that led to the village of Feldberg, where Christa had said you could get breakfast. Amazing how such a short way from the racing rush hour traffic, you were in a real village, little steep streets leading up to the church on the hill. Nothing open, it seemed, no one about. Various wine restaurants, the so-called *Heurige*, were closed for the winter. A pleasure, she thought, as she skidded up and down the still icy streets, not to have Franz there complaining that she'd forgotten to ask exactly where the Goldene Glocke was. It was a small-enough village. She passed a pharmacy, a small newsagent, and there it was—a wine restaurant with the usual garden on the side—all the tables removed now for the winter, but bright lights on the inside. She parked easily near the main door. She was so used to parking her little Toyota on the crowded Manhattan streets, this was a breeze. She went into the welcomingly warm Goldene Glocke. Christa was already there at a table in the window. She looked terrible. Eleanor felt immediately how inappropriate her own cheerful mood was. At the same time, she could feel a rising and almost pleasurable curiosity about the strange events at the Haus im Wald.

"You poor thing," she said and gave Christa a hug. "Have you ordered? You look as if you need a good cup of coffee."

"I can hardly believe," said Christa, "that you have turned up at a time like this. It is truly a miracle."

"You still believe in miracles? Why, by the way, are you in a Protestant home—a lifelong Catholic like you?"

"I had more and more problems with the Catholic Church in recent years—its attitude toward women, for example—it's a long story. Don't you remember, even in those days I was reading Dorothee Sölle? I gave you a book of hers, I remember."

"Oh yes." Eleanor had never read it. In those days, a pious German woman theologian hadn't exactly grabbed her attention. Now, perhaps. "Well, we all change as we get older," she said.

"You look exactly the same."

"Nonsense."

"Coffee? Rolls? Boiled egg?"

"All of the above," said Eleanor. "I'm hungry. But you, my dear girl—what a shock about your Frau Winkler!"

Christa's eyes filled with tears. "Yes, I can't tell you. First Herr Graf, and now this."

"God, nothing odd about this, is there?"

"No, of course not. Schwester Maria called me this morning to say they had found her dead when they went in to check, as they always do around seven. The doctor came at once. Said it was a heart attack. They took her away immediately. I didn't see her or anything—not that I necessarily would have wanted to—but so sudden, no chance to say good-bye. I wondered afterward"—she took a sip of the coffee that had arrived—"whether she was already dead or at least ill when I looked in last night." Again her eyes filled with tears.

"That's what I was going to ask. You went up there last night, didn't you?"

"Yes, I knocked and pushed the door open quietly, but she was in bed already, and only the little night-light was on. I assumed she had just dropped off to sleep, so I closed the door again and left. I should have checked. Maybe I could have done something about it."

"Surely not, she was very old, wasn't she? Was she still up and about? I wonder if I saw her at all."

"She was over ninety, but she was very much up and about. She did very well with a walker. If you were in the café yesterday afternoon, you might have seen her. She went almost every day for coffee and cake. It was her outing for the day."

Eleanor remembered a particular lady. "Did she wear a hair band and smile a lot?"

"Yes, that's right."

"Oh yes, I noticed her. She was sweet. She looked so excited picking out her piece of cake." She had left quite an impression on Eleanor because she had seemed so perky—a little woman, quite thin but sprightly, a red headband holding back her very wispy thin gray hair, her mouth chomping up and down over seemingly toothless gums in the manner of the very old, but with a totally cheery look. Yesterday, Eleanor remembered, she had on a bright green waistcoat that rose up slightly in the back because of her bent shoulders. She happened to have been sitting looking directly at that back, so she had observed it closely while the lady had looked all the cakes up and down and finally ordered a piece of black forest cake with cream and then hobbled over to a place in the window, obviously relishing every moment of this event.

"She certainly didn't look ready to die."

"She wasn't," said Christa. "That's what's so awful. It just doesn't seem possible."

"Still for her," said Eleanor, "it's not a bad way to go—peacefully in your sleep—better than a long illness."

"That's what we all say," said Christa, "a nice way to go. It looks like that from the outside. But when you're one of them, when you're on the inside, as it were, it feels very different. You don't measure your death against more horrible deaths. You measure it against life."

"Oh, Christa, why did you do this? Why did you put yourself in this position of being one of them? At your age?"

Christa smiled. "At my age," she repeated. "Have you ever been alone, Eleanor?"

"Of course."

"I mean really alone. Knowing that nobody was there, nobody was coming in the evening, not at the weekend, not even at Christmas. Alone. Period. I couldn't take it anymore. I could never cook. Frau Anker died. (Aha, thought Eleanor.) You're always told, make such moves early before you lose the strength to do it."

"But, Christa, you can hardly even be sixty-seven years old."

"That's OK. They'll take you at sixty-five if they happen to have room. I'd had my name down for three years, and when one of the nicer small apartments opened up in Melanchthon, I jumped at it. Believe me. And I'd spent all those years with my mother. The old are my natural habitat."

"But they die, my dear Christa, and you suffer."

"We all die, Eleanor. I can help a few people, perhaps. I can even be needed here. That's something. Frau Winkler so looked forward to seeing me in the evenings." Now Christa's tears poured. "I can't believe I'll never see her again. I never said good-bye."

"Now, now, my dear, what's this?" A sturdy old gentleman stood at their table.

Christa tried to wipe her eyes. "Oh, good morning, Herr Pokorny, let me introduce my friend Eleanor." He shook her strongly by the hand and looked at her with his piercing blue eyes under a shock of white hair. "Eleanor, this is the Reverend Pokorny. He lives in Melanchthon too. How are you, Herr Pokorny?"

"Well, as you see, still on my feet, still in the land of the dying." He did not seem aware that his usual little joke was not very amusing this morning.

"You've heard the news?"

"Yes, our poor Frau Winkler—and this awful business of Graf. Have you talked to the inspector yet? I'm on his agenda for this afternoon. Not that I have anything to say to him."

"We'll run you back," said Eleanor. "You walked here, I take it?" This old chap, she thought, must be a good walker.

"No, I have my faithful jalopy as usual."

"He has a splendid little electric vehicle," said Christa.

"Yes, my lifeline. Look in later, Frau Beck, if you want company."

"You see?" said Christa. "In the Haus im Wald, I do not live alone."

No, thought Eleanor, but you die alone, even in the Haus im Wald.

5

Franz was not sorry to be alone in the Zehenthofgasse. He had spent many hours in this apartment over the last ten years wishing that he were alone, here or anywhere, only to be away from the piercing, querulous voice of his mother, the voice that never stopped—that's how he thought of it—certainly never stopped long enough to hear anything he might have wanted to say himself. So in the end, maybe from the beginning, he rarely wanted to say anything to her at all. The only moment he could remember when they had been at all close was when they stood ten years ago at the coffin of his father. The shock of seeing him, his face artificially filled out, pink, and puffed up, not the sunken, pallid look of his months of illness, had brought them both suddenly, simultaneously, and quite uncharacteristically to tears. He had put his arm around his mother, remembered the shock of realizing how thin she was; and in that moment, he had thought, Perhaps now. But no, this moment had not been a prelude to some kind of genuine closeness between them. It was real, vivid, and then it was gone. They had both, he supposed, in their own ways, loved that courteous, chivalrous but self-contained gentleman of the old school who was his father. And so, for once in their lives, their never openly admitted disappointment in each other had been overcome in a moment of Schopenhauerian compassion—compassion for each other? For the dead man, violated by cosmetics in death as he could never have been in life? For the human condition, the man who must die? Even now that moment embarrassed him, so naked in its emotion—just as the thought of a particularly boisterous sex act afterward was slightly repulsive and always pushed quickly out of the mind. But push it out of the mind as you might, you never actually forgot it.

He made himself a second cup of coffee and hunted for his antihistamines. His headache tightened like a vise. How can I possibly deal with the situation here, he thought, if I cannot see out of my eyes? He lay down again in the small room that had been his since his father died. It had been his father's study, and Franz liked it. It had a fine old wooden desk with a portrait of Emperor Franz Josef hanging over it and book-lined walls. Austrian history, German history, military history. Of course, neither of his parents had been enthusiastic about his becoming an engineer. Well, maybe if he had made his career here as a Herr Professor on a high-powered technological faculty, but they had no understanding of his having left Austria in the fifties. His subsequent life in a not-very-famous college in the very foreign New York City meant nothing to them.

He knew very well why he had left Austria in the fifties. He'd been disgusted as a young man by the way his parents' generation had blindly settled for bourgeois respectability after the war, blotting out of their consciousness, it seemed, everything that had happened in the previous twenty years. Hypocrisy, he had thought at the time, though he often wondered now whether he was really still in the country that he had emigrated to with high hopes back then. The affluent middle class in the U.S. seemed similarly blind to the ugliness of many political realities of their own day. He was certainly glad to be retiring and to have his last semester in the classroom behind him. Typical of Mother to promise the desk to that silly little Adele, he thought. True, Adele had come often to help his mother. She was a nurse, the daughter of his cousin, but surely his mother knew that Franz himself had always coveted the desk. Franz Josef goes with me anyway, he thought. I am going to pack him up today.

And now there was the matter of the corner cupboard. He'd have to tell Ulrich. Why bother? Why not just ignore the whole thing? Let Ulrich take it away. But then if his mother found out, there would be hell to pay. And she'd be waiting to hear about the seven hundred euros—he must at least seriously hunt for them. He started with the desk. Piece by piece, he looked through the papers. Nothing but very old bills, ancient checkbooks, a few recent bank withdrawal slips of his own. His mother apparently never used this desk. How could she have misplaced seven hundred euros? Well, maybe she'd just made up the story to look as if she was making a generous gesture. No, that wasn't the sort of thing his mother would do. He turned his attention to the corner cupboard. Not very likely. It had a glass front, and there were trinkets on the shelves and little lace napkins and the like. Taking out a handful of the napkins, he found interleaved between them a red wallet and in it a bunch of banknotes held together with paper clips and a little piece of paper on which was written in Mother's very recent shaky handwriting: "For Franz to transport the carpets to America." Why had she done this? Why the carpets and not the desk, for example? Well, he wouldn't look a gift horse in the mouth. They were good carpets. He counted out the notes, exactly seven hundred euros. She would at least be pleased that he had found them. How had they missed them before? She'd been driving herself and them crazy at having forgotten where she put them. But she remembered well enough that she had put them somewhere and for this purpose. Thank God, she doesn't have Alzheimer's, he thought. At least that was one thing he didn't have to worry about inheriting. His father too had been very clearheaded up to the time of his death at eighty-six. More clearheaded than me, he thought glumly, blowing his nose. Neither of them had sinus troubles either. No one, his mother was wont to say, in *my* family has ever had sinus trouble. But, Mother, he used to think, I am in your family.

Getting up the courage to call Ulrich, he was standing over the phone when it suddenly rang. Did he have to answer it? Well, it might be Eleanor. It couldn't be his mother—she had refused to have a phone in her new room because of the cost. How would they keep in touch with her when they went back to the U.S.? they had asked. She had shown no interest in this question. The phone went on and on ringing. Finally, he picked it up.

"Fabian."

"Haus im Wald here. Herr Professor?"

"Yes."

"This is Sister Dolores. I'm so glad you're there. Your mother has taken a turn for the worse."

"The worse? What do you mean?" The pounding in his head intensified.

"We're not sure. After breakfast, we tried to get her up, but she was too weak to stand. She's not speaking to us. We've sent for the doctor." Sister Dolores was breathless. "Could you come?"

"Well, yes, my wife isn't there, is she?"

"No."

"She's gone with the car. I'll have to see how I can get there."

"Thank you, Herr Professor. Please do not delay."

She hung up. Do not delay? What was going on? Where was Eleanor? How typical that she was off gallivanting with one of her girlfriends when he really needed her. What should he do? Call a taxi? Was it that urgent? Weren't they overreacting out there? His mother often stayed in bed in the mornings because she didn't feel like getting up. Maybe they're just nervous because of the other woman's death and that crazy murder. Still, better just go. He fumbled through the phone book for the number of a taxi rank, called a cab, stuck the seven hundred euros in his inside pocket, and put on his coat. What about Eleanor? If she came back for him, she wouldn't know where he was. He couldn't remember the name of the breakfast place. She'd just have to turn around and drive back out there. He scribbled a note: "Took taxi to Haus im Wald. Mother worse" and stuck it on the kitchen table. He went down to the taxi, the vise very tight around his head.

Chapter 4

In the mornings, the front door of the Haus im Wald usually stood open for a while, even in the coldest weather. Only if snow were blowing in over the doorstep did Gruber, the doorman and porter, leave it closed when the housekeeper unlocked it for him. She always unlocked it promptly at eight in the morning and locked it equally promptly at six in the evening. But he left it wide open for an hour in the morning to let in the fresh air, as he put it. Director Schramm, whose office was on the ground floor, had sometimes complained about this because it wasted heat in the winter. But Gruber, a unionized worker, approaching retirement age himself, was one of the few people in the Haus im Wald who seemed impervious to the wishes of Director Schramm, following his own union rules, receiving union wages, working union hours, and maintaining his right to a work environment that suited him. Fresh air was important to his health, he insisted, and when it came down to it, even Director Schramm was not altogether sorry to feel the cold, clear air of the outside world flooding into the fetid atmosphere of the overheated house where some fifty people, many of them not very well, had tossed and turned the night away, dealing with their bodily functions as best they could and opening their own windows, as often as not, if they were able, in the morning. It was a sad day for most of them when they were not able to do this anymore, for the free, fresh, unionized air of the lobby could not reach the physically disenfranchised inmates of the upper floors.

1

It was warmer upstairs, Büchner thought. He had left the radiator on in his bedroom where no doubt it would be turned off by some zealous penny-pincher, but here in his borrowed office, he would keep it on full. Better try to make these people comfortable. He wished he could offer them coffee at least. Wachtmeister Schmidt knocked and walked in.

"Ah, Schmidt, good, got your sidekick with you? Good. Then you can split up and give him the job of completing these lists—the rest of the residents, nurses, etc.—try to get the names of all visitors on Sunday. Is there a sign-in list in the porter's office?"

"No, sir, people come and go as they please."

"Have you talked to the porter?"

"Yes, sir. A bit of a pain, sir, gives you lectures on his rights, and on yours if you give him a chance. He's 60 percent handicapped, he says, can't be expected to do this and that—you know the type."

Büchner laughed. "Which 60 percent?" he asked.

"Not the part that includes the mouth, he has a speech on everything."

"Well, take some time to talk to him right now. See what you can find out. He can surely give you an idea of who came in and out on Christmas Day. He was here, I suppose."

"Yes, double time, of course."

"Of course." Büchner had no problems with this. He was a union man himself. "Make it clear to him that regardless of past practice, while this investigation goes on, everyone who comes in the front door has to sign in and identify themselves."

"That'll take a bit of persuasion, sir."

"Persuasion nothing, Schmidt. Pull rank. Right now we're investigating a murder. Now let's see. Who's coming first? How did you set up the list?"

"Just the people living nearest to Graf, sir—opposite him and underneath. In the order I found them and the times when they could come."

"OK, fine. Go tackle Gruber then—but take your time. The more he can tell us, the better. Oh, and try to track down a young fellow known as Michael—handyman—works in the café. See if he could rustle us up some coffee to offer these characters, and me too."

There was a knock at the door. Büchner consulted his list. Lessing, the psychiatrist—not a bad start, he was looking forward to seeing him. A thin, straight woman walked in briskly, though with the aid of a cane. She had smooth, gray cropped hair, a small sharp face, and bright eyes behind rimless glasses.

"Lessing," she said. "Good morning."

Surprised for a moment, he quickly recovered himself, shook her by the hand, offered her an armchair by the little coffee table in the window, and sat down opposite her.

"Well, Frau Doktor, this is a bad business," he said.

"It is."

"I won't keep you long, just a few questions. You live next door to the Graf apartment, I believe? Were you at home on Christmas Day?

"I was."

"Alone? Family visiting for the holiday?"

"I have no close family."

"Did you hear anything odd?

"I didn't. My hearing is not bad, but normally not too much of what happens in the apartment next door penetrates the walls. That is one of the good things about this old building. If you mean did I hear the screams of the victim, no, I did not. There were people who came and went during the day, but I pay little attention to such comings and goings."

"You are a psychiatrist?"

"A retired psychiatrist, Herr Inspektor."

"Did you know Herr Graf?"

"If you mean," she said with a trace of smile, "am I prepared to present a psychoanalytic portrait of him, the answer is no. I do not live here in a professional capacity, but because I am old."

Büchner smiled. "But old habits die hard. You must look for the neurotic in the people you meet, just as I look for the criminal."

She smiled a little more. "Perhaps we are both looking for the same thing, Herr Inspektor."

"You mean that criminals are necessarily neurotic? But not all neurotics are criminal."

"No," she said. "I mean that all of us—criminals, neurotics, and the rest—are seeking to balance our personal needs against the demands of our society. We look for ways of finding and maintaining this equilibrium. The man who goes too far in one direction and damages society in his own interest, we call a criminal. The man who goes too far in the other direction and withdraws more and more, becoming increasingly unable to live the social life that is expected of him, we call a neurotic. Both are struggling with the same problem—lack of equilibrium in relating to their environment." She had obviously made this little speech on previous occasions, but she produced it with quiet conviction, if with a touch of self-parody.

"I take it," said Büchner, "that when you say *man*, you mean man or woman."

"I am of a generation, Herr Inspektor, that does not feel the need to spell out very gender-specific nuance. When I say *the man*, I assume that the intelligent listener is capable of understanding it as a general term."

"Just trying to prove, Frau Doktor, that I am up-to-date. I am of a generation that has to try harder."

She smiled and went on, "The man who is neither overwhelmed, intimidated, driven into himself by society, nor is on the other hand preying on society, willfully damaging it, this is the well-integrated man. Neither you nor I, in our professional capacities, deal too often with one of those."

"You're probably right."

"Do you consider yourself a well-integrated man, Herr Inspektor?"

The question caught him off balance, as rarely happened nowadays when he was himself playing the role of interrogator. He was tempted to try to answer the question. He would have liked to talk to this woman. But these were the temptations of the aging process creeping up on him again. Better stick to the case. “Frau Dr. Lessing,” he said, “we are here to talk about Herr Graf. Was he a well-integrated man?”

She thought carefully about the question. “I don’t think I knew him well enough to answer that. We talked politely when we met. He was always well turned out, always polite, never did anything noisy in his apartment. He seemed, in Haus im Wald terms, to have been quite a ladies’ man, one of the few men here who might have been held to be an eligible bachelor. In recent times, he sat in the café in the afternoons with one of the resident ladies. I sometimes go there myself.”

“Frau Hagen?”

“Ah, you’ve heard of her already.”

“Did she ever go to his apartment?

“Really, Herr Inspektor, do you expect me to answer that one?”

“You are not protecting the confidentiality of the psychiatrist’s couch. You are taking part in a murder investigation.”

“Of course, you’re right. Well, yes, I quite often saw her on our corridor. She sometimes came up with him after their coffee in the afternoon, I know that.”

“Was she there on Christmas Day?”

“I didn’t see her, but that doesn’t prove anything. I hardly went out of my apartment all day. I didn’t go down for the communal Christmas dinner. In any case, she wouldn’t have been there at the same time as his son. It was well-known that they didn’t get along.”

“But he wasn’t there on Christmas Day.”

“Oh yes, I think he was. I heard him in the doorway call, ‘Ciao, Papa,’ when he left at some point—I’m not sure when. One hears voices from the corridor, never through the walls.”

“You’re sure it was him?”

“How many people called Herr Graf Papa?”

“Just to recapitulate,” said Büchner, looking at his watch. “Between the hours of five and ten on the evening of Christmas Day, you were alone in your apartment.”

“Yes.”

“Can anyone corroborate this?”

Dr. Lessing smiled. “No, I’m afraid not,” she said.

"Very well. Thank you. You've been very helpful." He stood up to indicate that the conversation was over. "If anything else occurs to you, please let me know. And I'll think about your question, Frau Doktor."

"Which question?"

"Am I a well-integrated man?"

"For the sake of the Haus im Wald, we can only hope the answer is yes," she said and left the office smiling.

2

Büchner looked at his list and his watch. The next person was Sister Agatha, at nine thirty. He noticed that the other sister was not down on the list. Funny that. He'd have to check it. He could take a bit of a walk, however, before she came and maybe rustle up that cup of coffee—a little strengthening of the inner man before the redoubtable sister seemed like a good idea. At that moment, there was a knock at the door, and in walked Michael with a pot of coffee on a little silver tray and several cups.

"I was just thinking about you," said Büchner.

"About me?"

"Well, largely about the coffee, I admit. But thank you! Let me just ask you a question since you're here. The house is locked up between six in the evening and eight in the morning—am I right? No one can easily walk in then from the outside?"

"That's right. And there's only one door at that time that people can exit by, past the café and at the end of the lobby on the Martin Luther side. They can go out by that door, but they can't come in."

"So the only way to get in is with a key?"

"Yes, well, of course, there is a doorbell at the front door."

"And where does it ring if the porter isn't there—there's no night porter, I take it?"

"Right. The bell rings in the housekeeper's quarters. That's Frau Huber. It also rings there between one and two, the second hour of Gruber's lunch break—I fill in for him usually between twelve and one. Frau Huber has an intercom and can check who's there and, if necessary, ring through to another floor. Not many people come in after six. That's the end of official visiting hours in Martin Luther, and if the Melanchthon folks have guests, they buzz them in from their apartments or go down and open the front door themselves."

"They have keys?"

"Yes, all the Melanchthon people have a front door key as well as a key to their own apartments."

"And presumably someone in the house has keys to all the residents' rooms."

"Yes, there is a master key in the director's office, and Frau Huber has one, and well, I have one myself."

"What about Gruber?"

Michael laughed. "He doesn't keep keys. Against his principles. Having keys means having responsibility. I'm not paid, he always says, to carry responsibility for other people's property."

"He has a point."

"He's an old fuddy-duddy."

"That may be, but in the present circumstances, he is much harder to point a finger at than, say, you!"

Michael looked hurt. "Surely you don't suspect me, Herr Inspektor." He opened his big blue eyes very wide.

"Don't worry. Right now I suspect everybody and nobody. But where were you, actually, on the evening of Christmas Day?"

"I was visiting my grandmother, of course, in the Caritas home. Plenty of people can testify to that."

"And what time did you leave there?"

"I can't really remember. Oh, I was surely there till eight or so."

"And after that?"

"I went home—it's a depressing business having Oma in a home on Christmas Day. I went to bed pretty early."

"Alone?"

"Alone."

"Well, thanks for the coffee, Michael." Such a boy, it was hard not to use his first name.

"Have you got enough coffee for your next appointment?"

"For Sister Agatha? I don't know if she'll indulge."

"Surely not. If she's coming, I'd better get out of here fast."

"You don't care much for her?"

"Nobody around here cares for her very much, except of course for poor Sister Barbara."

"Poor?"

"Can you imagine sharing an apartment with Sister Agatha?"

"No, I cannot—there she probably is now."

"I'm off. See you later." He shot out of the door as Sister Agatha came in.

"Good morning, Herr Inspektor. I'm glad to see you were interviewing that young man. Not the most reliable of our employees."

"I wasn't interviewing him," said Büchner not quite truthfully. "He brought us coffee. Would you like some?"

"No, thank you. I have a lot to do this morning. Perhaps we can get straight to the point."

"Where is Sister Barbara?"

Sister Agatha looked momentarily flustered. "What do you mean?"

"A simple enough question. Why isn't she here? I asked to see all the residents, room by room."

"But I am here, Herr Inspektor."

"Yes, I do see that. But there is, I believe, another occupant of your apartment, namely, Sister Barbara."

"Why do you need to see both of us, Herr Inspektor? I can tell you all you need to know about Herr Graf from our point of view."

"You have one point of view between you?"

"Yes," she said flatly. "I would say so, yes."

"Well, I'm afraid that's not quite good enough for me. I will see Sister Barbara later."

"I cannot spare the time to come twice."

"That's not quite what I meant. I shall see Sister Barbara alone. And now perhaps you can tell me what you were doing on Christmas Day.

"What was I doing? I thought you wanted to talk to me about Herr Graf."

Büchner sighed audibly. "I have a great deal to do today, Sister, and it will help me a lot if you simply answer my questions."

"Very well," she said icily. "Sister Barbara and I ate dinner at one o'clock in the dining room—we consider this a duty to the community on Christmas Day—then we took a nap. Sister Barbara made a cup of tea at about four, as she usually does, and at five thirty, we were both in the chapel for half an hour. Then we went over to Martin Luther to look in on a couple of residents who have no family—we thought they would be alone."

"Namely?"

"Frau Winkler, for one, but Frau Beck was with her and the so-called Reverend Pokorny. They seemed to be having quite a little party, so we left and went to a couple of ladies one floor down who are suffering from incipient Alzheimer's and had no visitors. We stayed a little while with each of them then came back up here."

"And you came back to your apartment at about, what, half past six?"

"I suppose so. I don't quite remember."

"Did you see or hear anything unusual?

"No."

"And did you see Herr Graf at any time of the day?"

"No. We did not."

"And yet you were in his apartment at one point, were you not?"

"Whatever gives you that idea?"

"Something someone said. Perhaps I was mistaken. I got the impression—"

"Well, it was the wrong impression."

"Sister Agatha, have you any comments to make on the death of Frau Winkler?"

"Certainly not. What has that got to do with Herr Graf?"

"I am asking the questions, Sister."

"Perhaps I can go now," she said. "This kind of questioning strikes me as a waste of time."

"I will see Sister Barbara at noon," he said shortly and opened the door for her, but before she left, he said, "Oh, by the way, you said 'the so-called Reverend Pokorny'. Why did you say that?"

"Herr Pokorny," she said scathingly, "is a minister of the Baptist church. He is not an ordained clergyman of the established Protestant church."

"How does he come to be living in the Haus im Wald?"

"This is one of my own questions, Herr Inspektor. Herr Pokorny came back to Austria after . . ."—she hesitated—"a long period abroad. He is not even an Austrian originally. He has received a great deal of charity from the Lutheran church. More than that, I cannot say."

"The Christian church," said Büchner, "is presumably in the business of charity, even the Lutheran branch of it."

"I suggest that you look to your own business and allow us to mind our own. Good day, Herr Inspektor."

Sister Agatha walked out and closed the door with a bang.

3

"Seems like a great old guy," said Eleanor as they drove the short distance through the woods to the Haus im Wald.

"Yes, he's wonderful. Ninety-three years old and still getting about under his own steam."

"Ninety-three? He doesn't look it."

"That's what everybody says. He's a bit vain about it, of course, and is always bringing his age into the conversation. But that's typical. After a certain point, you want to be congratulated constantly just for being around."

"Priest, is he?" said Eleanor vaguely.

"Heavens, no, not what I would call a priest. He's a Baptist. Not too many of them in Austria. Comes from Hungary originally, a displaced person at the end of the war. I like him."

"Christa, aren't you setting yourself up for constant grief if your best friends are all over ninety?"

Christa's eyes filled with tears again, and Eleanor regretted what she had said. They pulled into a parking space in front of the house. "I'll come in with you for a moment, then I'll have to go back and get Franz."

"No time to go upstairs first. I'm supposed to be in the inspector's office at ten. Not looking forward to it. I've never been interrogated by a detective before."

"No, and you probably never will be again. Don't worry about it."

"No, well, you never worry about anything, do you?"

Where does she get that idea from? thought Eleanor. I spend my life worrying.

"I ran into this inspector last night, actually," Christa said. "Seems like a nice sort of chap. His name is Georg Büchner. How do you like that? Funny name for a policeman. He implied he was once a student activist too."

"Did he now? What does he look like?"

"Not my idea of a policeman—nor of Georg Büchner either. Sort of stooped, the way overly tall men are, and bespectacled."

"So that's the one. We saw him yesterday with a little round, scruffy, sweaty man—he didn't look like a policeman either."

"That was probably poor Erich Graf. Imagine if your father had been knocked about like that." Eleanor repressed a picture of her own father being knocked down and killed by some intruder in his own home. She sometimes had nightmares about this, and usually she was consumed with horrible guilt because in the nightmare, she knew she was the murderer. She never dreamed of actually committing the murder itself, though.

"Good morning, Sister Agatha," said Christa as the tall lady swept past, coming from the inspector's office, inclining her head slightly in their direction and looking like thunder.

"Doesn't look as if she enjoyed it much," said Eleanor.

"I bet he didn't either."

At that point, he opened the door. "Ah, Frau Beck," he said amicably. "What a pleasure to see a familiar face."

"Oh, Herr Büchner, thank you for saying that. This is my friend, Eleanor Fabian."

"Do you live here too?"

"Heavens, no! That is . . . I mean . . ."

"You don't have to apologize," said Christa. "No, she's visiting her mother-in-law who's just moved into the Martin Luther wing. We happen to be old friends."

"Well, Frau Fabian, won't you come in too?"

"Should I?"

"If you've been here a few days, you may have something to add."

Eleanor couldn't resist it, and Christa looked pleased. "Yes, do, it'll make it less frightening."

"I told you last night, there was nothing to be frightened of."

Christa again looked on the verge of tears. "But there is, Herr Büchner. I am frightened. A man has been brutally murdered a stone's throw away from my apartment. Why should I not be frightened?"

"Being frightened won't help. Exercising a little caution wouldn't hurt."

"Such as?"

"Keeping your door locked at night. Not wandering the halls after dark."

Christa blushed. "No, you're right. I was glad enough of an escort home last night."

"Well now, let's go through the formalities. Where were you, Frau Beck, between the hours of five and ten on the evening of Christmas Day?"

"Let me see, at about three, I'd got back to my apartment from the communal Christmas dinner."

"Was it well attended?"

"Oh yes, about twenty people were there, including guests. I came back upstairs with Pastor Pokorny, who also attended. I had a bit of a rest, then at some point before five o'clock, I went round and picked up the pastor, and we went over to Martin Luther. I took a bottle of sherry for myself and Frau Winkler. She likes—liked—a little tipple. Just a drop, you know."

"And Pastor Pokorny?"

"A lifelong teetotaler." Maybe that explains his ongoing sharpness of brain, thought Eleanor.

"We were both there until six thirty, but by then, Frau Winkler was dead tired, I mean to say, very tired, and we left. I went back to my room and watched TV for an hour or so."

"I see. Now, in that time, did you see or hear anything unusual?"

"No, Herr Büchner. Nothing."

"I seem to remember you said something the other night about Sister Agatha visiting Herr Graf on Christmas Day."

"Did I?" said Christa, rather flustered. "Oh, I can't remember. Perhaps she did. One is always seeing her in the corridors. She's often about."

"Did you or did you not see her go into or come out of Herr Graf's apartment?"

"Well, I might have. Yes. I can't quite remember. It might have been when I was coming back from dinner, about three, or perhaps when I picked up Herr Pokorny an hour or so later, but I might be mistaken."

"And Graf's son? Did you see or hear him?"

"No, definitely not."

"Have you ever been in Herr Graf's apartment, Frau Beck?"

"No, no," Christa was looking more and more upset. "I wasn't the sort of person he would have invited."

"Was Sister Agatha?"

"Oh dear, Herr Büchner, I simply don't know. I am too upset today, the death of Frau Winkler, you know."

"Yes, by the way, when you came out of her room last night, when we met in the corridor, what sort of state was she in?"

"Well, as I told you, she was asleep. Lying on her back, her mouth open."

"Did she usually sleep that way?"

"Yes, I believe so. At any rate, that's the only way I've ever seen her sleeping. I didn't think about it at the time. The staff had already turned off her lights, and I tiptoed in and opened her curtains for her. I usually did that before I left her in the evenings—she liked to see the moon when there was one and the sky getting light in the mornings. She took such pleasure in little things, you know. Oh dear."

Christa's eyes again filled with tears, and forgetting that this was an official interview, Eleanor fell into her society role and tried to change the subject. "How did you come by the name of Georg Büchner, Herr Inspektor?" she said. "It must be a great conversational ploy."

He smiled. "You might be surprised, Frau Fabian, at how many people in my line of work have never even heard of the name. Times have changed since the twenties. My grandfather, an old style Social Democrat, gave the name to my father in the days of Red Vienna—as a second name though—and he passed it on to me as my only name. So for my sins, my name is Georg Büchner, pure and simple, conversational ploy or not."

"Sorry, Herr Inspektor, I did not mean to take up your time."

"Yes, well, I'd better get on to the next customer," Büchner said jovially. "And you'd better take care of your friend here." The two women walked out into the corridor, Eleanor with her arm around Christa's shoulders.

4

Franz sat in the taxi, his head pounding. He closed his eyes against the glare of the sun on the snow. Taken a turn for the worse—he hated these silly euphemisms that women used—what did it mean? Suppose it meant that she was now—finally—dying? How often in the last ten years he had imagined her dying, well, not the specifics of it, but getting a phone call one day: "Your mother is dying." "Your mother is dead." And the fantasy carried with it an enormous sense of relief. Never again to have to contend with her in the flesh, to have to hold those nonconversations, to have to justify his existence to her. He had enough trouble justifying it to himself. If she were gone, really gone, wouldn't he feel like a different person? And yet on the occasions when she had really been ill and when it had looked as if she really would die, he had been overcome with a sense of panic, a terrible overpowering headache that felt like an enormous weight crushing his eyeballs. He felt this now in the taxi. He had to pull himself together. Soon he would be there and have to talk sensibly to Sister Dolores. What if, when he got there, she was dead? He felt as if his eyes were being pounded backward, backward into his brain.

"Seven euros, sir," said the taxi driver. "You all right?" Franz opened his eyes with difficulty, fumbled for his wallet, peeled off a ten-euro note from the seven hundred that he had stuffed in his inside pocket, gave it to the driver, and waved him off with his hand, much more than he would usually tip, but all he wanted was to get away from the glare of the sun. If only he were the sort of man to wear dark glasses, he thought, shades, he believed they were called nowadays. A comforting word, *shades*. He stumbled over the threshold of the Haus im Wald and could momentarily see nothing in what seemed to be the total darkness of the entrance hall. As his eyes adjusted, an officious voice from the porter's desk said, "Sign in, if you please, sir."

"Sign in?" he said, confused by this new event.

"Orders from higher-up, sir. Everyone must sign in. Name, time, room you're going to, reason for visit."

"Good God, man, reason for visit? My mother has taken a turn for the worse."

"Name, time, room number, visiting mother, quite sufficient, sir. I'm only following management orders, sir. Not my responsibility."

"No, no, of course not." Franz could just about see the pad of paper pushed toward him, headed Tuesday, December 27. Well, at least if she were dead when he got there, there'd be proof that he hadn't murdered her. Now he had a watertight alibi. What nonsense. He really did seem to be losing his mind. He walked along past the shop and past Director Schramm's office. At that moment, the door of the office next door opened; and he almost collided with his wife, coming out into the corridor with her arm around her friend's shoulders. "What are you doing here?" they said to each other simultaneously, equally ungraciously.

"I brought Christa to the interview with the inspector," said Eleanor, "and then I ended up going in with her. I'm taking her back to her flat. She doesn't feel good."

"It may surprise you to know that I do not feel so good myself," he said. "I had a phone call. My mother has apparently taken a turn for the worse." Now he had said it himself—twice.

"Worse? What do you mean worse?"

"Eleanor, I haven't the faintest idea. Perhaps you would accompany me, and we could find out."

Eleanor looked uncertainly from one to the other, and Christa said, "Please do go, Eleanor, I'll be perfectly all right."

"Are you sure?"

Franz groaned rudely and said, "Look I have to go, whether you come or not."

"I'll come, of course. I'll call you later, Christa."

"Fine. Thank you. Let me know about your mother. I'll worry . . . ," but Franz was already halfway along the corridor. When he looked back to see if Eleanor was following him, he saw an older woman in dark glasses, looking quite stunning, knock at the door of the inspector's office.

"Who's that?" said Franz over his shoulder.

"That is Frau Hagen."

"Who?"

"You remember the woman I told you about—she heard the news of Graf's death in the café and was absolutely shattered. I would love to have had a word with her—to see how she was." Typical. Franz stomped on up the stairs.

"How do you feel?" she asked, following him up. "Is your headache any better?"

"What do you think?"

"I think you are in a pretty bad temper, and I'm sorry I asked."

Franz groaned. This was silly. He had enough on his mind. The immediate question was, how would his mother be when they got there?

"Should we check with Sister Dolores first?" Eleanor said and went into the common room, then into the kitchen. No one to be found.

"Let's just go in," he said and pushed the door open. "Oh, for Christ's sake," he muttered again as they both saw the tall gray-clad figure sitting by the bedside, hands folded and eyes closed, apparently in prayer. "You have come then," she said to them with an unspoken *finally* in her voice. "I have been sitting with your mother because she is unwell. I can leave her now." She stood up as if that were all there was to say.

"But look here, Sister, how is she? I'd like to know."

"You'll have to speak to the doctor. She hasn't uttered a word today, apparently. When Sister Dolores came in this morning, she was lying on her back, her hands clamped on the gallows, as if she were trying to pull herself up. It was pulled right down on her chest. But she was unconscious, or perhaps one should say, asleep. I really couldn't say. They called me to sit with her till you came. And so I did. I shall go now."

"Thank you, Sister. That was very kind. We'll try to speak to the doctor." Sister Agatha bowed graciously in Eleanor's direction and, ignoring Franz, stepped into the corridor.

Franz stood staring down at his mother. She was breathing quietly, her eyes were closed, and somehow it did not look like a normal, peaceful sleep. "What do you think is wrong?" asked Eleanor nervously.

"How the hell should I know? I don't know any more than you do."

"Well, of course not, I just thought you might have an idea."

"Well, I don't. Let's try and find Sister Dolores."

At that point, his mother stirred and opened her eyes. "No, no!" she shouted, fixing her eyes on the gallows. She grabbed uncharacteristically at Franz's hand and, holding it in a tight grip, closed her eyes again.

"For God's sake, find the nurse," said Franz, and Eleanor ran out of the room. The vise around Franz's head was now matched by the bony tightness of his mother's hand closing on his. He tried to pull his hand away. Impossible. The worst kind of nightmare. Held in a grip of iron by his mother. He caught her wrist in his other hand and used all his strength to prize the hand from his wrist. His mother started to scream. The scream tore into his aching head. He would have to stop it somehow.

Eleanor and Sister Dolores came running in. "What is going on?" shouted Eleanor.

"Don't ask me," he said and went out into the corridor, laying his aching head against the cool wall. The screaming toned down into a whimpering and finally stopped.

"What did you do to her?" whispered Eleanor fiercely at him.

"Nothing, absolutely nothing. She seems to have lost her mind."

"They're trying to find the doctor. We'll have to wait for him to come."

"Not in there," said Franz.

"But someone has to sit with her."

"You do it," he said, the pain in his head overpowering him. "I'll sit in here," he said, pointing to the common room. "Please, Eleanor." How rarely I plead with her, he thought. He saw her face soften.

"OK," she said. "Get a glass of water and an aspirin. I'll fetch you when the doctor comes." With relief, he saw the door of room 12 close behind her.

5

Büchner opened the door to a lady, white-faced but composed, with dark-tinted glasses. She was the first of his visitors to look as if she might actually be mourning the dead man. Her very dark gray suit, cream silk shirt, dark purple scarf at the neck, looked carefully chosen. And she had a lovely face. One of those rare women, he thought, whom age cannot wither. A lined face, but beautifully lined. Not a woman who has suffered poverty, he thought.

"I am Ursula Hagen."

"Do sit down," he said. "I'm afraid the coffee is cold."

"Thank you, I have drunk enough coffee today." She smiled slightly.

"I have a few questions, which I am obliged to ask everyone who has been in contact with Herr Graf lately."

Again the slight smile. "Yes, and probably a few that you are not obliged to ask everyone."

"Meaning?"

"Herr Inspektor, you have undoubtedly talked to several people already; and since the Haus im Wald is a place where many people have few interests other than observing their neighbors, you will undoubtedly have heard that my relationship with Herr Graf was close."

"Yes, Frau Hagen, I have heard that you were friends."

"We were lovers, Herr Inspektor."

"I see," he said, taken aback despite himself at the boldness of this disclosure.

"You look shocked. None of the detectives I watch on TV ever look shocked, and they hear much worse things. I assumed you would be unshockable. I thought I should mention this right away, to save time."

"I am not shocked," he said. "But no one had mentioned it."

She pushed back a strand of her well-cut short pale blond hair in a gesture that seemed habitual and said, "Here we are old and, therefore, of a generation that avoids mentioning the unmentionable. It is still, in this house, unmentionable that elderly residents should make love to one another, whether in the marriage bed or out of it. Hans Graf and I, of course, made love out of it."

"Yes, I see." Büchner began to feel that she was getting the better of him and was enjoying his discomfort.

But then she took off her glasses for a moment and looked directly and sadly at him. "It is important to me that you hear this from me and do not pick it up from the innuendoes of others. I cared greatly for him, and I believe that he cared for me." Her voice shook slightly, and he could see that she had been crying. Her eyes, however, were made up in a way that would have made most women look like stage performers who had strayed inadvertently into the light of day. Not Ursula Hagen. She looked, he thought, quite lovely.

"I must," he said gently, "still ask you those questions that I am obliged to ask everybody."

"Go ahead."

"Where were you on Christmas Day, Frau Hagen?"

"I went to Hans' apartment at about eleven thirty in the morning, finished cooking a little dinner, we drank some wine and exchanged presents. He gave me this." She held out her hand with a silver-and-turquoise ring on the middle finger. "No, Herr Inspektor, not an engagement ring. We were too old for all that. But he knew I liked turquoise."

"And what did you give him?"

"Is that important?"

"I am not at the stage," he said, "where I know what is important and what is not."

"Very well, I'm afraid it was a silver-and-turquoise tiepin."

"Why are you afraid?"

"We sound like a couple of teenagers," she said. "It must seem absurd to you."

Frau Hagen, he wanted to say, I am not so young myself. I can imagine . . . He wanted to pay her a compliment of some kind. A quite irrelevant urge, he told himself sternly. Get back to the facts you really need. "So where were you then, after that?"

"We rested after our dinner." She blushed a little as if her earlier attempts at absolute frankness had been carefully rehearsed, and she had now lost her nerve, or perhaps only her vocabulary. "The wine made us sleepy. Then I made some coffee. And then I left, I can't remember exactly what time it was, because he thought his son might come, and his son does not like me very much—or shall we say, the idea of me. The fact is, we have hardly met, and Hans doesn't—didn't—see him very often. I went back to my apartment, watched a little television, and went to bed early, about nine o'clock, I suppose. I was tired. We were going to meet for coffee as usual in the café the following afternoon. But he never came . . ." Her voice trailed off. "I still can't take it in, Herr Inspektor. Who could have done this thing?"

"That's what I'm trying to find out. Do you have any suggestions? Did he have any obvious enemies? People with grudges against him?"

Frau Hagen was silent for a moment. "I don't know. I know nothing of his earlier life, his friends and acquaintances from the time of his marriage. His son . . ."

"Yes?"

"His son didn't get on very well with him. He had been very close to his mother, and well, Hans was a very attractive man. Perhaps there was some jealousy there—the son, on behalf of his mother, if you know what I mean."

"Did his son come on Christmas Day?"

"I assumed he had. Otherwise Hans would have called me in the evening. I just took it that he was there. But of course, I never saw Hans again."

"Was he well liked in the Haus im Wald?"

"I have only lived here for six months," she said, "and soon after my arrival, we became friends. Sometimes I thought people were jealous of us because of this unexpected bonus in our old age. There are quite a lot of, well, rather unattractive-looking people here. I suppose Hans and I cut a different sort of figure, and people don't always like that, you know."

Yes, Büchner knew. He had often seen a dangerously deep antagonism toward the rich and the beautiful, particularly if they were also happy—he was not altogether immune from it himself. This couple, even in old age, seemed to have been all of these enviable things.

"His best friend here," she said, "was Herr Ritter. Have you met him? Lives next door to me. They had been friends for a long time before I came. Nice little man with a highly developed aesthetic sense and a very fat and ugly wife. Oops!" She put her hand to her mouth in a girlish gesture and laughed. The laugh turned into a sigh and tears began to slither down her cheeks. "Herr Inspektor, I cannot cry here. My mascara will run. I put it on especially to deter myself from crying. Perhaps I have told you enough?"

"Thank you. Thank you for your openness. It makes my life simpler. Just one more question. Sister Agatha lives next door. Did she drop in on Christmas Day?"

"Good heavens, no. If there's one person in the Haus im Wald who did not care at all for Hans and, even less, by extension, for me, it was Sister Agatha. She would hardly 'drop in' on Hans any day of the week, still less on Christmas Day."

"I see," he said, taking her hand, a fine slender hand. "Accept my sympathy. This is a terrible thing."

"Terrible?" she said with a little smile, pushing back the strand of hair and looking slowly at him. She walked to the door that he held open for her and, pausing for a moment, she said, "It is the end of my life, Herr Inspektor, that's all."

Chapter 5

Food in the Haus im Wald was a major topic of conversation. The other physical necessities, sex and the later stages of the digestive system, were seldom discussed in the public places of the house, and perhaps not even in the private places. Widespread grumbling about the food provided by the management gave all the residents something to talk about and above all to be angry about, an important outlet since the civilized, well-brought-up Viennese burghers of sixty-five and over were hardly of a type to rage verbally against the dying of the light. But somewhere covered up inside them was, no doubt, the terrible anger of the old that they are no longer young and that their light is indeed dying. It was easy to rage against the food provided in the dining room where a hot meal was available every day between twelve and one and a cold meal between six and seven in the evening. The dining hours alone, which suited the management, were a source of annoyance—most of the walking elderly would have preferred to eat a little later. The Martin Luther people often ate in their rooms or in the common rooms on their floors, and since the Melanchthoners liked to cook in their own little kitchens, the management did not feel obliged to think up more than a very basic menu for which all residents paid an obligatory flat fee a month. They had figured out that they had to eat there at least six times a week if they were to get their money's worth. If they had paid more, the food might have been better; but as in the outside world, energy was expended on grumbling about the status quo, which occasioned little effort and brought few results. In any case, were not the residents of the Haus im Wald allowed to grumble about something? Being old may be better than being dead, but it is an aggravating business when all's said and done.

1

That's some lady, thought Büchner, warming his hands on the radiator. Not the murderer of Graf, surely, though like most of them, Frau Hagen had no actual alibi for the time of the crime. Passion though, passion she had. It gave one some hope. Imagine moving into an old folks' home and running into someone like her. Not very likely though. And in any case, he was no Hans Graf—rich, suave, good-looking, he wasn't. A knock at the door. That would be the Ritters. Well, if Frau Hagen was right, they ought to put paid to any fantasies of torrid passions in retirement. Fat and ugly, she had said. He thought with pleasure of Frau Hagen's little laugh, but quickly composed his features as Frau Ritter pushed her way into the room, leaning heavily on her walker, white ankle socks over thick lisle stockings—the first thing he saw, his gaze drawn downward to her aging legs by her obvious difficulty in walking.

"I apologize for bringing you here," he said. "I didn't realize. I should have come to you."

"Not at all," said Frau Ritter. "I get about. But I need to sit down now. Hildegard Ritter is my name, and that is my husband." She gestured in the direction of the little man who had come into the room behind her and closed the door.

Trim and neat, with a tonsure of suspiciously brown hair around a bald pate, he smiled pleasantly at Büchner, shook his proffered hand, and said, "Good morning, Herr Inspektor. We are happy to do anything we can to help. Hans Graf was our friend."

"He was your friend," said Frau Ritter. "I regarded him as an acquaintance."

"Hildegard," pleaded Herr Ritter and shrugged apologetically at Büchner.

"Perhaps, Herr Ritter, you could tell me something about him. I have not formed much of a picture of him yet."

Ritter looked at his wife. I can see, thought Büchner, that I may have to talk to these people separately.

"It's not easy for me to say much at the moment," said Herr Ritter, standing up and walking to the window. "I was very fond of Hans. We knew each other professionally before we moved in here, and afterward, well, I was very glad to have someone here I could talk to. I am—was an art dealer in my professional life, and Hans was an art lover, a collector himself in a small way. He did not, I think, suffer as much as I did on giving up his own home and selling his collection. But he understood that for me there was a kind of death in all that." His wife snorted. "Hildegard, you can say what you like. Hans understood." He turned to look out of the window. "And now he's gone." A silence fell on the room.

Büchner broke the silence. "I have heard, Herr Ritter, that Hans Graf may have acquired his art collection in ways considered dubious by some."

Herr Ritter turned and looked directly at Büchner. "Herr Inspektor, whatever you may have heard—and people say many malicious things behind other people's backs—whatever you may have heard, and whatever may have happened in a previous generation, I can assure you that Hans Graf made good a thousandfold for the sins of his fathers. I was able to help him in some of these matters, and I know."

Frau Ritter sniffed loudly. "That's enough, Hildegard," said the little man sharply, and Büchner was surprised to see her visibly subside. Another silence fell, and Herr Ritter again turned to look out of the window.

"Perhaps you would tell me, Frau Ritter, how you spent Christmas Day, let us say, after your Christmas dinner and into the evening?"

"We went down to have Christmas dinner in the dining room at one—they make it a bit later than usual in honor of the day—and then there is no evening meal, of course. They go to some extra trouble too—goose and so on—and we decided to go, though originally my husband wanted to cook in our apartment. He likes to cook."

"Yes," said Herr Ritter, turning sharply around, "and I wanted to invite Hans and Frau Hagen too, the way we used to."

"We used to invite Hans, before the advent of Frau Hagen. Things were different then."

"I wish, I wish, I wish," said little Herr Ritter, his voice rising to a shrill crescendo, "that we had invited them. Maybe this horrible thing wouldn't have happened."

"How could it have made any difference? They would surely have left us by three, and the murder took place after that, if I understand what the Herr Inspektor is asking us."

"Yes," said Büchner. "Let's get back to the answer to the question."

"Well, we left the dining room about a quarter to three, went back to our apartment, had a little nap, made some coffee about five, and watched some TV in the evening."

"Did you have any contact with anyone during that time?"

"Contact?"

"Well, did anybody come to see you? Christmas visits from grandchildren? Calls on the phone?"

"We have no children. No, there was nothing."

"So no one can confirm that you both spent the time in question at home?"

"Well, we can confirm for each other."

"Did you both sleep?"

"I never really sleep during the day," said Herr Ritter.

"And often not during the night," added his wife. "I slept very heavily. I do not usually drink wine, but for Christmas, they actually provided wine in the dining room. Unusual generosity."

"Not very good wine," said Herr Ritter.

"Well, did you hear anything or notice anything unusual in those hours? You live, I believe, directly below the Graf apartment. Can one hear anything that goes on up there? Radio? TV? Voices?"

"We sometimes hear"—he corrected himself with pain in his voice—"heard Hans' stereo player, but that was OK. I always liked what I heard. When we went down for dinner, he was playing Vivaldi's *Four Seasons*. As we left, I could hear the poignant melody of the Largo in the Winter movement. I shall never be able to listen to that again."

"Don't be so dramatic, Samuel," said Frau Ritter. "Later when we came back, it was very silent up there. They were 'resting' no doubt."

"As you no doubt proceeded to do yourselves."

"Yes," again Frau Ritter gave that unattractive snort, and Herr Ritter tried to look out of the window.

"You sleep lightly, Herr Ritter. Did you hear anything?"

"I believe I heard coming and going several times—footsteps, you know, the door, and so on. But no voices. I wasn't paying attention. And in the evening, we had the TV on—my wife likes to watch. And it is, I fear, rather loud." Büchner observed that neither of the two wore hearing aids. "I might have heard a thump, as of something falling on the floor, but that was earlier in the day, as I remember."

"When would that have been?"

"It must have been in the afternoon, probably when I was sitting reading after coming back from dinner, but I paid no attention."

"I see," said Büchner. "Well, thank you. You have been very helpful."

"Is that all?" asked Frau Ritter ungraciously. "I hope you had a good talk with Frau Hagen, Herr Inspektor. She and he were very close, if you know what I mean."

"I know what you mean, Frau Ritter. An enviable man, perhaps."

"And perhaps not, in view of what has happened?"

"That's enough, Hildegard." Herr Ritter ran, almost, to the door and opened it. She heaved her bulk to her feet.

"Better get going," she said. "We like to be there early. If they put out the soup before we arrive, it gets cold."

"Ah, you are eating in the dining room," said Büchner.

"Yes, we couldn't very well cook while we were talking to you, could we now?" Again the ungraciousness of the woman grated mightily on Büchner.

"I'll walk along with you then. Chance to get something to eat and meet some residents."

"Not good food, I'm afraid," said Herr Ritter. "We are not a gourmet establishment."

"It'll do," said Büchner, who had an urge to get this large woman out of his office as soon as possible. He turned the key in the lock and walked at a snail's pace, towering over the little man, his wife lumbering ahead with her walker, until they came to the dining room.

2

Eleanor sat at the bedside of her mother-in-law, listening to each rasping breath and looking at her small shriveled face. She remembered a time when Frau Fabian had been quite plump and seemed much bigger altogether. Now she looked so tiny. She was clutching the bedsheet with her little bony hands, and the gold wedding band looked loose on her finger. Eleanor held out her own ringless hand to compare it. She often took off her wedding ring these days. Some sort of a vague gesture of independence, she supposed. Already those telltale brown spots on the back of her hand. A little bit late for independence, especially of the vague variety. Would she too die like this, a little old lady in a "home," loved no longer by anybody? The terrible death of Graf came into her mind. Why was there something particularly horrifying about the murder of the old? Since they were nearer death anyway—they had, as younger people cheerfully said, their lives behind them—you would think that the brutal murder of an old man would be less horrifying than the brutal murder of a younger man. But it wasn't so. Perhaps, like me, she thought, people have visions of their own father, living alone, shuffling about the house late at night, old and vulnerable.

A knock at the door, and in walked a handsome middle-aged man with dark floppy hair, graying slightly at the temples, a ready smile for Eleanor as he stretched out his well-manicured, rather soft hand. "Dr. Hofer," he said.

"Oh," said Eleanor, "Are you *the* Dr. Hofer? The one Mother is so fond of?"

He seemed pleased at this. "I have certainly attended Frau Fabian for a number of years."

"Yes, my husband has told me about you. I am Eleanor Fabian, daughter-in-law. I'd better get my husband. He's resting in the common room. He'll want to speak to you."

She hastened out and found Franz sitting with closed eyes and a glass of water in his hand. Sister Dolores was preparing the table for the midday meal.

"Franz, you'll never guess who's there. Hofer."

"Oh my God, that's all we need." Turning to Sister Dolores, he said, "Isn't there a house doctor?"

"There are several doctors in regular attendance," she replied. "Dr. Hofer is the private doctor of a number of the ladies. He attended them before they ever came here, and they always love him. It cheers them up just to see him, though I don't know, frankly, what he's got that other doctors don't have."

"A highly polished bedside manner," said Franz, "for which he charges them an arm and a leg."

"That, of course," said Sister Dolores, "is none of my business."

"Anyway," said Eleanor, "we'd better get back in there and see him. How's your head?"

Franz gave her one of his withering looks. "No better for having to deal with Hofer," he said. "I'm not up to him at the best of times. I thought they'd have a real doctor here."

"Shh," said Eleanor, "he'll hear you."

Dr. Hofer turned to greet them. "Good to see you again, Professor Fabian," he said. "I'm sorry this has happened now, just when your mother has a chance to relax and feel she's being properly looked after."

"Well, what *has* happened, Doctor? That's what we'd like to know."

"Of course, we can't be sure at this stage. Your mother is suffering from a kind of old-age parkinsonism. It is the cause of convulsive movements, her occasional difficulty with speaking and so on. I prescribed a number of drugs to combat this." You certainly did, thought Eleanor. The bathroom cabinet in the Zehenthofgasse was full of little jars and bottles. One of the reasons Mother had to move into the home was that she seemed quite incapable of keeping track of all these medications. "But I believe she may have had a kind of fit."

"Fit?" said Franz. "What kind of fit?"

"The stress of the move, the various changes in her life, your visit—all these things combined might have brought on a particularly strong convulsive reaction."

"What can we expect now?" asked Franz. "A while ago she started screaming."

"Screaming? What brought that on?"

"Nothing in particular," said Franz.

Whatever did happen? wondered Eleanor. Well, he won't tell Hofer, that's for sure.

"We were told," she said to Hofer, "that when they found her more or less unconscious this morning, her hand was clamped on to that thing," she pointed toward the gallows.

"She was probably overcome by fear and clutched at it desperately."

"What was she afraid of?"

"My dear Professor, you probably know more about her inner fears than I do."

"With all that's going on in this place, murders, sudden deaths, and the like, free-floating anxiety seems to be the name of the game. As I remember, by the way, you recommended this move."

Hofer smiled. "Let us not exaggerate, Herr Professor. One murder."

"Did you sign the death certificate of that other woman? What was her name, Eleanor?"

"Frau Winkler. Really, Franz."

"Don't worry, Frau Fabian." Hofer's smile was tighter than before. "Your husband is upset. I did not attend Frau Winkler. I am a visiting doctor here, not an official house doctor. I come because my patients ask me to." And, thought Eleanor, because they have plenty of money in the bank. "I gave your mother an injection earlier, a mild tranquilizer. Hopefully, she will sleep and will have forgotten all about this episode when she wakes up. And"—he turned to Franz with a small bow on his way out—"you may certainly talk to the doctor who signed Frau Winkler's death certificate, though I am not sure what relevance that has. Good day to you both."

"So where does that leave us?" said Franz.

"Well, we can't do much but wait and see how she is when she wakes up."

"That Hofer is the pits."

"Franz, your mother adores him. She always tries to get her hair done just before he comes to see her. What's wrong with that? Why shouldn't an old woman get a bit of a lift out of a doctor's visit?"

"She got a bit of a lift, and he got thousands over the years. You forget, I've seen the bank statements and the bills."

"Chances are an old woman has to pay to get a bit of a lift. Who would pay court to your mother for nothing?"

"Are you trying to tell me that this was an erotic attachment on the part of my mother? That's sick."

"Sick? Who's to say what's sick and what's not sick?"

"Look, I'm not up to this sort of discussion right now."

You rarely are, thought Eleanor. "Why don't you go down and see if you can find something to eat for lunch. I had a huge breakfast with Christa. I'll stay here with Mother and hope to catch another doctor."

"Well, OK. I'll do that."

Eleanor watched him stalk stiffly out of the door. She looked again at the taut face on the pillow. Two people stiff with dislike of each other. No wonder Mother fell for the soft and supple movements of the charming Dr. Hofer. Eleanor reached out and tried to stroke the clawlike hand on the sheet, but as she gently touched it with her fingers, it twitched and jumped away. She sighed and settled down to wait.

3

Before they reached the dining room, Büchner excused himself and went to the men's room. He had no wish to eat his lunch with Frau Ritter, though he would have quite liked to talk some more to her husband. He looked back as he turned the corner and saw her appearing to remonstrate with him; the little man turned on his heel and disappeared in the direction of Melanchthon. He seemed to be genuinely upset at the loss of the dead man. No wonder he didn't feel like lunch. Büchner, however, was quite hungry.

Michael was in the men's room. The two men stood side by side at the urinal.

"Not busy in the dining room?" said Büchner.

"Not my job," said Michael. "I'm going to get the café ready for the afternoon. If you've finished for now in your office, I'll pick up the coffee cups."

"Any chance," said Büchner as they washed their hands, "of some fresh coffee in the room for two o'clock?"

"Sure. Glad to oblige."

Büchner went on to the dining room, wondering whose company he might seek out—or be landed with.

He stood at the door looking at the tables filled with elderly people. Usually, when he walked into a restaurant—he ate in a lot of restaurants and usually wanted to eat alone—he would see just a conglomeration of chairs and tables and bodies and movement. All that stood out was the empty chair he wanted, or preferably the empty table. Here, he had a vital interest in the inhabitants of the room; and as he stood there, he could feel his head organizing them into those he already knew, those he ought to get to know, such as the short gray-clad lady sitting opposite Sister Agatha, those who were completely unknown quantities—and those who were not there. He realized that he was scanning the faces hoping to see the lovely Frau Hagen. Unrealistic. She undoubtedly felt no more like eating in company than Herr Ritter did. Two vacant seats swam into the foreground of his gaze, one next to Frau Dr. Lessing, the other opposite Frau Ritter. He made straight for Dr. Lessing.

"May I?" he said.

"Please do join us," said Dr. Lessing. "May I introduce Herr Dr. Zimmermann, Frau Zimmermann, neighbors in Melanchthon, and this gentleman is Professor Fabian, a visitor in our establishment. Chefinspektor Büchner, Kripo Wien."

Büchner shook hands all round and sat down in the empty place at the head of the table, Dr. Lessing on his right and the visiting Professor Fabian on his left. Soup was just being served, and Büchner was glad to see that it was *Frittatensuppe*, one of his favorites, and it was steaming hot. "Nothing like a hot soup," he said cheerfully.

Franz was looking around nervously. "Do you have a napkin?" he asked Büchner.

"No, apparently not."

"Ah," said Dr. Lessing. "We must ask for a couple for you. This is one of those antiquated establishments where we all have individual cloth napkins, and they are placed in little plastic envelopes with our names on them outside the door. We collect them as we come in and leave them there when we go out."

Büchner thought squeamishly of his childhood where napkins had to last a week, and by the end of the week, they lay on the table in their little rings, exhibiting the ugly traces of the week's meals—no matter how you folded them, by the end of the week, you couldn't hide the smears of gravy, jam, whatever. Not a pretty sight. The waitress brought two paper napkins for the guests. That's more like it, thought Büchner.

"You are thinking of moving into the Haus im Wald?" he said to the other guest, his neighbor on the left.

Franz looked crossly at him. "No, are you?" he said rudely.

Dr. Lessing intervened soothingly. "Professor Fabian is, I think, at that stage in his life where he does not want to be reminded that such a thing could happen to him."

"I'm sorry," said Franz. "I have a stunning headache, and I shouldn't be inflicting myself on other people. But I thought some food might help."

"Bringing your mother in here was undoubtedly a stressful thing," said Dr. Lessing.

"My headaches," said Franz stiffly, "are caused by chronic sinus infection."

"Ah, yes," said Dr. Lessing, concentrating on her soup.

"I don't suppose," said Büchner, "that you can say that with impunity to a psychoanalyst."

"You are a psychoanalyst?" said Franz.

"Was, I am now very much retired. So you can say anything you like to me."

"I don't buy the notion," said Franz, "that one is responsible for one's own physical pain. A doctor in New York once said to me, 'Take more responsibility for your headache and less aspirin.' Absolute rubbish. Feeling responsible for it makes it worse, not better. That kind of thing just makes you reach for the aspirin bottle."

"And does that help, Professor?" said Dr. Lessing. "How many aspirins have you taken today?"

Büchner laughed, as did Frau Zimmermann. Herr Dr. Zimmermann, who wore hearing aids in both ears, seemed to be paying no attention to the conversation. The second course had arrived, a slice of roast pork in a gravy that looked none too appetizing.

"Sorry about the food," said Dr. Lessing.

"It's food," said Büchner. "Do you eat here often?"

"About six times a week. Otherwise, I cook for myself."

"You like to cook? I don't," said Büchner.

"Most of us here," said Frau Zimmermann, a cheerful looking lady with a crop of well-coiffed blond curls, sitting on Franz's left, "make our own meals a lot of the time. Have you tried dropping wheat products from your diet, Herr Professor? There are people who get rid of headaches that way."

Büchner saw him turn, visibly annoyed, to look at her, and he took the opportunity to speak quietly to Dr. Lessing. "I've been thinking," he said, "of your definition of a well-integrated man. In my job, I see so many isolated individuals, neurotic, I would say, certainly alienated. One has to assume that with so many neurotic individuals about, society itself must be neurotic. In which case a man who is well-integrated into it may have to be neurotic. A sane man would not want to be integrated into a madhouse."

"It is our job," said Dr. Lessing, "yours and mine, to try to stop society tipping over into the madhouse, to keep the balance of the sane, I by helping the neurotic to maintain reasonable contact with society, not fleeing it nor overwhelmed by it, and you by removing the criminal to a place where he cannot overturn standard social strictures and harm his fellow men. We try to increase the critical mass of the well integrated."

Franz, Büchner noticed, had quickly given up listening to Frau Zimmermann and caught the end of the exchange between the inspector and Dr. Lessing. He finished his meal quickly and pushed back his chair. "If you'll excuse me," he said, "I'm not well enough integrated for this conversation."

"I'm sorry," said Büchner. "I would have been interested to know where you place the role of professor on the sanity spectrum."

"You'd better talk to my wife. She goes in for that kind of conversation."

"Your wife? Was that the lady I met this morning with Frau Beck?"

"That's right. We are both visiting my mother. I really must go. She is not at all well today." He bowed to the table and left in a hurry.

"Not exactly a charming man," said Dr. Lessing. "But here *is* one, doing his daily rounds. You'll have met Herr Direktor Schramm?"

The director greeted the table, "Everything all right?" and then said to Büchner, "Getting all you want, Herr Inspektor?"

"Oh, certainly," said Büchner, digging his spoon into what looked like a mess of tapioca. "Always liked tapioca at school, Herr Direktor, we used to call it frogspawn."

"I mean are you getting all the help you want in your work?" said Schramm, a shade more coldly.

"Certainly, but I look forward to our little talk. If you have a chance at the end of the day, perhaps I could wrap up some points with you. Say four thirty?"

"Very well, till then." He moved on to the next table.

"A well-integrated man?" he asked Dr. Lessing.

"I'm really not sure. Well organized, well educated, well preserved, well dressed, but well integrated? I think one would have to take the question very seriously in his case. But I must take my leave. A friend of mine is coming to drive me to a concert this afternoon. I am unfortunately now dependent on the kindness of friends to get about. Frau Zimmermann still drives, you know, such a boon."

"Oh yes," said Frau Zimmermann. "I couldn't live without it."

"The day may come . . ." said Dr. Lessing.

"I try to think positively," said Frau Zimmermann. "What is your concert?"

"The Salzburg soloists are playing chamber music this afternoon in the Brahms Room of the Musikverein. Wonderful young people."

"Well," said Büchner, "I have to get on to more mundane things." They all stood up and walked out of the room behind the affable Director Schramm. Was he, thought Büchner, one of the well-integrated center? Or was he on the neurotic, surely not criminal fringe? And what about the others? He could hardly hope in one morning to have got very far with his search for the person who was upsetting the equilibrium in this social microcosm, the Haus im Wald. And his afternoon guests, Pastor Pokorny and Sister Barbara, were not very likely customers, though Pokorny, it would seem, had a less-than-simple past. But who, in that generation, didn't? He would have liked to take a short nap like everyone else in the house. He could pop up to his room in Martin Luther for ten minutes. On the way out of the dining room, he stopped at the table with the box of named plastic envelopes and flipped through them. Somehow macabre that Hans Graf's was still there. On an impulse, he took it, thrust it into his inside pocket, and headed back to Martin Luther.

4

Franz was glad to be away from the dining room. The food and several glasses of water that he had drunk didn't seem to have done much for his headache, and now the roast pork and potato dumpling sat heavily on his stomach. He needed to take a walk in the fresh air perhaps—but he had to go upstairs first and see what was happening. When he went into room 12 in Martin Luther, Eleanor was still sitting there, and his mother still lying there, breathing loudly, her mouth slightly open, her eyes closed.

"Nothing new?" he asked.

"No. You? Have a good lunch?"

"No," said Franz. "The food is mediocre, and the company irritating."

"Why the latter?"

"I don't expect to be regaled with psychobabble in the depths of the Vienna Woods. If I wanted that, I'd go to California for Christmas."

"Chance would be a fine thing," said Eleanor. "Oh, if only we were in California!"

"That's hardly the point."

"Well, why didn't you sit by yourself?"

"You can't. The tables are set for six, and when I got there, they were all pretty occupied. I chose a table where there were only three, but that inspector came in and sat between me and an elderly psychiatrist."

"Psychiatrist?" Eleanor perked up. 'What's he like?"

"She, my dear, she, it's a woman who thinks she knows everything. Started commenting on my headaches, of all things, but I quickly put an end to that. And there was another silly woman who went on about food allergies. Didn't pay much attention to her either."

"I bet you didn't. What did you think of the inspector?"

"His main concern seemed to be to impress the lady psychiatrist with how clever he is. You'd think he'd have better things to do under the circumstances. Why isn't he going round checking fingerprints and all that jazz?"

"Oh, Franz, what do you know about what detectives do."

"Nothing. But I don't want to have lunch with them either. Are you hungry, by the way?"

"No, but I'm beginning to feel the need for fresh air."

"Just what I was thinking. Shall I sit here while you take a walk?"

"That would be wonderful. Then I'll do the same for you."

Franz again found himself alone with the small wizened person who was his mother. Mother. Had he really spent nine months in that body sixty-six years ago? His head ached and ached, and his stomach churned. He thought of a colleague of his, male, who had spent a whole term's sabbatical once with his own mother who had Alzheimer's and all kinds of physical problems. She had been in a nursing home, and his colleague, an only son, had felt very guilty about that. He'd visited her every day through that semester, and the care wasn't very good, so she'd developed a rash all over her body. Shocked by this and unable to arouse the interest of the staff in the problem, he'd begun to wash her himself, all over, and put ointment on. "Can you imagine," he'd said to Franz when it was all over, "putting ointment in your mother's vagina?" Eleanor had found this very moving and admirable. It had made him feel sick, and his head reeled now at the thought. He stood up and walked over to the window. He opened the door onto the balcony. A large black bird that was perched on the railing outside flew away, and the wind blew snow off the roof into his face. Was Eleanor really out there walking in those cold woods?

He went back into the room and closed the door quietly. The cold air had only made his head worse. On balance, he was glad Eleanor was there with him. It would have been even more hellish if he had been alone. In a way, he was surprised she had come. She had not seemed to want to spend a lot of time with him lately and took every excuse to go off on her own or with one of her friends or to stay with her aged father. She had an overdeveloped sense of duty where parents were concerned. That's probably why she was here. Nothing to do with me or with her, in a way, just conforming automatically to the standards of behavior planted in her at an early age. Well, why was he here himself? Hardly out of love for that angry little woman on the bed behind him. Was it out of duty? He had been tempted not to come; after all, she was now in professional care, but Eleanor had insisted that there was no way to explain to Ingrid that they were leaving it all to her, all the work of the move to say nothing of all the guilt of putting Mother in a home. He could have lived with that himself. Just not to be here, to be in his own study at home with his books—he could have put up with quite a burden of guilt for that.

Behind him his mother had started to make choking sounds in her throat, and for a long second or so, he contemplated remaining motionless where he was, looking out of the window. Maybe she would just die. The sounds got louder, and he turned to see her once again clutching the gallows and trying to pull herself up as she stared seemingly terrified at where he stood against the window. Hofer had said she was frightened.

"Mother, it's me, Franz."

"Stay away from me," she seemed to be saying, gasping for breath. This was awful. The bell for the sister hung over the bed, and he would have to lean over her to ring. She might start screaming again. Maybe he should go for help. But should he leave her? For what seemed like a long time, he stood transfixed, staring at her, and she at him. Then she fell back on the pillow and was quite silent.

For a while, he couldn't move. Then he went out into the corridor, holding a hand on his own aching head, and went into the common room where Sister Dolores was spoon-feeding a very old gentleman in a wheelchair with a spoon. He said, "Sister, I think we need help. A doctor. A real doctor, not that Hofer chap."

She looked at the old man, who had his mouth open, and then said in desperation, "Could you just finish up here? Just tiny spoonfuls, and I'll go check on your mother."

Oh my God. He took the spoon and steered it toward the old man's mouth. He had no idea how to do this. The tapioca pudding slithered largely down his chin, and the man looked helplessly at him, his pale watery blue eyes wide open.

"I'm sorry," said Franz. "I'll try again."

He did better the second time, and the man hoarsely said, "Thank you." That was nice; he'd actually got a word of gratitude. He couldn't ever remember gratitude of any kind from his mother. She rarely said thank you to him at all.

Sister Dolores came back with a shocked look on her face. "Professor Fabian, your mother has gone."

"Gone, gone where?"

"She has stopped breathing." Sister Dolores was dialing a phone number. "Is the doctor with you? Absolute emergency. Immediately to Martin Luther, room 12. Now! Now!"

Franz turned around rapidly to run into his mother's room, and in the second he turned, he felt he was losing his balance. He couldn't save himself from falling. He tried to clutch at the nearest chair but failed, and the footrest of the old man's wheelchair was in the way of his head. He lost consciousness.

5

Büchner was usually pretty good at catnapping. Not only could he drop right off to sleep, but he also had some of his best ideas at the moment of waking up. Into his mind would swim something someone had said, or better yet, something he should say to someone, but perfectly formulated, better than he ever managed when fully awake. If he could get up quickly enough, he could write it down. Today, however, he had difficulty falling asleep, tired though he was. He shouldn't have eaten two of those dumplings; they weren't even very good. He used to have a stomach like iron, but he wasn't that young anymore. A bad idea being in a place like this at his age. The shape of things to come was altogether too present. And winter was also present in this room, he realized. It wasn't warm. Someone *had* turned off the radiator, and the wind was beating, of all things, hailstones against his window—a sudden squall. Might as well get up. He'd got under the bedcovers fully dressed, and now he got up, shivered, and put on his overcoat. He looked out of the window to see Frau Fabian striding off toward the woods on the footpath in front of the house. A brave woman walking in weather like this. A brisk walk, however, would be a nice thing. Did he have time? Not really. He wanted to take a look around Martin Luther before starting on his afternoon interviews. He went out again, leaving the radiator on, walked upstairs and along the corridor, and stopped outside the door of the recently departed Frau Winkler. He remembered Michael saying that the rooms in this wing were always open. He tried the door. It was locked. I don't suppose we fingerprinted in there, he thought. Hadn't seriously connected it with the Graf case. Still he'd like to have a look inside, as unobtrusively as possible. Quickest thing was to pop down and ask Michael to open it sub rosa.

He found him immediately in the café. "I need your master key briefly, Michael," he said.

"I guess you have a right, Herr Inspektor."

"I guess I do, Michael."

"I'd be glad if you'd drop it off when you're through," he said and handed it over.

Büchner went back upstairs. There was no one on the corridor. He unlocked the door to room 24 and slipped inside. The room had been thoroughly cleaned, and the bed stripped. Nothing to see really. The bed was in the corner, facing the big window on the end wall and the door onto the balcony. On an impulse, he lay down on the bed to see what actual view you would have from there. He pulled down on the gallows. Yes, you could pull yourself up on it. If you didn't give it a real tug to send it back up, it stayed hanging down, its triangular shape swaying against your view of the window. With his head on the uncovered pillow, he could see largely sky through the window. Last night Frau Winkler would have seen the moon, and silhouetted against the sky was the concrete balustrade of the balcony—ugly, these balconies—better to have an uninterrupted view of the sky and the treetops. Feeling now suddenly that he could fall asleep after all, he jumped up. Didn't want someone to catch him in the seemingly perverse act of sleeping in a bed recently occupied by a dead old woman. He looked at his watch. He really was losing his grip. He was going to be late for Sister Barbara.

Hurrying downstairs, he found her standing outside his door. "So sorry," he said. "Do come in. Have a cup of coffee. Oh!" The thought of coffee reminded him of Michael and the key. "Make yourself at home. I'll be back in a minute."

When he came back, she was drinking her coffee and looking calmly around her. He had somehow expected a nervous woman, but she didn't appear to be that at all. There was a slightly blank look in her eyes.

"Are you the Georg Büchner," she asked him, "who was active in the student movement here in the late sixties?"

"Well, yes. My name, for my sins, is Georg Büchner, and I was active at one point in the student movement."

She smiled. A short stout woman, she had a pink unmade-up face and a ready smile. "So was I."

"Well, fancy that," he said, genuinely surprised. "I don't meet many of the old comrades nowadays."

"You wouldn't remember me in any case. I was a nobody, a bit older than the rest of you, I used to make coffee for the group, hand out pamphlets, that sort of thing. I remember you because of your name."

He laughed. "Yes, a name like mine is hard to forget."

"For us old revolutionaries anyway."

"We certainly took different paths, you into the church and me into the police!"

"I didn't go into the church until a lot later. It was Agatha who finally convinced me that the way to deal with my life's problems was to sublimate them in the service of God."

He looked closely at her but detected no irony in what she said. "Ah, yes, you have a formidable friend there. Sister Agatha didn't think I should speak to you at all."

Barbara replied solemnly, "She saved my life. She tries to save me from most things. And sometimes, I try to save her, though she doesn't really notice that."

"In this case, I really wanted to speak to each individual. Perhaps you can tell me what you know about Hans Graf."

"We've lived next door to him for five years, ever since we moved in. We were on normally good terms with him, not super friendly. He is, was, more worldly than we are. He was never noisy in his apartment. He never asked us for anything. We would pass him in the corridor quite often. He was always polite."

"And his friend, Frau Hagen?"

Barbara looked at him for a long time before she answered. "Yes, she too. A lovely woman." Büchner saw no trace of the cattiness that had marked other people's comments.

"It was suggested to me that Sister Agatha visited him on Christmas Day."

"Oh no, that's not possible. We were together the whole time. And anyway, why should she?"

"I have no idea. Did you sleep in the afternoon?"

"Yes."

"Do you sleep in the same room?"

"Why, yes, Georg. It is a two-room apartment, living room and bedroom. Should I call a Chefinspektor by his first name?"

"Once a comrade, always a comrade," said Büchner. "Is the apartment big enough for both of you?"

"Of course. You should see the double rooms in a charitable institution! I did volunteer work in them for years. I remember twin ladies of ninety who could not bear to be separated, and they had to be fitted once into a single room, about half the size of the Martin Luther rooms. The people here do not know their own good fortune."

"I know what you mean. So you did not hear Sister Agatha leave the apartment on Christmas Day in the afternoon."

"I most certainly did not."

"Nor anything unusual in Herr Graf's apartment?"

"Again, no."

"Were you both in your apartment throughout the evening?"

After a momentary hesitation, Barbara said, "Yes. At about five thirty, we spent half an hour in the chapel, and after that, about half an hour in Martin Luther, then we came back, closed the door of our apartment, and stayed there."

"Well, that should do it for now then. Good to meet an old comrade."

They shook hands, and Barbara left, the picture of composure as she had arrived. Outside, Pastor Pokorny was waiting, leaning on his cane. "Sorry to keep you waiting, Reverend."

"Herr Pokorny will do," said the old man, smiling. "That's OK. But I'll be glad to sit down. I *am* ninety-three you know."

"Yes, I know, but I would never have guessed it. Have you lived here long?"

"The last six years. I lived alone until then, ever since I came back to Austria from England—I ended up in England after the war, and my daughter still lives there. She began to be too worried about my living alone, so I moved in here."

"What took you to England, Herr Pastor, if I may ask?"

"You may presumably ask what you like, Herr Inspektor. That goes with your job. And I have no secrets. It's a long story though, for which you have no time, I'm sure."

"The short version?"

Pokorny laughed. "The more interesting question is what brought me back to Austria. Many people fleeing the Nazis ended up in England—I was no exception there. I was put into a camp in Hungary—the country of my birth—because the Baptists were regarded then as a dangerous sect. I was transferred to an Austrian camp where I managed to survive the war years and ended up in a DP camp in Holland. From there I was rescued by the Baptist Union and taken to England. I was grateful for this. I married and had a daughter. When my wife died, I just wanted to end my days in Central Europe. The Austrians gave me a chance to do this when I retired from the active ministry in England. I love Vienna, and the Lutherans, as you see, have been kind to me. That, in a nutshell, is my story. I have enjoyed my life here. I was a resident here before poor Graf moved in."

"Did you know him well?"

"Not well. You may have noticed, Herr Inspektor, that residents here fall into at least two categories. They do not divide along lines of age or sex, but more along lines of . . ."—he hesitated—"sophistication. Herr Graf counted among the sophisticates. I do not. That nice Sister Barbara who just left does not. Frau Beck, the youngest resident, does not." Büchner could see what he meant. But was it sophistication? Or class? Or religious belief?

"You went to the communal dinner on Christmas Day, I heard."

"Yes, then I took a long nap. At my age, conversation with a group of people is much more tiring than tête-à-tête. And then I walked over with Frau Beck to visit Frau Winkler. And now she has gone too. To be honest, her passing has upset me personally far more than the horrible death of Herr Graf. She was a dear lady, widow of a pastor, who also suffered under the Nazis, you know, and definitely one of us, the nonsophisticates."

"Do you think there's anything odd about her death?"

"No, except that I would not have thought that she was ready to die."

"What time did you leave her room and go back to your own?"

"Oh, about six thirty, I suppose. I usually watch the TV news in the evening and go to bed early. Find I can't keep my eyes open much after nine—though, alas, they are again wide open after five in the morning!"

"Well, thanks for coming, Herr Pokorny. We'll talk again, I'm sure."

"At your disposal, sir." He got up carefully, but Büchner noticed that he did not use his hands on the chair, or his cane, to help him to rise. This old man still had muscles. Amazing for his age. But could he knock an able-bodied man down? Maybe. Pokorny walked out, swinging his walking stick more in the manner of a long-distance walker than of a feeble old man.

A knock at the door and Michael came in. "Come for the coffee cups?" asked Büchner.

"I'll take them, but have you heard the latest? The mother of that professor chap has just died, the prof has knocked himself out in the kitchen, and his wife is nowhere to be found."

"She's in the woods," said Büchner. "I saw her from the window. She went along that footpath that goes from the front driveway into the woods. Try and find Schmidt to go after her. I'd better get up to Martin Luther pronto." He looked at his watch. Two thirty in the afternoon. Not twenty-four hours since he'd arrived at the Haus im Wald and already two more people had died here. Natural deaths, no doubt, but how much bleaker could the deep midwinter get?

Chapter 6

It is not uncommon in an old people's home to walk along a corridor and see a once-closed door, behind which an individual had lived and breathed only yesterday, now standing open, the floor polished, the bed stripped, the window open. Such a door stands open perhaps only for a day in the Haus im Wald because the waiting list is long, and within twenty-four hours, new relatives are there, looking, measuring, thinking of how to prepare their loved one, or not-so-loved one, for the impending move. And Director Schramm surely abhors a vacuum. He has his bills to pay, and empty rooms pay no bills. Locking room 24 on the orders of the local constabulary after the sudden departure of Frau Winkler is an imposition. Bad enough that the even more desirable apartment 32 in Melanchthon is cordoned off and unusable for an indefinite length of time. The passing of Frau Winkler was, Schramm had protested, a natural event. Wachtmeister Schmidt had smiled and allowed that dying at ninety-three was natural enough, but the room had to remain locked for now. It's regulations, he had said, his voice suggesting that on his territory, bureaucracy was a stronger force than nature. A natural death. A seeming commonplace perhaps in the Haus im Wald, but when, really, does a death seem natural to the living? Or indeed to the dying?

1

Eleanor was glad to be out of the house. It was bitterly cold, and what had looked like a snow flurry as she pushed open the front door looked now more like a flurry of hailstones. Oh well. She pulled up the hood of her down coat, tied it tightly under her chin, and strode down the path toward the wood, her head bent forward into the wind. Such a pleasure to take big steps and feel her leg muscles tightening. A few years ago, she had done some strength training in her local health club in Manhattan and had never felt so good in her life, before or since. She'd have to start again. You only had to look at all these ladies in the Haus im Wald, shuffling along the corridors, putting one foot so carefully in front of the other, clumpy laced shoes, fat ankles, thick stockings. What they needed in this place was a gym, not a chapel, a whole bevy of female strength trainers, not male charmers like the delightful Dr. Hofer, armed with pills. She'd defended Mother's right to be enamored of him, but better for her if she'd been in the hands of a strong, good-looking woman like her own trainer, Angela, someone who would have helped her stand on her own feet for a few more years, not sink steadily into a helpless stupor. She drew back her shoulders, took deep breaths the way Angela had taught her. "One deep breath is as good as a tranquilizer any day," she used to say. Eleanor walked quickly now, trying to avoid the temptation of looking down at her own feet, and instead looking ahead at the path she was walking on. Look where you're going, she said to herself. With this snow underfoot, you could fall flat on your face here, and there's absolutely no one to help you.

The path was very wide, and the trees were quite dense in places. It must be lovely in the summer. A bit bleak now, but protected at least from the hailstones. So far, there was only one path. Better look out. In a wood, you could easily follow a breakaway path almost without noticing it, and then it could be difficult to find the way back. She was just coming to a sort of crossroads—four paths leading off in different directions, all looking much the same. On one of them, she could see a small shrine a few paces along. That would identify it for her. She went up to it and read:

In memory
of our dear children
Herta Frankl
and Ilse Dworak
who on 12 January 1946
at the age of ten and eleven years
three hundred meters to the west in this wood
died in an accidental explosion.

She shivered and looked around her. January 1946, that cheerless time after the war. It would have been cold and snowy, just like this, children playing in the snow, in the trees, a sudden loud explosion, and two of them blown to pieces. Would their parents have waited and waited in vain and finally set out in search of them? Or were there other children, running, running, perhaps hurt, and perhaps bleeding, through the woods to find someone, to tell someone? There were fresh flowers on the shrine. Herta and Ilse were still not forgotten, almost sixty years later; but the wood seemed more sinister to her now, a place where war could store up its cruel legacy. She went on walking along that same path, thinking perhaps she ought to turn round and go back, but not wanting to, when suddenly she saw something move in the undergrowth under the trees. It seemed to be somebody's leg. A camouflaged leg, that's what it looked like, a brown-and-green trousered leg. Looking closer, she saw that it belonged to a young man lying flat on his stomach with a rifle in his hand. A sudden rush of fear, then the young man said, "It's all right, ma'am, army exercises."

"Army exercises?" she said incredulously. Within sight of that shrine? "This sort of thing still goes on?"

"It certainly does," he said. "There are more of us in that direction." He pointed in the direction she had been walking in.

"I hope you're not going to shoot that thing." He couldn't be more than eighteen years old, she thought. He opened the gun and showed her the bullets, grinning.

"My God," she said.

"Don't worry, only blanks—dummy cartridges." But the wood seemed less inviting by the minute.

"Stay warm," she said fatuously to the young man and turned around to retrace her steps. She passed the shrine again, was at the crossroads, and of course, couldn't remember which path she had come down before. All she knew was that it wasn't the one past the shrine. Was it the one immediately ahead or the one to the right? They all looked the same in the snow. It was too cold to dither about, and she took a chance on the first to the right. She thought she could see her own footsteps, but the snow was blowing all the time from the branches, and the light was dim.

What time was it? Two thirty. She ought to be going back. Franz would be getting distinctly restive. She didn't like the feeling of not being sure she was on the right path. It occurred to her suddenly that perhaps she was being a bit casual wandering in the woods alone when there was supposedly a murderer on the loose. Typical that Franz had not thought about that. She seemed to have gone much farther along this path than when she was walking this way before. Oh God, she groaned, better walk back to the shrine and try one of the other paths. How could she be so stupid? She plodded on, and finally she could see the crossroads again, and there standing in the middle of it, looking around at the various paths, was a tall figure, wearing a big black belted coat and what looked like a balaclava helmet. This time she was really frightened. The figure turned and came at a fast pace toward her. She thought of running but was rooted to the spot.

"Frau Fabian," said the figure, pulling off his helmet. "I've been looking for you."

Unable to speak, she stared at him. He looked familiar. "Michael," he said, "Michael Neumann. I've been sent to find you."

"Oh." She closed her eyes for a moment in relief. She felt tears behind her eyelids. "I'm glad you've come. I was a bit lost. Stupid of me."

"It's this way. We must hurry."

"Is there something wrong?" she asked as they walked briskly down the right path.

"Well, your husband fell and hit his head. He's come round, but it was a bit of a shock, and I'm afraid his mother . . ."

"Yes, what? She's probably furious that Franz could be so stupid as to fall down."

"Well, no, not really. It seems that she died. Quite suddenly."

Eleanor stopped. None of this seemed real. Mother couldn't have died just like that, could she? "Are you sure?"

"That's what I was told, but the sooner we get back the better so that you can see for yourself."

"Yes, of course."

Eleanor was out of breath, trying to keep up with the young man. A big comedown from those minutes on this path in the other direction when she'd felt so strong and determined. Her legs felt weak, her head in a muddle. She saw the Haus im Wald looming up as the path emerged from the wood, and she didn't feel ready for it.

2

Büchner locked his door behind him. He'd made sure he had a key to this office, and he stepped out at a brisk pace to the second floor of Martin Luther. This time he'd better be there to take charge himself. He passed the door of the common room and saw the professor stretched out on the couch, leaning over him a handsome middle-aged man, presumably a doctor. That could wait. He wanted to get to the scene of the death. Sister Dolores was standing with the director at the bedside where Frau Fabian lay. They were trying to turn her on to her back, and her left foot was somehow stuck in the railing at the side of the bed. Schramm uttered a grunt of irritation as he tried to force out the foot.

"Stop that at once," said Büchner.

Schramm turned. "You have no right, sir," he began.

"I have every right. I am conducting a murder investigation here, you may remember. Every death that occurs here at the moment is my business. What in the world are you doing?"

The director looked about to explode. Sister Dolores said mildly, "Only preparing the body for the undertakers, sir. They'll be here in an hour and will take her away. We've called her niece who lives in the village, and she'll tell us what arrangements were in place for this eventuality. She signed the forms when we admitted Frau Fabian. The professor is—"

"I know about the professor. But this body is going nowhere at the moment. I am phoning the police mortuary right now, the crime squad will come, and then the body will be taken there for an autopsy."

"This is outrageous," said Schramm. "The family will be appalled. I am appalled."

"Herr Direktor Schramm, perhaps you will realize once and for all that a murder has been committed on your premises. Since then, in less than twenty-four hours, two people have died. That makes six deaths in the month of December in the Haus im Wald. A bit much, even for the bleak midwinter. No doubt it's all very natural, with the exception of the unfortunate Herr Graf, who was struck to the ground with a fatal blow to the head. This, may I remind you, means that there is a pretty vicious murderer hereabouts. I have no choice but to look very carefully at the circumstances of death in this new case. Kindly leave everything as it is, touch nothing more in this room, go back to your office, and cancel the funeral home for now. Sister, I would appreciate it if you could find Wachtmeister Schmidt for me." She looked nervously at Schramm.

"Do as the inspector says. Don't worry. This will all be sorted out soon," and turning to Büchner, he said stiffly, "It is very hard for us to accept the kind of world you appear to live in."

"My kind of world right now is situated here in the Haus im Wald. I could also wish it were not. But from now on, I want to be officially informed by you of everything that happens in it. I do not want to have to pick up rumors from the café, which is how I found out about this. And now I would like to get on with my job. Please give me the key to this room. I will lock it until my colleagues arrive." He took out his cell phone and called police headquarters. It was important to get the police doctor here as soon as possible. Already the body had been moved.

As Schramm left, Büchner turned himself to look at the body. So small. He had an impulse himself to cover it with a sheet;

it was so undignified, lying there with nightdress pulled about and exposing the tiny little legs up to the thigh, skin wrinkled and mottled, and the left foot still caught in the rail. A strange contortion in death. His colleagues would be here in half an hour. He'd better go and see what sort of shape the professor was in. As he locked the door of room 12 behind him, Eleanor came panting along the corridor, her coat and hood covered in wet snow, followed by Michael.

"They found you. Good. Your husband is in there." They all went into the common room. The doctor, if that's what he was, was still there. He looks like a TV star, thought Büchner.

"Why, Dr. Hofer," said Eleanor, "this is Chefinspektor Büchner."

The two men shook hands, eyed each other coolly, and Büchner said, "Are you the house doctor?"

"No, visiting private patients. Frau Fabian is—was—a long-term patient of mine." A slight groan from Franz caused them to look around. He still looked to be only semiconscious.

"For God's sake, Franz, what's going on?" said Eleanor.

"I'm sorry," he said. "I don't want to open my eyes at the moment."

"We've called an ambulance," Hofer said. "He'll have to go to the hospital for an MRI of his head. He took a nasty crack on it, right above the right eye. He fell forward and landed with his head hitting the edge of the footrest of a patient's wheelchair."

"Oh, Franz," said Eleanor, helplessly. "However did you do this?"

"Don't ask me," he said. "I have no idea."

"He does suffer from positional vertigo," Eleanor said to Hofer. "He can lose his balance if he turns or makes sudden movements of his head. He's usually very careful. But maybe the shock of hearing about his mother—"

"Mother?" said Franz.

"Did he lose consciousness?" Eleanor asked Hofer.

"Yes, it seems so. For around sixty seconds. A slight concussion. He doesn't remember much about the circumstances at this point. He ought to be all right, but it will have to be checked. He'll have a monumental black eye at the very least."

"Will you go with him or stay here?" said Büchner to Eleanor. "I'd like a family member to be here when we examine the body and the room."

Eleanor flinched. "What do you mean?"

"Because of the circumstances at the Haus im Wald, I have called in the crime squad."

"Is that necessary—" began Hofer.

Büchner cut into his question. "Yes, I know she was over ninety, a natural time to die and all that, but I'm doing my job in a house where murder has been committed. Frau Fabian and her room will be carefully examined. I'd like to talk to you in private, Herr Dr. Hofer, before you leave the Haus im Wald. Could you come to my office downstairs at three thirty?"

"Very well."

Two strapping young men from the ambulance service came in with a stretcher and helped Professor Fabian on to it.

"I suppose I can come too in the ambulance," said Eleanor. "If Ingrid, our cousin, is coming, you'll have a family member in attendance, Herr Inspektor, won't you? Oh, Ingrid, thank God." She came in, white-faced and shaken.

"We have to go," said Eleanor. "I'll be back, of course. Inspektor Büchner will explain everything."

Oh, will he, thought Büchner wearily, guiding the professor's cousin to the locked door of room 12.

3

Eleanor followed the stretcher into the elevator, trying vainly to mop some of the wetness off her coat. She'd pulled off her hood and, catching sight of her reflection in the mirror of the elevator, thought how awful she looked. Above all, how old. Her hair looked exactly the way she hated it, straggly gray strands falling in too long bangs over her forehead and hanging straight down at the sides of her lined, well, almost wrinkled face. Her glasses were slipping down her wet and shiny nose, still red from the ill-fated walk in the freezing forest. Oh God. What did it matter? No one was looking at her. There were bigger problems. Yet somehow, she thought, if she had only looked all right, she could have dealt better with the crisis—it was a crisis, wasn't it? she thought vaguely, still scarcely taking in the reality of what had happened.

She climbed up the big step into the ambulance, grateful for and yet resenting the helpful hand of one of the young men. Franz was already ensconced on his stretcher bed and covered with a blanket. His eyes were still closed. They set off at high speed with the hooter of the ambulance blaring.

"Where are we going?" she asked the fair-headed young man who was sitting with them.

"AKH," he said, "the general hospital on the Gürtel—has the biggest accident unit in the city."

"Quite a job you have here," she said, falling into polite conversation by force of habit. She saw Franz stir irritably on his bed of pain. No doubt he would prefer silence. He hated it when she struck up conversations with perfect strangers. What the hell. She had a right to get through this thing in her own way. "Have you been doing it long?"

"Six months. Another two to go. Soon they're going to cut it down to six months altogether. I'm doing my stint in community service."

"Community service?"

"You know, the alternative to military service." Of course, the Austrians still had conscription.

"Well, this seems a lot more useful than lying about in the Vienna Woods in the snow, playing at being soldiers."

"Yes, that's what I thought. And there's also the danger that it won't stop at playing. Our guys get sent to places like Bosnia nowadays." Or Afghanistan, thought Eleanor. Better not get into that. It would give Franz a hemorrhage.

"You like the work?"

"Yeah," he said casually. "I'm thinking of taking it up for real when my time's up. They'll count this time toward your training. OK, here we are." The ambulance screeched to a halt, and the young man sprang out to get a hospital stretcher. Franz was loaded on, and they wheeled him to the admissions desk.

"Thank you so much," said Eleanor, "and good luck in your career."

"Oh, for heaven's sake," muttered Franz. "Where do you think you are? A garden party?"

At least he's coming back to normal, thought Eleanor. She signed him in: no, he had no insurance in Austria; yes, he was a U.S. citizen; yes, she supposed he was a tourist at the moment. Born in Austria, 1938, male, "confessionless"—what did that mean? Oh yes, of course, no affiliation to a religion. Profession? Professor, now retired. He had fallen and hit his head, unconscious for one minute. He can't remember what happened. She pointed to the swelling around the right eye and the cut over the brow, which Nurse Dolores had covered with a Band-Aid. They were sent off through the long corridors to the radiography unit in the back of the building.

Before they took him, the nurse in charge said, "Please give all valuables to your wife."

Franz took off his watch, emptied his pockets, gave her his wallet, then, putting his hand in his inside pocket, said, "Eleanor, it's gone."

"What's gone?"

"The seven hundred euros."

"What seven hundred euros?"

"You know, for the carpets."

"But we couldn't find it."

He groaned. "I can't go into all that now, I'm telling you, it's gone."

"Ready, sir?" said the nurse, and he was whisked away. Eleanor took off, finally, her very wet coat, draping it over the chair in front of her. The wet had seeped through to the down lining. Ugh. If only it were a little warmer in here. She went to the ladies' room and dried off the front of her hair with a paper towel, trying to comb it into some sort of shape. Then she went back and sat down.

How long would it be? She didn't even have a book or a newspaper. How could she think of reading in any case? She needed to get her head around what had happened. She had been almost enjoying the whole scene there in the Haus im Wald, she realized, this morning when she set out for the day, glad of the coincidence of finding Christa—God, she must call Christa—and more titillated than anything else by the whole murder thing. But now, Mother was dead. Had Franz grasped this yet? She said it to herself several times, Mother is dead. Mother is dead. It made no impact. It didn't seem true. More like a dream, like that walk in the woods, ghosts of dead children, soldiers in the undergrowth, could she be asleep? Oh, for heaven's sake. Try to think straight. Mother is dead. The inspector is, at this moment, examining her room. Her poor little body is being carted off to a police morgue to be pulled about and even cut open by impersonal hands. She thought of the hand on the sheet earlier today, how she had wanted to touch it, to comfort it. Now she would never have the chance again. She waited, hoping for a few tears. Nothing. She really hadn't like Franz's mother. But she'd felt sorry for her. Always in the shadow of a successful man, her husband, always suiting her life to his, always hearing people say how charming he was. Disappointed in their only son who simply wasn't charming. Nor was she. Their lack of charm had not united them; it had made it impossible for them to come together. They grated on each other, and both of them had so much wanted the love of the charming senior Herr Fabian, who had treated them both with extreme courtesy, paying compliments and opening doors—but loving them? She had herself once loved Franz. She had known from the beginning that he was a difficult man to be close to, and he really wasn't the sort of man she was usually attracted to—rather short, tending to be plump—but still, a dapper Continental European sort of look and a small goatee beard. And she'd liked his seeming independence of the opinions of other people, his intellectual certainty—he always knew what he thought—and then his desire for her. That was what had tipped her over into loving him. He had really wanted her. Where had all that gone? What she felt for him now was a sort of irritated boredom. Because she sensed that was what he felt for her? Possibly that was what his mother had felt for him too, and she rarely bothered to try and hide it. But Mother was dead. Would this make a difference?

Mother was dead, and they were searching her room. Surely that was idiotic. But the horrible death of the suave, well-dressed Herr Graf hung over everything. Oh dear, she'd better call Christa. There was a phone outside the waiting room.

She seemed to have awakened Christa out of an afternoon nap, because at first she couldn't grasp who was on the phone and what had happened. She reacted with shock. "Shall I come to the hospital?" she asked at once.

"No, no," said Eleanor, thinking that was all Franz needed at this point. "I expect Franz will be out soon. I'll have the ambulance take us back to the Zehenthofgasse, and then I'd better come back to the Haus im Wald to see what's going on. And our car is there in any case. I'll get in touch as soon as I can."

"Yes," said Christa, "I can't believe it. Frau Winkler and now your mother-in-law!"

Eleanor hung up and thought of Frau Winkler. She saw her again as she had been the day before Christmas, with her funny little red headband, her perky smile, her excitement at picking out the cake she wanted. So alive, and now she was dead. Eleanor sat in the waiting room, put her head in her hands, and finally felt the relief of tears.

4

"My condolences," said Büchner to Ingrid. "This is a very sad event. I gather you were instrumental in bringing Frau Fabian in here."

"Yes," she said. "My aunt was very much alone in recent years since my uncle died. Franz was in America, and I kept an eye on things. My daughter Adele is a nurse, and she would go several mornings a week to bathe Tante Bertha, and then a visiting nurse went in the evenings to get her into bed, but it was all too much for us. But this, I didn't expect this." She looked at the bed making a move toward it.

"Please don't touch anything, Frau Konrad. The crime squad will be here shortly."

"Crime squad?"

"Yes, we have to take every precaution. I expect you know a murder took place just two days ago here. We are treating all deaths as suspicious at the moment."

"But Tante Bertha, she only just arrived. Why would her death have anything to do with a murder?"

She's right, of course, thought Büchner. Highly unlikely. But he had no idea yet what the motive for the one obvious murder had been. It wasn't particularly reasonable, he knew that, to regard the other deaths as suspicious; but still, his insistence on the crime squad, fingerprinting, autopsy, etc., had a lot to do with his mounting dislike for Schramm and a rather petty desire to put him in his place. Not the motive of a well-integrated man, he thought. The police officer and two men and a woman appeared at the door. "Ah, good," he said. "Do what you have to do. Frau Konrad won't be in your way. She's the niece of the dead woman and is just standing by. Sister Dolores is along the corridor if you need anything. I'll leave you to it." He shook hands with Frau Konrad. "Perhaps you would please check before you go that nothing is missing from the room as you remember it. We'll need your phone number," he said. "Any problems, I'll be downstairs. I'm very sorry about all this."

When he got to his office, Dr. Hofer was waiting outside. "Thank you for coming, Herr Doktor," he said. "Do come in and have a seat."

Dr. Hofer took off his coat with some relief. "Warm in here," he said.

"Yes. I'm afraid the chill of my room in Martin Luther got to me, and I've had the radiator on full here all day. Shall I open a window?"

"Thank you. That would be nice. Staying here overnight, are you?"

"For a day or two. Now look here, Herr Doktor, I realize as well as you do that the deaths of these two ladies probably have nothing to do with the quite clear-cut case of the murder of Herr Graf."

Hofer looked quizzically at him.

Slightly annoyed with himself, Büchner said, "I mean, the Graf case is obviously a murder and not a natural death—an expression we seem to hear a lot of around here. The two ladies, however, do seem to have died suddenly. No one was expecting either death. I'd like your straightforward professional opinion on them."

"I have attended Frau Fabian for a number of years. You may not know, Herr Inspektor, that I happen to practice acupuncture as well as being a normally licensed medical practitioner. Unlike many doctors nowadays, I visit patients in their own homes. Frau Fabian was afflicted with old-age parkinsonism and also suffered the pain of arthritis. Regular acupuncture seemed to help her."

"How regular?"

"Sometimes two or three times a week."

"Was this covered by her health insurance?"

"No."

"And would you have gone on attending Frau Fabian here?"

"Yes. She asked me to do so only yesterday."

"And what do you think was the cause of death?

"Convulsions, constriction of breathing causing the heart to stop."

"Had she suffered anything like this before?"

"It was my impression that she had suffered one violent convulsion before I arrived in the Haus im Wald this morning. She was subject to the jerky movements of parkinsonism, but this seems to have been a particularly violent episode. I prescribed an injection of a mild tranquilizer when I arrived, in the hope that she would sleep peacefully. Your autopsy should confirm this."

"What time was this?"

"About nine thirty."

"And the next time you were called to her room?"

"She had stopped breathing. I could not revive her."

"Sleeping a little too peacefully?"

"I'm not sure I care for that remark, Herr Inspektor."

"Sorry, just a little joke. And what about Frau Winkler?"

"I didn't know Frau Winkler. She was never a patient of mine."

Büchner thought of Pastor Pokorny's categories. The sophisticates to whom Frau Winkler did not belong were probably the only ones who could afford Hofer.

"Did you attend any of the other residents who died in December?"

"One of them. A ninety-year-old woman who succumbed to what you might call"—he smiled—" a clear-cut case of liver cancer. She was very ill for the last month, and I did not see her then. I should perhaps tell you, however, that Herr Graf was a patient of mine. I was very shocked at the manner of his passing."

"And what did you do for him?"

"He had heard of my practice of acupuncture and called me in some months ago to see if I could help alleviate severe back pain. I tried, and I believe it helped him. He seemed to think so, at any rate, and was quite grateful to me. Oddly enough, he called me just before Christmas to see if I would come back and try some more treatment. I went early on Christmas Eve and gave him an acupuncture treatment then. I would have looked in there again today."

"Did he give you the impression that anything was wrong? Anything he was worried about?"

"On the contrary. He was exceedingly cheerful. Quite hyper, in fact, looking forward to the Christmas holiday. He was always the center of attention here—many people were charmed by him. And he had a special friend, you know. Well, of course, you know by now. Frau Hagen. He was going to spend the holiday with her. He said to me, 'Do what you can for me, Doctor. Apart from this backache, I'm the happiest man in the world.'"

"Quite an assertion for a seventy-six-year-old man."

"Indeed."

"And did you get rid of the backache?"

"Hardly, in that one session."

"No, I suppose not. Herr Doktor, is there anything you can tell me about the Haus im Wald, after how many years of familiarity with it?"

"Ten years."

"Anything that might help us with our investigation?"

Dr. Hofer appeared to think seriously about the question. "In these ten years, I've never witnessed any irregularity of any kind, if that's what you mean."

"And Schramm. How do you view Direktor Schramm?"

"He is an affable man. I cannot say I know him well. There are things that one might do nowadays in an institution like this that he does not do—more innovative geriatric care, shall we say—but he runs a tight ship. I admire a man who can make money and do good at the same time, don't you?"

"Does he make so much money?"

"Schramm is a rich man. He lives in an exceedingly good part of town in a charming villa with an expensive wife and two very spoiled daughters. And all this on the strength of running a residence for the aged. Not bad, eh?"

"And where do you live, Dr. Hofer?"

"In an exceedingly good part of town in a charming villa." Hofer laughed. "My expensive wife, however, has divorced me and is living off generous alimony payments."

"And all on the strength of Chinese medicine?"

Hofer's smile faded. "Not exactly. I have a traditional practice too."

"Of course."

A knock at the door. "That will be our affable, old-fashioned Herr Direktor," said Büchner.

Hofer stood up. He gave Büchner his card. "You can reach me if you need me. Given your height, Herr Inspektor, and—if I may say so—your somewhat dubious posture, you may one day also suffer from backache."

Büchner looked at the card after Hofer had left—yes, it was certainly an expensive part of town. These characters in the health industry had it made. Still, he couldn't believe it was such a great life—sticking needles into old ladies, and gentlemen too. Hofer had an eye though: he did occasionally have backache himself. And it was interesting that Hofer had a connection to Graf.

"Chilly in here," said Schramm as he came in. Then looking at the window and running a hand proprietarily over the radiator, he added, "Heating the Vienna Woods, are we, Herr Inspektor?"

"Herr Direktor, I think we've got off a bit on the wrong foot. Let's sit down somewhere more pleasant and try to have a friendly chat. How about your splendid café? Excellent idea, by the way, having a café for the residents."

"Very well. There's a small booth at the terrace end where we can be undisturbed. Let's go."

Büchner closed the window and, in a gesture of goodwill, turned down the radiator before they left the room.

5

The two men walked through the café to the booth by the window, Schramm bowing and greeting on all sides. At four thirty, the café was quite full, still some Christmas visitors. Each man ordered a pot of coffee. Büchner sat quietly for a while, trying seriously to overcome his dislike of the other man. He had always found he did much better in getting real information from people if he could find some point of contact with them, something he could like or sympathize with, than if he started off with more or less conscious hostility toward them. But there was something irritating to him about the way Schramm sat there with his perfectly cut hair and his carefully manicured hands, his slight overweight well disguised in his very expensive suit, surveying the scene around him. Lord of all he surveys, thought Büchner. But then, he is the boss of the place, and he's made a success of it. People seemed to count themselves lucky if they could get in here. Well, of course, that might change a bit if news of the murder spread and if it were not solved rather promptly. It must be rough on Schramm dealing with this. No wonder he was so on edge. Maybe that was a way to reach the man, Schramm, to get past his facade. "Herr Direktor," he said, trying to achieve a genuinely interested but neutral, nonthreatening tone, "it must be a very big shock for you having a murder happen on your excellent premises."

Scanning Büchner's face suspiciously, Schramm seemed satisfied and said simply, "Yes, Herr Inspektor, it is. I have not absorbed it yet."

"No, it usually takes awhile for the reality of something like this to sink in. The sooner we can get to the bottom of it, the better for all of us. You know the Haus im Wald better than anyone, I'm sure. Perhaps you can help me."

"I've been trying to do that, Herr Inspektor." Schramm promptly bristled.

"I know you have. And I appreciate it, but I would really like to regard you as an ally in my investigation and not as an adversary. I realize that I have to some extent been adopting an adversarial attitude toward you, and I am trying to drop it."

"Well, that's good. I didn't care for it at all,"

Büchner was immediately annoyed again. Why did one always expect one's own concessions to be matched by concessions on the other side? Giving an inch to some people seemed only to confirm their own sense of absolute rectitude. Drop the attempt at fellow feeling, he said to himself, and get on with it. "You were not actually in the Haus im Wald at the time of the murder?"

"No. I was not. I took my family to Kärnten for a skiing vacation over Christmas. My two girls love to ski."

"Two girls?"

"Yes, I have two teenage daughters. I had a phone call from here on the second Christmas Day and gave instructions to cooperate with you as much as possible, then I got in my car and drove back. Of course."

"You were in Kärnten then on Christmas Day itself?"

"Yes, drove there on Christmas Eve."

"How long a drive is that for you?"

"Oh, about four or five hours on a good day."

"And people can testify to your being on the ski slopes on Christmas Day?"

"Herr Inspektor! Of course." Schramm looked distinctly annoyed.

"Just routine questions. Who informed you of the situation here?"

"Sister Agatha. You have met her, I believe."

"Does she hold an actual position at the Haus im Wald?"

"Not exactly. But she is a deaconess of the founding organization, the Lutheran church. She sits on the advisory board of the house, actually; and since she moved in herself, she likes to make herself useful in various ways." Schramm seemed to be choosing his words rather carefully.

"Are you glad of her help?"

A slight pause. "Yes, of course. All help is useful in a place like this. We have an excellent housekeeper and a competent nursing staff, but also a number of volunteers, who are also ladies of the Protestant church. They come and do various useful things, talking to the lonelier patients in Martin Luther, reading to them sometimes, helping to feed them if necessary, doing bits of shopping sometimes. Not all the residents are blessed with concerned relatives."

"Is that the sort of thing Sister Agatha does?"

"Her friend, Sister Barbara, actually does a lot of that. Sister Agatha's preferences seem to lie more in the . . . supervisory area. She goes about and sees who needs what, and then she organizes the volunteers, that sort of thing. It has become natural for the nursing staff to contact her when for example, I am not in the house, if something goes wrong. That is how she came to be the person to inform me of what had happened."

"Do you remember exactly what she said and when she said it?"

"Well, it must have been between twelve and twelve thirty because we had just returned from our morning on the slopes and were settling down to an excellent lunch. I was called from the table to the phone. Let me see, I was so shocked that I'm not sure if I remember exactly what she said."

"Did she sound upset?"

"Well, no, I can't say she did, but then Sister Agatha rarely sounds upset. Her first words were something like, 'I'm sorry to disturb you. I have some bad news,' and then she said Hans Graf had been found dead. 'Struck in the head,' she said. 'He's lying dead on his carpet.' I remember that, it was so shocking."

"And you say this was just after noon?"

"Yes, it must have been. She didn't say much more. I said I'd come at once, and she said a chief inspector was being sent to investigate, and I said, he can use the office next to mine."

"That was very thoughtful of you in a moment of great shock."

"It is my job to be thoughtful."

Certainly, self-deprecation was not one of his traits, thought Büchner. "Do you have any idea at all of why Hans Graf may have been murdered?"

"I have been pondering this, of course, haven't we all? Could it have been what they call on TV an outside job? A thief? Graf was a rich man."

"It's possible. But there are no signs of a break-in, and the murder apparently took place after the doors were locked to the outside. So anyone who came into the building would have had to identify himself on the intercom. Or herself. Nothing obvious is missing. Wallet still stuffed with banknotes in his inside pocket. So far, no one has checked his personal belongings. His son claims not to have the faintest idea what he had in the apartment."

"Have you asked Frau Hagen or Herr Ritter? They were, I believe, his closest friends."

"Thank you, I shall," said Büchner, thinking suddenly of the silver and turquoise tiepin. He had looked at Graf's belongings, the ones that had been on the body when it was brought into the police morgue. No tiepin. Still, maybe he didn't have it on at the time of the murder. Somehow one thought he would have, since he had just been given it. Büchner had a sudden picture of Frau Hagen leaning forward and fastening the pin lovingly on the tie—a silver blue tie—of Herr Graf. He felt a sexual stirring at the thought.

"He was, I believe, a well-liked man," said Schramm. Well loved, one might also say, Büchner thought. He had himself not wanted love lately, too much like trouble; but in this moment, it seemed a most desirable thing. He tried to concentrate on the rich tones of Schramm's voice. "People liked him. The only motive I can think of for such a crime, if it was a personal one, is jealousy. He was a . . . an enviable man."

Indeed he was, thought Büchner. "Can you think of anyone here who might have been so envious of his relationship with Frau Hagen that they would kill for it."

"No," said Schramm quickly. "Surely an absurd notion. This is a Viennese rest home for the elderly, not a hotbed of Hollywood passion."

"Oh, quite," said Büchner. "I was only speculating." There had been a moment there where Schramm had almost opened up. But then he had swung into his usual defensive posture. He must get back to Dr. Lessing and question her a bit more closely about her line on the well-integrated man.

"Excuse me, Herr Inspektor," a voice said. "I'm sorry to interrupt, but I just brought my husband home from the hospital and took a cab back here to get our car and check up on Mother's room. The door is locked. I wonder if you can tell me what has happened. I don't want to disturb you, but I don't know what I'm supposed to do next."

"That's OK, Frau Fabian. Have you met Herr Direktor Schramm? Frau Fabian is the daughter-in-law of the elder Frau Fabian, who died so suddenly today. She and her husband are visiting from New York." Schramm stood up. "My deepest sympathy, Frau Fabian. I expect you know that the body of your mother-in-law had to be . . . taken away."

"Yes, I know," said Eleanor distractedly. "What should I do now?"

"Sit down and have a cup of coffee."

"I'd like a cup of tea," she said. This woman, thought Büchner, looks a wreck.

Schramm remained standing and said to Büchner, "Will that be all for now? I should probably get back to the office."

"Yes, of course, thank you for your time."

"Coffee on me, of course," said Schramm and, with a bow to Eleanor, "and the tea too, my dear lady." Not a big success, thought Büchner, my attempt at rapprochement.

Eleanor hung her wet coat over the back of her chair and sat down. She put cream and a large spoonful of sugar into her tea. "I need this, Herr Inspektor." She smiled at him.

A nice smile, he thought. "You have certainly had a terrible day. How is your husband?"

"Recovering. The scan of his head didn't show any immediate problems. They told him to go home and rest for a day or two. But now we have to deal with this death. Franz did not even seem to know that his mother had died. The bang on his head must have blotted all that out."

"It must have all been a shock. The Haus im Wald seems to be full of shocks."

"I can hardly believe that this time yesterday I was sitting here cheerfully drinking my tea when I heard about the unknown Graf's death."

"Yes," said Büchner, looking at his watch. Almost twenty-four hours since he had arrived at the Haus im Wald himself.

"Want anything else?" said the cheerful voice of Michael. "We'll be closing up shortly."

"No thanks," said Eleanor. "You've done enough for me today! This young man rescued me in the woods when I lost my way, Herr Inspektor."

"Ah, I thought Wachtmeister Schmidt was sent to look for you."

"Couldn't find him in a hurry," said Michael, "so I went myself."

"And very grateful I am too," said Eleanor, beginning to look better after the tea. "So what do I do now, Herr Inspektor?"

"Nothing at this point. They'll call you from the police station when they have finished their work."

"Oh, by the way, Herr Inspektor, my husband thinks that seven hundred euros are missing from his inside jacket pocket. It wasn't there when he got to the hospital and had to turn in his belongings. And he definitely remembered having it with him when he came to the Haus im Wald."

"Seven hundred euros? Quite a lot of cash to be carrying loose in his pocket."

"It's a long story, but anyway, it seems to be missing. When can we look into Mother's room? Presumably all the furniture will have to be removed now."

"I'd like the door to stay locked for now," he said. "Check with me tomorrow."

"I think I'll look up my friend Christa, before leaving," said Eleanor, "so I'd better be off. Bye, Herr Inspektor. Thanks for the tea."

"Thank the management," he said and bowed as she struggled back into her wet coat and left.

So the end of a working day, he thought, and only three locked doors to show for it. He'd better sit down at once and write up his notes on the whole situation. He needed to know where he stood. He'd like to have a talk with someone, but Schmidt, while a competent-enough lad, did not seem much of a conversational partner, and all the others were more or less suspects. Less rather than more, on the whole. None of them so far seemed to fit the bill. What he would really like to do was invite Frau Hagen out to dinner, but that would be inappropriate behavior on almost any count. Oh well, back to the office and out with the notes.

"How about a drink with an old comrade?" Sister Barbara appeared from nowhere.

"A *drink*, Sister?" he replied.

"Well, *you* can have a drink. I have my motor scooter outside. You can hop on the back, and we'll go to the Goldene Glocke in Feldberg."

"I don't mind if I do," he said, feeling distinctly cheerier. He fetched his coat and scarf and set off through the snow with his unexpected companion.

Chapter 7

One does not have to be in an institution for very long before all life on the outside begins to pale into insignificance. Attention is rapidly focused on other inmates, on helpers and employees, and in particular, on anyone who has, or seems to have, authority. Relatives, thinking to bring into the Haus im Wald news of the outside world as well as fruit and flowers, find themselves regaled instead with the latest failure of Sister Agatha to answer a call, or the way in which Sister Dolores pays instant attention to the needs of one person and none at all to another. Visitors may yawn, but such stories gain animated attention in the communal dining room, where they are the stuff of everyday life. Martin Luther residents do not go out anymore into the outside world, nor do they expect to. The drama of their lives is played out within their own walls. The residents of Melanchthon also find that the small dramas involving one another consume more of their remaining life energies than any larger dramas in the outside world. Even visitors are drawn into these if they stay more than a day or so. But when the residents of either wing stop concerning themselves with the drama inside the walls, you can be pretty sure that their time on the stage of life is coming to an end.

1

Eleanor dripped her way through the lobby toward the staircase of the Melanchthon wing. Just past the shop in the lobby was a notice pointing to the chapel. Heavens, she thought, will we now have to organize a funeral for Franz's mother? She had called herself a Protestant, and certainly she wasn't a Roman Catholic, but she hadn't attended a church for years, as far as Eleanor knew. What do you do about funerals in a case like that? Do you have to have one? Ingrid would know. Probably Christa too. She'd better find out because it was the last thing that Franz would want to think about. Why not look into the chapel for a minute to see what it was like? Maybe a small service here would be enough. There might be some sort of Haus im Wald chaplain.

She looked in through the door. It was a plain room and had a table made of light-colored wood at the far end with an unadorned wooden cross on it. To the side was a lectern with a large open Bible. On either side of a narrow aisle, there were about twelve rows of pews with red plush kneeling cushions. Eleanor felt a sudden impulse to go and kneel down—and do what? Pray? To whom? To what? For what? In any case, she was much too wet. Still, she walked in and down the little center aisle, curious about what page the Bible was open at. Ecclesiastes. Well, whoever read from it last in this place may well have been thinking of mortality. *Because man goeth to his long home, and the mourners go about in the streets.* She could not resist the temptation to read on aloud: *"Or ever the silver cord be loosed or the golden bowl be broken, or the pitcher be broken at the fountain, or the wheel broken at the cistern."* She paused, touched by the beauty of the words.

A voice taking up the verses from the back of the room startled her: *"Then shall the dust return to the earth as it was, and the spirit shall return unto God who gave it."*

"Oh dear," she said, flustered. "Pastor Pokorny. Caught in the act, I'm afraid. It's hard to resist the sound of one's own voice reading such a beautiful passage."

She walked toward him, and he smiled benignly, "Well, yes, my dear Mrs. Fabian, if you had read on, you would have come to the admonition: *Vanity, vanity, saith the preacher, all is vanity.* But this is an admonition *for* preachers too, you know, if you read *vanity* in the way most of us understand it. I like the sound of my own voice as well as the next man. Quite probably, Frau Beck left the Bible open at that page. I had suggested the last chapter of Ecclesiastes as a reading for Frau Winkler's funeral service. Perhaps she was practicing reading it. A piece of pure poetry, you know, not everyone's favorite funeral reading, but it's a favorite of mine."

"I was just going up to see Christa actually and only stopped in here on an impulse. I'm afraid I'm very wet." She looked apologetically at the damp trail she had made up and down the aisle. "It's been a dreadful day."

"Yes, I heard about your mother-in-law—I'm so sorry. I have not known such a couple of days since I moved into the Haus im Wald. Do you know how that chapter in Ecclesiastes begins? The preacher urges you to remember your Creator in the days of your youth, before the evil days—*the years draw nigh when thou shalt say, I have no pleasure in them.* I have had pleasure in my life, Frau Fabian, but I am beginning to feel that those sad years, alas, are drawing nigh."

He had looked so buoyant and full of life this morning, Eleanor thought, but now in the dim light of the little chapel, there was a shadow in his eyes, his shoulders seemed suddenly bent, and even his strong voice quavered.

"I shall sit here for a while and think," he said. "What is happening to us, the old folk of the Haus im Wald?" He turned away. "Good night, my dear." He walked to the front of the chapel, down the center aisle, leaning on his cane with one hand and holding the backs of the pews with the other as he passed. He sat down. *"Or ever the silver cord be loosed,"* she heard him say aloud as she went out through the door, *"or the golden bowl be broken."*

I must hurry, she thought. What am I doing dawdling around here? And she almost ran up the two flights of stairs to Christa's apartment. She knocked at the door, and Christa immediately opened it.

"My dear girl, you are so wet. Take that stuff off at once."

"I don't think there's any point. I would only have to put it right back on again. I just came to see how you are and say hello and good-bye."

"Oh, I thought you could have had a bit of supper with me." She gestured to her little coffee table where she had already put out bread and wurst and cheese.

Eleanor knew that she must have spent a good hour clearing up the space around this table to make it habitable for a guest, and she would have liked nothing better than to take off her wet things, sink down on the couch, and have a good talk. "But, Christa, I simply dare not. Franz is back in the flat, home from the hospital after the concussion, and I am already late. I ran into your Pastor Pokorny in the chapel."

"The chapel?"

"Yes," Eleanor felt rather silly about this. "I just went in on an impulse, and there was the Bible open at a wonderful chapter in Ecclesiastes."

"Yes, I was trying it out for Frau Winkler's little funeral service. It's a favorite of Pastor Pokorny's, but somehow it seems to me more suitable for a man than for a little lady like Frau Winkler. In fact it would probably be just the thing for Herr Graf's funeral, if they are having one for him. Maybe that is really what is on the pastor's mind. All of us just keep thinking about that murder. The chapter ends with that verse about how God will bring every work unto judgment—*every secret thing, whether it be good, or whether it be evil.* There's a horrible sense of evil, don't you think, hanging about the place at the moment?"

"Heavens, Christa, I wish I could get you out of here for a while. You have nothing to do with any of this, and yet you got so upset in the inspector's office today."

"I got in an awful muddle, I know, when he asked me about Sister Agatha. But you see, Eleanor, I *did* see her coming out of Graf's apartment. For some reason, I didn't want to say so, perhaps because I don't particularly like her and so wanted to bend over backward rather than point the finger at her. But the fact is that I saw her coming out of his apartment. I am nearsighted, it's true, and I was only looking along the corridor from the staircase, but I do remember her coming out of his apartment at some point."

"Well, you must tell the inspector the truth."

"I can't take any more of this cross-examination stuff." Christa was crying again.

"OK, OK, it probably isn't that important because the murder in any case was surely later. Christa, dear, please eat something, then lock your door, and go to bed."

"Lock my door!" The tears fell again.

"Well, you know what I mean. Put that little chain thing across now when I leave, and I'll be back to see you tomorrow. We have to deal with Mother's death too, you know."

"Yes, I'm sorry. I'm sorry. I'll be better tomorrow. I hope you find Franz better tonight."

I doubt that, thought Eleanor as she hurried down the stairs and out of the side door, grateful not to run into any other residents of the Haus im Wald on the way.

2

Well, here's a switch, thought the inspector. Me sitting on the back of a small motor scooter, my arms around the ample waist of a chubby deaconess of advanced years. He almost laughed aloud.

"Cold?" shouted Sister Barbara, half turning her head.

"Yes," he shouted back, "but fine! Glad to be out of there."

"Know what you mean!" She skidded on the wet snow as they turned into the road to go through the woods. "Oops! Don't worry! I've been driving one of these things ever since our student days. Not far now!"

Oddly enough, he didn't worry, and the cold air in his face was, for the moment, exhilarating. It drove all thought out of his head and left him only with sheer physical sensation.

Entering the village, Barbara shouted, "Goldene Glocke, OK?"

"Fine!" he shouted again, and they skidded to a halt in front of its bright lights.

"You go on in," she said. "I know a place to put the scooter round the back."

At six o'clock, the Goldene Glocke was just beginning to fill up. The only place open in the village, probably, at this time of year, though in the summer the whole area round about would be buzzing with people, out from the city to drink the new wine in the gardens of the Heuriger. This place, he looked around him, was set up like a Heuriger—you could have waiter service at your table, or you could go and collect whatever you wanted at the buffet. He lingered at the hot end of the buffet. I shall eat *Stelze* with sauerkraut, he decided. Just what I need on a night like this. But first I'll find a table. There was an empty one in the back, next to the big window that looked on to the garden, where in summer the long tables would be full.

"This OK?"

Sister Barbara had come in, her face bright red from the cold. "Fine. Can't wait to warm up."

The waiter came. Büchner ordered a beer, and Sister Barbara an apple juice. "You eating?" he asked.

"No, I'll have a snack with Agatha later. We had a meal at lunchtime, and we usually just have something light in the evening when she's back from doing her rounds."

"Her rounds?"

"Yes, she usually checks on the people in Martin Luther, sees if everything's all right in the common rooms, and so on. I often go too and see if people need help eating, for example. You can't just stick food down in front of really old people, you know. They just toy with it and leave most of it on the plate. That's what happens half the time in nursing homes unless someone is paying attention. And Agatha certainly pays attention. She tries to make sure that somebody helps them."

"Ah yes, and you are often that somebody, I suppose."

Sister Barbara laughed. "Well, yes, that's my role. That's fine. It suits me. Maybe you'd like me to come to the buffet with you and give you a hand with picking out your dinner?"

"Thanks a lot," he took a large swallow of beer, laughed, and made his way to the buffet.

"So how is she managing this evening?" he asked when he came back with his Stelze. "Did you tell her you were taking this old man out to dinner?"

"Yes, of course. I think she felt a bit guilty about sending you to bed without any supper last night, and she actually suggested I should make sure you ate tonight."

Feeling slightly disappointed to discover that this whole outing had been Sister Agatha's idea, he said, "Oh, Sister Barbara"—with an ironic emphasis on the *Sister*—"and I thought you just wanted to catch up with an old comrade."

"Well, of course, I did. I do. I am very happy to see someone from my own past." Again there was a directness about her way of speaking, no jocularity, no irony. "It really is the distant past now."

"Yes, hard to believe that the big year 1968 was almost forty years ago"

"Remember that May? Twenty thousand students on the barricades in the Sorbonne. Barricades, I thought, just like the French Revolution."

"Yes," said Büchner. "I was so fired up by that, the very thought of the magnitude of it, the fact that they had to put in ten thousand policemen to deal with it! And of all things, a young German as the student leader!"

"I know," she said, "Daniel Cohn-Bendit. A name to conjure with in those days."

"Sure was. Remember his slogan, 'A radical change in the university means a radical change in society.' We really believed that back then."

"Ever see him on TV?" she said. "He's quite often on German TV talk shows—I think he's in the European Parliament now, with the Greens, isn't he? Still a fiery speaker—but what happened to his radical change in society?"

"We thought it was just around the corner in Vienna too when you and I were shooting our mouths off in the so-called Association of Socialist Students. Sorry, don't mean to mock."

"Well, you were shooting your mouth off. I was just making the coffee."

"I made lots of speeches in those days. Democratization of all spheres of life—that was the big slogan."

"What in the world got you out of all that and into the police? Did you go to the big demo in Salzburg where we let the pig loose in the protest against the federal army?" They laughed. "But the police were pretty brutal that day—that wasn't funny—with their rubber truncheons and all."

"They had to protect the army from the students. We were all against the army. 'Drop acid, not bombs!'" They laughed again, and Büchner ordered another beer. "I suppose the problem was, it gradually dawned on me that we were enjoying it all too much. And when the Aktivisten started their performances, remember, they would stand naked on the stage in the big lecture hall and pee and shit and masturbate—I began to think, they are no different from the Dadaists in Zürich in the First World War. *Épater le bourgeois*. Sure, we shocked the bourgeoisie, and sure, we achieved quite an opening up of the university—but 'democratization of society'? Not a hope in hell."

"Is that why you went into the police?"

"Well, you know, I did some reading about the '68 Sorbonne show, and I'd always been so impressed with the way the students defended themselves against the tear gas, the cudgels of the police, and all that, and then I discovered that their success stemmed in good measure from the fact that the police were under strict orders not to endanger life! In other words, they could be brutal up to a point, but their brutality stopped well before dead bodies."

"OK, but we had our own instances of police brutality. You haven't forgotten Ohnesorg—that German student shot by the police in Berlin. That really set off the radical student movement there. About '67, wasn't it? And remember poor old Rudi Dutschke."

"Yes, but Dutschke was shot by some crazy person, not by the police. Oh hell, I'm not trying to defend the police. Well, maybe at some level I am. But that wasn't my point. My point was that the whole thing was a far cry from the French Revolution, and I thought then, who were we trying to kid? So I began to think, I've had it with students and universities. I was studying German literature, remember. It all seemed so out of touch. When I went into the police, I thought I wanted to tackle the problems of society from within the power structure. I wanted to see what the world was like from another angle."

"And what is it like, Georg?"

He finished the second beer slowly with one long last swallow. He felt she deserved a serious answer but wasn't sure he was up to giving one. "What is the world like in the Haus im Wald, Barbara? A bunch of people trying to survive, trying to do good, some of them, trying to make money, trying to find love and companionship, trying to find God, solitude, meaning, trying to preserve their own dignity, trying to avenge themselves for their raw deal in life, or to seek justice for themselves in one way or another. I am in the justice business, that's how I see it, I like to think there is some justice somewhere and maybe I can help it along. That's all. That's all that's left of my big ideas."

She looked directly at him. "Justice, yes. A fine idea. But one man's justice is another man's punishment."

"That's the life of the lawman, yes,"

"But here, now, in the Haus im Wald, if you bring the killer of Hans Graf to justice, you may bring punishment and even death to another person, or persons."

"That's true, Barbara. Do you have a problem with that?"

"If I were in your shoes, I might have."

"But I wear the shoes of a policeman."

"Yes," she said solemnly, even sadly. "That's so. Can't get around that."

"Look, Barbara, do you have something to tell me about this murder?"

"No, no. I just wanted to get a sense of where you stood these days, what your priorities were, in the war of ideas, I mean. I have to get back, I think." She made no move to get up, however, and they sat for a while in what might have seemed to be a companionable silence, if Büchner had not had the feeling that Barbara had sunk back into her own world. She stared rather dully into space.

"Better get going," he said finally. "It's been great to breathe the air of the world outside the Haus im Wald."

"Yes, sometimes one feels no other world exists except the one inside." They stood up and went out the back way to where the little motor scooter stood gathering wet snow. Barbara wiped it off with a cloth from the saddlebag, and they set off back through the cold night.

3

Franz had been drifting in and out of consciousness in his little room in the Zehenthofgasse for what seemed like a long time. The pain in his head seemed to have receded since he had taken the strong analgesic in the hospital. When Eleanor came back, she would have filled the prescription they gave him, and he would have another couple of pills to see him through the night. He gingerly touched his right temple with his fingers. Very sore to touch. He had taken quite a crack. I wonder, he thought, how it looks? He put on the bedside lamp, carefully eased himself out of bed, and peered into the small round mirror hanging on the wall. My God, they were right about the black eye, though it was more of a reddish blue at the moment. But it covered the whole of the right eye cavity and spread down into the cheek and across the nose. The whole area seemed to be swelling up. Grotesque. His first thought was, Mother will be enraged that I could do something like this to myself. Then it began to come back to him. Eleanor had said in the hospital that Mother was dead.Was this possible, or was this whole thing some crazy nightmare?

He got back into bed and closed his eyes again, trying to shut out the events of the day and fall back into his not unpleasant, semidrugged sleep. It didn't work. The drug was obviously wearing off. Where the hell was Eleanor? Still at that madhouse to which they had taken his mother for her to be properly looked after? They'd looked after her, all right. What had happened to her, really? He thought of the moment in her room that he most wanted to forget but probably never would, the moment when she had been gripping his wrist and he'd tried to get free and she'd started screaming. If she really was dead, was he responsible for her death? He would never have to say so to anybody else—he had been completely alone in the room with her—but he remembered now the frenzied way he'd tried to pry her fingers from his wrist and how, when she'd started to scream, he had felt an uncontrollable urge to keep her quiet; and he had, for a fraction of a second at least, put his one free hand over her mouth. Of course, that was a crazy thing to do, and it hardly even stopped her. She went right on screaming, but she had loosened her grip on his wrist, and he remembered now the immense relief of that. Would he have kept his hand over her mouth if she hadn't let him go? Was this how murders happened? In desperate moments when the suffering inflicted on one person by another simply became unendurable? Maybe something like this had happened with Graf. Whom could he have been hurting so much that they just had to strike out at him? This was idle speculation. He hadn't actually committed murder himself, had he? But suppose he had not taken his hand away, and suppose that nurse—what was her name?—had come in with Eleanor and found his mother dead under his hand. He would not be lying here with a black eye; he would be in custody, being interrogated by that pip-squeak detective. Thus does one's life hang on a thread. In any case, though he wasn't going to be found out, he probably had contributed to her rapid demise, first by the hand-over-the-mouth episode, and then later by simply not reacting when she began to make weird noises in her throat. But still, wait a minute, she had been very unwell that morning, had taken a turn for the worse, remember, he'd been sent for by the hospital. Maybe the autopsy would bring some concrete information. If only it would prove that that ass, Hofer, had poisoned her with his medicines, he would be the one being interrogated by Pip-squeak. They deserved each other. Oh, my aching head. He was trying to find a comfortable place on the pillow for his head when he heard the key turn in the lock. Thank God, Eleanor in the nick of time with the pills.

She came into the room on tiptoe, looking totally bedraggled. "You're still wet," he said.

"Yes, I can't wait to get out of these things and into a hot bath. How are you feeling?"

"Pretty bad," he said. "Where are the pills?'

"Here. I'll just fetch some water."

"Please."

She came back, opened the packet, fumbling with the cover on the little plastic container. Franz groaned. She struggled on, and finally it came off. He swallowed two pills.

"You can have two more in six hours. Can I get you something to eat?"

"Don't even mention the word," he said, closing his eyes again and turning over to face the wall. Eleanor turned out the light and closed the door, he thought, with a bang. Can't worry about that. He tried to do what doctors were always telling him to do with headaches: relax into the pain. Sometimes he felt this was almost working, but only for seconds at a time, then the relaxing became a suffocating sinking. He fell now into the hole where there was nothing but pain.

4

"How about a cup of coffee with Agatha and me before you turn in? The night is very young for a professional man like you."

A little surprised at this invitation, Büchner looked at his watch. "Well, yes, I'm not usually tucked up in bed by eight o'clock. But do you think Agatha will want to see me at this time of night?"

"She said I should bring you back."

"And you always do what she says?" It was again a slight pang of annoyance that made him say this in a mocking tone.

"Yes, pretty much," said Barbara, again without apology or irony. Did she take everything literally, or was she just very much under control?

"OK, I accept."

"I have a place to put the scooter," she said. "Perhaps you could just wait for me for a moment in the lobby?"

"How do I get in?"

"Here, take the front door key. The residents of Melanchthon all have one. We are grown-ups, you know, with a life in the outside world, though it may not always seem like it."

"OK." He let himself in, feeling not quite revulsion but certainly some antipathy as he entered the warm lobby of the Haus im Wald.

Two men were coming up to the front door as he walked through it. One was Michael, with coat on, ready to leave, and the other was little Herr Ritter. They greeted him, clearly a little surprised to see him, and Herr Ritter said quickly, "Good evening, Herr Inspektor, we are just coming from the evening meal."

"Ah yes," said Büchner. "You missed lunch, did you not?"

"My, my, you certainly keep an eye on us, Herr Inspektor."

"My job, Herr Ritter. Off home, Michael?"

"Yes, a long day today. Will you want breakfast again in the morning, Herr Inspektor?"

"If you think you'll be here before eight."

"Certainly, I will. Well, good night, Herr Ritter, Herr Inspektor, just running for the bus to Feldberg," and he left.

"A good boy," said Herr Ritter. "We're all fond of him here."

"All?"

"Well, almost all. Hans Graf thought the world of him. He was trying to use his influence to help the boy get his grandmother a room in Martin Luther."

"His influence?"

"Hans was a rich man, and very rich people can sometimes get things done. He was leaving a sizable legacy to the Haus im Wald, you know, something they rather like here, for obvious reasons. Sister Agatha, however, has a different kind of influence, and she is not so well-disposed toward young Michael. Ah, Sister Barbara? A cold night to be out and about."

She came in rubbing her hands. "Indeed. Good evening, Herr Ritter. Well, shall we?"

All three made their way silently up the staircase, and at the second floor, Büchner said, "Good night then, Herr Ritter. I'm having coffee with the ladies. If you're up early in the morning, why don't you join Michael and me for early-morning coffee in the café? It would have to be at seven thirty. I'd like the chance of a bit of a chat with you"—he paused—"on your own."

Herr Ritter smiled wryly. "Yes, I see. Well, I'll try. A very good night to you both."

And off he goes to that dreadful wife of his, thought Büchner. "An odd couple, the Ritters," he said as they made their way to the next floor.

"Is there any other kind?" said Sister Barbara and smiled, but benignly. She opened the door of the apartment. Yes, it was a very pleasant room, this end room with its two windows, one facing you as you went in and one long low one on the right wall.

"And who lives under you?" said Büchner, losing touch for a moment with the floor plan in his head. "Not the Ritters, they are under the ill-fated Herr Graf."

"No, the Zimmermanns. Another odd couple, if you like. Tax accountants, both of them, in their former lives, and they did very well out of it, built up quite a business together. They're divorced."

"An odd kind of divorce, living together in an apartment this size."

"Yes, apparently they had a long and acrimonious divorce, but went on living in the same house on separate floors, quarrelling with each other in two separate apartments for twenty years, but when he got to be eighty years old, they must have decided they would give the status quo ante another try and live in the same four walls. Got to be too tiring, I suppose, climbing the stairs just to quarrel. He shouts a lot—Herr Zimmermann—you hear him sometimes as you walk past, but I don't think she pays much attention."

"Did they have anything to do with Herr Graf?"

"Frau Zimmermann does his taxes every year. Did, I should probably say. She does most of the tax work for people round here—another life's habit they don't want to give up. Herr Zimmermann is a bit past it, but she's still bright as a button."

Well, thought Büchner, there's someone who might have insight into the private financial life of Herr Graf. Better talk to them tomorrow. Where, he wondered, is Sister Agatha?

Barbara came back from the kitchen, where she had put on the coffee. "Where is Agatha, I wonder," she said.

"I was wondering too. Still doing her Christian duty over in Martin Luther?"

"Possibly. It's after seven o'clock already. She should be back soon—unless some other dreadful thing has happened over there again."

"Better drink my coffee and go over there then!"

The door opened, and in came Sister Agatha. "I do apologize, Herr Inspektor, that I was not here to greet you."

"Don't apologize, Sister. I am enjoying the coffee and a talk with Barbara."

Agatha looked sharply at him. Barbara said quickly, "You won't have coffee, will you, Agatha?"

"Thanks, I'll stick to my peppermint tea at this time of night."

She sat down in the armchair opposite Büchner, looking tired and, he thought, almost human. She closed her eyes for a moment and rubbed her forehead with her fingers.

"Headache?" said Barbara.

"I'm all right. Just tired. It was a long day."

"For all of us," said Büchner.

"And how is your investigation going, Inspektor?"

"I shall sit down in my room tonight and go over my notes," he said. "Do either of you have anything to add that might help me?"

The two women looked at each other, and there was a silence.

"Barbara thinks," said Agatha, with some difficulty, "that I should tell you one or two things, before you hear them from someone else. I do not think they have any relevance to the murder, but they are what they are. I knew Hans Graf many years ago. We were engaged to be married. My family was then wealthy, as was his, and our engagement was very much approved by both families. Shortly before the wedding day, Hans Graf broke off the engagement. He did not"—she paused—"love me enough, that was what he said. It was a minor scandal in our circle, and I was deeply humiliated by it. As it turns out, I do not regret it. My life has been a good one, and his, from what one hears, was marked by a series of . . . unsuitable relationships. I was, I admit, not pleased when he moved in here, but whereas he still has the wealth to get what he wants—he is a big fish in the small pond of this neighborhood—I do not. Barbara and I can afford to be here only because we are deaconesses and there are special arrangements made. And when he came and promptly took up one of his"—she paused again—"classic relationships, with Frau Hagen, well, shall we say, it has taken a great deal of Christian charity to put up with this, and there are no doubt a number of residents who will be only too willing to testify that there was not much love lost between us, as one might say."

"No one has said it," said Büchner, "but I appreciate your filling in this piece of the background. Does it explain in any way, perhaps, why one resident thinks she saw you coming out of Graf's apartment on Christmas Day in the afternoon?"

"Absolute nonsense—as I have already told you, I wasn't there."

"Then that remains a mystery. Ladies, I think I should retire and do my homework."

"I think you will find," said Sister Agatha with a slight smile, "that your room is a little warmer tonight. I went in this evening and turned up the heat."

"Thank you," said Büchner. "And thanks for the coffee. Good night to you both." He was not sure whether to be grateful for Sister Agatha's showing a human face or annoyed at the thought of her calmly letting herself into his bedroom. Privacy, he thought, is not a feature of life in the Haus im Wald, that's for sure.

5

Leaving the sisters' apartment, Büchner walked toward the staircase and stopped at the door of number 32, still with the cord across it, forbidding entry to all but authorized personnel. I am authorized personnel, he thought and tried the door handle. The door was open. Why wasn't it locked? Does Schmidt really think that a sign saying Keep Out is enough! Annoyed at the idea that anyone could have been walking in and out all day long, he walked in quickly himself and closed the door behind him, surprised to see a key in the lock on the inside. He walked through the room and closed the curtains before turning on the light. The light switch next to the window turned on the bright ceiling light, and the first thing he saw was the chalk outline of the body, still bright white on the carpet. The second thing he saw—and he caught his breath with surprise—was a living person sitting deep in the winged armchair, who had not been visible before in the shadows, but was now blinking in the sudden light and looking straight at him.

Smiling with embarrassment, she said, "I'm sorry if I startled you, Herr Inspektor. I must say, I'm relieved it's you."

"Frau Hagen! What in the world are you doing, sitting here in the dark, in a room where . . ."

"A room where a man was murdered? Is that what you want to say, Herr Inspektor? That man was Hans Graf. Soon this room and all it meant to me will be gone. I could not resist trying the door handle this evening, and when I found out the door was open, I could not resist walking in."

"Yes, well, the same thing more or less happened to me! It ought to have been locked, I need hardly say. Did you notice the key on the inside?"

"Key? No, I didn't. I'll leave now, of course." She smiled at him and stood up.

"No," he said. "We are here now. Why don't we talk for a moment?"

"I don't think I have very much to say." But she did sit down again. She looked older tonight, he thought. The bright light showed up the lines on her face, and she sat with her shoulders hunched forward, quite different from the rather brave and upright show she had managed this morning in his office. It seemed strange to him now that he had found her almost sexually attractive before.

"Perhaps you could turn off that bright light," she said, as if reading his thoughts. "There is a little lamp over there on the desk. We always used to put that on. Quite enough light at our age."

He laughed politely, but did as she suggested.

"There was a time," she said, "when bright lights were my life. But not anymore. I shall live in the shadows now."

"You are an opera singer?" he said.

"Was, Herr Inspektor, very much was. I am not one of those singers who goes on until everyone wishes they would stop. I stopped quite early—I was tired of worrying about my voice every minute of every day. I wanted to talk and eat and drink when I felt like it and not always have to deny myself to save my voice. In the last year, particularly, it was wonderful never to have to worry about it."

"Did you know Hans Graf in your singing days?"

"No. I did not. Apparently, he heard me sing a number of times. His favorite role was my Marschallin in the *Rosenkavalier*—ironic really now, the aging beauty who loses her young lover to youthful beauty. Do you remember the moment in the opera where the Marschallin is singing about the mysteriousness of time passing?" Frau Hagen sang quietly: *"How can it really be / That I once was little Resi / And one day I will be an old woman, the old Marschallin! / 'Look, there she goes, old Princess Resi.'"*

She still has a lovely voice, thought Büchner, moved.

"The Marschallin simply can't fathom it," Frau Hagen went on, "because she is the same person as the little girl and the old woman." She uttered a bitter little laugh. "The same, yes, but not the same. At the end of the opera, when it is all over for her and the young people are happy, the Marschallin sings a sort of deep sigh of resignation, almost an octave." Frau Hagen sang it now, *"Ja-ja,"* and added, "I remember the last time I sang that sigh in the State Opera and knew it was the last time I would sigh beautifully in public for my lost youth. Hans apparently saw that last performance, and he used to say, he fell in love with me there and then." She smiled sadly. "I'm sorry. You don't have to listen to this nonsense. All that is over now for me. Now I am really sighing. An old woman, and I have lost my old lover—to what? To whom?" She got up angrily, and he saw the actress in her as her voice rang out theatrically, "Who did it, Herr Inspektor? Are you going to find out?"

"We should perhaps not hold this conversation here," he said. "If anyone hears it, they may be dismayed at voices sounding in the closed room."

"I'm sorry. I'll leave. Of course. You probably have more serious things to do than to listen to an old woman trying to hold on to memories of something that has gone. As the Marschallin says, *Whoever embraces too tightly holds on to nothing.* I tried so hard to hold on to my last bit of happiness, and I lost it."

"But you were not responsible for the loss, surely. Hans Graf was brutally murdered. He did not escape from you because of your tight embrace."

"We do not know, do we, Herr Inspektor, what the motive for the killing was."

"You mean, you think it might have had something to do with you? If you have any concrete notion of that, you should tell me."

"You and I did talk the last time about jealousy. But I did not mention, I think, that he had had some odd notes in recent weeks that made some mention of me. He told me that. I never saw them, but he did say over Christmas that someone had been sending him little notes about the way his relationship with me lowered the tone of the establishment. Unsigned, he said."

"Well, Frau Hagen, why didn't you mention this the last time we spoke?"

"He didn't take them seriously. There's always gossip in a place like this. He thought it was hilarious that anyone should pay attention to our liaison. And so did I. We both felt, if you know what I mean, in love and untouchable. Silly at our age. But there it was. It's only now, thinking of the Marschallin, that this came back to me."

"I'll have a look through the apartment, though I hardly think our men would have overlooked something like that."

"Good night, Herr Inspektor. I'll leave you to it." She took one last long look at the room from the doorway, looked for a moment at the key in the door on her way out, and left.

Well, that's a funny business, thought Büchner. Poison pen letters? No one else had mentioned anything like this. The crime team had gone through the apartment and found very little, no murder weapon, no obvious signs of break-in or any disorder in drawers or closets. The apartment had looked in perfect shape, except for the grisly spectacle on the carpet. I suppose we are going to have to fingerprint all these residents, he thought, his heart sinking at the prospect of broaching this topic with Schramm and the rest. Slipping on his own plastic gloves, he opened the desk in Graf's little office and looked through it. Bills, bank statements, insurance forms—no anonymous letters. Graf would have thrown them away, as likely as not. Probably assumed they were from some frustrated elderly spinster. From Agatha, maybe, given their history. But Büchner doubted that Graf would have thought that. Even he, who hardly knew her, did not think that Agatha would stoop to writing anonymous letters. Still, he would like to have seen one of them. He looked quickly through the bedroom drawers—one held assorted cuff links, tiepins, and so on. No yellow stickers. No silver-and-turquoise tiepin either, he thought. That was odd. He needed someone who had known Graf well to look through and see if anything else might be missing.

Better get back to his room and finally get down to some serious analysis of all this. He'd picked up enough atmospheric vibrations for a while. He went to the door and looked at the key in the lock. Could Schmidt have left it there? Hardly. Or Frau Hagen? She might well have had a key to Graf's apartment. But if this was a key he had given her, why had she not said so? He extracted it carefully, still wearing his gloves, locked the door on the outside, and put the key in a small plastic bag. He heard the sound of the next door opening, and the head of Dr. Lessing appeared gingerly around it.

"Oh, it's you, Herr Inspektor. That's a relief. I began to think there were ghosts next door."

"Sorry to have disturbed you, Frau Doktor. I've locked up now. Good night."

At another time, he would have jumped at the chance of a word with this lady, but he'd had enough words with ladies for one day.

Chapter 8

Not one of the residents of the Haus im Wald was born later than the 1930s. Even Frau Beck, who was younger than most, first saw the light of day before the fateful summer of 1939. The prewar vintage of the residents colored their attitudes to many things. No doubt everything would be different when the postwar generations began to invade the sanctuaries of sheltered living, but for the time being, residents retained many of the characteristics of earlier times, such as an exaggerated respect for doctors, an unwillingness to question them, an automatic acceptance of whatever they chose to diagnose or prescribe. The lives of those who were doctors to this generation were much easier than the lives of those who took care of the middle-aged. The latter had to deal with constant cross-examination, second opinions, and worst of all, the Internet which turned younger-generation patients into instant experts on whatever ailed them. There was, however, no computer room in the Haus im Wald. The office computer was used exclusively by office staff, and only the Zimmermanns had a laptop on which the enterprising seventy-five-year-old Frau Zimmermann worked with her tax forms. When it came to medical information, therefore, the residents still believed that their doctors knew best. Frau Dr. Lessing, a medical doctor herself, was no doubt more skeptical than most; but on the whole, among residents of the Haus im Wald, faith in the doctor was held to be not a sign of weakness, but a support for ongoing life.

1

Eleanor closed the door on her husband with a bit of a bang. It was childish, of course; the man was not well. Still, a word of thanks wouldn't have come amiss. She turned on the water in the bath. Then she went wearily into the kitchen, made a cup of tea and a cheese sandwich, and carried it into the bathroom. I shall have it all in a hot bath, she thought, pouring bath salts into the steaming water and turning on the little electric heater on the wall. Finally, she could take off her wet shoes and stockings. She put the tray with her supper on the soap rack that stretched across the bath and, naked, stepped in and sat down in the high foam. The phone rang. No no no, she thought. Let it ring. She lay in the bath, allowing herself to relax. What was more soothing than to feel the warm soap bubbles all over your body, to let your mind go blank, to turn on the tap and put even more water in until only your head poked up out of the water. Wonderful for her shoulder, which had been hurting on and off all day. One good thing about the Zehenthofgasse was that there was plenty of hot water.

Who could that have been on the phone? she wondered, munching on her sandwich. Ingrid and Ulrich, maybe. Or, oh dear, maybe Christa. The poor girl had seemed in a pretty bad way. Anyway, whoever it was would call again. Her mind drifted back over the day. Unbelievable that last night they had been worrying about things like who should get the corner cupboard and where were the seven hundred euros for Mother's carpets. And now tonight, all that didn't matter a damn. Mother was dead. Though come to think of it, where *were* the seven hundred euros? Very odd that Franz thought they had disappeared from his pocket. She tried to focus her mind on the sequence of events during the day. When had he mentioned the euros? At the hospital? Then he must have lost them sometime between his taxi ride to the Haus im Wald and his arriving at the hospital. She would have seen them if they'd dropped out of his pocket in the ambulance, and a bunch of banknotes didn't just drop unnoticed out of your pocket. Could someone have taken them? But out of his inside pocket? She could feel her head clouding over and her eyes closing. Lord, she probably shouldn't go to sleep in this deep soapy water. Another unexplained death in the morning. It had always struck her that if she wanted to commit suicide, this would be the way to go. But if you went to sleep and your head slipped under the soapsuds, would you drown or just wake up spluttering? She wasn't going to try it out quite yet. So Mother had gone, she kept coming back to that. How did she really feel about it? She had never actually liked her, but she had often felt sorry for her. Franz's attitude to her had been difficult to take. He just barely did his duty, visiting her once a year, telephoning perhaps once every few weeks, and then only because Eleanor kept saying, "Isn't it time you called your mother?" She had visited her herself several times in these recent years since the death of Franz's father. She knew that the old lady had been very lonely. So did Franz. But it hadn't moved him to do anything about it. She thought of his voice when his mother would occasionally phone him. "Oh, hello," he would say in a flat dull way with a downward intonation. Never, "Hello, Mother!" He hardly ever called her anything at all. And now there it was, she had died, and there had been that odd business of her holding on to him, screaming. What had he done? Didn't bear thinking about really. She let out some of the water and tried running in some hot. But the water was cooling down, even here in the Zehenthofgasse. At least Franz would be fast asleep by now. She could watch a bit of TV and go straight to bed. The height of bliss! Well, that said something. This old-folks-home atmosphere was really getting to her. She felt somehow older than when she had arrived. And at the same time, minute by minute, less satisfied with the way she was living. She and Franz had been married getting on for thirty years. Surely there was no point in contemplating leaving him at this age. And yet with the picture of herself living in an old folks' home (she couldn't stop calling it that) so vividly before her eyes, she was beginning to feel quite desperate to grab a little bit of life now while there was still time and to enjoy life in a way that she and Franz didn't seem to do together anymore. But how could she possibly do this? Here was Christa, scarcely older than she was, already completely resigned to ending her days in the Haus im Wald. But she was no Christa. Never had been. At sixty-three, she could probably even fall in love again, though as the soapsuds cooled down and started to subside and she could see her sixty-three-year-old body, it was hard to imagine falling excitedly into bed with somebody new. Well, she certainly didn't fall excitedly into bed with Franz anymore, nor he with her. Lord, she'd better get out and see how he was doing. The water was cooling down distinctly in any case.

She clambered out of the bath, dried herself, and got right into her pajamas and dressing gown, thinking longingly of sleep. As soon as she opened the bathroom door, she could hear from the way Franz was moving in bed that he wasn't asleep. She went to his door and looked cautiously around it. "Are you asleep?" she whispered hopefully.

"No," he said very loudly. "These pills don't seem to have any effect at all."

"Maybe they will soon."

"I took them ages ago. Where have you been?"

"In the bath. Trying to warm up."

"I think I'm going to throw up," said Franz.

"Oh God." She ran to the bathroom, brought a bowl, and held his head. He vomited violently into the bowl and fell back on his pillow, sweating streams.

"Franz!" she said desperately. "This is terrible."

"I'll be all right," he said weakly, falling back on the pillow. "Glass of water please. Turn the light out, would you?"

What am I to do? she thought. He needs a doctor. I need a doctor. I can't cope with this on my own. She went to the telephone where there was still a list of emergency numbers. The only name she recognized was Hofer's. Franz couldn't stand him, but she knew he made house calls, and he might come; it wasn't so late, only 9:00 p.m. If she left it any later, she might end up having to get an ambulance and take Franz back to the hospital. Hofer was better than that. And he lived in Döbling too.

She dialed the number, and Hofer himself answered.

"Eleanor Fabian here. I'm very sorry to disturb you, Dr. Hofer, but I do not know where to turn, and your number was by the phone. We are in my mother-in-law's apartment in the

Zehenthofgasse, and my husband seems to me to be dreadfully ill."

"And what are his symptoms?"

"A blinding headache, which the analgesic I got for him doesn't seem to touch, and now he's started vomiting."

"Would you like me to come and have a look at him?"

"Well, yes, I'd be very grateful."

"And does your husband want me to come?"

"Right now, Dr. Hofer, I'm not at all sure he knows what he wants."

"Very well, I can probably be there in about ten minutes."

"Thank you, thank you. You know where we are. No more than ten minutes? I appreciate it greatly."

She quickly threw on a sweater and a pair of pants and went back to Franz. "Try to breathe deeply," she said. "It helps to stop the vomiting. Just hold on. The doctor is coming." It was a sign of how bad he felt that he said nothing. And even when she said, "Dr. Hofer, he was the only one I knew how to find quickly, and he knows where we are," even then, Franz hardly reacted. He seemed to be concentrating on trying to breathe deeply. She sat by the bed, willing Hofer to arrive quickly.

The ring at the doorbell was a relief, and Eleanor brought the doctor straight into the study. "Let's have a look at you," he said in classic doctor parlance. Franz remained silent while the doctor checked him front and back with the stethoscope, took his temperature, felt his pulse, and looked with a little lamp into his eyes.

"Headache very bad?"

Franz nodded dumbly.

"Any blurred vision?"

"Not that I can tell."

"Do you remember the fall?"

"I could hardly forget it."

"Well, yes, you could actually. This would tell us something about the severity of the concussion. I need a precise answer to the question." Franz looked slightly mortified—outdoing him at his own game, thought Eleanor.

"Very well, speaking precisely, I do not remember actually falling or what caused me to fall. I do remember coming to, facedown on the floor, with a blinding headache."

Hofer turned his questions to Eleanor. "Has he vomited more than once?"

Before she could reply, Franz said, "No, but the headache is very bad, and the pills seem to have lost their effect."

Hofer looked at the prescription. "They are only acetaminophen, you know. What you call Tylenol, I believe. It is not usual to give people who have suffered concussion too strong an analgesic. I'm sure you would agree, Professor Fabian, that it is not a good idea to overprescribe!" He turned again to Eleanor. "Did he have an electroencephalogram in the hospital?

"Yes, there appeared to be no particular problem."

"Well, Professor Fabian, I think if your wife can rustle up some sort of ice pack and put it on your head for twenty minutes at a time, that may be the best we can do for the moment. Another two Tylenol in six hours. And keep drinking lots of liquids. I think you will be all right in the morning. You and your wife should simply watch out for new symptoms in the next couple of weeks."

Franz said nothing. Eleanor accompanied the doctor into the sitting room. Thank you, Doctor. I'm sorry if I got you here for nothing. I just felt at my wits' end."

"I understand. Are you in pain yourself, Frau Fabian?" He talked quite differently now, she noticed. There was an attractively gentle note in his voice.

"Well, yes, as a matter of fact, I wrenched my shoulder moving furniture around in here a couple of days ago. How did you know?"

"You seemed to be holding your shoulder in an unnatural way. I have an eye for these things. Just sit for a second on this low-backed chair."

She did and felt immense pleasure at the way his strong, gentle fingers manipulated her shoulders and the back of her neck.

"Just breathe deeply."

She did. After a few minutes, he said, "Well, there we are, Frau Fabian. Not a complete waste of time, this visit, was it?" and he smiled.

"No, no, not at all. That was wonderful. Thank you."

"Don't let that husband of yours drive you into rheumatic spasms." He smiled again. "Good night, Frau Fabian."

Well, she thought, all those old ladies knew a thing or two. Dr. Hofer certainly had a way with him. And he had dealt pretty efficiently with Franz too. She went into the kitchen, found a plastic bag of frozen peas in the icebox, wrapped it in a cloth, and took it into Franz's room with a large pitcher of water and two more Tylenol. She put the peas on his head. "There," she said, "hold that. The peas are for now, the Tylenol is for later, and I'm going to bed." And without waiting for an answer, she left the room and firmly closed the door.

2

The lights were dim in the lobby of the Haus im Wald as Büchner walked through it. Schramm saves on the electric bills at night, he thought. I can't blame him for that. He took out the key from his pocket and looked at it through the plastic, comparing it with the two other two keys he had—one to his office and one to the Fabian room in Martin Luther. Even in the dim light, this one looked somehow different. A thought struck him. He walked along the corridor to his office, and using his plastic gloves, he tried it in the lock. It turned easily, and he let himself in with it. Well. That was interesting. The key left in the lock was a master key and probably opened any door in the place. So it wasn't a key that Frau Hagen would have got from Herr Graf. He picked up his notes from the desk and double-locked his door on the way out, though why he should bother to do that, he didn't know, since master keys seemed to be floating freely about the building. The door next to his opened in that moment, and out came Director Schramm.

"Oh, it's you, Herr Inspektor. I wondered who was opening and closing doors at this time of night."

"Working late, Herr Direktor?"

"Yes, I sometimes come back to do paperwork in the evenings when everything is quiet."

"Could I just step inside for a second? There's something I'd like to ask you."

Schramm bowed slightly and pointed Büchner to a chair opposite his desk.

"I would be interested to know," said Büchner, "how the key system operates in the building. I have the impression that people are fairly casual about locking their doors, and of course, in the Martin Luther wing, doors will have to be kept open as a matter of course for the care of the patients. But there is, I presume, a properly established master-key system?"

"Yes, of course," said Schramm. "It is crucial in such a situation to exercise proper control over who has keys to what rooms. The residents in Melanchthon all have two keys—both of the 'change variety,' i.e., they fit only one lock. One fits the front door, and the other the individual apartment. These keys are, of course, identified by sequence number, not the same, obviously, as the actual number of the apartment. And then there is a master key that allows authorized persons access to all locks. There are only two authorized persons. I am one, and the housekeeper, Frau Huber, who lives on the premises and has been employed here for almost ten years, is the other."

"I see. And how easy is it, do you suppose, to duplicate these keys?"

"The master keys? Impossible without my express permission. They are part of a high-security key system, and no licensed locksmith in Vienna may make a duplicate without written permission from me."

"Well, perhaps you can explain then, Herr Dircktor, how it is that I have just found what appears to be a master key in the lock inside Herr Graf's apartment?" He took the key and showed it to Schramm, who flushed.

"Impossible," he said. "But yes, the number 15566RHS is the number of the master key." He reached out to look at it more closely.

"Do not take it out of the bag," said Büchner.

"If it were duplicated by a reputable locksmith with my permission, the name of the locksmith would be imprinted on the back. This one is blank. What does that mean?"

"I was hoping you would tell me. Could you check whether your own master key is where it is supposed to be?"

Schramm took out his key ring. The key was there. "And this one cannot be Frau Huber's key because hers, like mine, has the name on the back of Hoffmannn, the locksmith."

"Perhaps," said Büchner, thinking of his young friend Michael, but not mentioning him, "there are more master keys floating about the building. This one would, I take it, also open the front door?"

"Yes," said Schramm, "it would."

"I'll leave you with the puzzle then. But I will keep this stray master key. I will need to check it for fingerprints. I'm afraid we are reaching a point where it will be necessary to fingerprint the mobile residents and the employees of the Haus im Wald."

Schramm looked as if he were about to remonstrate, but taking a deep breath, he said, "You must do your job."

Büchner's little room was pleasantly warm when he got there. This, at least, he had Sister Agatha to thank for. He tossed his papers on the table, took his shoes off, and lay down on the bed, letting the events of the day run through his head. Odd details surfaced: Michael's key, Agatha coming out of Graf's apartment, Dr. Lessing's hearing Graf's son on Christmas Day, Fabian's story about losing seven hundred euros, the key in the lock of Graf's room . . . sometimes a collection of inexplicable oddities added up to something that began to make sense, but he couldn't see it here. And then the two old ladies dying within hours of each other—he couldn't get them out of his head, and yet a connection with Graf seemed unlikely. His cell phone rang. He took it out of his inside pocket, remembering as he did so that he had something else in there.

"Büchner," he said.

"Schmidt," came the reply. "News on the autopsies, sir. Graf did not die immediately from the blow on the head, but from respiratory and heart failure following intracranial bleeding, probably some hours later. And the contents of the stomach show no medications, well, except aspirin and sildenafil citrate"—he paused—"that's Viagra, sir—equivalent to a 100 mg dose taken up to nine hours before death."

"I need to digest that one," said Büchner, "if you'll pardon the expression. And the old lady, Frau Fabian?"

"Congestive heart failure, sir. She'd taken two medications, Levodopa and Alprazolam."

"OK, thank you, Herr Schmidt, I'll talk to the doctor early in the morning. Get here early yourself, we need to set up general fingerprinting."

"Yes, sir. Eight thirty soon enough?'

"Fine, I'll be in the office on the ground floor."

Well, what does all that add up to? Then he put his hand in his inside pocket again and brought out what he had almost forgotten, the plastic envelope containing Hans Graf's last table napkin. He hesitated before opening it. There was something not quite pleasant in the thought of seeing the last traces of food enjoyed by someone whose stomach's contents had just been so coldly analyzed. He opened it and took out one of the rather expensive white damask napkins that the Haus im Wald provided for its residents. Some slightly stomach-churning traces of gravy. And then, as he carefully unfolded it on to the bed, he saw that a slip of paper was adhering to the inside fold—a yellow sticker. Printed on it in almost childlike letters was the crude rhyme:

DIRTY OLD MAN YOU KNOW WHO
THAT OLD LADY'LL BE THE DEATH OF YOU

This was the sort of thing Hans Graf had found hilarious? He had died, no doubt, before finding this one. It struck Büchner as more stomach-churning than the gravy. He went to the window and threw it open. Schramm's expensive heat could go out of the window. He needed air. He took in the cold air in greedy gulps. There was no moon tonight. The clouds seemed to be pressing down on the house. He felt a pain in his chest and closed the window. A house of heart attacks, he thought. I'd better get some sleep.

3

Franz was surprised when he woke up in the morning to see from the bedside clock that it was eight o'clock. The events of yesterday slowly came back to him. He was surprised that he could see at all, if it came to that. He must have been asleep for some hours. He moved his head gingerly from side to side on the pillow and was again surprised to discover that his headache was not too bad. He remembered taking two Tylenol around 4:00 a.m. with a glass of water—the pain had still been pretty bad then. Maybe now he'd really got over the worst of it. He rolled over, put his feet on the floor, and was shocked to find his right foot in a cold wet mess. What was this? He stooped down to look—soggy green peas! So that's what Eleanor had slapped on his head last night after the visit of the dreadful Hofer. One way or another, he would get that man before all this was over. He went to the bathroom and then into the kitchen. Eleanor was already sitting there with her inevitable cup of tea, fully dressed and somehow spruced up. Makeup at eight in the morning?

"Going to take the world by storm?" he asked.

"Yes, maybe. And you?"

"Well, I do feel better," he admitted.

"So Dr. Hofer's methods worked." She sounded smug.

"Nothing to do with him. He didn't really do anything."

"He did a lot for me. He put my mind at rest and gave me a night's sleep."

"Ah, yes, well Hofer is a ladies' doctor."

"Jealous?" she said, almost coquettishly.

He felt unreasonably angry. "Any chance of a cup of coffee?"

"The instant coffee is on the counter, and the water only needs to be boiled. Do you good to move about a bit." She went on reading the *Standard*.

"Did you go out already and buy the newspaper? That's new."

"Yes, as you say, taking the world by storm."

"Well," he said, "I'm going to take that Dr. Hofer by storm if I get half a chance. I am trying to absorb the fact that my mother has died, and I want to know exactly what she died of and what he has been prescribing for her."

"Oh, Franz, back off. He's a nice guy, and he came out to see you last night when I called."

"When *you* called, yes, and he treated me like an idiot."

"Franz, he was absolutely right. No, no, not that you're an idiot, but that there was really nothing to worry about. Look, you slept in the night, and you do feel better."

"That may be. Nonetheless." Typical that she should take Hofer's part. In any case, he was going to get on to it right away. "I'm going to contact that inspector right away and see if he has the results of the autopsy." Eleanor groaned. "I have a perfect right. She was my mother."

"What are you really concerned about, your mother or getting at Dr. Hofer?"

Franz turned on his heel, went into the other room, and dialed the number of the Haus im Wald.

"Please connect me with Chefinspektor Büchner."

He tapped his fingers on the desk while they seemed to be trying various numbers, then he was on the line.

"Good morning, Herr Inspektor. Franz Fabian here."

"Ah yes. Good morning, Herr Professor. How are you? What can I do for you?"

"Thank you, I am better. I am calling to ask for the results of the autopsy on my mother.

"I have only the outlines, Professor Fabian. I haven't spoken to the doctor myself yet, but it appears that she died of heart failure."

"Well, yes, so do most people ultimately, but what caused it?"

"This is not a question always answered by autopsy."

"What medications did they find?"

"Levodopa and a trace of Alprazolam." Franz scribbled this down.

"And who was the prescribing doctor?"

"I'm afraid I cannot tell you that."

"Do you mean you cannot because you do not know, or you may not because it is not allowed?"

The inspector sighed audibly. "Because at this point, I do not know."

"Isn't that the sort of thing you are supposed to know?"

"Forgive me, Professor, I must go now. Perhaps we might talk later. I will be here all day, and no doubt you will be arriving at some point."

"I most certainly will."

Franz strode to the laptop in his room. Google was on his home page, and he quickly typed in Levodopa. He took a few notes and then typed in Alprazolam. He stormed into the kitchen.

"You see? A killer combination. He'd given her Levodopa for parkinsonism—I know she's been having that for a long time, and it can cause, I quote, 'extreme emotional states, particularly anxiety,' and the dosage has to be carefully watched in elderly patients, and then remember he told us he'd given her a 'mild tranquilizer'—well, Aprazolam should be 'very cautiously prescribed for the over sixties' and, he added triumphantly, 'an overdose can be fatal.'"

"For heaven's sake, Franz, you know perfectly well that pulling this stuff at random off the Internet can be very dangerous."

"Not as dangerous as prescribing wildly to the old, the way Hofer has done for years—at great profit."

"You have no actual idea whether he prescribed the Levodopa—and in any case, do you know the dosages of anything?"

"Well, no, but I shall find out."

"Oh, go ahead. I want no part of this."

"Fallen for Hofer, have you, like the other old ladies?"

"I am trying," said Eleanor, "to keep my temper. There's the telephone. I'd better get it."

Franz drank his coffee and took two more Tylenol. He knew that he was being slightly silly, but he could feel a certain enjoyment at the thought of confronting Hofer again. And later when he had all the facts, he would do some serious research on the Internet.

When Eleanor came back, she said, "Why don't you get dressed? We'd better drive out to the Haus im Wald. Ingrid was planning to go today to find out what to do about the furniture and the things in the room, and we should be there."

"Was that Ingrid?"

"No." There was a pause.

"Well, who was it then?"

"It was Christa. She tried to get me last night when I was in the bath, and I didn't answer. She had a bad night, and she wants to talk."

Franz rolled his eyes. "I see. Well, the first person I want to talk to out there is Hofer."

"I hope you'll thank him for coming to see you last night."

"I'll thank him, all right. And you'd better pick up that mess of peas from the carpet in the study. It escaped from its plastic cover when I stepped on it. That's one carpet we won't be rolling up to take with us. Which reminds me. The mysterious disappearing seven hundred euros. I don't suppose our clever-dick detective has found out who took it."

"Does it occur to clever-dick you that perhaps you just carelessly lost it?"

"No, it does not." He got in the shower and was glad to feel the stream of hot water on the back of his head and shoulders. Did Eleanor realize how wearying their constant snippy repartee was? Imagine a relationship where you just exchanged thoughts, quietly and calmly, and maybe even agreed about things. Was such a relationship possible? He had married Eleanor thinking she was a very different sort of woman from his mother, and now here they were, talking at each other, hardly even expecting to be listened to, still less understood. Could you stop this sort of thing once it had become a habit? He stepped carefully out of the shower and turned around to find the bath towel—just the sort of movement to trigger vertigo, and he couldn't risk another bang on the head. He dressed and went out to find Eleanor combing her hair in front of the hall mirror. Actually, she looked pretty good today.

"It's OK," he said. "It was a bad day yesterday. Maybe we can do better today."

"Maybe," she said as they walked out to the car, "but I doubt it."

4

Büchner felt as if the big black birds had been cawing all night long. Do they ever sleep, he wondered, as he tossed and turned between five and seven, trying to catch just a little more sleep. He needed to be fresh and rested to face the day. He had hoped for that sudden flash of insight he sometimes had at the moment when he woke up, but the waking process this morning was too long-drawn-out and too haunted by the birds, who seemed to be mocking him.

Big black birds who swoop and swarm and swerve
Cawing in hundreds, loud in winter skies.

The lines repeated in his head—swooping, swarming, swerving—drowning out any hope of his subconscious mind's helping him to think a useful thought. Might as well get up and go down to the café. At least he could expect a good cup of coffee and something to eat. Little Herr Ritter might come. He wanted to tackle Michael on the topic of keys. Better get there before Herr Ritter in that case.

By seven thirty, he was at the door of the café. He could already smell the coffee—that was nice. Michael let him in. He didn't look as if he had slept well either—black rings under his handsome eyes.

"Good morning, Michael. Sleep well?"

"Not particularly. You?"

"No. I guess we all have too much on our minds."

"You can say that again."

They sat down at the counter, where Michael had already set three places. "Herr Ritter called down to say he was coming too."

"Good, but I have to ask you something first. Schramm has told me that there are only two master keys in the whole establishment. He has one, Frau Huber the other. But I know for a fact that you have one because you lent it to me yesterday when I wanted to get into the Winkler room."

"Did you say that to Schramm?"

"No."

"Well, you could have. He knows I've got one because he gave it to me. But he'd be annoyed that I lent it to you because nobody is supposed to know I've got it."

"Why is that?"

"He knows it's handy for me to have one, given all the jobs I do, but actually he doesn't want Sister Agatha to know that he gave me one because he doesn't want to give one to her."

Büchner couldn't help laughing at this. "It's like a girls' boarding school around here! Doesn't it seem a bit silly?"

"Well, you know, when they put in the new system of locks, about a year ago, a master-key system, Schramm made a big deal out of the fact that since security was being emphasized everywhere, he was going to make sure that the reputation for safety here was a good one, and there would only be one master key, and he would keep it. Obviously, this wasn't practical because for one thing, he's not always here! So he had to give out a couple, and he gave one to me. Actually, none of these, as he probably told you, is the original key, not the one he carries around either. All the originals, master and change keys, are locked in a cabinet in his office, as the company advised him when they put the whole system in. Only copies are issued."

"And who has the key to the cabinet?" Büchner laughed again.

"Well, he does, of course. No one else has one of those."

It all seemed a bit ridiculous to Büchner, since if these were cylinder locks, as they probably were, they were not hard to pick. He could do it himself in pretty short order. And he suspected that Michael probably could too. "Ever picked a lock?" he asked.

"Herr Inspektor!" Michael grinned. "What do you take me for?"

"For a clever chap," said Büchner. "But tell me, do you have your master key safely at the moment, because one has turned up in an odd place."

Michael pulled out his key ring. "Sure," he said, and there it was. Büchner took a look at it—obviously one sanctioned by Schramm; it had the same official Hoffmann name on the back.

"OK. Just wondered." A knock at the café door announced the arrival of Herr Ritter. He peeped around the door and hopped in, looking spruce as usual, but not quite chipper. There was a nervousness about the way he looked from one man to the other, as if wondering what they had been talking about. "Well," he said, "I am here."

"Yes, indeed. Good morning. The coffee is all ready, thanks to Michael."

"I'll go scramble a couple of eggs for you, Herr Inspektor, OK? Herr Ritter?"

"No, no thanks, coffee is just fine." He sat on the bar stool, his feet dangling just short of the floor. "Well, Herr Inspektor, was there anything special you wanted to ask me?"

"Just a couple of things. When we talked yesterday, it seemed to me that there was a considerable divergence of opinion between you and your wife in your attitudes to Hans Graf and, well, also to Frau Hagen. Is there a reason for that?"

"I'm afraid, Herr Inspektor, there are divergences of opinion between my wife and myself on many matters. But she is a good woman at heart, and I owe her a great deal."

"That may be, but it does not answer my question." Michael came back with the eggs. "Would you prefer to talk about this alone?" asked Büchner.

Herr Ritter gave a slight laugh. "No need. Michael knows it all anyway. We often talk to each other, and I have no dark secrets, not even from my wife. I have often wished I had."

"Do you think she has any from you?"

"What do you mean?"

"Was her dislike of Graf and Frau Hagen such that she might have taken actual steps to harm them?"

"You are surely not suggesting, Herr Inspektor, that Hildegard might have murdered Hans. You can't be serious."

"I grant you, it conjures up an incongruous picture, but so far most of the pictures I can conjure in which a resident of the Haus im Wald crashes a blunt instrument into the head of Hans Graf are pretty incongruous. In any case, I have some evidence that someone was actually trying to hurt these two in other ways."

"Are you thinking of the yellow-sticker writer?"

"Ah, you know about this."

"Hans and I laughed about it. He mentioned to me that he had a couple, and I told him that I had too. If you are wondering whether Hildegard, who showed her dislike of the two so openly, could be the yellow-sticker writer, I'm afraid you will have to think again. Mine certainly did not come from her!"

"Do you still have one?"

"Good heavens, no. I threw them out immediately. I only had a couple, both before Hans' death."

"And?"

Herr Ritter looked questioningly at Michael.

"Oh, go on, tell him," said Michael. "It's all nonsense, so what does it matter?"

"Very well. They were offensive little rhymes, such as 'Old fag Ritter needs to be fitter,' that kind of nonsense. I don't remember the exact words—another used the expression 'old fruit'—the implication was obvious—and that one had something like 'Hands off Mike' in it."

Herr Ritter and Michael laughed. "Do you really find it funny?" asked Büchner.

"Well, not really," said Herr Ritter. "But in a long life, you learn to laugh at many things. At any rate, I can assure you that Hildegard would not be writing such notes to me! Though it suggests an older generation person. I mean, who says fag nowadays, or fruit? In any case, it's absolute nonsense. I have never laid a hand on Michael, as he will testify. I do not deny I enjoy looking at him. Who in this house, male or female, does not? But looking is all I have done with anybody for many, many years."

"Has either of you heard of anyone else receiving a yellow sticker?"

The two men looked at each other, and this time, they really laughed, giggled in fact like two schoolboys.

"There was," said Michael, "the morning I came in and found the porter Gruber spluttering over a yellow sticker on the notice board that said, 'Hey Gruber, hands off Huber.' That's when we really knew this whole thing was just some joker having fun, if a rather nasty kind of fun."

The telephone rang, and Michael, who answered it, said, "It's for you, Herr Inspektor—that Professor Fabian."

"Would you guys excuse me for a minute?" said Büchner.

"I'd better get back, in any case," said Herr Ritter. "Hildegard will wonder what I'm up to." Michael went with him to the door and left Büchner to his phone call. He found himself increasingly irritated in the course of it. Yes, Fabian had a right to know the results of the autopsy, but did he have to be quite so rude in his manner of asking about it? All these people were beginning to get mightily on his nerves.

He went back along the corridor to his office but first knocked at Schramm's door. The director was there. "It occurred to me," said Büchner, "that you must have a key cabinet in your office where you keep the originals of all your keys. You forgot to mention that last night."

"I did not think it was important. I am the only one with access to that cabinet."

"Perhaps you wouldn't mind opening it for me to see."

Sighing deeply, Director Schramm opened a closet behind his desk in which there was a cabinet with a combination lock. He punched in four numbers, and the door swung open. A look of astonishment appeared on his face. "The master key is not there," he said.

"Please do not touch anything more," said Büchner. "I'm afraid the fingerprinting must begin in earnest."

"That will upset everybody very much," said Schramm.

"Herr Direktor, please consider two facts: One, a murder has been committed, so there is in all probability a murderer loose in the house. Two, someone unknown now has a key that opens every room in the house and has made, it seems, at least one unauthorized duplicate. Together these facts mean that no one is really safe in this house anymore."

Schramm sat down heavily, and Büchner left the room.

Chapter 9

Most of the residents of the Haus im Wald had a radio of some kind, and many of them kept it tuned to Ö1—Österreich Eins—the cultural channel of ORF, the national Austrian broadcasting company. One recent news report became an immediate topic of conversation among the residents. It dealt with growing concern in Austria that while car accidents on the whole were on the decrease, those involving the elderly were on the increase. Those residents who had long since given up driving a car congratulated themselves volubly for having done so, even though some of them had only given up under pressure from family members. Those few residents who still had a car and drove it, such as Frau Zimmermann, were obliged to defend themselves over lunch where there used also to be talk of the way Herr Graf could sometimes be seen driving his large BMW very fast out of the driveway and onto the road through the woods. Well, many residents thought now, with a certain repressed satisfaction, he will not do that again. The sisters did not deign to discuss their motor scooters, formerly used in their work of visiting the poor and the sick, but it was sometimes remarked that Sister Barbara had a reckless way of taking corners. Pastor Pokorny's electric vehicle came under discussion not for its speed but for its slowness, that he still rode it into the village on a road where normal vehicles had to give him a wide berth; this probably shouldn't be allowed, it was said, though not to him directly. Many residents knew that the loss of mobility had helped put them where they were. The highly respected Ö1 might suggest that they had done the right thing, that the roads of Austria were safer without them, but it could not take away their envy of those who could still put their hands on the wheel, their foot on the gas pedal, and drive away.

1

The Fabians walked out of the building to their little rented Volkswagen, parked along the road in the Zehenthofgasse. Franz automatically unlocked the door on the driver's side.

"Don't you think perhaps . . . ?" said Eleanor tentatively.

"What?" he paused, key in hand.

"Well, that I should drive. Sensible, perhaps, given your accident, and so on."

"And so on?" he repeated, with ironic emphasis. "Are you trying to say I'm past driving the car?"

"Don't be absurd, Franz. Go ahead. Drive! I just thought, with your headache and the sun and so on. I only meant, if you didn't drive, you'd be able to keep your eyes shut."

He looked at the sky, bright blue this morning, and a brilliant morning sun. "OK. I see what you mean. Go ahead." And he meekly walked around to the passenger side.

That was easy, she thought. Let's hope the day goes on like this. She got into the driver's seat and turned on the engine. It took a few tries—it had been a very cold night—but the engine turned over, and off they went.

"Well," said Franz, "and what is the plan of action today?"

"I haven't really got one, have you? There are some things we have to see to, your mother's room for one. That means getting permission from the inspector. And we'll have to talk to Ingrid about what to do with the furniture and all the clothes and stuff—they can't come back into the Zehenthofgasse. And then there's the funeral—"

"Please, Eleanor!" Franz interrupted her, his eyes closed and an expression of extreme suffering on his face. "Not all at once. One thing at a time."

"OK, but you asked for a plan of action."

"That," he explained carefully as if to a child, "was an attempt at irony."

"Well, what do *you* think we should do?" Here we go, thought Eleanor. All the practical decisions will be put off.

"Don't you think we first need to know how and why my mother died?" he asked.

"She died of a heart attack. They told us."

"That," he said firmly, "is not enough for me."

"But what's the point of making a huge fuss about it? She's dead. We have our flights back to the States next week. We have to get on with the practical side of it."

"You are at liberty to do what you like. My first priority is the autopsy, that is, the inspector and Hofer. Why don't you just go and have your chat with your troubled lady friend and leave me to it."

"I certainly will leave you to it," said Eleanor, anger rising in her throat. "And you can rest assured that I will also take my flight back next week and leave you to deal with whatever hasn't been done." She stepped on the gas.

"For Christ's sake, Eleanor," he opened his eyes and peered forward into the sun, low on the horizon. "It's crazy to drive so fast with this kind of visibility." He was right. She slowed down as they came off the expressway and onto the small road leading to Feldberg. "Watch out for that old man!" he said as they entered the main street.

Eleanor did a wide curve around Pastor Pokorny, who was steering his little vehicle into the entrance to the parking lot of the Goldene Glocke. She pulled in herself and honked her horn: "Grüß Gott, Herr Pokorny," she called cheerfully. He waved back.

"Oh, for Christ's sake, Eleanor," said Franz again. "Must you?"

Eleanor drove on and said crossly, "You are not very nice. He is such a lovely old man."

"Lovely old men tend to chatter on, and I have things to do."

"If you were really interested in finding out what is going on in the Haus im Wald rather than just scoring points off Hofer and Büchner, you'd be interested in talking to any and all of the residents," she said.

"Ah, Miss Eleanor Marple herself," said Franz. "Out to solve the Mystery of the Haus im Wald single-handed."

"Oh, shut up," said Eleanor, and she pulled into an empty space near the entrance. "You go and do what you like. I'll see you later."

They stopped at the front desk. On the form that Gruber pushed in front of her, Eleanor filled in Christa's name and apartment number and wrote in the last column, *Visiting friend.*

"You too, sir?"

Franz thought for a moment and wrote in the last column, *Direktor Schramm.*

"Do you have an appointment, sir?"

"Well, no."

"Then you'll have to wait here until I can find out when he will see you." Gruber pointed to a small wooden chair near the desk. Eleanor laughed.

"So long," she said, "see you around," and walked along to the staircase, paying no attention to Franz's loudly whispered, "For Christ's sake, Eleanor."

"Watch your language, sir," said Gruber. "This is a Christian establishment."

Eleanor laughed to herself going up the stairs. Franz might think he can talk down Hofer, she thought, but he's met his match in Gruber.

She walked up to the third floor and knocked at the door of number 35.

"Who's there?"

"Me, of course, Eleanor." She heard the chain being taken off, and Christa stood there, still in her dressing gown. She looked terrible, as if she hadn't slept all night.

"Come in, come in quickly," she said and put the chain back across the door as soon as Eleanor was inside.

"What in the world is the matter? You look awful, Christa."

"I feel awful." She collapsed on the sofa. The remnants of the carefully prepared supper for two were still on the table. Nothing had been washed up.

Eleanor said, "Look, have you had any breakfast?"

"I can't eat."

"Now don't be silly. You have to have something. Try to calm down, and I'll make a cup of tea."

"You English and your cups of tea. It will take more than a cup of tea to calm me down today."

"Nevertheless," said Eleanor, thinking that in any case she needed one herself. She went into the kitchen, ignoring Christa's remonstrances, unearthed a teakettle from the muddle on the counter, and lit the gas under it. "So what happened?" she said.

"After you left, I put the chain across, as you had suggested, and had some supper. I felt very nervous and actually tried to phone you, just to talk, but you didn't answer. I thought I might try again a bit later, so I lay down here on the couch and was so tired I must have fallen asleep almost straightaway. Then in the night, I don't know what time it was, I was woken up by someone outside in the corridor. I thought there was even a soft knock at my door, a sort of soft muffled sound as if a gloved hand was touching the door. I was terrified. I couldn't see the door very well without my glasses, and it was pretty dark. I didn't want to put a light on, but I crept up to the door and put my ear against it. I could swear I heard someone breathing. I stayed there by the door for ages. There may have been shuffling footsteps—I really could hardly tell anymore. Finally, I went back to the couch. I just lay there, rigid with fear, I don't know how long for. The chain was still on, and the door was closed, of course."

"Was it still locked?

"I didn't dare touch it to find out. I had the key in my dressing gown pocket where I'd put it the night before. I was just petrified."

"Did you think of calling the inspector? He's only over in Martin Luther."

"No, for one thing, I didn't have his number, and for another, well, I thought, maybe I'd imagined the whole thing. I didn't go to bed. I just stayed out here on the couch fully clothed until it began to get light, and then I called Pastor Pokorny because I know he's awake at first light. He didn't answer though, so I did open my door a crack and look out, and I could swear the door to Graf's apartment was open. So I closed mine again in a hurry and just sat here trembling for about half an hour, then I tried the pastor again and got him, and he came along, fully dressed—you see, he always gets up so early—and he said the door to Graf's apartment was certainly closed then and maybe I had imagined the whole thing. What do you think, Eleanor, do you think I'm losing my mind?"

"Of course not," said Eleanor firmly, though the possibility had occurred to her. "Here, drink this tea. Take a bath, then we'll go and tell the inspector about all this."

"He'll think I'm crazy."

"I'm sure he's entirely used to dealing with crazy people," Eleanor said, realizing at once that it was the wrong thing to say. "Now, don't cry, Christa dear, I'll run you a nice hot bath. Everything is going to be fine."

But is it? she wondered as the water gushed and foamed hot into the bathtub on top of the bath salts that she had liberally thrown into the somewhat grimy bath. What if there really were someone creeping around the building at night, listening at doors, and breathing heavily? Maybe she should stay the night with Christa tonight and see for herself. Miss Eleanor Marple indeed.

2

Büchner sat down at his desk and looked at his watch. Just after eight. He could call the autopsy lab now and get some details before Schmidt arrived at eight thirty. He hadn't just been trying to frighten Schramm into a greater degree of cooperation. He was beginning to be seriously worried himself about what was going on in the house. He had felt reasonably sure in the beginning that the whole thing was some sort of personal vendetta against Graf alone, but the idea that someone was stealing keys and someone—the same person or another?—was sending anonymous notes to various residents, this seemed to widen the field of motivation as well as the actual danger to the community. He dialed the number of the autopsy lab and was glad when Dr. Wierzbicki answered. Büchner had often worked with him and liked his forthcoming but factual style.

"Guten Morgen, Herr Doktor. Büchner here."

"Guten Morgen, Herr Inspektor. I was expecting you. Where do you want me to begin?"

"First of all, Graf. Time of death, cause of death. The first estimate from the doctor on the scene around noon on Monday was that death probably occurred some fourteen to sixteen hours earlier and was probably caused by a severe blow to the head with a blunt instrument. We have been proceeding on the assumption, therefore, that the murder took place between eight and ten the evening before, that is, on Christmas Day. But it sounds as if we may have to revise this idea."

"Well, the amount and distribution of rigor mortis, the extent of digestion of the last meal—I regret to say, the poor man's Christmas dinner—the body temperature and that of the room in which the body lay overnight, the degree of putrefaction, all these point to seven to ten the evening before as the time of death. However, the cause of death is clearly an intracranial hematoma."

"Which means?"

"It means that the blow to the head itself, which was not as severe a blow as it might have initially seemed to us, in fact caused a blood vessel to rupture between the brain and the skull. And that could have taken place hours earlier. Emergency medical treatment immediately following the blow might have saved his life, but without that, nothing could stop the hemorrhaging into the brain. He lay, probably unconscious, maybe comatose, until respiratory failure and heart failure brought about his actual death."

"And all the blood on the carpet?"

"Largely from superficial blood vessels broken by the blow and some cerebrospinal fluid from the ear. But the blood that killed was inside the head."

Büchner shivered involuntarily. "Yes, thank you, I think I get the picture. But, Doctor, this does change our picture of when the unfortunate Herr Graf was actually struck on the head, does it not? It could have been anytime between, say, noon and eight o'clock in the evening when death seemed to have occurred?"

"Well, I would say a few hours before the actual death, certainly not before noon, since he had eaten his Christmas dinner, but probably no later than four."

Büchner breathed deeply. That did change the picture. "Oh, and the contents of the stomach, Herr Doktor? Christmas dinner and Viagra, I hear."

"Yes, he probably took the Viagra about two hours before his dinner."

"And"—Büchner overcame a certain squeamishness in asking this next question—"had he had sexual intercourse in the hours before his death?"

"No, Herr Inspektor. Either the Viagra didn't do the trick or the murderer intervened with the blunt instrument."

"Yes, I see." The picture of the lovely and tragic Frau Hagen rose before Büchner's eyes and made it impossible for him to enter into any sort of humorous exchange on this topic. He certainly needed to think it all through again.

"And what about the old lady, Frau Fabian?"

"Congestive heart failure. Hardly unusual in a ninety-year-old."

"Contents of stomach? Levodopa and Alprazolam?"

"Yes, just the usual prescribed doses for geriatric parkinsonism."

Into Büchner's head came a seminar he had recently been obliged to attend on crime and the elderly, where one of the often-repeated warnings had been: *beware of the word* just—*just the usual symptoms, just old age, just demented*. But right now, he didn't have time to think about that. Someone was knocking at his door, and he needed to rethink the whole Graf case. "Thank you, Doctor, you've been most helpful. I might get back to you with more questions."

"Fine, we'll be releasing the body of Frau Fabian then?"

"Oh yes. I'd better warn you that you may be getting a call from her son, Professor Fabian—not the easiest man to deal with."

"I'll do my best, Inspektor."

"I'm sure you will, Herr Doktor. Auf Wiederhören."

At the door was Schmidt.

"Guten Morgen, Herr Schmidt, we've got to get a move on. Where can we do the fingerprinting?"

"Simplest place would be in the lobby, sir. There's a table and chair there, and we can bring in everything from the van."

"Fine. Put a note under every door in Melanchthon, people are to come between ten and twelve. Same note to all the staff including"—he laughed slightly—"the director. Explain to anyone who complains, the only way to be fair is to cover absolutely everybody. Then nobody should feel singled out. Whoever doesn't come is singling himself out—they are all bright enough to see that. As soon as we have all the prints in and listed, I want them compared with the prints you found in Graf's apartment and any that might still be on this key." He handed him the key in the plastic bag. "I'd like this back as soon as possible. And could you send a few more people to see me at intervals this morning? Gruber, the porter for one, the Zimmermanns from apartment 23, Frau Huber, the housekeeper, oh, and I'd like to see that young Graf again, if you can get him on the phone."

"Very well, sir, I'll get going." There was a knock at the door.

"Ah, Michael, with the coffee. Thank you. Getting to be quite a routine."

"Anything else you need?" said Michael, setting out the tray of coffee and the cups.

"No. Well, just tell me one thing, Michael. You told me you were visiting your grandmother on Christmas Day. Were you here at all? Earlier in the day, I mean."

"Yes, I gave Frau Huber a hand preparing the dining room for the Christmas dinner. But I left around noon, I think it was."

"I see. Just wondered."

As Michael left, Büchner heard the voice of Professor Fabian at Schramm's door. "I need to speak to you, Herr Direktor, and also to the inspector." Büchner closed his door quickly. He didn't feel like dealing with the irate Professor Fabian just yet.

3

After sitting for half an hour on the small wooden chair in the foyer, Franz was fit to be tied. It was almost nine o'clock now, and he was sure Schramm had been there all the time. He certainly hadn't seen him arrive in his car and come in through the front door, and these Austrian bureaucrats tended to start their days early. Finally, the phone rang at Gruber's desk, and he said officiously, "The Herr Direktor will see you now," and accompanied him to the office door as if this were the Imperial Court and Franz a petitioner.

"You may knock," Gruber said pompously.

Franz tried to wither him with a look, failed, and so obediently knocked as Gruber walked back to his desk. There was a word in German for the way Gruber walked—*gravitätisch*—and Franz thought of it now. It was the way butlers walked in Viennese drama, a solemn, stiff, self-important swagger.

Emperor Schramm called out loudly, "Come in."

He did stand up when Franz entered the room, but he did not come out from behind his desk.

"Grüß Gott, Herr Professor." He gestured toward the high-backed chair facing him across the desk.

Franz sat down, noticing that there were two armchairs and a little coffee table by the window. No move was made in that direction. Well, he would not be intimidated by the emperor.

"I am here, Herr Direktor Schramm, because my mother died yesterday on your premises in strange circumstances. Strange enough at any rate for the police to feel obliged to perform an autopsy. I would like to know the results and also to hear your explanation. My mother had only been here for a week when this happened, and when she came in, there was no indication that death was around the corner. I understand that there have been several other recent deaths, one clearly a murder. I am, to say the least of it, disturbed by all this."

Schramm fixed his deep brown eyes on Franz. He wore rimless half-glasses at his desk, and he looked sternly over the top of them. Franz's own eyes were aching, and to his annoyance, they began to water as he tried to stare down the steely gaze of his interlocutor. He wished, not for the first time in recent days, that he had dark glasses. This pompous ass might think he was crying.

"You do not look well, Herr Professor." Schramm's voice took on an irritatingly condescending tone. "I understand you fell yesterday. I am sorry."

"Thank you. I am not here to look for sympathy, but for explanations."

"I'm not sure what explanations I can give you other than the ones you have already. Your mother died of congestive heart failure—not an unusual death for a ninety-four-year-old woman. Of course, I know that the loss of a mother is a terrible thing at any age, and you have my deepest sympathy and, I'm sure, the sympathy of all the residents of the Haus im Wald. If we can help you in any way with funeral arrangements—"

Franz interrupted the practiced flow of this little speech, tapping his fingers angrily on Schramm's large mahogany desk. "I want the precise results of the autopsy, man. I want to know what doctor prescribed what drugs to my mother. And incidentally, I want to know what happened to the seven hundred euros that disappeared out of my pocket when I was here yesterday."

"Seven hundred euros?" This did finally seem to catch Direktor Schramm off guard. "This is the first I've heard of that."

"Well, it's certainly not the last. If you do not have detailed information yourself about these things, perhaps you would be so good as to get that inspector in here to lay out some of the facts. He was presumably the one who requested an autopsy."

"I will call him and tell him you would like to speak to him." Schramm picked up the phone, and Franz heard it ring several times in the next room before Büchner answered.

"Grüss Gott, Herr Inspektor. I am sorry to disturb you. I have Professor Fabian here who wishes to speak to you. Very well, I'll tell him you'll see him in ten minutes' time."

Schramm turned to Franz. "He will see you—" he began.

"Yes," Franz interrupted. "I heard you—in ten minutes' time. So I am to go in there?"

"Yes," said Schramm, standing up and extending his hand. "Perhaps you would be so good as to wait in the lobby as I have business to transact here on the telephone."

Feeling distinctly upstaged, Franz walked to the door, his eyes stinging. He took out a handkerchief and blew his nose loudly. Turning in the doorway, he remembered that there were practical things to discuss. "There is the matter of my mother's room." he said.

"Please ask the inspector when he proposes to release it," said Schramm.

"And then there are the fees that we have paid to the Haus im Wald."

"All the paperwork was done through the bank on the signature of your cousin, Frau Konrad, who had power of attorney," said Schramm. "You had better go over the matter with her first. Auf Wiedersehen, Professor Fabian." He picked up the phone and began to dial.

Franz stalked back to Gruber's desk. He didn't intend to sit on that silly chair any longer. He walked out through the front door and did a couple of turns around the snowy driveway. The sun on the snow made him feel dizzy, and he went back in.

"Please sign in, sir."

"Don't be absurd. I was here a minute ago."

"Regulations. Who are you going to see now?"

Franz groaned and filled in, *Chefinspektor Büchner.*

"Do you have an appointment, sir?"

I don't believe this, thought Franz, but since his head was beginning to ache, he meekly said yes, looked at his watch, and said, "Eight minutes past nine." Gruber slowly wrote down 9:08. This time, at least, he did not accompany him. Going to see a lesser functionary of the Imperial Court, of course.

Franz knocked at Büchner's door. Büchner opened it, shook him by the hand, and motioned him to an armchair at the small coffee table. "Would you like a cup of coffee?" he asked.

"Well, yes, as a matter of fact, I would," said Franz. What was this, a good-cop-bad-cop routine that the two men had worked out? They wanted to get rid of him—he was sure of that—in short order.

"How can I help you?" said Büchner, leaning back in the other armchair and smiling benignly.

"First of all, can you please give me the precise results of the autopsy report."

Looking at the paper in front of him, Büchner replied, "Your mother died at about one o'clock yesterday afternoon."

"I know that. I was there."

Büchner smiled patiently: "Yes, but I understand you were not quite compos mentis at the time."

"Just give me the cause of death, Herr Inspektor."

"The cause of death was congestive heart failure. The contents of the stomach showed the meal she had eaten the previous evening, as well as the medication, Levodopa, one dose, 400 mg, administered the previous evening, and one dose of Alprazolam, .25 mg, administered about two hours before death. I have not yet talked to the prescribing doctors about the dosage, but am assured by the police doctors that these are normal enough doses."

"Normal by what standards?"

"I'm afraid I have not yet looked further into this myself. My first concern at the moment, I must admit, is the death of Graf, quite clearly caused by another person."

"And what did he die of?"

"I am not at liberty to give you all the details there, Herr Professor. You will understand that. Suffice to say that he was struck on the head and suffered an intracranial hematoma. Altogether different, you see, from the case of your mother."

This was true. Franz made notes of the details, thinking he would check it all later; but in the meantime, "Have you talked to the doctors who prescribed for my mother?" he asked.

"Not since I received the report," said Büchner. "But I know that the Levodopa was a standing prescription from before the time when your mother was admitted, and her private visiting doctor, Dr. Hofer, prescribed the Alprazolam yesterday morning because of her extreme agitation. Needless to say, you are at liberty to follow up on this yourself."

"And you may rest assured, I will."

"No doubt. But while you are here, Professor Fabian, what is this odd story that keeps cropping up of your having lost seven hundred euros?"

"I had seven hundred euros in my inside pocket"—he opened his jacket to show the pocket to Büchner—"when I arrived here yesterday. When I got to the hospital an hour or so later, the money was no longer there. The pocket, you can see, is quite deep. The notes could hardly just have fallen out."

"Who was actually present? After your fall, I mean."

"Well, I was unconscious for perhaps one minute, but during that time, as far as I know, only Sister Dolores and some poor old man in a wheelchair were there. Dr. Hofer was somewhere around, and then Direktor Schramm seemed to be about—I don't remember seeing him, but I think I heard his voice. I wasn't seeing very much at all at the time. Then Eleanor, my wife, appeared. She'd been fetched from the woods by that young man from the café, what's his name? And then my cousin Ingrid arrived, and then Eleanor and I were taken in the ambulance to the hospital. When I had to show my passport and other papers, I saw that the wad of notes had gone. It was money, you see, that I had found in the apartment. My mother had lost it, a long story, and I found it and was bringing it to show her. I knew she would be pleased, but then she never did see it after all." Franz stopped, shocked to feel his own emotions at this thought. Tears suddenly welled up in his eyes, different tears from the ones that had blinded him in Schramm's room.

"Are you all right?" asked Büchner.

"Yes, yes. My eyes, you know, the fall and the sun." Franz blew his nose again. "I think I shall go now, Herr Inspektor. I do not feel very well." He stood up, feeling shaky on his feet. He sat down again.

"Hold on. I'll get the housekeeper. I think you had better go and lie down for a bit. Rest assured, I'll look into the mysterious missing euros."

Looking at the telephone list on his desk, he dialed the number of Frau Huber. "Perhaps you could give us a hand here, "he said, and a bustling fat woman in a uniform appeared almost immediately. "The professor is not feeling well," Büchner said to her. "You're coming to see me later, I believe, for a chat?"

"I am indeed," she said, putting out a chubby arm for Franz to lean on: "Come with me, my dear sir, I have heard all about it. Your poor mother. Oh, and look at your poor head! No wonder you are not feeling well."

Franz felt strangely happy as she led him away.

4

Büchner wanted to look at the notes he had made in the blessedly quiet half hour before the irritable professor had appeared, but promptly at nine thirty, there was a knock at the door, and he knew the morning's interviews were beginning. He opened the door and ushered in the Zimmermanns. He remembered meeting them briefly at lunch yesterday. Frau Zimmermann, short and plump, with a round face, lined but apple-cheeked, and a neat head of very blond curls, bounced in first and shook him cheerfully by the hand. "Gruß Gott, Herr Inspektor. Our turn at last."

"Yes, Frau Zimmermann, thanks for coming." Büchner bowed slightly to the anything-but-cheerful-looking gentleman, bald, red faced, and apoplectic, leaning on a cane, wearing two hearing aids. "Guten Morgen, Herr Doktor," he said loudly. He had observed the *Dr.* on the apartment door and never missed the opportunity of using a title with the older generation Viennese.

"No need to shout," said Herr Zimmermann. "With these things in, I hear altogether too much."

"Do sit down," said Büchner. "Coffee?"

Frau Zimmermann happily accepted a cup, helping herself liberally to cream and sugar.

"Let's get on with it," said Herr Zimmermann. "What can we do for you?"

"Just a few routine questions in the matter of Herr Graf's death. You live, do you not, on the floor below Herr Graf's apartment, also in the front of the building?"

"We do."

"That must be that very pleasant apartment with windows on both walls in the sitting room. I've seen the one above yours where the sisters live."

"They probably know a good deal more about Graf than we do," said Frau Zimmermann.

"Because they lived next door to him?"

"Yes, that, and"—Frau Zimmermann leaned confidentially toward him—"Sister Agatha, you know, knew him in the past.

They were once engaged, many years ago. That's no secret. Everyone from Döbling knew about it, and lots of people here are from Döbling."

"I expect so," said Büchner, thinking, yes, it was one of the most expensive areas in the city. "You also lived in Döbling?"

"Spent all our married life there," said Zimmermann. "Very nice house. Renovated to my own design. Had our own offices on the ground floor."

"We spent our later unmarried life there too, on separate floors," said Frau Zimmermann perkily. "We are divorced, you know. The present arrangement is one of convenience—trying to pool the resources of old age and help our children at the same time. It is only an experiment. Our daughter and her family happen to need a house at the moment, so they are living there. We might well go back to the old arrangement. Old age finances are not so simple, Herr Inspektor. You are too young to know about all that." This lady, thought Büchner, who looks so conventional, has a lot of spunk.

"Not here to discuss our finances," barked Zimmermann. "Let's get on with it."

"Where were you," asked Büchner, "between the hours of noon and nine o'clock on Christmas Day?"

"We both went down for Christmas dinner in the dining room at one," said Frau Zimmermann. "Back to the apartment at three. Then my ex"—she giggled at Büchner—"took a nap in his room, and I drove over to see our daughter and her children in our house. I was back here at about seven."

"You have a car?"

"I certainly do. I would never have agreed to this arrangement if I could not have kept my car. That was one of the stipulations in the contract. That and the separate rooms."

"You have a contract?"

"Of course," said Frau Zimmermann. "We have both spent our professional lives working on the domestic finances of other people. Nothing that is not fixed in a signed and notarized document counts for anything in this day and age. That is one of the things Herr Zimmermann and I agree on."

"Not here to discuss our finances," said Herr Zimmermann. "How often do I have to say this? My wife is a talker, Herr Inspektor. She will keep us here all day if you don't get to the point."

"Well, Herr Zimmermann, you went to sleep in your apartment at three o'clock? Did you see or hear anything out of the ordinary after your . . . ex-wife left?"

"Didn't hear a thing, of course, while I was sleeping. Without these things in"—he pointed to his hearing aids—"I wouldn't hear if a bomb went off."

"And when you woke up?"

"Made a cup of coffee, may have been four thirty or so. Still light anyway, just about. Sat in the armchair looking out of the side window, my favorite place. Saw a couple of people on that footpath leading into the woods. Nothing unusual about that. People often go for walks there."

"Who did you see?"

"Can't say exactly. Sight not hundred percent anymore. Looked like a couple with two children and a little sled, visitors probably going for a walk after Christmas dinner. And then maybe one of the sisters—looked like that gray hood they wear."

"And what time was that?"

"Light enough to see something. Must have been before five."

"Which sister?"

"Haven't the foggiest. Didn't care at the time. Don't care for either of them very much. One's too nosy, the other's too friendly."

"My ex, I should tell you, Herr Inspektor, doesn't care for anybody very much."

"Did you care for Herr Graf?" Büchner asked Herr Zimmermann.

"Civil enough. Paid his bills on time."

"His bills?"

"We," said Frau Zimmermann, then dropping her voice, "actually I," and raising her voice again, "prepared his tax returns for him. This was our job, you know, tax counseling, and I may be seventy-five years old, but I like to keep my hand in. If a man can be a pope at seventy-five, I always say, I can certainly be a tax accountant. I got into computers before I gave up full-time work." Sotto voce, "He never did." Louder, "And so I can do everything from my room."

"Admirable," said Büchner. "So you did this for Graf?"

"Yes. He was a good client. He was, you undoubtedly know, a rich man, an investment banker in his day."

"Yes," said Büchner. "It has occurred to me to wonder why such a man would choose"—he paused, looking for the right word—"sheltered living when he might well have afforded to be looked after in his own home."

Frau Zimmermann smiled. "Rich men are often rich from a lifetime of doing the careful thing with their money. Herr Graf had invested his money very well, of course, but we in our generation have seen currency devalued, and savings and investments lost in our families more than once. This is, of course, hardly a cheap solution, but it is prudent. It is a comfortable and safe place for an elderly man of independent wealth to live and die." She paused, no doubt considering the implications of what she had just said. "Well, that's what we used to think. And Herr Graf had, in any case, potential financial obligations that might have suggested prudence."

"Kathi," interrupted Herr Zimmermann. "You are talking too much. The inspector has his own official ways of checking Herr Graf's financial situation without your betraying confidences entrusted to you as his tax adviser."

"Of course," said Büchner. "I was interested in having some impression from you of whether he might have had enemies, people who had enough against him to commit a violent act."

"His son resented him greatly," said Frau Zimmermann, "because of his leaving his mother. But he is hardly a violent boy. And Herr Graf provided very well for him."

"In his will, do you mean?"

"In his lifetime. As indeed he has provided for others."

"Kathi!" said Herr Zimmermann.

"Thank you," said Büchner. "We shall, as you say, be looking officially into his financial circumstances." Then suddenly he asked, "Did you really like him?"

"I liked him," said Frau Zimmermann. "I am very sad that he has gone."

"Not so sad about the bequest," said Herr Zimmermann.

Frau Zimmermann blushed. "Now who is being indiscreet?"

"He was a great one for the ladies, "said Herr Zimmermann. "They all loved him." He gave a great barking laugh. "And he loved quite a few of them. Not least our own prima donna, the lady Hagen. A whole lot of ladies would have liked to knock *her* on the head."

"That's quite enough, Richard," said Frau Zimmermann and stood up. "Please let us know if we can help you any further, Herr Inspektor."

"One last question, Frau Zimmermann. You came home from your daughter's at about seven in the evening of Christmas Day, you said. Did you see anyone on your way in? In the parking lot? The lobby? The elevator?"

She thought for a moment. "Dr. Hofer was just driving away. I thought nothing of that. He's always popping in and out. And I passed Frau Huber in the lobby, she was locking the door at seven, later than usual, she said, because of Christmas Day. Oh, and Pastor Pokorny was in the elevator going up. He mentioned that he had been in the chapel. I can't think of anyone else."

"Thank you," said Büchner. "You've been most helpful." And he saw them out. He sat at his desk and looked at his notes. Nothing seemed to fit. People always seemed to be popping in and out, and often in places where they hadn't said they'd been. Was it that he was getting old and couldn't piece things together anymore, or were his eyewitnesses so old that they got everything wrong? Or was someone deliberately lying? Would he really have to recall all these people and ask them the same questions all over again? Maybe the fingerprinting would narrow the field. But in the meantime, he had already recalled young Graf. There was a knock now. Perhaps he was here. He opened it. No, it was the professor's wife and her tearful friend. Once more into the breach, he thought, and ushered them in with as much polite interest as he could muster.

5

"We apologize for coming unannounced," said Eleanor as they sat down at the coffee table.

"Sorry about the dirty cups," said Büchner. "I'm afraid we're out of coffee."

"We've just had tea," said Eleanor. "We wanted to see you right away."

"I have another appointment at ten," said Büchner, "but I'm glad you came. I need to know what is going on in this establishment."

"Oh," Christa burst out. "I wish I knew, Herr Büchner. Everything has changed in the last couple of days. I always felt so safe here, so protected, and now . . ." Oh, Lord, thought Eleanor, she's going to cry again.

"Don't cry, Christa dear. Just tell the inspector what happened."

Christa took a deep breath. "Last night," she said, "I'd fallen asleep on the couch in my living room, and I was awakened by someone outside in the corridor and what sounded like someone touching my door."

"Softly, you said," interposed Eleanor, "as if the person had gloves on."

"What time was this?"

"I'm afraid I don't know. It was very dark." *That's* not much help, thought Eleanor. It's dark these days from five in the evening till after seven in the morning.

"I was afraid to open the door, but when I crept up to it and listened, I thought I heard someone breathing outside." She shuddered at the thought. "I didn't take the chain off or anything."

"Ah, you had the chain across. Good!" said Büchner encouragingly.

"After a while, it stopped, and I just lay on the couch until it began to get light. Everything was quiet, so I peeked out at some point into the corridor without taking the chain off. There was no one about, but the door opposite, Herr Graf's door, you know, seemed to be ajar. After a while, I called Pastor Pokorny because he is always so helpful and reassuring, and I know he wakes early. He came round straightaway, but he thought perhaps I had imagined it all."

"You forgot to say, Christa," said Eleanor, "that the first time you called him, he didn't answer."

"No, well, that's not important. He was probably in the bathroom or something."

"What time was that?" Büchner asked.

"I'm not sure."

"Well, Christa," Eleanor again, "if it was first light as you said, it must have been after seven."

"In any case, I couldn't see the time. I didn't have my glasses on."

"Did you have them on when you looked out at Graf's door?"

"Well, no, and I am very nearsighted."

"Ah, but," said Eleanor, "there is the matter of the heavy breathing, Herr Inspektor."

"Heavy, was it?" asked Büchner.

"Well, I could hear it through the door, or thought I could."

"Quite so."

"What can I do?" said Christa. "I will be so frightened tonight."

"Perhaps you can go and stay with your friend," said Büchner helpfully.

Eleanor, seeing hope dawn on Christa's face, said quickly, "Oh no, that wouldn't do. There is no room in the apartment in the Zehenthofgasse." And, she thought, Franz would be livid at having Christa on the living room couch! "I can stay the night with Christa. I can sleep on her couch and keep an eye on things."

"And what will your husband say to that? He doesn't seem so well himself."

Eleanor was about to remark that she didn't much care at this point what her husband would say to anything, when she took in the second of Büchner's sentences. "Oh, have you seen him then?"

"Yes, he came to see me. He seemed quite unwell, and the housekeeper took him to lie down."

Good Lord, thought Eleanor. He must feel pretty bad if he puts up with something like that. "Where did they go?" she said. "I'd better find him."

"The housekeeper's apartment is on the ground floor of Martin Luther, on the opposite side of the house to these offices, near the elevator. Frau Huber is the lady's name—seems like a kind person. Quite took your husband under her wing."

Good Lord, thought Eleanor again. Franz under the wing of that officious fat lady? This doesn't sound very likely.

"Here is my cell phone number, Frau Beck. Whether or not Frau Fabian stays the night, you may call at any time, and you certainly should if you have another bad experience. And if anything happens in the course of the day that makes it unnecessary for Frau Fabian to stay the night, I will call you."

"Thank you, Herr Inspektor," said Eleanor. "Do you mean that you are close to finding out? Oh dear, I was looking forward to doing a bit of sleuthing myself."

"Perhaps you have read too many detective novels, Frau Fabian. Please remember that this is real life. And be very careful!"

Typical, thought Eleanor. "Oh, I was only joking," she said pleasantly. "Come along, Christa, we'll go and check on poor Franz."

"Of course. Thank you, Herr Inspektor."

"Thank *you*," said Büchner as a knock on the door signaled the next visitor. In came Frau Huber.

"We were just talking about you," said Büchner. "I was telling Frau Fabian how kind you were to her husband. She was just coming to look for him."

"Such a lovely man," said Frau Huber.

Eleanor wondered if they were talking about the same person—she noticed that even Büchner looked a little nonplussed. "My husband? Professor Fabian?" she said doubtfully.

"He's been through an awful lot in the last day or so," said Frau Huber. "His poor face is all beat-up, and he has lost his mother."

But he loathed his mother, Eleanor thought, restraining herself from saying so. "Yes, well, I'll go and see him."

"I think perhaps you had better not." An unexpectedly steely tone had entered Frau Huber's motherly voice. "I just put him to lie down in my apartment, and what he needs is an hour's sleep. Perhaps you could come back about noontime."

Eleanor wondered about arguing with her, but then again, she thought, why should she? A couple of hours off might be rather nice. "Come along, Christa," she said. "Thank you, Frau Huber, you are very kind. I'll be back at noon, Herr Inspektor. Happy sleuthing!"

"Let's go," she said to Christa when they were outside the door. "Let's drive off and have a real breakfast somewhere. I've got the car, after all. Franz is under the fat lady's wing, and there's nothing to keep us in this place a moment longer. Let's get out of here."

Christa's face lit up. "Oh yes, Eleanor, yes," she said. "Let's get out!"

Chapter 10

Very few of the residents who still walked the carpeted halls of the Haus im Wald did so with an upright back and a brisk step. Herr Graf had been one of them. His friend, Herr Ritter, was another. But on the whole, stoops and shuffles were the order of the day. Visiting relatives were often surprised to discover that a few weeks after taking up residence, those who had previously put one foot in front of the other in a quite normal way had already begun to move their feet carefully along the floor, looking down as they did so. Those who had long since ceased to walk much outside their own four walls before moving in now scarcely ventured out of their apartments without at least a cane or, in many cases, a walker. Frau Ritter was one of these. She got about quite a lot in the house because she liked to know what was going on, but she was never without her walker—the old-fashioned kind of four-legged metal frame with wheels on the front legs and rubber feet on the back ones. She often stopped and leaned on it and looked about her. It was in that sense a useful device for the inquisitive. There was a more modern kind, a three-wheeler with a much tighter turning radius, no fixed legs but soft-touch brakes. This was popular in the Haus im Wald because it was foldable and could be used easily in the café or inside an apartment. Pastor Pokorny's daughter had given him one, but he still despised the idea and kept it at the back of a closet. He liked the sturdy cane he had used over many years for hiking, and he was not afraid of falling. But then he had not yet fallen. How often, in descriptions of the downward trajectory of the elderly, did one hear the sentence, "And then he fell." It tended to mark the hiatus between confidence in light and life and a sense of encroaching darkness.

1

Frau Huber walked sturdily and purposefully into Büchner's office and settled herself comfortably in the armchair, filling it completely. Contained as it was in her quite smart navy-blue-and-white uniform, her very ample figure did not have that gone-to-seed look that he had found so unattractive in the equally large Frau Ritter. Frau Ritter was, of course, considerably older, he supposed. Frau Huber had an ageless look, useful probably in her job of supervising the living conditions of the aged.

"Well now, young man," she said, "what do you want to ask me?"

So she considers herself older than I am, thought Büchner.

She looked disapprovingly at the dirty cups and the empty coffeepot. "Would you like me to do something about all this first?"

"I'll give Michael a call," he said. "If he's in the café, he will deal with it."

She looked at her watch. "Ten fifteen," she said. "He's supposed to be doing some repair jobs in Martin Luther. But you can try."

Büchner dialed the café number. Michael answered and said he would bring fresh coffee at once. Frau Huber made no comment.

"First of all, Frau Huber," said Büchner, "thank you for helping me out with Professor Fabian. I was quite shocked myself when he walked in here this morning with that tremendous black eye."

"Yes, the face, of course, is not the main problem—that bruising will go away—but the poor dear seems to be a very upset man indeed."

"Yes, I suppose so," said Büchner, though the poor dear had seemed to him more irritable and aggressive than upset. "You seem to bring out the best in people, Frau Huber. And since you must know everyone here so well, I'd like to ask you a few questions about them."

At that point, Michael came in. He greeted Frau Huber with none of the nervousness with which he encountered Sister Agatha, Büchner noted. When he had gone, Büchner asked her, "That young man, for example. There seem to be various opinions about him. Does he work under your supervision?"

"Yes, I supervise his work, practically speaking, though in terms of the official organization of the Haus im Wald, he reports to Herr Direktor Schramm, as do I, and as does the doorman, Gruber. But I give Michael his day's work plan, and he usually keeps to it very well. Gruber, of course, is a law unto himself."

"What are Michael's working hours?"

"Basically nine till five, but he keeps flexible hours—he may sometimes come late, but he also often stays late."

"And he was here on Christmas Day, I gather?"

"Yes, he came at about ten to help set up in the dining room and left at twelve thirty, before people started eating."

"Twelve thirty? Are you sure?"

"Yes, I had asked if he could stay a bit longer, but he said he had to visit his grandmother. He's very attached to her, I know that."

"What did you do yourself on Christmas Day?"

"I was up early as usual and in the kitchen at eight to make sure everything was getting under way for the dinner. I was there most of the morning and ate my Christmas dinner with the residents at one, supervised the clearing up, and got back to my apartment about four. Then I slept for a while. There was no evening meal on Christmas Day, so I stayed in my apartment, watched TV, and went to bed about ten o'clock."

"Were you in the lobby in the evening at all?"

"As far as I can remember, only to lock the front door at seven—an hour later than usual because it was Christmas Day."

"Did you notice anything unusual in the course of the day? Over dinner, or later?"

She thought for a moment. "Not really. I was surprised that the Ritters came for dinner. They usually cook for themselves on

Christmas Day. I sat at a table with the sisters, Pastor Pokorny, and Frau Beck. An unfortunate combination because Sister Agatha is very condescending to Pastor Pokorny. There wasn't much of a Christmas spirit in the sisters. Even Sister Barbara did not seem to make her usual efforts to be cheerful. I assumed the problem was that Sister Agatha was not happy with her table companions."

"Nor with you either?"

"She would be condescending to me too if she could because of my position as a domestic of sorts," said Frau Huber, laughing comfortably. "But she can't. She needs me, you see."

"She does?"

"Yes, she loves to take charge and, basically, boss people around. She does quite a lot of that with the nurses and the old bedridden residents. But when it comes to running the house"—Frau Huber exuded cheerful confidence—"I am in charge, and she knows it. I have the ear of the director, who has relied on me for close to ten years, and"—she paused and smiled again—"I have the keys of the house, and she doesn't."

"Well, that brings me to another question: you have a master key?"

"I do."

"And where do you keep it?"

Frau Huber pointed to a key ring on the belt around her waist. The keys nestled comfortably in the soft spot in front of her well-covered hip bone.

"Do you ever hang them up anywhere?"

"No. At night I put them on my bedside table."

"Do you know whether anyone has a master key apart from Direktor Schramm?"

Frau Huber hesitated. "Well, as a matter of fact, Michael does. But we—the director and I—would not want this to be known."

"You both place considerable trust in this young man."

"Yes, we do. He has worked here for five years, and he does a lot for all of us."

"And no other master keys have been given out as far as you know?"

"No, Herr Inspektor. It would not be a good idea."

"One more question: what was your opinion of Herr Graf?"

"A charming and generous man. An asset to the house. Gave generously to the maintenance and renovation fund—and generous tips to the staff at Christmas."

"Did that include yourself? And Michael?"

Frau Huber looked slightly embarrassed. "I am not allowed to take tips from residents."

"So you did not?"

"Well, Herr Graf had a gentleman's way of giving presents. They were not really tips."

"And this Christmas?"

"He knew that my TV was not functioning properly, so several days before Christmas, he brought me a new one with a big screen—went to get it himself and brought it here in his car."

"And Michael?"

"You had better ask him yourself. He was at liberty to take tips. And Herr Graf would normally have given him something for Christmas. A generous gentleman. He will be much missed."

"Why, Frau Huber, would anyone have hit him on the head?"

"Perhaps," she said, "he was more generous to some than to others. You know, Herr Inspektor, in my opinion, Herr Graf was generous because he was kindhearted. Others might say"—and her benign look slipped slightly at this point—"that he knew whose palm to grease."

"And whose palm did he grease, Frau Huber, other than, in the most gentlemanly way, yours?"

"I'm afraid that's something you'll have to find out for yourself, Herr Inspektor. I haven't the faintest idea. You were asking me to speculate, and so I did."

Silence fell for a moment, and then Frau Huber said, "If you have nothing else to ask, Herr Inspektor, I'd better go back and check up on that poor Professor Fabian."

"Yes, of course. If you think of anything else that I ought to know, Frau Huber, I hope you will get in touch with me."

She stood up, Büchner noticed, without using her arms to propel her out of the chair, despite her undoubtedly considerable weight. "Don't forget the fingerprinting," he added as they walked to the door. "Oh, and by the way, it occurs to me, have you heard any rumors about little anonymous notes being passed out to residents on yellow stickers?'

Her face, as she shook his hand at the door, turned a dull red. "No," she said. "No, I haven't. Auf Wiedersehen, Herr Inspektor."

Alone, Büchner heaved a sigh. Had she received stickers so embarrassing that she was afraid to mention them? The palm-greasing innuendo reminded him that he needed to take a close official look at Graf's financial situation. He looked through the list of phone numbers that Schmidt had prepared, dialed the number of Graf's attorney, and left an urgent message. From palm greasing, his mind jumped back to fingerprinting. Better check that this is under way, he thought and walked along the corridor to the table set up near Gruber's desk. Frau Dr. Lessing was in the act of rolling her index finger on the inkpad.

"So this is what it has come to, Herr Inspektor," she said good-humoredly, wiping the traces of ink off her finger with the individual disposable wipe held out officiously for her by Gruber, who seemed to be not displeased with his role as policeman's aide. He was peeling the wipes carefully off a little pad, offering each person precisely one.

"I'm afraid, as you say, it has come to this," said Büchner. "Will you be at lunch today, Frau Doktor? It would be pleasant to continue our conversation."

"No," she said. "I am cooking this morning. But why don't you join me in my apartment if you are free at twelve?"

"That would be a pleasure," said Büchner and returned to his office with a lighter step.

2

The two women got into the car, and Eleanor drove off with a flourish, very fast down the driveway into the road.

"Only Herr Graf," said Christa, "used to zoom in and out of the place like that."

"Oh, he did, did he? I wish I had known your Herr Graf."

"He wasn't my Herr Graf. I hardly knew him, really. But in the Haus im Wald, he was larger than life, and all of us old ladies, who watched him doing things like zooming in and out of the driveway, had something of a pang for all the things we would never have again, and maybe, as in my case, never really had."

"Christa, for heaven's sake, you're not an old lady. You could still have all sorts of things if you really wanted to." And if you got out of here, she added in her head.

"Where are you going?" asked Christa nervously as Eleanor drove blithely through Feldberg and headed onto the expressway.

"We're driving into the world," she said and started to sing at the top of her voice:

Heili, heilo, wir fahren
Fahren in die Welt.

Christa chimed in happily—she had always liked to sing, and they sang now in parts:

Heili, heilo, wir fahren
Fahren in die Welt . . . ohne Geld

"That old *ohne Geld*—no money—joke," said Christa who had added it to the line, "certainly applies to me right now, because I just walked out literally without a cent. Good thing I put my coat on at least before we left the apartment—I had thought of going for a walk while you looked for Franz. But where are we going, Eleanor? I can't go too far into the wide world with no money in my pocket."

"We are going," said Eleanor triumphantly, "into the Inner City. To hell with Feldberg. It's about time you got out into the real world."

"But can we do that? What about Franz?"

"To hell with Franz. In any case, the fat lady was probably right. In his state, he's better off resting. Doesn't mean we have to kick our heels in the dreary old Haus im Wald all day."

"Oh, Eleanor."

"I know, I know, it's not necessarily all dreary, but right now, we need a break. You thought so too back there."

"Yes, I did."

"So sit back, take a deep breath, and enjoy it. Look, we're already off the expressway and zooming along through Heiligenstadt. All we have to do here is turn right, go straight along this short stretch to the Saarplatz, and make sure not to get stuck behind a bus. Then we just have to follow the tramlines into the Ring, and halfway round it, find somewhere to park, and then go sit in a really snazzy coffee place—not one of those musty old coffeehouses. Today is a day for the modern world. It's not much more than a half-hour drive altogether. Vienna is a small town, you know, it's not London or New York."

"The speed you drive certainly makes it seem pretty small."

"No point in dawdling around. Everyone here drives pretty fast, and if you're slow, you're a hazard to everyone else."

"Yes. That's why I gave up driving long ago. I got tired of everybody honking at me and trying to force me to drive faster."

"I can imagine," said Eleanor, taking a fast turn onto the Silbergasse just ahead of the bus. "Close your eyes, my dear girl, and relax. I'm a good driver, I really am. I took a course on defensive driving not so long ago—attack is the best means of defense, in a manner of speaking." She laughed.

"Just remember," said Christa, who wasn't laughing, "that in this country, you have to stop for pedestrians at the zebra crossing. You just completely ignored an old lady about to step into the street!"

"Sick of old ladies," said Eleanor. "*Heili, heilo*, we're driving—driving into the world!"

They sang the whole song right through to the last verse:

The birds of summer fly
Away from wood and field
It's time to say good-bye
We're off to see the world.

"Amazing," said Eleanor, "how one remembers all the words of things one learned when young." They went through their forty-year-old repertoire of youth-camp hiking songs, singing all the way down the Billrothstraße, the Nußdorferstraße, the Währingerstraße to the Ring, Christa slowly but visibly relaxing. Then they drove around the Ring itself.

"I much prefer the other way round the Ring," Eleanor said, "the way the trams go, past the *Parlament*, the museums, and so on, but still, don't you feel now as if you're in the big city and the Haus im Wald is light-years away?" said Eleanor.

"I'm not sure that's how I want to feel," said Christa, tightening up again. "Please stop telling me how to feel."

She's right, thought Eleanor. I hate it when people do that to me. "Sorry. Anyway, let's find a place to park. There's the State Opera. I'll cut down to the left off the Ring—then we'll find a one-hour parking place and walk back to the Kärntnerstrasse."

"It's your lucky day today," said Christa as Eleanor squeezed the car into a small space with the practiced touch of a Manhattan driver.

"What did I tell you? This is our day out, and God is on our side."

There was less snow underfoot than out in the woods, but it was bitterly cold and windy as they crossed over the Ring to the Opera.

"Right here on the corner," said Eleanor, "is the new Sacher café—not the old one with plush seats and crotchety waiters in tailcoats and bow ties. Wait till you see it."

"I like the old one round the corner."

"Oh, Christa, it doesn't hurt to try something new."

"Do I have to get up on one of those?" said Christa when they went in, and she saw the tall short-backed stools, black and shiny, standing at the little square high tables with glass tops. The walls were covered with mirrors, the bar gleaming with black marble and chrome.

"Yes, you do," said Eleanor, hoisting herself up at a table by the window and pushing a stool toward Christa. She watched as Christa made several efforts to get her bottom up onto the stool. Good Lord, she thought, it really is difficult for her. But why? She's not overweight. Finally, by leaning her arms on the tabletop and putting one foot on the rung of the stool, she managed it.

"Oh God," she said, panting. "And now I'm looking directly at myself in the mirror. I don't need that."

"Well, don't get down again. I'll move my chair around so that you can look at me instead." Christa did look pretty awful today, she thought. Her hair was straggly, no makeup, that old green loden coat—all totally out of place in this chichi café scene. A young waitress in a very short pleated skirt came and cheerfully took their order. They both ordered a mélange and a piece of Sacher torte with whipped cream.

"So much for our hearty breakfast," said Christa, already looking more cheerful. "You, Eleanor, are looking very good today, do you know that?"

Eleanor felt, ridiculously, as if she were blushing. "Well," she said, "I did make a bit of an effort—don't know why exactly." She had washed her hair, and when she had seen it in one of the mirrors as she walked into the café, it had actually looked quite good. She had a good short haircut, and when she took trouble to comb and brush it, the gray in it, no meager amount, looked rather like carefully placed streaks for which she would have paid a lot of money, if that's what they had been. The secret, she thought, is somehow to look expensive. Then you can enjoy sitting in a place like this.

"Do you hear that, Christa?" A music tape was running as in every other café. "Sidney Bechet's 'Petite Fleur'! Oh, if that doesn't take you back. Wouldn't you give anything to be young again?"

"It's no good thinking like that."

"Oh yes, it is," said Eleanor passionately. "Just listen to that music. Close your eyes. We could be twenty-one again."

"Here comes the Sacher torte," said Christa, "that does more for me than the music. I say, Eleanor, don't open your eyes yet. You'll never guess who just came in and sat down at the bar—I can see him in the mirror."

"Who, for heaven's sake?"

"Dr. Hofer."

Eleanor felt a stab of combined pleasure and shock, something she hadn't felt for a long time. The thought of that moment of shoulder massage last night flooded back into her mind, and she admitted to herself that this was the reason that she had got out of bed with such enthusiasm that morning, done her hair, and dressed herself up. For Dr. Hofer? Like all the other old ladies, Franz would say.

"Oh, Eleanor!"

"What now?"

"You'll never guess who he's meeting here."

"Come on, Christa, don't keep doing this. Just tell me."

"Frau Hagen! Looking absolutely exquisite, all in black. He just kissed her hand in its long black glove."

And now a terrible pang—what of, jealousy? What nonsense, thought Eleanor. "I don't want them to see us," she said quickly.

"Why not?"

Eleanor tried to think of a plausible reason and fell back on her Miss Marple role. "Because, my dear Christa, something very odd is going on in the Haus im Wald, and those two are leading players. What are they doing meeting here like this? Let's just sit quietly and see what happens. Can they see us?"

"Not unless they happen to look in the right mirror," said Christa. "They seem to be very focused on each other right now. But we don't want to look as if we are spying on them."

"Let's just eat our cake. What are *they* having?"

"Fom here it looks like a small glass of *Sekt* each—or prosecco perhaps."

"Of course," said Eleanor with a sigh.

"What do you mean, of course?"

"Oh, nothing," she said. With Sidney Bechet playing in the background, what she would really like to have been doing was sitting at the bar drinking prosecco with Dr. Hofer. "I'm only listening to the music."

"'Extraordinary how potent cheap music is,' somebody once said," said Christa.

"Noel Coward," said Eleanor. "And he should know. But I agree with him. Not that I consider Sidney Bechet to be cheap music, but a tune like 'Petite Fleur' certainly has the particular potency that cheap music has."

"What potency?"

"Oh heavens, Christa, you know," she said incautiously. "I suppose, put at its crudest, it basically means, it makes you feel like having sex."

"Does this music make you feel like having sex?"

"Good Lord, no, I was just speaking generally." Again Miss Marple rescued her from this impossible conversation. "It is extremely odd," she said, "that Frau Hagen, in her deepest grief, should be here, sitting at a bar with Hofer. If only we could hear what they are talking about."

They finished eating their cake in silence, as if somehow that would make the conversation on the far side of the bar more audible. The Sidney Bechet tape went on to the tune of "When I Grow Too Old to Dream." I really am too old to dream, thought Eleanor. I should give it up. She heard the rest of the words in her head: *When I grow too old to dream, I'll have you to remember.* When you're young, she thought, this sounds very romantic. When you actually are too old, it sounds more bitter than sweet.

"Talking of cheap music," she said to Christa, "song lyrics certainly change in their potency over time. I remember when my father was looking after my mother—I was in their bedroom early one morning—he removed the pot of urine from the commode, and as he was carrying it out of the room, the radio was playing that old song about undying love—*You ask how long I'll love you*—or some such. He was plodding through the bedroom door with the pot of urine, and the young guy on the radio was crooning cheerfully, *'Until the twelfth of never, and that's a long, long time.'* Believe me, it took on a distinctly ironic tone—I mean, this was what the twelfth of never looked like now."

"Times do change," said Christa. "We wouldn't have been sitting here like this forty years ago drinking coffee and talking about pots of urine. That's OK. In a way, it's a nice story. At least your mother had your father. She was lucky."

Yes, but was he? thought Eleanor. He had looked after her invalid mother for ten years, and that's a long, long time.

"Hey, that didn't last long," said Christa. "They're leaving. He's paying. They're going out into the Kärntnerstrasse. I can't see them now."

They must have gone in different directions because within seconds, Dr. Hofer passed the window where they were sitting, walking toward the Augustinerstrasse. “Oh Lord,” said Eleanor as he looked in and saw them, smiled in what seemed to her a mocking way, raised his hat, and walked on. “Now he knows we saw them.”

“So what?” said Christa. “It doesn’t make any difference.”

“It does to me. We’d better go back to the Haus im Wald.” The sight of Christa climbing carefully down from the table, clutching it with her hand, and looking nervously at where she was putting her feet on the rungs of the stool made her feel intensely depressed. “Let’s go,” she said and paid the bill. Her hair didn’t look half as good to her in the mirror on the way out as it had on the way in.

3

“Herr Schmidt?” said Büchner on the telephone in his office. “Do you think you could spare Gruber for a quarter of an hour? I think Graf Jr. is coming at eleven thirty. I could fit Gruber in now, if you can manage without him.”

Schmidt, talking from the lobby on his cell phone, laughed. “Sure, Herr Inspektor. He’s very helpful, but I’ll manage for fifteen minutes.”

Büchner put down the phone. This young Schmidt, he thought, will go far. He really knows how to deal with the local population. He wasn’t sure he would do as well himself with the redoubtable Gruber. Stick to the facts and pull rank. The Grubers of this world had a respect for authority.

“Ah, Herr Gruber, come in.” A stocky man, surely all of sixty, but strong looking and straight-backed. What was it Schmidt had said about his being 60 percent handicapped? He certainly didn’t look it. He motioned him to the upright chair in front of the desk, which he had placed precisely opposite his own. Gruber sat down, still straight-backed.

Forgetting his resolution, Büchner commented, “You have a military bearing, Herr Gruber. Did you have an army career?”

"I did not, "said Gruber firmly, and he volunteered nothing more. No doubt it was against his principles to give any more information than that actually asked for.

"Thank you for being helpful to Wachtmeister Schmidt."

"Only doing my job," said Gruber.

"Quite. You seem to do it very well. I will not keep you very long. Since you keep a careful watch of what goes on in this house, you may be able to help me with a few things. There seem to be some discrepancies in the residents' accounts of the comings and goings on Christmas Day."

Gruber nodded, as if this were no surprise to him.

"Perhaps you would first tell me what your normal working hours are, and were they any different on Christmas Day?"

"I work the regulation eight hours a day on weekdays, start at eight and finish at six with a two-hour lunch break, twelve till two. At the weekends, I come in from twelve till six, one hour break, one till two, earning time and a half on Saturdays and double time on Sundays, union wages. The Sunday hours and rates were in effect for Christmas Day, except that I stayed till seven in honor of the day."

"So on Christmas Day, you sat at the porter's desk from noon until seven in the evening?"

"Except for some time between one and one thirty, when I collected a Christmas dinner made up for me by Frau Huber and brought it back to my desk. I didn't take my official lunch hour. There are always a lot of visitors for Christmas, and the front door needs to be open, but we have to keep the house secure."

"I gather there was no system of signing in?"

"No, sir. Herr Direktor Schramm never required this."

"Did you know all the visitors who came?"

"No, I did not. There were quite a number. Until now it has not been our practice to ask people to identify themselves, though new visitors frequently stop by the desk and give their names and ask for directions."

"Were there any such on Christmas Day?"

"A few. The rest, I knew most of them well by sight, if not by name."

"Did you know anyone who visited Frau Winkler in Martin Luther?"

"No, I do not remember her ever having a visitor."

"And the new resident, Frau Fabian?"

"I was not aware of the Fabian relatives on Christmas Day. I have had . . . dealings . . . with Professor Fabian since."

"I can imagine. And for Herr Graf?"

"Not to my knowledge."

"Would you recognize Herr Graf's son if you saw him?"

"I would."

"Did he pass you on Christmas Day?"

"He did not."

"You're absolutely sure?"

"If I were not, I would not have said so."

"Of course not, Herr Gruber. From your desk, you can see the entrance to the Melanchthon staircase, can you not, and the elevator? And the entrance to the café and the corridor to Martin Luther on the opposite side of the lobby?"

"I can."

"Could anyone come through the front door and go up the stairs to Melanchthon without your seeing them? Or come out of the elevator and go, let us say, to the chapel without your seeing them?"

"Not unless they deliberately waited until I had stepped away from my desk for a moment. But they would have to come through the front door or out of the elevator and look to see if I was there first. Someone wishing to escape attention, I suppose that is what you mean, would thus have to risk being seen."

"You would have made a good policeman, Herr Gruber."

"I . . . perhaps so." It had looked for a moment as if Gruber was about to volunteer a personal remark, but he did not.

"Now, this is quite important, Herr Gruber, from the point of view of corroborating other people's stories. No doubt residents came and went through the lobby all day, and you cannot be expected to remember every one of them, but to the best of your recollection, did you see Pastor Pokorny in the lobby?"

Gruber thought for a moment. "Yes, he came back from Martin Luther with Frau Beck at one point—sometime after six—and then he came down alone, to go to the chapel as usual. That was sometime before I left. He is a devout man, you know."

"Quite. And did you see Frau Huber in that hour?"

"She came at seven as usual to lock the front door before I left. I do not keep a key. It is not my responsibility."

"No, of course not. And did you see Dr. Hofer around this time?"

"Yes, he left just before seven, just before Frau Huber came with the key."

"Do you know when he had arrived?"

Gruber looked chagrined. "I do not."

"So either he walked in when you had stepped away from the desk or he came before you arrived."

"In the latter case, someone, probably Frau Huber, would have to have buzzed him in. Outside hours, there is a bell and an intercom connecting to Frau Huber's apartment."

"Yes. Do you recollect when you might have stepped away from the desk?"

After a short silence, Gruber replied stiffly, "I am obliged because of certain physical problems to visit the men's room every two hours."

"I see," said Büchner, trying to register no reaction in his face. "So then, let us say, around three and five p.m.?"

"Precisely at three and five p.m.," said Gruber. He looked at his watch.

"Oh dear," said Büchner. "Do you need to—"

Gruber interrupted him abruptly, "I informed Wachtmeister Schmidt that I would be back in fifteen minutes."

"Yes, of course. One last quick question: did you see either Sister Agatha or Sister Barbara cross the lobby from Melanchthon and go out of the front door between four and five?"

"Yes, Sister Barbara went past, wearing her cloak and hood, greeted me, and said she was going out for a breath of air. I said it was cold and getting dark. She said she would be back soon. And she was, just after five o'clock."

"Ah, yes, just after you . . . well, yes. Thank you. You have been extremely helpful. A man who keeps his eyes and ears open and knows how to state a fact."

"That is my job, Herr Inspektor, as no doubt it is yours."

"Indeed. Auf Wiedersehen, Herr Gruber, keep up the good work."

Gruber almost smiled. "And the same to you, Herr Inspektor." He walked stiffly to the door, turned, nodded, and left.

Well, thought Büchner, that really was helpful. He looked at his notes. One: Frau Lessing does seem to have been quite mistaken in thinking the younger Herr Graf was there on Christmas Day. Two: Pokorny, Hofer, and Sister Barbara all did things on Christmas Day that they did not tell me about. Were they trying to hide things, or were these things all too trivial for them to remember? He seemed to be drowning in a sea of trivia. In the next couple of hours, the fingerprinting might at least suggest who was actually in Graf's room on Christmas Day. Though, of course, the absence of people's fingerprints did not conclusively prove that they were not there. No actual murder weapon had yet been found, but there were enough hefty canes floating around this building—most people either owned or could easily acquire a *blunt instrument* of that kind. He had noticed that the rooms he had been in all had a stand near the door to hold canes, umbrellas, and such like. Walking about with a cane, even if one did not usually do it, would hardly attract attention. And since it now transpired that the blow itself need not have been such a violent thing in itself, there were many among the residents who could have landed it, ludicrous though the image might be that rose to the mind in most hypothetical scenarios. Certainly, Michael and Dr. Hofer had the strength and were apparently in the building. The sisters? Well, yes, they were able-bodied enough to ride motor scooters. Pastor Pokorny was quite handy with his wooden walking stick and still had muscle power at ninety-three. And even Herr Ritter? He was agile, but so small; and his wife so large, but lacking in agility. The Zimmermanns? Herr Zimmermann was unsteady on his feet, but certainly large; and Frau Zimmermann was an all-around, tough little lady. Frau Doktor Lessing was very trim. One would have thought that in an old people's home, there would scarcely be a physically plausible perpetrator of a violent crime. But physical disability was relative. Look at Gruber—"60 percent handicapped"—but clearly with strong arms, shoulders, and legs, which were all you needed, say, to play golf or knock down an elderly gentleman, while Frau Beck was the youngest and supposedly fittest, but if she tried to take a swing at a person, or indeed a golf ball, she would surely miss. But all this was absurd—where was the motive? One would have intuitively sensed that some motives were highly unlikely in an old people's home. "Crime of Passion in Home for the Elderly"—this would have struck him as a bit of a joke in the past. Not so much after a couple of days in this place. Eleven thirty-five—a knock at the door. Must be Graf Jr. He stifled a yawn. After Gruber's observations, he didn't expect much from this gentleman. More to be hoped from lunch with Dr. Lessing. He perked up at this thought and called out, "Come in!"

4

Franz opened his eyes to see a totally unfamiliar blue-and-green woven pattern in front of his face. He put out a hand and felt the wool. He seemed to be lying on a couch with his face toward the back of it. Where the hell was he? His head was aching, his face was aching, his body was aching. He turned over gingerly and saw a cane leaning against a chair, then he remembered. He remembered who had put the cane there and why. He remembered feeling ill in the inspector's office. Had he made a complete fool of himself? He closed his eyes again, remembering how willing he had been to put himself literally into the hands of that nice woman who had put the cane there, in case, she had said, he needed to go to the bathroom when she was out—he should use it since he might be unsteady on his feet. This kind of solicitude normally irritated him, but he had been relieved at the time, had let her take over and tell him what to do. She had put him to sit on this couch, and God, yes, she had bent down, untied his shoelaces, and taken his shoes off for him, saying comforting things like, "You'll be all right, Professor, just relax." He remembered feeling her ample bosom against his knees while she did it, and not minding this in the least. Then she'd put a blanket over him, told him to lie down and close his eyes and go to sleep. And he'd done that, feeling peaceful, it seemed, for the first time since they'd arrived and started dealing with his mother's move. She's dead, he thought now. Mother is dead. And a slight wave of nausea went through him at the thought. He heard the key turn now in the lock and tried to sit up.

"Ah, Professor Fabian," said Frau Huber. "Are you feeling better? I looked in about half an hour ago, but you were fast asleep."

"Yes, thank you," said Franz, feeling foolish now at the thought of how he had earlier abandoned himself almost lasciviously to her care. It was hardly his style. "Yes, thank you," he repeated. "I have been asleep. What time is it now?"

"It's just after noon," she said. "You've been asleep for a couple of hours."

"Thank you," he said again. "I must have needed it. I'm afraid this bang on my head has rather unmanned me."

"Surely not," said Frau Huber, smiling, it seemed to him, almost coquettishly.

"Well, I mean, it has taken it out of me." Again he felt ridiculous. It was totally absurd that this very large lady in a uniform seemed to him at this moment to be almost seductive. The knock on his head must have addled his brain. "I'd better try to get moving," he said. "You've been very kind, but I have quite a lot of business to attend to, you know, after the death of my mother and so on."

"I think you'd better eat some lunch before you start trying to move about again. You were quite faint in the inspector's office. Did you eat breakfast?"

Franz tried to think back to breakfast time. "I honestly can't remember," he said. "Have you seen my wife?"

"Not since she left the inspector's office a couple of hours ago. Where is she supposed to be?"

"I don't know," he said. It was really hard to focus on the events of the morning.

"My dear Professor Fabian, I will make you a nice sandwich and a cup of peppermint tea. You're not leaving here until you get your head together and are sure your legs can carry you."

"You're very kind," he said and was not at all sorry to lie back down on the couch. A bell rang loudly in the kitchen. Franz jumped.

"It's only the front doorbell," she said. She went into the kitchen and called through the intercom, "Who's there?"

She buzzed the person in, came back, and said, "It's Dr. Hofer, perhaps he ought to have a look at you."

"I don't know about that, but I did want to speak to him today, I remember that."

"I'll go and see if he can pop in for a minute." She hastened into the lobby, coming back a moment later with Dr. Hofer. "I'll make that sandwich," she said and went back to the kitchen.

"Well, Herr Professor, what's this I hear? A collapse in the inspector's office?"

"Not exactly a collapse." With the exit of Frau Huber, Franz felt his good humor rapidly evaporating. "I didn't feel well, and Frau Huber kindly brought me back here to lie down."

"Ah, yes, a very kind lady, Frau Huber." Hofer had a way of making his every remark sound ironic. Not at all, Franz thought, the way he talked to his lady patients.

"I wanted to ask you a few questions, Dr. Hofer, arising out of the autopsy report on my mother."

"Ah, I have been brought here on false pretenses. I understood that you needed medical attention yourself."

"Whether or not I need it, I can manage without it at the moment," said Franz, his old acerbic self, but with formal politeness asserting itself. "Not that I am ungrateful for your making a house call last night."

"I will, of course, be sending a bill for that," said Hofer, and again Franz wasn't sure if this was seriously or ironically meant.

"Please do," said Franz. "I am also prepared to pay for your professional opinion on the autopsy report." He took out a piece of paper from his pocket where he had jotted down the facts that he had. "My mother had apparently received Levodopa the night before she died. Do you know who prescribed this and how much?"

"I know that I did not do the prescribing. It would have been her general practitioner, Dr. Dietrich, in Döbling. She came into the Haus im Wald bringing with her the medications she had previously received. The dosage was 600 mg."

"Does it strike you as a reasonable dose for a woman of her age?"

"Your mother was suffering from late-onset parkinsonism." Hofer seemed to be taking pains to sound patient and was coming across clearly as long-suffering. "She had been taking Levodopa for about five years to try to improve her quality of life—talking, walking, etc. L-dopa is tolerated quite well by many patients aged eighty and older. She probably started with a lower dose, but doses are increased as time goes on and resistance to the drug grows."

Franz was finding it quite hard to concentrate on what the mellifluous voice of Dr. Hofer was actually saying, but he battled on with his questions. "And then you, that morning, prescribed Alprazolam. How much?"

"A moderate dose, .25mg. She was very agitated, and Alprazolam has a quite quick effect in reducing anxiety. It is a mild tranquilizer."

"But I gather that in certain cases it can be fatal."

"Ah, Professor Fabian, I detect an Internet aficionado! If you look further, you will find that it has only been fatal in cases of an overdose, and the dose I gave her, as borne out in the autopsy, was far from an overdose."

"In a ninety-year-old? And on top of the Levodopa?"

"There is no danger of interaction."

Well, he was bound to say that, wasn't he? thought Franz. He would check it all out on the Internet as soon as he got back to his laptop. But now he felt very tired again. Frau Huber brought in a tray, pleasantly laden with steaming peppermint tea, attractive open sandwiches, white spreading cheese, pink spreading wurst on brown bread, decorated daintily with green chives and parsley.

"Frau Huber has an aesthetic sense in the preparation of food," said Hofer. "You are lucky to have fallen into her hands, Professor."

"I am certainly grateful to her," he said, wishing that Hofer would just leave, and feeling a sensual need to sink his teeth into the soft, enticing sandwiches. "I should probably eat something now and go to try and find my wife."

"The last time I saw her," said Hofer, "she was sitting in the Sacher cafe in the Kärntnerstrasse in town."

"What?"

"She was sitting—"

"Yes, I heard. But that's hardly possible," said Franz, now totally confused. "I can't remember her having said anything about going anywhere."

"Professor," said Hofer, "you know, if you are having serious trouble remembering recent events, you might have to check yourself into the emergency room of the hospital again. It might be a delayed reaction of some kind to your fall."

"Nonsense," said Franz. "I'm perfectly all right."

"Eat your sandwiches, my dear sir," said Frau Huber. "You'll feel better for that."

"Yes, indeed. I'll say good-bye then, Dr. Hofer."

"Auf Wiedersehen, Herr Professor, but remember what I said."

"That's asking the impossible, isn't it, Herr Doktor, if I'm having a hard time remembering recent events."

"Ever the literalist," said Dr. Hofer, bowed slightly and coldly. "Auf Wiedersehen."

He left, and as he did, the bell in the kitchen rang again.

"Who is it this time?" said Frau Huber and went to see, while Franz fell upon his sandwiches with real relish. She came back.

"It is your wife, Professor, she asked if you were still here. I said yes. She's coming right along."

Franz felt a stab of disappointment. Why? What had he been hoping for? Nothing, he supposed. He just hadn't wanted to emerge from the womb so soon.

5

Eleanor and Christa drove back to the Haus im Wald in a more subdued mood than when they were driving into the city. Eleanor did not feel in the least like singing, and the city streets on the way from the Ring to the Gürtel and on out to Grinzing, piled higher and higher with distinctly dirty snow the farther out they drove, looked less and less inviting. They passed several large hostile posters of the Freedom Party that she simply hadn't noticed on the way in, proclaiming in large letters, VIENNA MUST NOT BECOME ISTANBUL. "The underside of Viennese politics," Eleanor remarked. "Not pretty." Christa, who had never cared to discuss politics, said nothing. They drove in silence back up to the Silbergasse and along to Heiligenstadt and the expressway. Christa had her eyes closed, and Eleanor felt distinctly deflated. As the wooded areas on either side of the road intensified after Feldberg and the trees seemed to get higher and higher, she felt more and more oppressed at the thought of returning to the Haus im Wald. "Shades of the prison house begin to close around the growing boy," she said.

"What growing boy?" said Christa.

"Not literally," said Eleanor. "I was just meditating on our return from youth to the house of old age."

"That's not what Wordsworth was talking about," said Christa, who had been an English teacher.

"Of course not. But shades of the prison house closing in on us feels like an appropriate image, nonetheless."

"Not a helpful one. Not to me, at any rate. At this point."

"No. I'm sorry." They drove in silence until they pulled into the driveway of the Haus im Wald. Eleanor parked in the visitors' section, and they crunched through the snow to the front door. "Better ring the bell," said Christa. "I don't seem to have my key, and it's Gruber's lunchtime. It's after twelve."

"Heavens, is it? Franz is probably furious by now."

"Frau Huber will answer the bell. You can ask if she knows where he is."

Eleanor did this, then turned to Christa. "He's still with her. Lying down! I'd better go and see what's going on. Shall I check with you later?"

"Please do. I'll be in my apartment. I have to eat sometime, and I have to prepare some things in the chapel for the little service for Frau Winkler tomorrow. But you'll be able to find me."

"Fine. I think, by the way, it would be a good idea if I stay with you tonight."

"Would you really do that, Eleanor? I would be very glad. I dread the night."

"OK. I'll put it to Franz. Now I'd better go."

She walked through the lobby and knocked at the door of Frau Huber's apartment.

"Frau Fabian, do come in. Your husband is just finishing a little lunch I made for him. He does not seem to be very well, the poor dear."

The poor dear, thought Eleanor. Well, that's a new one. She went into the little sitting room to find Franz sitting on a blue-and-green-patterned couch with a matching crocheted blanket over his knees, drinking something from a floral-patterned cup.

"My goodness, Franz," she said. "What's up?"

"Apparently, I almost passed out in the inspector's office," he said. "And Frau Huber brought me back here."

"Yes, I can see that. But what have you been doing? What are you drinking?"

"Peppermint tea."

"But you don't like peppermint tea."

"Frau Huber seems to think it will be good for me."

"Oh, she does, does she?"

"What were you doing in the city?"

"The city? How did you know I was in the city?"

"Your friend, Dr. Hofer, dropped in here to see me, and he said he'd seen you there. Seemed odd to me."

"Seems odd to me that you are here being dropped in on by Dr. Hofer, whom you can't stand."

"It was Frau Huber's idea. She thought I should see a doctor. I took the opportunity of asking him a few questions about my mother. But I'm not up to much today, I must admit."

"Probably you should go back to the apartment and lie down there."

"Yes, probably," said Franz, making no attempt to stand up. "What *were* you doing in the city?"

"Well, you seemed to be well taken care of by Frau Huber, so I thought it would be good for Christa to get right away from here, completely away from the whole atmosphere. We just went and had coffee and came back."

"What about Ingrid and Mother's room?"

"Oh Lord, I forgot all about that. I'd better go and see what I can find out. But don't you want to go home?"

"Home?" said Franz vaguely, and stretched his legs out on the couch again, pulling the little crocheted blanket over himself. "Maybe I can just stay here until you know what is going on."

"OK, I'll go and ask Frau Huber. Then I'll take you home and leave you there. I've promised Christa I'll stay in her apartment tonight."

"You've what?!"

There was a banging at the door. Eleanor went into the hallway to see Frau Huber open the door to a very breathless Christa. "Please come," she said. "I need help, in the chapel."

"In the chapel?" said Eleanor incredulously as she and Frau Huber hastened across the lobby.

"Yes," panted Christa. "On my way down to get a bit of lunch, I looked in there to check if the flowers had come for the memorial service and . . ." They had reached the chapel door.

"Oh dear, oh dear," said Frau Huber. On the floor near the altar table was Pastor Pokorny. The tablecloth had apparently been pulled off the table, and white lilies were scattered around an overturned vase near his right hand, which was clutching at the tablecloth. He was lying facedown and seemed to be struggling to get up.

"I tried to help him," said Christa, "but he's too heavy for me."

"Of course, he is," said Frau Huber. "Pastor Pokorny. Just lie still, we'll get help."

He was making whimpering sounds. "I fell," he said. "If I could just get up onto my knees, I could stand, but I can't. I've been trying and trying . . ." His voice was thin and tremulous.

"Just lie still. Perhaps," she turned to Christa, "you would run to Martin Luther and get help—two nurses—one alone is not allowed to lift a person. On second thoughts, don't run. We don't want any more falls around here."

Frau Huber got one of the plush cushions from a pew and eased it under the pastor's head. "Just try to relax, Herr Pastor, someone will soon be here. What happened?"

"I don't know. I caught my foot in something, maybe my own cane. I fell forward, tried to save myself by grabbing on to the table, but the cloth came off in my hand. Simply can't get up!" Again he tried to push himself up onto his knees, and again failed. Tears of frustration began to mingle with the blood from grazes on his face that had come with the fall.

"Oh, Frau Huber, I'm sure we can get him up together," said Eleanor.

"We'll wait for help," said Frau Huber firmly. "We might only make things worse. Try to stay still, Herr Pastor."

"I want to get up," he said desperately.

Two nurses came into the chapel with a wheelchair, and together, each putting an arm carefully under his arms, they tried raising him to his knees. He gave a yelp of pain, and they lowered him back to the floor. "That won't work," said one of them. "He probably bashed his knees when he fell." Carefully they turned him onto his back and raised him to a sitting position. On his face was a look of pure outrage, as if he could not believe that this was happening to him. "Could someone put the wheelchair behind him and hold it still?" said one of the nurses. Frau Huber did, and the two nurses, arms under his arms, raised him into it. Everyone breathed a sigh of relief.

"Now what?" said one nurse.

"I want to go back to my apartment," said Pastor Pokorny, his voice still quavering.

"I'm afraid that won't do," said Frau Huber firmly. "If you have difficulty walking, you'll need care, and that means Martin Luther."

"No, no," said the pastor loudly. "I'm sure I can walk." He tried to push himself out of the chair and put weight on his feet. But he fell back panting into the chair.

"Martin Luther, I'm afraid," said Frau Huber. "At least for a night or so."

"Well, for a night or so," said Pastor Pokorny, putting his head back and closing his eyes.

Sister Agatha appeared in the doorway. "I hear there's been an accident?"

"Pastor Pokorny has fallen," said Frau Huber. "He will need attention. Can he be put up in Martin Luther for now?"

"Room 25 on the third floor can be used," said Sister Agatha. "Wheel him over there, and I'll get a doctor." She turned to Christa and Eleanor, "You can leave him to us." And the little group trundled away toward Martin Luther and its carpetless rooms. Eleanor felt they should intervene but didn't know how.

"That's the last straw," said Christa and started to cry.

"Try not to worry," said Eleanor. "He may get over it quickly and soon be back in his own place."

"Not very likely," said Frau Huber as she gathered up the lilies from the floor. "He is ninety-three years old. I must send someone to clear all this up." She picked up the vase and examined it. "Cracked," she said, dropped it into the wastepaper basket by the door, and went out with the armful of lilies.

"When I said the last straw," said Christa through her tears, "I meant, room 25 is Frau Winkler's room. And tomorrow is her funeral."

They left the chapel. *Or ever the silver cord be loosed*, Eleanor heard the strong old voice of Pastor Pokorny in her head, *or the golden bowl be broken.*

Chapter 11

In the Martin Luther wing, there were several residents who had, as we so pleasantly say, lost their memories, as if this were a matter of simple carelessness. Sometimes it even seems to be that. Memories come and go, and lost ones can sometimes be retrieved by sheer concentration or willpower, but sometimes they cannot. Listeners to Österreich Eins in the Haus im Wald were hearing programs these days in honor of various Austrian anniversaries that were to take place in the year ahead, such as the end of the Second World War, and many of the learned commentators dealt with the collective memory of the Austrians. Some younger scholars seemed to think that this memory had been lost as far as the decade preceding 1945 was concerned. All the residents of the Haus im Wald were old enough to have some recollection of the war years. Even the youngest, Frau Beck, born in 1939, could have had at least vague memories of the bombs that destroyed much of Vienna in 1944 and '45, while residents as old as Pastor Pokorny, born during the First World War, and already in their early twenties when enthusiastic crowds of Austrians greeted Hitler in the streets of Vienna, must all, you would think, still know where they had been on those surely unforgettable days in the middle of March 1938. Those who had passed their midseventies and were not yet eighty, such as Sister Agatha, Frau Dr. Lessing, and the late, lamented Herr Graf himself, were in their teens when much of Austrian youth was marching to the rousing choruses of the Hitler Youth, so they too must have had memories, unless they had chosen to lose them. One would not actually know, however, what or if they remembered. By mutual consent, it seemed, "the war" was a taboo subject. Or perhaps in some cases, a memory so repressed that it really was irretrievably lost.

1

When Erich Graf walked into the office for the second time, Büchner thought at once that he had a less hangdog air than he had the day before yesterday. He looked less sweaty, less rumpled, less nervous, more like a man—a sexist thought, and what did it really mean? Büchner asked himself as he extended his hand. Even Graf's handshake was less limp.

"Like some coffee, Herr Graf? I think there's still some in the pot, though it may not be very warm."

"That's OK. A cup of coffee would be nice."

"Better than scotch, eh?"

"Scotch?" Graf looked puzzled. "Oh yes, of course, you only had the hard stuff when I was here before. Well, I'm in better shape this time anyway."

They sat down in the two armchairs.

"You've had a chance to get over the shock at least," Büchner said.

Graf seemed to hesitate for a moment, then he said firmly, more firmly than he had said anything the last time, "Yes, I have. And not only the shock. Well, I was shocked, of course, but apart from the ugliness of his death, I was also hit by a huge wave of what I can only call disappointment—disappointment and frustration at all the unfinished business. I hadn't said good-bye to him, of course, but the fact is that I hadn't ever really said to him what I felt about him, and he had always given me the impression that I was nothing but a disappointment to him, no big reputation, careerwise, no wife and children, no real money—you know. And I never knew how to counter any of this, since it was never actually said."

"I know exactly what you mean."

"You do?" Erich sounded surprised.

"Yes, as a matter of fact, I think I do. We're probably the same generation, you and I, postwar offspring. Parents occupied with the famous rebuilding of the country, working hard to forget the past, rebuild the future, wanting to give everything to the children they saw in front of them, without really seeing who these children were."

"Exactly. My father wanted to give me a good life. He worked hard enough for this, God knows, but when I didn't want to throw myself with enthusiasm into the good life as he saw it, he just couldn't take it in, really didn't have time, didn't ever talk—not to me anyway. From an early age, I had the feeling he didn't really like me. And deep down, I hated him for that. I suppose that's a foolish thing to say to someone who is looking for motives for his murder. But I didn't murder him, so I'm not particularly afraid of telling the truth."

"And so you hated him?"

"I also admired him, well, envied him anyway, but also in some ways despised him."

"Despised him?"

"Yes, when I realized as a teenager how he had dragged his feet about admitting that some of his property, artworks, and so on had, to put it bluntly, been stolen from Jews. Not by him, of course, he was far too young at the time when our illustrious forefathers were helping themselves to other people's property. And he did make amends in a big way later, but too late to help some people, I'm sure. Not that he didn't help me, he made me a small allowance too in recent years. But none of it really wiped out for me what I saw as an arrogant lack of concern in the days of his greatest strength."

"You also envied him?"

"Yes. He was handsome, big, strong, successful, women fell for him. When I was twenty and he was fifty, any girl I brought home was immediately taken with him, and I faded into the background. A cliché, I suppose, in the family lives of successful men."

"So what has changed, Herr Graf, since his death?"

Graf thought for a minute. "Well, again it may be rather foolish of me under the circumstances to admit that his death, now that I have taken it in, has somehow lifted a weight off me."

"I don't think you're foolish to admit it. I doubt in fact whether you would admit it if you had been the one who struck the fatal blow."

"Ah, but this kind of talk might be held to be a clever ruse. I assure you, Herr Inspektor, it is not. In any case, when you see the will, you'll see that it presents you with a quite down-to-earth motive for murder, except that I had never seen the will before." He laughed, a more open laugh than the nervous giggle that had punctuated their previous conversation.

"So you have seen the will? I was going to talk to Dr. Schönholz, your father's attorney, this afternoon."

"Dr. Schönholz called in the main beneficiaries of the will to his office in the city this morning and read it to us."

"I see." Büchner, curious as he was, tried not to show it.

"I am, as it turns out, the main beneficiary. Frau Hagen also received a substantial bequest, as did"—he paused—"Dr. Hofer."

"Hofer!" Büchner could not disguise his surprise.

Graf laughed again. "Yes, a bit of a surprise. When I walked in and saw him sitting there, I thought first of all that perhaps he was just dancing attendance on the lady Hagen. But no, he had been summoned by Schönholz too."

"Well, fancy that."

"Fancy that, indeed. Schramm was there also—various smaller bequests went to the Haus im Wald and to some of the staff. Since I was not necessarily expecting to inherit anything at all, it is quite a stunning feeling to be the proud possessor of what is to me a small fortune, namely, a stock portfolio of some five hundred thousand euros and several pieces of real estate. My father was a rich man, Herr Inspektor, even after paying out quite massive amounts in restitution. He worked hard to build his assets in the decades after the war, and the properties he acquired then accrued in value in the last thirty years. But I should also say that what he wrote in his will about his bequest to me has also, at least temporarily, removed a burden from me. You will no doubt read the will, and you will see what I mean." Graf finished his coffee and leaned back in his chair. "The end of a chapter, you see, Herr Inspektor, for me. The end." He closed his eyes for a few seconds and took a deep breath.

"Thank you, Herr Graf, for telling me all this. I am afraid, however, that I am only at the beginning as far as my investigation of this murder is concerned."

"Yes, of course, that's a mystery to me too. I doubt whether I can help you much. There is the envy factor, of course. I was probably not the only person who was envious of him, and envy can be a vicious sort of thing."

"Yes, it can. But I do also have one concrete question that I must ask you again about the day of the murder. One resident seems sure that you visited your father on Christmas Day. But you have clearly stated that you did not. You do not wish to change that testimony?"

"No. I wasn't here that day. I came, as I told you, on the next day only because of a certain presentiment after receiving several unidentified phone calls."

"Yes. Thank you. One more thing, I wonder if you would come with me to your father's apartment for just a few minutes. I know you have said you did not visit often, but still, if you were to look around carefully, something might strike you—something missing, for example, or out of place."

For the first time in this interview, Graf began fiddling with the fabric of the arms of the chair. "I don't much want to go in there again. But if you insist . . ."

"I would be grateful. I have to be in the apartment next door at noon, so we will not be there long."

"Very well." The two men left the office. "Oh, by the way," said Büchner as they walked to the lobby, "it might be a good idea, for the sake of completeness, if you were to get yourself fingerprinted. We're doing it to practically everybody who can walk and talk."

Graf laughed. "Beat you to it, Herr Inspektor. I offered myself up on the way in."

"You did? Well, thank you." Büchner automatically headed for the stairs in Melanchthon. They walked up the stairs to the third floor. Büchner noticed that Graf was huffing and puffing as they went up the last flight. Not in great shape, he thought. Overweight for his height. Thank God, I haven't got to that point. I can still walk a couple of flights of stairs without losing breath—a sign of age, congratulating myself on something like that. He checked the door to apartment 32; it was locked. He opened it, and they went in. "Perhaps you would put on these gloves," he suggested.

"No point in adding to the fingerprint confusion." He put on a pair himself.

"What should I be looking for, Herr Inspektor?"

"Any differences in the apartment from previous visits, or indeed since the time when you found the body."

"Well, that's new," Graf said, pointing at the carpet in the living room.

Büchner, following his pointing finger, was startled to see a yellow sticker in the chalk mark on the carpet in the place where the head of the victim had lain in its own blood. He gingerly picked up the sticker. Who could possibly have put it there? The three known key holders—Schramm, Frau Huber, and Michael—could of course have got in, and the mysterious person who had somehow managed to remove the original master key from Schramm's office safe. But who would have written this? The lines again made up a rhyming couplet in the same crude printing:

HERE LAY THE BODY OF AN AGING LECHER
DID HE LAY THE LADY? YOU BET, YOU BETCHA

Büchner put the sticker carefully into a plastic bag.

"What's this?" said Graf.

"There appears to be a joker at work in this place, who leaves little notes about the place. Have you heard anything about it?"

"No, well, I wasn't here very often, was I? What sort of little notes?"

"Probably the less said about them, the better at this point. Let's look around a bit more."

They walked into the bedroom, and Büchner opened the top two drawers of the bureau. "This seems to have been where your father kept things like watches, glasses, tiepins, rings, and so on. Do you have any idea of what might have been here? Is anything you remember missing?"

"I'm not really the person to ask," said Graf. "In his will, he left the contents of the apartment to me, so I suppose this stuff is now mine, with the exception of a waistcoat watch and chain, which had belonged to his father and which he left, oddly enough, to the porter, Gruber, and a set of gold cuff links, which he left, equally oddly in my opinion, to Michael, the young man who works in the café."

Still wearing his gloves, Büchner opened the various little cases in the two drawers. "There's a watch and chain," he said. "Do you recognize it? I do not see any gold cuff links."

"The watch had my grandfather's initials on the back. That's the one. The cuff links, I don't know. He often wore gold cuff links. I can't see why there shouldn't be any here."

"I'll have Schmidt look carefully through the other drawers and make an inventory, unless you would like to do it yourself, or at least be present while he's doing it."

"No thanks," said Graf. "Just being here now is beginning to drag me down again. I'd like to leave, if you don't mind. I'll have to come back sometime when you guys have finished your work. Right now, it somehow makes me feel sick."

"I know what you mean," said Büchner, and he really did. For the second time in this conversation. Funny the fellow feeling that he seemed suddenly to have for this man, who had quite put him off the first time he met him. "Thank you for coming, in any case. The end of a chapter, remember?" He shook his hand and smiled encouragingly.

"Thank you, Herr Inspektor, thank you."

Büchner looked at his watch as he saw him out. Almost noon. He'd better go along to Dr. Lessing. Odd those missing cuff links. And no sign of the silver-and-turquoise tiepin either. No pattern in any of it. Bits and pieces of information. He couldn't even begin to distinguish important facts from unimportant ones. He locked the door, glad to leave the dead man's room behind him and wishing he did not have to carry that nasty yellow sticker with him. Even in its plastic bag, it made his pocket feel dirty.

2

The two women stood outside the chapel, watching the large lady moving her weight purposefully from one foot to the other through the lobby and past the café. The lilies bobbed their heads over her shoulder as she disappeared around the corner.

"I hope she'll bring those lilies back," said Christa petulantly.

"Of course, she will," said Eleanor. "When is the service tomorrow?"

"At nine thirty. Pastor Pokorny was going to conduct it."

"Maybe he still will," said Eleanor. "Look, when they get him settled in over there, we'll go and see him. Weren't you going to lunch? Could I come too, do you think? Franz had sandwiches prepared by the fair hand of Frau Huber, so I don't have to worry about him." There was something annoying, she thought, about the way Franz had been, as it were, captured by Frau Huber. But why should it annoy her? Surely she wasn't jealous. Not of that fat, uniformed, bossy lady. Absurd. "I'll just pop into the ladies," she said. "You can see if there would be a place for me at lunch."

The ladies' room was just outside the dining room. Eleanor went in and into one of the stalls. She was slightly shocked to hear what sounded like a woman crying quietly in the next stall. Her first instinct was to flush the toilet quickly and get out to escape the embarrassment of finding out who it was, but Miss Eleanor Marple told her quickly to stay where she was, bend down, and see if she could identify the feet of the lady through the gap between the bottom of the partition wall and the floor. She could only see a pair of black leather shoes that could have belonged to anybody, and not even Miss Marple could persuade her to stand on the toilet seat and look over the top of the partition. In any case, the snuffling sounds had now stopped, and the toilet was flushing next door. Eleanor quickly flushed hers and stepped out to the washbasins, almost colliding with one of the sisters, not Agatha, the other one. What was her name? They had never been introduced. But this was hardly the time or the place for social niceties. The sister, red-eyed, smiled politely and said hello. They stood at the paper towel dispenser with dripping hands, each deferring to the other, then both reaching for the same piece, drawing back with nervous oh-I'm-sorry's and after-you's, until Eleanor determinedly took a piece, dried her hands, and walked out, leaving the sister—she could see in the mirror—dabbing at her eyes with the damp towel.

Well, well, thought Eleanor, what's all that about? She went into the dining room and saw Christa waving to her from a table, which still had two empty places. She crossed the room to this table, and Christa said to her table companions, "This is my friend Eleanor Fabian."

"We have met," said Herr Ritter, standing up immediately and drawing back the empty chair next to him for Eleanor. She was genuinely pleased to see him again. "Why, Herr Ritter," she said, "I am so glad to see you. And Frau Ritter," she extended her hand to the lady who was sitting opposite him.

"We heard," said Frau Ritter, "that your mother-in-law died suddenly."

"Yes," said Herr Ritter. "We are so sorry. Please accept our sympathy."

"Thank you," said Eleanor. "It was a shock."

"It was," said Sister Agatha, who was sitting opposite Christa at the end of the table. "We were all very upset about it. Ah, Barbara," she said to the other sister who came in and found herself motioned to the seat opposite Eleanor. "Sister Barbara, Frau Fabian," said Agatha. The two women shook hands. How embarrassing, thought Eleanor. She must know I heard her crying. Why in the world was she crying in the toilet, of all places. Well, I can hardly ask her here.

"It's Wiener schnitzel today," said Christa with an attempt at brightness. "One of the better offerings of the kitchen."

"Not to be compared, of course," said Herr Ritter, "with Figlmüller's, but not bad. You may notice that the dining room is pretty full."

"What's Figlmüller?" asked Eleanor, glad of a neutral topic of conversation.

"That's where you get the biggest and best Wiener schnitzel in Vienna," said Herr Ritter. "They have one restaurant in the city center and one out in Grinzing, not so far from here."

"How have I managed to miss that?" said Eleanor. "This one looks pretty good to me anyway." She squeezed a wedge of lemon on it and tucked in with some enthusiasm. "When I was a student here in the early '60s and didn't know much about Vienna at all, I had a landlady who taught me how to make a Wiener schnitzel.

She used to beat the meat to paper-thinness—much thinner than this. Meat was much more scarce in those days, of course."

"It certainly was," said Frau Ritter.

Eleanor, aware that she was burbling on to fill what seemed to her an ominous silence from the two sisters, said, "Yes, well, she told me it was even worse right after the war when they could hardly get hold of meat at all, they beat whatever they could get even thinner, and they couldn't dip it in even one egg yolk because they had no eggs. She claimed things had been much better before. She was full of nostalgia for earlier times, that lady. In fact she was the only Viennese I ever met who openly described herself as a Nazi. I remember coming into the kitchen on the morning of April 20 and finding her crying. I asked what was the matter, and she said, 'Today is the Führer's birthday.'" Now total silence fell upon the table. Eleanor had often told this story in other places, and it had usually been regarded as quite amusing. Not, she thought to herself, here. Oh dear. A mistake. Her table companions addressed themselves in silence to their Wiener schnitzels. "I'm sorry," she said lamely, and Sister Barbara looked across the table at Eleanor and said with a smile. "Why? No one can blame you for finding someone crying." Eleanor was touched by this, taking it as forgiveness for her earlier unintended intrusion.

"No, no, of course not, thank you," she said.

"What in the world are you talking about, Barbara?" said Sister Agatha. "That was hardly the point."

"Oh, wasn't it?" said Sister Barbara mildly. "And how long will you be staying in this country?" she asked Eleanor.

"We were planning to fly back to the United States next week. But things are rather in disarray, as you can imagine."

"Well," said Sister Agatha, "there will presumably be little to keep you here now that your mother-in-law has passed away."

"It's not so simple," said Eleanor, feeling quite cross at Sister Agatha's presumption in saying this, even though she was actually of much the same opinion. "The recent strange events at the Haus im Wald have, for example, meant that my mother-in-law's body was carted off to the police morgue and cut open in an autopsy."

"Do we really need to discuss this at the dining table?" asked Frau Ritter, nonetheless spearing a large piece of Wiener schnitzel and chewing on it with gusto.

"I am beginning to wonder," said Eleanor, "just what one *is* allowed to discuss at the dining table in the Haus im Wald." She heard Christa catch her breath at this. Now I've gone too far, she thought.

Herr Ritter intervened in gentlemanly fashion. "My dear Mrs. Fabian, you must forgive us. We are all a bit on edge at the moment. The loss of our dear friend Hans Graf has upset us all, and we may not be reacting very politely."

"Speak for yourself, Herr Ritter," said Sister Agatha. "Personally, I do not feel upset, nor do I consider that I have been reacting impolitely."

Herr Ritter smiled patiently. "I apologize, Sister. I do not presume to speak for you. Let me say rather then that *I* am very upset, because that is a fact."

"Oh," said Eleanor, a little too effusively, "but *you* are always so polite and kind, upset or not."

"Eleanor," said Christa, "would you like some dessert? It's ginger pudding with custard today. Usually that's quite nice."

"None of their puddings," said Frau Ritter, "are actually that nice."

"But you will have some, my dear?" asked her husband, only a shade acerbically.

"Yes, I will. One has to cat something."

"It *is* possible," said Sister Agatha, "to eat nothing for dessert, especially if one tends to be overweight."

At this, Sister Barbara pushed her chair back from the table, as if she couldn't take any of it any longer, and said in a low voice, "You will have to excuse me. Auf Wiedersehen."

The others all accepted a sizable portion of ginger pudding in silence.

"Did you all," said Christa, "see the notice about the service tomorrow for Frau Winkler? It will be at nine thirty in the morning."

"Mr. Pokorny," said Sister Agatha, "will hardly now be conducting the service."

"Why ever not?" asked Herr Ritter. "What has happened to *him*?"

"He fell," said Sister Agatha, "and is now in the Martin Luther wing."

"Surely not," said Herr Ritter with genuine agitation. "He is in such splendid shape for his age. Why did they take him there?"

"*We* took him there," said Sister Agatha, "because that is where he belongs."

"He doesn't belong there for good, Herr Ritter," said Christa, flushing. "He has gone there to recover from the fall."

Sister Agatha merely sniffed.

"What a terrible week it has been so far," said Herr Ritter. "What will be the next thing?"

"Oh, Herr Ritter," said Eleanor, "there doesn't have to be a next thing. We all just have to be careful and watch out for each other."

"Yes, my dear, I like your optimism."

"She is of a younger generation," said Frau Ritter darkly. "She can afford to be optimistic. And talking of the younger generation, where is that detective today?"

"Presumably detecting," said Herr Ritter.

"Well, if so, he's doing it in a funny place," said Sister Agatha. "I saw him just before lunch going into Frau Dr. Lessing's apartment on our floor. And they are not here, so they must be having a cozy lunch up there."

"What kind of a psychiatrist is Frau Dr. Lessing?" asked Eleanor. Again there was a silence, and she wondered what was wrong with *this* question.

"A retired one," answered Frau Ritter firmly, eating her last mouthful of ginger pudding. "Come along, Samuel," she said to her husband. "We'll have coffee upstairs." And she began the cumbersome business of rising from the table and pushing back her chair while her husband fetched the walker. "Auf Wiedersehen," she said. Her husband bowed politely and said to Eleanor, "I hope the rest of your stay with us will be less upsetting than it has been so far."

"Thank you," she said. "I do too."

"We'll go as well," said Christa, standing up with some relief. "I'll also make coffee upstairs. Auf Wiedersehen."

Leaving Sister Agatha sitting alone at the table, Eleanor followed Christa out of the dining room.

3

Dr. Lessing opened the door immediately at his knock. "On the dot of twelve," she said. "That's nice."

"I was looking forward to this," said Büchner. "I would hardly be late."

The room that he entered was very pleasant. It lacked the windows on two walls that so much enhanced the sisters' apartment at the other end of the corridor, but there was still plenty of light from the long windows on the side overlooking the driveway and the road into the woods. The furniture was simple: straight lines, light wood, a round glass dining table, now attractively set for lunch, two armchairs at a coffee table in the window, one wall lined with bookcases, a couple of throw rugs on the well-polished wooden floor. The atmosphere was calm and somehow neutral. Büchner remembered the same atmosphere in the one psychiatrist's office he had frequented in his life some fifteen years earlier for a couple of months.

"Can I offer you a glass of wine, Herr Inspektor? I presume we should eat immediately since you will want to get back to work."

Noting with some relief that she was choosing not to regard this conversation as part of his work, he said, "A small glass of wine would be nice. But as you say, I shall shortly have to get back to the job."

She went into her little kitchen, came back with a bottle of good Wachauer wine, and handed it to him with a corkscrew. "Not a sexist act," she said. "It's just that I have to get the soup." He opened the bottle and poured two small glasses. She came back with a steaming tureen of liver dumpling soup and set it in the middle of the table. "I hope you like *Leberknödelsuppe*," she said. "I thought you needed something substantial to keep up your strength. We'll just have cheese and salad afterward."

"Excellent," he said.

She raised her glass to him. "Here's to your pursuit of justice in the Haus im Wald!" They drank, and as he was helping himself to the soup, she said, "And are you in hot pursuit, Herr Inspektor? Or am I not allowed to ask such questions since I am among the potentially guilty?"

He looked seriously at her. "If I were on the job, Frau Dr. Lessing, I would have to regard you as one of a number of suspects. Living next door to the murdered man, having no alibi, no one to corroborate your movements for the day of the murder, and you are perhaps quite strong enough to have knocked this man down with a cane, especially if you took him by surprise. You have apparently no motive, but nor does anyone else, as far as I have been able to discover so far, among the residents."

She smiled. "But at this moment, as we have said, you are not on the job. So perhaps we can forget this theoretically possible but highly unlikely eventuality."

"I would like that," said Büchner. "This Leberknödelsuppe is excellent!"

"I cannot take much credit. I didn't make the dumplings myself."

"Whatever brought you to the Haus im Wald, Frau Doktor, if I may ask?"

"At the age of seventy-five a year ago, I finally gave up my last patients. I lived alone. And I had increasingly severe arthritis. Is that enough of an answer? You will find, Herr Inspektor, that after the age of seventy, one begins to ask oneself, what will happen to me when I can no longer drive my car, do my own shopping, my gardening? That is, if one is alone. Are you, by any chance, alone in life, Herr Inspektor, if I may ask?"

"Well, yes, as a matter of fact, I am. I have never been married, nor ever really wanted to be, and I haven't thought much about my old age."

"A few days here should change that." She laughed. "But don't worry, as soon as you are out of here, you will quickly forget it all—until you are about seventy. Then it will all come back to you."

"This room actually reminds me of my own one excursion into psychotherapy," he said. "About fifteen years ago, I was about forty and involved with a younger woman who wanted very much to get married and have children. It got so that she could hardly talk about anything else. I half wanted this too, but I half wanted to hold on to my own freedom. I simply couldn't make up my mind, which half had the strongest pull. It was quite a torment. You will not think this a good characteristic in a police officer. Decisiveness and resolution would seem to be a sine qua non for the job."

She thought for a moment. "I suppose so. But isn't there a sense in which being able to hold on to two or more versions of a possible reality simultaneously in one's mind is also a sine qua non for a good detective? I mean, ultimately you have to come down in favor of one or the other, but if you cannot see with equal clarity more than one possible picture of the reality of the situation, then you stand a chance of simply blotting out the right picture with another."

She collected the soup plates, took them into the kitchen, and came back with a cheese board, a baguette, and a green salad. She poured them both one more small glass of wine.

"I'm sure you're right about the job," said Büchner and laughed. "However, believe me, you have a hard time trying to explain to people that your ability to see two equally plausible versions of your own life at once is a part of your perspicacity as a detective. Someone who is waiting year after year for you simply to make a decision, for them or against them, sees it, if you will pardon the expression, as a cop-out."

"What did she do, the lady in question?"

"She left me in the end, as I knew she would."

"So you were left willy-nilly with one version of reality, the solitary one."

"Yes. Though in a peculiar way, the other version never really disappears from my head. I can pull it back when I want to. Into my head, that is. I only went to an analyst back then for a couple of months—it was my girlfriend's idea—and once he showed me some pictures that I have never forgotten. One, when you looked at it first, showed a white chalice on a black background, then you looked at it again, and it showed two heads in profile, black on a white background. If you kept looking at it, you could shift it yourself from one to the other, but you could never hold on to the two ways at once. I suppose you've seen lots of such pictures."

Dr. Lessing smiled. "Yes, of course. I was something of a Gestalt therapist myself. Are you beginning to shift possible shapes of the Haus im Wald reality in your head by now?"

Büchner sipped his wine thoughtfully. "Well, no, Frau Doktor, not really, I must admit. I was thinking to myself before I came here that I do not really have any picture, no foreground shapes, no background colors—all I have is a wealth of detail. Loads of bits and pieces, none of them adding up to anything in particular."

"Did your psychiatrist show you those other pictures, not the ambiguous ones that you've mentioned, but the ones of incomplete objects, lines, and blobs, all in their right position in a particular picture, but much of the detail left out. You, the patient, with your eye, your mind's eye, shall we say, have to fill in the blank spaces to assemble the picture, to effect what we gestaltists call *closure*."

"I don't remember one of those, but I can imagine what you mean. Well, OK, here's one blob and a blank space in which you yourself are involved. You told me that you heard Graf's son leaving his apartment on Christmas Day. He called out 'Ciao, Papa' as he left. You heard it clearly, you said. Are you still sure of that?

"Yes. I heard it. I was alone here. I didn't listen to the radio until the evening, and I heard this at some point in the earlier part of the day—I cannot say when—I was not much interested in it at the time. I heard the voice, faintly, the door close, and the footsteps go past my door, presumably to the stairwell."

"And yet Graf Jr. says he most definitely was not here. And Gruber, who knows him, was at his desk most of the day and did not see him come into the house or go out. How do we 'effect closure' on these particular lines?"

"Herr Inspektor, first of all, you do not 'effect closure' on individual lines and blobs, you only do so when the whole picture jumps out of the page at you. Usually, it does not do so when you stare fixedly at the individual parts and try to force meaning into them. You have to shift your gaze freely from one part to the other, in as relaxed a way as possible. But I do not want to push this analogy too far. Obviously, in your position, you need to examine the details too, with as freely shifting a gaze as possible. There are various possible versions of this little incident that spring to mind. One: Erich Graf is lying. He was here but no one happened to see him. He killed his father and left, calling dramatically at the open door, 'Ciao, Papa.' Two: I am lying. I want to cast suspicion on Erich Graf either because I murdered Herr Graf myself or my best friend did. Both these versions strike me as forced and unlikely. So what other version is possible? Well, maybe someone else, other than Erich Graf, came out of that room and said, 'Ciao, Papa.' I asked you, when you questioned me the other day, how many people called Hans Graf father. At the time, I meant this ironically. But perhaps after all, it is the most freewheeling, least-forced question to ask. There is, one discovers in years of analysis, always a question to ask that opens up the field of inquiry. Closure, in the gestaltist sense, actually means revealing the shape that lies hidden in the details, freeing up the mind of the beholder, if you like, to see it. But come, Herr Inspektor, sit over there in the armchair for five minutes and let your thoughts float freely while I go and make you a cup of coffee so that you can get back on the job."

Büchner sat in the high-backed, upright but comfortable armchair, put his head back, and closed his eyes. He tried to let the lines and blobs of the scene in the Haus im Wald float freely before his eyes. Sleepy from the wine, he himself floated into pleasant unconsciousness for a few minutes and woke to find a demitasse of good black coffee in front of him and Frau Dr. Lessing sitting opposite, observing him gravely but benignly. I think she quite likes me, was his first thought. And I like her.

"What sort of psychiatry did you practice, Frau Doktor?" He sipped his coffee. "I mean, you say gestaltist, but on whom, for whom?"

"I think I would prefer to say, with whom. Well, I worked with all sorts of private patients, but I also did work with the courts on the assessment of soundness of mind, diminished responsibility, and so on. And I acquired a bit of a reputation for dealing with sexual problems, sexual offenders at one end of the spectrum and sexual relational problems at the other."

"I see." Why should he be surprised at this from this trim little gray-haired intellectual lady? But he was, though he tried not to show it.

"I studied," she went on, "in Vienna in the early fifties, in the aftermath of the war when such things as the disgraceful expulsion of Sigmund Freud were still quite recent history, though history that everyone was busily forgetting. There were many factors in my developing this specialty, but now I'm afraid you have to get back to work."

He looked at his watch. Yes. It was one o'clock, and by two o'clock, he needed to be in the city to talk to Schönholz and look at the will. He stood up, and towering over the diminutive lady, he said, "Thank you very much. This has been a most pleasant and helpful interlude. I hope I may talk to you again."

"I hope so. I have enjoyed it too."

He shook her hand and was sorry to leave.

4

Franz snuggled luxuriously into the couch, lying on his side and holding the little crocheted blanket up to his face. He pulled a corner of it up over his ear. Why was this funny little blanket so comforting to him? He had an absurdly childish desire to keep it for himself. He had his briefcase with him. Maybe he could put it in there and take it away with him. What absolute nonsense! Not for the first time that day, he felt he was sinking back into childhood. Or worse, reaching forward into second childhood. How he had enjoyed the little lunch on a tray. Meals on a tray had been a rare treat when he was a child. Only when he was ill. That was the only time his mother really softened toward him, lighting the wood-burning stove in his bedroom, another rare occurrence, and coming upstairs to see him, bringing tiny meals to tempt his appetite. Again the thought flooded his consciousness. Mother is dead. No chance now that those moments of demonstrated affection could ever recur. He felt tears creeping down the side of his face into the crocheted blanket. He was fully aware that they were tears of self-pity, not of grief. He felt very, very sorry for himself. He knew he ought to snap out of it, but it was not an uncomfortable feeling. He really wanted to submerge himself in it, under his blanket, though he wouldn't want all those women trooping back from whatever it was that carried them all away awhile ago to find him weeping into his blanket. He heard the front door open and fumbled in his pocket for a handkerchief.

Thank God, it was only Frau Huber. She tiptoed in with an armful of lilies.

"Ah, Professor, you're awake. Just let me put these flowers in water."

He dried his eyes and dabbed ineffectually at the corner of the blanket. His head ached, and he had no desire to stand up. "What's happening?" he asked when Frau Huber came back.

"Don't worry your head about it," she said. "Just one of the old gentlemen fell down. It's always happening around here."

"Yes, well, it happened to me yesterday."

"That was quite different," she said. "You had had a dreadful shock. And you are not one of our old gentlemen." She pulled up a chair to the couch and sat very close to him.

"I don't know about that," he said. "Ever since I've been here, I keep getting mistaken for one of the residents."

"I find that very strange, Herr Professor. You look like a man of the world to me. Oh, but your poor head," and she stretched out a hand and stroked his forehead gently. What gentle hands she has, he thought, but strong.

"Your blanket is quite wet," she said.

"Yes, I'm afraid I wept a few tears when you were gone."

"You poor dear! The loss of your mother, of course."

"Well, yes, that's it, of course." He could feel his rational mind deserting him. He wanted to hold this hand that was moving so softly over his head. He took it in his own hand and impulsively carried it to his lips.

"Oh, you poor dear," said Frau Huber again, and moving closer, she slowly put her hand in under the crocheted blanket, opened a button on his shirt, felt inside it, and stroked the bare skin of his chest. He closed his eyes, oblivious to everything except the sensation of sheer happiness and extreme desire. Slowly she moved her hand down toward the zipper of his pants. Oh yes, he heard a voice saying in his head, yes. The doorbell rang loudly several times. Frau Huber pushed her chair back, and he opened his eyes to see that she looked entirely calm and not in the least fazed by what seemed to him a crass and cruel interruption. She stood up as if from a normal conversation and went to answer the door. He sat up. Whatever am I doing? he asked himself and threw aside the crocheted blanket, which suddenly seemed slightly disgusting to him.

Frau Huber came back, followed by the director with Franz's cousin Ingrid.

"Franz, you look dreadful," said Ingrid.

"He's had a fainting attack," said Frau Huber. "He's been resting."

Franz was horribly aware of being red-faced and sweating, as well as bruised and black-eyed. His head was pounding again. "Guten Tag, Ingrid. Yes, I know I look awful—the bruises and so on. Did Eleanor find you?"

"I haven't heard a word from Eleanor. I finally went to ask Director Schramm if he knew what was going on, and he kindly brought me here."

Did the whole of the Haus im Wald know that he'd been sleeping on Frau Huber's couch? Or not sleeping, as the case may be. Another erotic jolt ran through his body, and he could feel Frau Huber looking at him. He'd better get out of here.

"Well, Herr Professor," said Schramm, "at least your cousin has now found you. She and I were beginning to wonder if you and your wife had vanished into thin air. I have already told Frau Konrad that the police have given us permission to open up the room of your late mother tomorrow so you can begin to make arrangements for the removal of the furniture. Do you want them to bring your mother's body back here?"

Franz felt a stab of anger at Eleanor. Surely she was supposed to be dealing with all that. He didn't have a clue what to do with his mother's body.

"I think it would be best," said Ingrid, "if they take her straight to the funeral home in Feldberg. You will have to decide," she said to Franz, "on such things as coffins and burial—or perhaps cremation?"

Franz felt quite desperate. "I need to talk to my wife," he said.

"Certainly," said Frau Huber. "But where is she?"

"I did see her in the dining room at lunchtime," said Schramm. "But of course, that's over now."

Franz looked desperately from one to the other. He seemed to have lost the ability to focus on practical problems.

"Franz," said Ingrid firmly. "I will take you back to the Zehenthofgasse right now. We'll talk about what to do with Tante Bertha, and then you can rest there. Perhaps," she sniffed, "Eleanor will turn up."

"Very well," said Franz meekly.

"I'll fetch my car. I parked at the back of the house." She went out.

"Am I leaving you in safe hands?" said Schramm to Franz.

Franz's mouth dropped open rather stupidly.

"Well, of course, you are," purred Frau Huber. "I will accompany him to the car." Schramm took his leave.

She fetched Franz's coat, helped him on with it, then put his scarf gently around his neck. "What a pity you can't stay here and rest," she said. "But never mind. Come along, lean on me." Taking his briefcase in her left hand, she held out her right arm for him to lean on. They went out to the car. Franz had his arm through hers and was almost painfully aware of the feel of her large breast. His knees were weak, and he leaned on her, thinking all the time, What is the matter with me? She helped him into the car.

"Thank you, Frau Huber," said Ingrid imperiously.

"You're most welcome," said Frau Huber with an exaggerated obsequiousness.

Franz groaned slightly as the car pulled out, and he put his head back with his eyes closed.

"I'm glad to get you out of the clutches of that woman," said Ingrid. "Such a bossy sort of a know-it-all. Why ever did Eleanor leave you with her?"

Franz made a vague gesture with his right hand, suggesting helpless ignorance, his mind and body arrested in midsentence by the image of the clutches of that woman.

"I can't talk just now," he said.

He tried to think back past the hours on Frau Huber's couch to the things he had intended to do this morning. He'd been so determined, that much he remembered, to deal with Dr. Hofer, to tackle the detective, to get the better of the two men. And he had failed miserably, but he couldn't remember how, what had gone wrong. Maybe he could still pull himself together today and do something sensible.

"Thank you, Ingrid," he said as they came near the Zehenthofgasse. "I appreciate your kindness in bringing me back, but I think I need to be alone. That fall really knocked it out of me. I'll have Eleanor call you about . . . about the arrangements."

"Yes, Franz, that's what you said before."

"I'm sorry. I haven't got a clue what she's been doing all day today."

"Could she be in the apartment?" she asked as they pulled up outside.

"No, the car's not there. We'll call you later. Thanks again, Ingrid."

Ingrid revved up her car rather angrily, reversed much too quickly, skidding on the snowy surface, and swung back out into the street. Franz didn't care. He just wanted to be alone.

5

"I'm not sorry to get out of there," said Eleanor as they left the dining room.

"No, nor am I," said Christa. "Come on, let's go upstairs and have a cup of coffee and try to relax for a minute."

They walked up to the third floor of Melanchthon, passing the lanky detective who was running down the steps, two at a time.

"Guten Tag, ladies," he said, saluting them cheerfully, military-style, as he ran. "See you later."

"He looks as if he had a cheerier lunch than we did," said Eleanor. "Those characters were a real downer. You can hardly open your mouth, it seems, without offending someone."

"There are some things, my dear," said Christa, "that it's really better not to mention, such as Hitler's birthday."

"Oh, for heaven's sake," said Eleanor as Christa opened the door of her apartment. "Hitler's been dead for sixty years. His actual birthday was about a century ago."

"Yes, well, some people around here were actually born close to a century ago. And in any case, Herr Ritter is a half-Jew."

"A half-Jew?" repeated Eleanor incredulously. "Is that kind of Nazi vocabulary still used around here? It's straight out of the Nuremberg Laws!"

Christa flushed. "Well, you know what I mean. His father was Jewish—so I believe."

"Well, so what?"

"Eleanor, we're dealing with the prewar generation here," said Christa doggedly. "Some things are just better not mentioned. No one talks about Herr Ritter being Jewish, and no one but no one talks about Hitler. I'll make some coffee."

Eleanor followed her into the kitchen, strewn as usual with unwashed cups and saucers. "I really haven't got time," she said. "I have to rescue Franz from the clutches of Frau Huber, though I must say he looked pretty cozy on her couch."

"Didn't you say we could check up on the Reverend Pokorny?"

"Oh yes, well, we'll have to be quick. By the way, I had a funny experience before lunch. I came upon Sister Barbara crying in the toilet. What do you make of that?"

"Crying?"

"Yes, I heard someone sobbing quietly. She stopped as soon as she heard me, then she came out of the stall looking very red-eyed."

"Did you say anything?"

"Good Lord, no. I am not completely your bull in a china shop, Christa, whatever you may think. But what do you think was wrong with her?"

"I have no idea. But if she was crying in the toilet, it must have been because she didn't want to do it in front of Agatha in their apartment."

"Good thinking! Is she afraid of Agatha, do you think?"

"Hard to say. Agatha tends to intimidate everybody. But the two of them are pretty inseparable."

"Do you think they have, you know, that sort of relationship?"

"What sort of relationship?

"Oh, Christa, you know what I mean. More than a normal friendship."

"Heavens, I shouldn't think so. They are retired deaconesses after all."

"What world do you live in, Christa? These things go on everywhere. I bet nunneries are rife with it."

"Eleanor, sometimes you are absurd," said Christa. "Come on, let's get over to Martin Luther."

"OK, then I simply must track down Franz. I'll have to drive him back to the apartment and then come back here later. Do I need to bring sheets or anything for the couch?"

"You really are coming?"

"Of course, I am."

"I think I've got some clean sheets," said Christa uncertainly.

"Don't worry. I'll bring all I need."

They went down the stairs and through the lobby. "I see the fingerprinters have gone. Did you get yours done? I did. Maybe by now they already know whodunit."

"Yes, I did get mine done," said Christa with a sigh. "You make it all sound like a game."

"Sorry," said Eleanor, remembering that for Christa, going over to Frau Winkler's room was fraught with memories that she didn't have herself. They walked up the stairs, past the floor where Franz's mother had lived for one ill-fated week. "Christa, I keep forgetting I'm supposed to be doing something about Mother's room! I forgot even to call Franz's cousin Ingrid. I'm getting completely scatterbrained."

"Well, you're in the right place then," said Christa, and they walked along the corridor to room 24.

"Uncanny," said Eleanor. "It's exactly above Mother's room. What do you think they did with all Frau Winkler's furniture?"

"She didn't bring much with her. Her room was furnished with the regulation hospital bed and the standard stuff supplied by the house if the resident doesn't have or doesn't want her own. Frau Winkler was a widow for many years—her husband was a Lutheran pastor who died during the war. That's something else people don't talk about. She lived on a very small pension, I know that."

They knocked at the door. There was no answer, so they tiptoed into the room. Pastor Pokorny was lying on his back, propped up on his pillows. His eyes were shut, Band-Aids adorned his face, his mouth was open, and his dentures were in a glass on the night table.

"How dreadfully old he looks all of a sudden," whispered Christa. "Come outside for a minute." In the corridor, she said, "Look, I'm going to sit here with him, hopefully until he wakes up. I don't want him to wake up and have a shock at being where he is."

"Good idea," said Eleanor. "There've been enough shocks around here lately. Best to keep an eye on him. I'll go and look for Franz. Don't expect to hear from me till later this afternoon or this evening."

Eleanor went down and found the door to Frau Huber's apartment ajar. She knocked and then called out, "Frau Huber!" There was no answer. She waited awhile then went in and gingerly pushed open the door to the room where she had left Franz. He was nowhere to be seen. She looked around and saw a pad of yellow stickers lying on the little escritoire. She tore off one of the stickers and went back to the door with it. Taking a pen out of her bag, she wrote: "Frau Huber, if you see my husband, please tell him I'm looking for him. EF" And she stuck the note on the inside of the slightly open door.

She went to the lobby. "Herr Gruber, have you by any chance seen my husband?" she asked.

"Yes, Frau Fabian," he answered. "He came to the door here about half an hour ago, supported by Frau Huber."

"Supported?"

"He had his arm through hers and seemed to be leaning quite heavily on her."

"If you say so. It doesn't much sound like my husband."

"She helped him into a car driven by a lady whom I have seen before."

Must have been Ingrid, Eleanor thought. "Where were they going?"

"I have no idea. You might ask Frau Huber. She seemed to be quite involved in it all."

"I just went to her apartment. She doesn't seem to be there, but the door is standing open, at all events, just ajar."

"That is very unlike Frau Huber. Perhaps I should check."

The two of them walked back to the apartment, and Gruber knocked. Still no answer. He put his head around the door, called Frau Huber, and then jumped back as if something had bit him. "There's another," he said, obviously shocked, and held on to the open door as if he did not want to go any farther.

"Another what?" said Eleanor.

"Another yellow sticker. It's better if you don't see it," he said and reached inside, took the yellow sticker, and crushed it in his hand.

"Herr Gruber," Eleanor said. "Why did you do that? I put that there."

"You did? But you haven't been here long enough. This has been going on for weeks."

"Whatever are you talking about? Take a look at it. I wrote it to tell Frau Huber I was looking for my husband."

Gruber smoothed it out and read it. "I see," he said. "I apologize."

"What did you think it was?"

"I suggest you forget what I said, Frau Fabian. Better not mention it to anybody."

"Now look here, Herr Gruber," said Eleanor heatedly. "I'm getting a bit tired of not being able to mention things around here."

"What is all the shouting about?" said Frau Huber, coming out of her bedroom, smoothing down the apron part of her uniform, and looking smug, rosy-cheeked, and self-possessed as usual. "I was having a nap."

"Do you usually nap with your front door open?" asked Eleanor crossly.

"My dear Frau Fabian, we are not living in New York here."

"I have lived," said Eleanor, "for thirty-five years in New York, and I have never had anything to do with a murder until I came to stay in the lovely Haus im Wald. And what's all this about yellow stickers?"

Frau Huber fixed Gruber with a baleful look. "There was a misunderstanding," he said. "Frau Fabian had put a yellow sticker on your front door with a note about her husband."

"I was looking for my husband. I was worried about him."

"Then I suggest you go back to your apartment. His cousin came and fetched him. And if you are so worried about your husband, perhaps you should pay a little more attention to him."

"Good day to you," said Eleanor and turned on her heel, boiling inside but, as she very well knew, completely routed. The fact that Gruber was also going back to his post with his tail between his legs was little comfort. Fellow feeling from him was unlikely.

She turned to go out of the front door to her car with a curt Auf Wiedersehen.

It was a surprise to her when Gruber answered, "Auf Wiedersehen, Frau Fabian," and then, with a distinctly malevolent tone in his usually neutral voice, said, "One day, Frau Huber will fall flat on her face."

"All I can say, Herr Gruber, is that I hope I am there to see it."

Gruber coughed discreetly. "Please forget I said that, Frau Fabian. I overstepped the mark." But they smiled at each other in parting. It was the first time Eleanor had seen Gruber smile.

6

Franz took off his coat. What a relief to be alone in the apartment. He remembered that he had wanted to look up stuff on the Internet. He could at least try to do that. He fumbled in his pocket and found the notes he had scribbled down when he was talking to the detective. They didn't seem very helpful now, and he could hardly remember why he had written Levodopa *40 mg, Alprazolam .25 mg (Hofer)*, and the words *intracranial hematoma*—what was that about? It had the word *Graf* after it. Was that what the detective said Graf had died of? He went into the study, opened up his laptop, which had Google as his home page, and typed in *intracranial hematoma.*

Referred to the Mayo Clinic Web site, he came right away upon a very clearly set out page from something called Ohio Health. This described the way a blood vessel may rupture between your skull and your brain, and blood then leaks between the two. The pounding in his head increased as he read further, and it reached a crescendo at the sentence: *Signs and symptoms of an intracranial hematoma may occur from immediately to several weeks or more after a blow to your head.* He closed his eyes again and could almost feel the blood leaking under his skull. He opened them and read the list of symptoms—*headache, nausea, vomiting*—I've had all that, he thought and read on: *As more and more blood flows into the narrow space between your brain and skull, other signs and symptoms become apparent, such as progressive lethargy and unconsciousness.* I've been lethargic for hours. *Mild head trauma is more likely to cause a hematoma if you are elderly.* I am, let's face it, elderly. *If the hematoma keeps growing, a progressive decline in consciousness occurs, possibly resulting in death.* Shock waves increased with each sentence. *Hematomas with the onset of prominent symptoms occurring within forty-eight hours are often fatal.* When was my fall—yesterday? The day before? *The risk is greater for those that take aspirin daily.* Aspirin, oh my God. Where was Eleanor? There was no one to help him. It had happened to Herr Graf alone in his apartment. Blood leaking under his skull. Oh my God. I am alone, so very alone. Where are they all? Was he supposed to know? Somebody had said something today about memory loss, who had said that? What? Where? It was no good; he just couldn't remember. He more or less deliberately let his head fall forward. Pain shot through him as his bruised forehead made contact with the hard plastic of the computer. He lost consciousness.

Chapter 12

There were various reasons why the residents of the Haus im Wald had turned to "assisted living" Some, such as the relatively young Frau Beck, had done so out of sheer loneliness and a kind of psychic helplessness. Many were driven by a worsening physical condition to seek security and safety—the intellectually independent Frau Dr. Lessing was an example—while others, the late Herr Graf for one, seemed to be governed by a desire prudently to husband their resources, physical and financial. But then there were those, especially in the carpetless Martin Luther wing, who were not so much self-motivated to seek out the Haus im Wald as a refuge for their old age, but who were "put there" when all their efforts to maintain their independence had failed. Some had repeatedly fallen, but more often than not, they had succumbed to something that was another taboo topic of Haus im Wald conversation, namely, incontinence. What comfort was it to say, as the self-help books do, that incontinence is a medical condition, not a personal weakness? What comfort to know that some 50 percent of all residents in homes for the elderly suffered from it or that it is the most common reason in the so-called civilized world for families to give up on caring for their elderly at home? Frau Fabian Sr. had been felled by it, her niece Ingrid having given her absent son, Franz, many graphic examples of how the situation could no longer be dealt with. At the younger end of the elderly spectrum, there were few sixty-year-olds who could handle, for example, post-prostate-surgery symptoms with the iron discipline of Herr Gruber, working at bladder training with a rigorous program of urinating on schedule so that he remained, against all odds, in control of his own body. To be in control of the mind and lose control of the body—is this not the cruelest fate that awaits the old?

1

Büchner ran down the stairs two at a time, greeting the American lady and her friend as he ran—no time for niceties, he had to get into the city to see Graf's attorney. Stopping off in the men's room, he almost collided with Gruber, who was coming out. They nodded to each other. Büchner looked at his watch and smiled. One minute after one o'clock. A man of his word, Gruber. Admirable. Büchner smiled to himself again. He felt in a good mood after lunch with Dr. Lessing. Perhaps this visit to Schönholz and an examination of Graf's will would begin to help him draw lines between some of the dots in the picture. Schönholz' office was in the Inner City, in the Hegelstrasse. He could park his car in the Bergstrasse, where he lived himself, then take a tram around the Ring to the Schwarzenbergplatz, and walk a block to the attorney's office.

"Auf Wiedersehen, Herr Gruber," he called as he went out of the front door. "Back soon! Hold the fort!" Why was he being so hearty and jovial with everybody? It wasn't as if he had made much progress this morning, though for some reason, he felt as if he had. What had he actually done? He started up his car and skidded his way, a shade too fast, down the drive to the road. Well, he had, at least to his own personal satisfaction, eliminated Graf Jr. as a suspect. What Graf had said about his relationship with his father rang true, and it did not sound like a murderous one. A highly personal reaction on his part, he realized. It had brought to mind his relationship with his own father, whom he had certainly never wanted to murder, fraught though the relationship was till the end. Büchner Sr., sent to the Russian front at the age of nineteen, 'fortunate' to survive three years as a POW in Russia, returned home, one of the many 'late homecomers' three years after the end of the war in 1948, physically and mentally devastated, but determined to make a go of life in the new Austria.

Working night and day in the furniture business of his new wife's family, he had made a good living, but rarely had time for his son and had no sympathy at all with the student movement of the sixties—young people, as he saw it, with the great good fortune to be at the university, throwing it all away with their long hair and pot-smoking and violent language. In one sense, thought Büchner now, their situation had certainly been similar to that of Graf and his father—they had never really talked about any of this. But his own father had died young at the age of forty-three, of late results of his war-deprived years, said the doctors, and of compulsive overwork, thought the son who shortly thereafter left the university and went into the police force, something again that his father would never have understood. He had been too young, however, to feel a sense of relief of the kind that Graf described at the demise of his father—only a kind of emptiness, a bleak knowledge that he had never known his father nor his father him. His father had left no last words for him in a will either. Büchner was immensely curious to see Graf's will.

Thinking, and driving on automatic pilot, he found himself already sailing down the long Billrothstraße through the outer districts of the city itself. Yes, he was glad to be out of the hothouse atmosphere of the Haus im Wald, and yet at the same time, he was fascinated by it. He hadn't even been there for two full days yet, but it seemed much longer. He would go back for one more night. At such times, he was glad that he had no one at home to whom he had to account for his comings and goings; and at the station, he had long been senior enough to please himself as to how he conducted his investigations. He had had enough successes as a detective to give him a pretty free hand. He knew plenty of people who put in for early retirement from the force before the age of sixty, and he was already fifty-five. Maybe he would soon have to think about it. But what then? He pulled into a parking spot in the Bergstrasse. His apartment was an attic floor at the top of an old house that faced the famous Bergstrasse 39, now the Freud Museum. This rented attic apartment at the back of the house on the second courtyard had been his home since the days when he shared it with two fellow students in the student movement. He had never wanted to move out. It had a big old stone terrace, a sort of shabby loggia, where he liked to sit on summer evenings, nursing a scotch, looking at the rooftops of Vienna, and musing about whatever case he happened to be working on. What would he muse on when he had retired? he wondered. But there would be no sitting and musing now—just a quick dash in and out. He pulled his mail out of the mailbox by the front door, took the rickety elevator to the top floor, walked up one flight to the apartment under the roof, went in, grabbed some clean underwear and a shirt, even a tie, and stuffed them all with the mail into his briefcase. Then he ran down the stairs and up the Bergstrasse to the tram stop on the corner. One stop, then a quick change onto the tram around the Ring to the Schwarzenbergplatz, and in ten minutes, he was walking over the Ring and along the Hegelstrasse.

He walked up two flights of a wide stone staircase, worn down in the middle of each step by generations of feet, and at precisely 2:00 p.m., he rang the bell of Schönholz' office.

"Grüss Gott, Herr Chefinspektor," said the distinguished-looking, quietly spoken silver-haired man, who was obviously Gotthold Schönholz.

"Guten Tag, Herr Doktor," said Büchner, avoiding even in these august and conservative surroundings the customary religious greeting—a small gesture of loyalty to his own socialist past. He was rather painfully aware that the lawyer was wearing a very good suit and he was not. The two men shook hands, and Büchner sat down in the large leather armchair across the desk from the attorney.

"This is a very sad and unexpected business," said Schönholz.

"Yes, it is. Did you know Herr Graf for very long?"

Herr Schönholz smiled. "You could say that. My father was his attorney, and I took over when my father died in 1980. I was his attorney for twenty-five years."

"I am here," said Büchner, "primarily to take a look at Herr Graf's will, but you might be able to help me to understand this case in other ways too."

There was a pause; then Herr Schönholz said carefully, "It was not a personal relationship, you know, Herr Inspektor. We did not, as it were, mix socially. In our firm, we have always been concerned not to mix business and pleasure. Our relationships with our clients are cordial but, at the same time, personally distanced."

"I understand that. Nonetheless, you might, because of dealing with his business affairs over the years, have some idea as to whether he had any major problems, any conflicts, any people in his business life who bore grudges against him, anyone, to put it bluntly, who might have wanted him dead."

"Herr Graf was a rich and successful man, Herr Inspektor." I'm getting a bit tired of hearing that one, thought Büchner. "Such men are not universally loved." And that one too. "But I cannot say that I know of anyone in his business life who might have hated him to that extent, no, I cannot. He had a very good name in the firm of investment bankers where he spent many years. He was known to be helpful to junior partners, and he was, it was obvious, adored by people like the office staff. Herr Graf was what is known as a charmer."

"So I have heard, and yet someone was so little charmed by him as to strike him a blow on the head that felled him to the ground and ultimately killed him."

Herr Schönholz blanched at this directness. "Yes, that is something that goes beyond my powers of imagination and quite exceeds my capacity for interpretation." Büchner waited. Schönholz went on. "Perhaps you would like to look at the will? He made it only three months ago. It was signed and witnessed here in my office, and as in his previous wills, I was named executor. I have kept it on file with his instructions to read it aloud to the main beneficiaries in the event of his death. This I have already done."

He handed it over the desk to Büchner, who with great curiosity opened it to the first page. "The Last Will and Testament of Johannes Erich Graf." So Graf gave his son his own second name as a first name, just as his own father had given him his second name, Georg, which was how Büchner came to have the name that seldom failed to cause people of a certain class to do a double take. He ran his eye quickly over the opening paragraphs regarding domicile, revocation of previous wills and codicils, payment of debts and funeral expenses, until he came to the first paragraph of actual bequests. Here he began to read slowly and carefully:

> One-half of all the rest, residue, and remainder of the property, both real, personal, and mixed and wheresoever situate, which I may own or be entitled to at the time of my death, I give, devise, and bequeath to my son, Erich Wilhelm Graf, with the following proviso that he receive in toto all the contents of my apartment in the Haus im Wald, with the exception of the small bequests listed below, and that he also receive my automobile, if such I possess at the time of my death. In making this bequest, I wish to make the following statement to my son.

And then following, written in Graf's own hand:

> *My dear son, for you are my dear son though I have never known how to show this to you, I remember as if it were yesterday the day you were born and I held you in my arms and thought with overwhelming happiness, "A boy, a boy all my own." I wanted to give you the world. You never wanted the world I had to give. Now it is too late for us to know each other. In leaving you a large part of the material residue of the life that I led and you despised, I hope you will not reject it as you have rejected me, but see it as a gift of love to the boy who was, on that happiest day of my life, all my own.*

I need time to take this in, thought Büchner. I'll have to ask for a copy. Is this a moving declaration from beyond the grave? Graf Jr. seemed moved by it—or is it a piece of empty sentiment too little and too late? These two possibilities shifted and took each other's place before his eyes like the white chalice on the black groundwork and the two black profiles on the white background. Graf, loving father; Graf, charming hypocrite. He could after all have tried much harder to reach his son in his lifetime. When he wrote this, he couldn't have known there was so little time left. But then again, his son—Büchner thought of their first meeting—was not easily lovable nor reachable. But he had to get on and read the other bequests.

> One-third of the rest, residue, and remainder of the property, I give, devise, and bequeath to Ursula Hagen, who has brought me much happiness.
>
> One-third of the rest, residue, and remainder of the property, I give, devise, and bequeath to Karl Hofer, who has been a mainstay of my health and comfort in the Haus im Wald.
>
> One-third of the rest, residue, and remainder of the property, I give, devise, and bequeath to the renovation and restoration fund of the Haus im Wald, administered at present by the director, Jürgen Schramm. This is in gratitude for the safe haven that I have found there.

Not so safe after all, thought Büchner.

> The following small bequests are tokens of my gratitude and regard for individuals and should be apportioned before the estate is divided.
>
> To my friend Samuel Ritter, the paintings in my apartments and those in storage, for him to keep or dispose of as he sees fit. He will know what to do with them. If he should predecease me, they should revert to my estate. Thank you, old friend.
>
> To my tax accountant in recent years, Frau Katharina Zimmermann, ten thousand euros as a small token of thanks for much practical bookkeeping help in recent years.
>
> To Manfred Gruber, the gold watch and chain inscribed with my grandfather's name, with thanks for loyal service."
>
> To Michael Neumann, the set of gold embossed cuff links, with thanks for loyal service and many lighter moments.

That was the end of the bequest section. Büchner read through quickly to the end of the document. Gotthold Schönholz was named as executor of the will. He looked up at Schönholz, who had sat in silence throughout his reading.

"Interesting document," Büchner said, taking a few deep breaths. It had for some reason quite disturbed him; he wasn't sure why. "I would be most grateful for a copy of this," he said. "As you must realize, anyone benefiting from a will or even hoping to do so has to be regarded as having a motive to get rid of the person who made the will."

"Yes, of course. The police have a right to a copy."

"You drafted it only three months ago, you said?"

"Yes. Previous wills had divided the estate between Erich and his mother. At her death, he changed it to two thirds to his son and one-third to the Haus im Wald. The addition of the two new major beneficiaries came with the new will three months ago."

"Were you surprised at this?

"Surprise is not a part of my mandate. As I told you, we are not accustomed in the firm of Schönholz and Eberhard to become involved in personal matters."

"Did the beneficiaries know before the death of Herr Graf that they were beneficiaries?"

"Not from me. Of that I can assure you. Of course, I really cannot say whether he divulged the information himself. I met Frau Hagen and Dr. Hofer for the first time at the reading of the will."

He took out of his drawer a copy of the will. "I would appreciate it, Herr Inspektor, if you would sign for this."

"Certainly." Büchner signed, put the document into his already-bulging briefcase, not altogether happy that his boxer shorts were immediately visible when he opened it up. He stuffed them back in and made his farewells.

A lot to think about there, a lot to think about. He walked this time rather slowly down the stairs onto the cold street, shivering as the wind blew open his coat, which he had not bothered to button up properly. The icy blast was a shock after the overheated office of the supremely discreet Herr Dr. Schönholz.

2

Good old Gruber, thought Eleanor as she drove away from the Haus im Wald. Who would have thought it? A real heart beats in that ramrod torso. Anyone who feels that much hostility to the abominable Frau Huber can't be all bad. But what was all that stuff about yellow stickers? Gruber had seemed so appalled when he saw hers. There really were an awful lot of funny things going on out there. Sister Barbara crying in the toilet, people fooling around at Christa's door at night—unless, of course, Christa had imagined that. Well, she'd have a chance to check that out tonight. Maybe she could find a way of actually talking to Sister Barbara alone. Christa was surely right when she said she must have been crying in the toilet because she was afraid to do it in the apartment. Could she be afraid of Sister Agatha? This lady did strike Eleanor as being a rather nasty piece of work. Different from Huber, but still nasty. She and Huber must surely be at daggers drawn. Poking her nose into everything and trying to organize everybody. Poor Pastor Pokorny had essentially been carted off to Martin Luther by Agatha, and it was clear that she had no respect for the old man anyway; she seemed actually to relish the opportunity to tuck him up in bed and leave him there. Would he ever get out again? Maybe Sister Agatha was a pathological man-hater and *she* had murdered Graf. And now she was trying to intimidate Christa because Christa had seen her coming out of Graf's apartment on Christmas Day. And Sister Barbara was crying because she knew and was afraid to say so. She smiled to herself as she turned off the expressway at Heiligenstadt. "Not bad, Eleanor," she said, "not bad." At least it's a hypothesis, the first I've figured out so far. But soon, she thought, sobering up as she approached the Zehenthofgasse, soon I have to deal with Ingrid and Franz. Funny. No sign of Ingrid's car. Careful not to slip on the icy steps, she let herself in through the front door and went up in the elevator.

"Franz!" she called. There was no answer. Maybe he was resting. She tiptoed into the living room. No one there. Into the study. No one there. She tried to push open the bathroom door. It was locked. "Franz, are you in there?" she called. Silence—she could hear the sound of water running in the washbasin. This seemed to go on and on. "Franz, please open the door," she shouted now and banged on the door. Franz opened it a crack, an unpleasant smell greeted her, and he went back to the washbasin.

"I'm trying to clear things up," he said pathetically. "Can't you wait a minute? I'm not well."

"For heaven's sake, let me help you." She pushed the door open wide and could see Franz, standing there with nothing on below the waist, trying to wash something out in the sink. He seemed to be almost in tears.

"What in the world has happened?"

"I don't know," he said. "I'm in a terrible muddle. My head is very bad. I tried to look stuff up on the Internet. I think I've got a hematoma—blood leaking slowly under the skull. I had a huge panic attack, fell forward onto the computer, passed out I think, and when I came to, I had peed in my trousers—and other things too. Oh God, I'm just trying to clear up. It's very hard when you're alone." Now he began to cry in earnest.

Eleanor was horrified. She'd never seen him like this. "Well, you're not alone now, Franz. Just leave all that. Get in the shower for a minute, and wash yourself off. I'll deal with the rest." She turned the shower on for him, made sure it was running warm; and when he stepped in, she ran some more water over the messy clothes in the sink, trying not to breathe in while she was doing it, dumped them all in a bowl, and carried them out to the kitchen where there was a washing machine. Thank God, his mother isn't here, she thought. She would never let them use her washing machine; she still thought of them as young and unable to deal responsibly with appliances. Young, ha-ha. If she could see Franz now. Well, she couldn't. She is dead. And in a peculiar way, that seems to be the problem. Can't think about that now, must see what he's doing. Franz was stepping out of the shower.

"There, that's better, isn't it?" she said, trying to sound encouraging, but with an awful sinking feeling. Irritating though Franz could be in his somewhat pompous sureness that he was always right, at this moment, she would have given anything for him to be restored to that state. This pathetic, almost-sniveling Franz was more than she could bear.

"Look," she said. "You've had a terrible couple of days. Wouldn't you like to lie down?"

"I think I need to go to the emergency room of the hospital. I've remembered now, that's what Hofer told me to do if I was having memory problems."

"They can't be that serious if you've just remembered that." She more or less automatically snapped back. But then, seeing with horror his eyes fill with tears again, she said, "Well, OK, Franz, if you think it's necessary, of course, we'll go there at once." She took the big bath towel that he was holding rather helplessly in front of him and rubbed his shoulders and back with it. "Everything will be all right," she said.

"I've got all the symptoms of intracranial hematoma, you see. Headache, nausea, lethargy, progressive decline in consciousness—all that stuff. And now on top of all that, incontinence."

"Incontinence? That is a symptom of intracranial hematoma?" she said skeptically.

"Well, no, but it's a part of being elderly, and hematoma from a blow on the head is more likely to lead to death if you are elderly, and"—he paused, to give added significance to the utterance—"if you take aspirin regularly."

Eleanor had a strong desire to laugh, but seeing how serious he was, she restrained herself. "Oh, come on, Franz, most things are more likely to lead to death if you are elderly. And you aren't even particularly elderly! And you're certainly not incontinent! You said you had a panic attack and passed out. People can lose control of their bowels in moments of extreme fear, soldiers on the battlefield, and all that, one is always reading about it."

"Always?" questioned Franz, and Eleanor was relieved at this flash of his normal pedantic self.

"In any case, if it makes you feel better, I'll certainly drive you to the hospital. How did you come upon this hematoma thing?"

"I'd noted down various things in my conversation with the detective, and intracranial hematoma was, if I remember rightly, what Graf died of in the Haus im Wald. I looked it up, and it seemed to fit my symptoms—it can take anything from hours to days for it to lead to death. So while we are standing here talking, the blood may be seeping into the brain."

Interesting, thought Eleanor, distracted for a moment from Franz's plight by the question of how many hours Graf might have lain there in his apartment with the blood slowly seeping into his brain. But she followed Franz into the study where he had his clothes and helped to find the things he wanted. Amazing that he just sat there and let her put his socks on for him. God, she thought, I hope this isn't the shape of things to come. But I'd better take this seriously. Maybe he really does have a cranial hematoma. She realized that she didn't believe it for a minute. "Did you say Hofer told you to go to the emergency room?"

"Yes, well, of course, he didn't know anything about this hematoma, but he meant if things didn't improve."

Eleanor made a quick exit and left Franz trying to knot his tie. Hematoma here or there, he was not proposing to go out without a tie. She closed the door of the living room and tried quickly to call Dr. Hofer. She only got his answering machine. In a low voice, she said that she was taking her husband to the emergency room of the AKH, apparently on his advice, and would use his name as a referring doctor; she hoped he didn't mind. Then she hung up. She had thought of asking him to come to the hospital, but hadn't quite dared.

"We'd better go right away," she said to Franz, "if it's an emergency."

"If? Do you have any doubt?"

She helped him on with his coat, and he said, "Were you talking to someone on the phone?" The hematoma sure didn't affect his hearing.

"Just leaving a message for Christa," she said. "Nothing important." Quick with the lie, wasn't she, these days? Still, it wasn't worth bothering Franz with the thought of Dr. Hofer at this point. Just get him to the hospital. She was happy right now to keep the thought of Dr. Hofer all to herself.

3

Sitting on the tram around the Ring with his briefcase on his knees, Büchner was tempted to take out the will and have another look at it. But the tram was crowded, and his briefcase stuffed so full that he risked dropping something on the floor of the tram, wet as it was from the dirty melting snow on people's boots. This wouldn't do the will any good, nor his boxer shorts either, if it came to that. The letter to the son, he realized, was what was burning a hole in his pocket. He ought to be focusing on the bequests, but in a peculiar way, that letter seemed to hold a key to Graf's character, though one he hadn't really got hold of yet. Or did the idea of a father's voice speaking from beyond the grave capture his imagination for other reasons? He hadn't thought so intensely of his own father for years, the father whose middle name he bore, who had never made a will, still less written a statement for his son to read after his death. Georg's mother had inherited enough to live on, but had left no fortune to her policeman son when she died some years ago. She had had little understanding for the career he had chosen for himself. Sometimes, he thought, as he changed trams at the Schottentor and rode the one stop back to his car in the Bergstrasse, he had no understanding for it himself. It is what it is, he thought, looking longingly at the door to his apartment building. He'd have liked nothing better at this moment than to go up there to his comfortable, shabby place and read at leisure the words of the dead father. But this dead father, he reminded himself, was a victim of murder, and he needed to get back to the scene of the crime.

He turned the car back up the Währingerstrasse toward Döbling. He could read the will in his little room there that evening. The cawing of the big black birds would be an appropriate accompaniment for the voice of the dead father. Once in a great while, he would think he still knew how the voice of his own father had sounded, but that was probably a fantasy. It had more likely faded completely from his memory. Even his face was hard to recall. Erich Graf was, by comparison, a lucky man. In many ways. And yet his father must have been an even more difficult father to have—not made easier by having him for so much longer. The more Büchner heard of the dead man, he realized, the less he liked him. *Rich, powerful, charming*—these words cropped up again and again, but something was missing. The only person who seemed to talk of him with genuine passion and to be suffering his death with genuine grief was Frau Hagen. Well, not quite the only one. Herr Ritter too seemed immensely sad at his passing, and the *Good-bye, old friend* of the will rang true, truer somehow than the brief lines about the other beneficiaries. One person missing from the "loyal service" list was, it now occurred to Büchner, Frau Huber. Was anyone else missing? Into his mind suddenly came the freewheeling question that Frau Dr. Lessing had posed as a way of opening up the field of inquiry: how many people called Hans Graf Papa? The immediate and obvious answer was, other than Erich Graf, no one. Surely none of the people that Graf had named in his will. Sometimes, especially in fiction, illegitimate sons popped out of the woodwork, demanding acknowledgment of their birthright, or wreaking revenge for the treatment of their mother, or some such. But this had never happened in his workaday world of crime resolution in late-twentieth-century Vienna. Illegitimate sons—or daughters—were not that much of a dark secret anymore. He ran his mind over the men who had cropped up so far in this case and could not imagine any of them in this role. Michael was, he supposed, a son figure, by virtue of his being young; but if he were really Graf's illegitimate son and knew it, would Graf have the nerve to leave him only a pair of gold cuff links, in view of the considerable fortune to go to his "real" son, Erich, bearer of the middle name?

Dealing with the heavy traffic on the expressway, he let the whole case slip out of his head for a few minutes. But once through Feldberg and into the woods, it came crowding back, and he began to hope against hope for some new ideas from the fingerprinting. He parked the car, looked at his watch; it was after three. Scarcely had he arrived and taken off his coat when Schmidt was knocking at his door. Büchner sat down, motioning him to sit down, and said, "Let's have it then, Herr Schmidt. What do the prints tell us?"

Schmidt grinned, clearly enjoying this role of the great revealer. "Well, sir, they have all shown up for fingerprinting—that is, all the residents of Melanchthon and all the staff, with two exceptions." He paused.

"Cut the suspense, Schmidt. Who are they?"

"One is Herr Zimmermann, sir. His wife said, when she came to be fingerprinted, he objected on principle. He wasn't a criminal and didn't choose to be treated like one."

"Only one of those, that's not bad. Who was the other?"

"One of the sisters, sir. Not the tall one, the other, Sister Barbara."

"I see." Büchner was surprised at this. Zimmermann was an eccentric man, markedly irascible, and altogether of a generation liable to stand on its dignity, but Barbara? "Any reason given?"

"No, sir, she just didn't turn up."

"And how do the prints in Graf's room match up? The routine set from right after the murder, and the second set, after we discovered the door had been opened."

"Nothing really new in the second set, as far as we could see, except that the door handle itself seemed to have been wiped clean. Both sets, of course, have Graf's own prints all over the place, all obvious places—point of entry, doors to other rooms, telephone, computer, and so on. The only other recognizable prints anywhere but the living room are those of Frau Hagen. But then in the living room, there are various identifiable prints in the first set, point of entry, polished chair arms, etc., namely," he read off a list, "Sister Agatha, Frau Hagen, Dr. Hofer, Frau Huber, Herr Neumann, Herr Ritter—alphabetical order, sir."

"Quite the center of traffic in the Haus im Wald, Herr Graf's room."

"Yes, sir, I would say so, sir. And there are a couple of sets of unidentifiable prints at the point of entry."

"I take it you mean the apartment door," said Büchner, who was beginning as usual to find the police jargon slightly absurd. "What about the master key? Any prints?"

"Absolutely none. Wiped clean. You'll want that back, sir." He handed it to him.

"Thanks. Anything else, other than fingerprints?"

"We did search the woods near the house and came across one regulation cane lying under the recent snow near the path in the undergrowth. It might, of course, simply have been lost, though a person who has difficulty walking and needs a cane is hardly likely to lose it on a walk in the woods."

"Any identifiable traces?"

"This sort of cane is a regulation cane, issued to anyone who needs one in the Haus im Wald, and there are no fingerprints on it, no hair, blood, or anything else. Of course, a normal person wears gloves in this cold weather in any case, and it's been washed plenty by the falling snow."

"Well done, Schmidt. Efficient job on the fingerprinting."

An efficient job, he thought as Schmidt left, but it doesn't get us much farther forward. A whole lot of people seemed to have been in Graf's apartment in the days before the murder, but not necessarily on the day of the murder itself. Certainly Sister Agatha, Michael, and Frau Huber had not mentioned being in the apartment—though, come to think of it, Sister Agatha was there right after the body was found. She had explicitly denied being there on Christmas Day. And as usual, the absence of fingerprints meant little, chances are that anyone deliberately up to no good would have carefully avoided leaving fingerprints, as in the case of the key. Interesting though that Barbara had failed to present herself for fingerprinting. He really needed to speak to the sisters again. He dialed the number of their apartment, but no one answered. Probably doing their Christian duty in Martin Luther. I'll take a walk upstairs, he thought, drop by my room and have a look around.

Büchner went up the stairs and into his small guest room. The bed had been neatly made. Who does that? he wondered. And the radiator was still on, lower than he had left it, however. He put his shirt and underwear in a drawer and put the copy of the will underneath them. As if that would deter a real thief. This place had an infantilizing effect: he felt like a naughty boy hiding a girlie magazine from his mother. He went out, locking the door behind him. For what purpose? People wandered in and out of his room with ease, it seemed.

And now, the sisters. Where might they be? He walked along the corridor, looked into the community room, no one there, on up to the next floor. Everything was very quiet. Afternoon nap time, he supposed. Then he saw the door of Frau Winkler's room opening, and coming backward out of it, with a very red and frightened face, was Frau Beck. She seemed to be trying to pull something over the threshold, but her exertions were getting her nowhere. He heard her say in an agitated whisper, "I can't! I can't!"

"Can I help you, Frau Beck?" He stepped forward and saw what she was pulling vainly on: a wheelchair in which sat a little old man in a hospital gown, a bruise under his right eye and Band-Aids all over his face. It took Büchner awhile to realize that it was Pastor Pokorny. "Good Lord," he said.

"Oh, Herr Inspektor," said Christa, panting and frightened, but more resolute than he had seen her before, "Yes. Yes, please. You can help me."

4

"Better close your eyes in the car," said Eleanor. "You don't want to make your head worse. Put that rug around you." She reached toward the backseat to get it.

"No, no," said Franz. "If anything, I'm hot. Maybe I'm running a temperature."

"Was that one of the symptoms?" She got into the driver's seat.

"I can't remember. Look, I know you don't believe it. But I do feel pretty terrible."

"I believe that," said Eleanor. "You look pretty terrible. Close your eyes, and try to relax."

"Has it ever occurred to you that telling someone to relax usually has the opposite effect?"

"Well, yes, it has occurred to me, as a matter of fact. Do you have a better idea? I would quite like to relax myself."

"There are other ways," he said.

"You looked pretty relaxed on Frau Huber's couch. What was her secret?"

Franz blushed. "You're right," he said. "I'll just close my eyes."

Good heavens, thought Eleanor, he's actually blushing. Surely that fat lady didn't get up to anything. Or Franz himself. Well, hardly, in his condition. No wonder he's got a hematoma. She laughed to herself. Didn't believe a word of it. In any case, she'd better not pursue the point in case he really does have a hematoma. Don't want to make him any more uptight than he is. They were already driving around the Gürtel, only a short way now to the AKH. She drove in silence until they got to the emergency entrance. "You go in and announce yourself at the desk," she said. "I'll be there as soon as I've parked."

Franz didn't make a move. Oh hell, she thought, got out, walked around the car through the slush, and opened the door on his side.

"Come along," she said, giving him her arm and helping him out. The shape of things to come, indeed. "You can manage, can't you?" she said. "Just go in through that door. The desk is on the left, remember?"

"How should I remember? The last time I was carried in and had my eyes shut."

"Yes, well, this time you'd better keep them open. You'll have to walk in. I can't leave the car here." Already another car was honking at her. She waved her hand in a stately manner to the driver and walked with Franz to the door. He leaned heavily on her. "Look, there's a bench. Just sit there, and I'll be back." Another handwave to the irate driver behind her, and she got the car out of the way. She had to park downstairs in the parking garage. By the time she got back to the emergency room entrance, Franz was standing at the desk.

"I've told them," he said to her, "that I was here yesterday. They're getting out the file."

"At least we won't have to give them all that personal information again."

"Very well, Herr Professor, here it is," said the young woman behind the counter. She had come back with the file, handed it to Franz, and said he should take it with him to radiology. "Oh, just a moment," she said, taking it back and looking at the personnel fact sheet. "What is the name of your doctor? Did he refer you to the emergency room?" Eleanor and Franz answered simultaneously, one saying yes, the other no.

"Yes, he did," said Eleanor. "His name is Hofer. It isn't in the first file, we have consulted him since."

"And he sent you here?"

"No," said Franz.

"Franz, Dr. Hofer told you to come here if you had any more trouble."

"Does he know that you are here now?" asked the young woman.

"Yes. I left a message on his answering machine." The young woman filled in the last offending space on the form and handed it to them. "You have to go all the way to the back of the hospital, down that corridor, then down in the elevator one floor. Give this form to the admitting doctor. Auf Wiedersehen."

"And just when did you leave a message on Hofer's answering machine?"

"Just before we left the apartment, actually."

"So that's what you were doing. Leaving a message for Christa, my foot. Why didn't you tell me the truth?"

"I didn't want a whole scene about Hofer at that point. And I thought it would be useful at the hospital to have a referring doctor's name," she said. And I secretly hoped, she thought, that he might show up and give us a hand. "I don't see," she said, quickly moving from the defensive to the aggressive mode, "that you are suffering much in the way of memory loss. Why would you remember something as trivial as a phone call to Christa?"

"When you go into a room, close the door, and start muttering on the phone, I know perfectly well that you're hiding something, and, trivial or not, I don't like it."

"What's that got to do with memory loss?"

"Let's quit the amateur diagnosing and see what the experts have to say."

"Good idea." They walked in silence through the long corridors. There'd been no offer of a wheelchair this time at the emergency desk, and now that Franz was annoyed about something, he seemed to have forgotten his difficulty in walking. He certainly wasn't hanging on her arm anymore, but was striding resolutely along, putting his feet down with his customary determined thump-thump. Their downstairs neighbors in Manhattan always complained about heavy footfalls in their apartment, and they certainly weren't hers. They got into the visitors' elevator—a man was being pushed out of the service elevator on a stretcher, his skull bandaged, looking as if he'd come out of surgery.

"Hematomas," said Franz, "usually require surgery to remove the blood."

"You see?" said Eleanor. "You remember every word of that damned Internet thing. Where's the memory loss?"

"I had a lot of trouble earlier today remembering things."

"Earlier!" said Eleanor triumphantly. "You see? Didn't you say 'progressive'—'progressive decline' in something or other? You seem to be progressing upward, not declining."

"This is a stupid argument," said Franz. "You are pushing me to the point where I almost want a hematoma, just to prove I'm right."

"Yes, of course, I'm sorry. It's stupid." She was reaching the point herself where she wanted him not to have a hematoma, not to save him from surgery or death, but just to prove that *she* was right. That was marriage for you. Well, hers anyway. They had reached the office, and Franz said firmly, "You stay here. I'd rather go in alone."

"Fine. You'll have to do all the talking at this stage in any case. I don't have the vocabulary for this sort of thing in German." She went into the small waiting room where there were two comfortable-looking armchairs. She sat down and closed her eyes.

"Frau Fabian?" said a quiet voice above her.

"Dr. Hofer!" She pushed herself up from the low chair, somewhat mortified that this was not so easy. She almost bumped into him with her head as she stumbled slightly on gaining a standing position.

"Don't get up," said Hofer belatedly, sitting down himself on the other easy chair and stretching out his elegantly clad legs in a relaxed way. Lovely shoes, she thought.

"How nice of you to come," she said, sitting down again and hearing in the back of her mind Franz saying, Where do you think you are—a garden party?

"I got your message and thought I had better check up on the situation. You know, the elder Frau Fabian was a patient of mine for many years, and her death was a shock to me. It must have been a great shock for the professor. What seems to be the matter at the moment?"

"Well, you see, of course he's been feeling unwell. You saw him yourself last night. But then, for some reason—I probably shouldn't tell you this, I know doctors don't like it—he looked up intracranial hematoma on the Internet and convinced himself he had one."

"However did he come upon that?" asked Hofer, quizzical amusement on his face.

"It was something to do with that detective out at the Haus im Wald. Apparently, he told Franz that this was the cause of death in the case of Herr Graf, and because Franz had also had a blow on the head, and"—she laughed deprecatingly—"because he began classifying himself as elderly, he got fixated on the idea that he had one too."

Dr. Hofer did not laugh with her. The look of amusement on his face tightened into something more like wariness. "This is what they say caused Graf's death?"

"I believe so. That's how I understood it anyway. Don't take my word for it. Anyway, that's what happened. He thought he had all the symptoms—headache, nausea, vomiting, progressive lack of consciousness, memory loss—"

"Lack of consciousness?" said Hofer skeptically. "He seemed quite conscious when I saw him earlier in Frau Huber's apartment. That's also what I gathered from her."

"Oh, really? What did she say?"

"Nothing much. She seemed to find him quite delightful."

"Delightful?" Eleanor stared at him blankly, but recovered herself. "Well, that's nice. But anyway, no, I don't think he was losing consciousness, though he worked himself into such a state at the computer that he apparently did faint or something." She decided to spare him the details of the "or something." After all, he wasn't really Franz's doctor. Let Franz tell all to the examining physician if he saw fit.

The door of the office opened, and Franz appeared, this time in a wheelchair. They could see him from the waiting room, and both got to their feet, Hofer, she noted, with grace and agility. She did better this time herself, being prepared for difficulties. She was not quite prepared, however, to see Franz in a wheelchair, nor for the look of combined relief and triumph on his face.

"Ah, Dr. Hofer," he said magnanimously. "I didn't expect to see you here. Though we gave your name at the admitting desk. I hope that is no problem." Why the cordiality? wondered Eleanor.

"Not at all," said Hofer.

"The doctors have decided," said Franz rather grandly, "to keep me here overnight under observation. They saw no point in doing another MRI, but, given my age and the severity of the symptoms since the accident, they want to be on the safe side. But I don't want to hold up this gentleman." He waved a hand at the orderly. "He's taking me up to a bed. You may come with me if you like. But, Dr. Hofer, do not waste any more of your . . . valuable . . . time."

"I'll just see you settled in," said Hofer. "Where are you taking him?"

"Room 802, sir. Eighth floor." The orderly wheeled Franz into the service elevator and turned the wheelchair around. As the doors closed, Franz waved airily at the two of them.

"Well, that's a surprise," said Eleanor.

"Not really. The AKH knows all about Americans and their propensity for litigation. They don't want some uninsured American tourist dying after being denied treatment by them."

"You don't actually think that Franz will die, do you?" They were waiting for the visitors' elevator.

"No, frankly, I don't. But of course, it is true that a minor head injury can cause an intracranial hematoma—not likely, since they apparently saw no signs of hemorrhaging in the head yesterday. They are just being extra careful. I mean, I imagine he has high blood pressure in any case—he certainly looks like it—and he has been very tense in recent days, not surprisingly, of course, and at his age, the heart can do odd things too, you know."

"Yes," she said, looking sideways at him in the elevator. How old was he? He looked very fit. His whole body seemed positively to exude relaxation—maybe all that Eastern medicine. "Do you go in for meditation?" she asked.

"Well, yes, as a matter of fact. Why do you ask?"

"I don't know. You seem so relaxed."

He smiled and held back the door on the eighth floor with one hand while shepherding her out of the door with the other. "You should try it," he said, and his smile had this time that element of mockery that she thought she had seen through the window of the café that morning when he raised his hat to her and Christa. Did he realize then that they'd been observing his tête-à-tête with Frau Hagen? She wished she had a way of bringing that into the conversation; she was so curious about what he had been doing there, drinking champagne or some such with that lovely lady.

They had reached room 802, and Eleanor looked in to see Franz being helped into hospital garb in a small but pleasant single room.

"He'll be all right now," she said to Hofer.

"Yes. I'll take my leave then. I'll call the hospital later to check on his condition. I somehow doubt," he smiled, "that there will be a problem. But you never know."

"Do you think," asked Eleanor impulsively, "that Frau Hagen is really upset at the death of Herr Graf?"

Hofer looked sharply at her, his implacable composure for once seemingly disturbed. "You ask strange questions, Frau Fabian. What makes you ask me this?"

"Oh, I don't know. I thought, since you know her, well, you know, I've been concerned about her—I was there when she heard the news, you know." Totally flustered, she gave up. "I'm sorry," she said. "Just burbling on. Thank you for all your help. It was so kind of you to come."

"Not at all," said Hofer, "*Küss die Hand*," and he planted a polite kiss in the air somewhere slightly above the fingertips of her right hand, which he took lightly and held for half a second. He walked away. The end of the garden party, she groaned inwardly, noticing, as she put her right hand on the door handle, that her fingernails were dirty. The last straw, she thought.

5

"I can't get the chair," said Christa, continuing to tug on it, "over this ledge thing, whatever it is."

"Hold on," said Büchner. "It's only a little ridge in the floor. Let me do it."

She relinquished her hold on the chair, which began to roll backward into the room. "Easy does it," said Büchner. "I've got it. But what's going on?"

"No time to explain," said Christa breathlessly. "I'm taking him home, that's all."

"Home?"

"Yes, to his apartment. I can't talk about it now. It's almost three thirty, and everybody will have finished having their naps, and Sister Agatha may be up here any minute. We have to get him out of here before she comes."

We? thought Büchner with some trepidation. He couldn't see Pastor Pokorny's face from where he was. "Is this what he wants?"

The voice of the pastor boomed out, "It's what I want!"

Christa was hurrying ahead to press the button for the elevator, and Büchner, beginning to get the hang of how the wheelchair worked, threw caution to the winds and speeded up his pace to a trot. "Keep your feet on the footrest, Pastor, and hold on tight. Here we go."

Pastor Pokorny roared with laughter as Büchner, scarcely missing a beat, rolled him onto the elevator.

"Thank God, nobody in it," said Christa.

"Thank God, indeed," said the pastor.

"And nobody getting on here either," said Christa as they passed the first floor. "We're in luck."

"Now what is all this about?" said Büchner, but the elevator was already at the ground floor.

"No time to talk now, "said Christa. "This will be the hard part. We have to get past the café, past Gruber's desk, and into the other elevator. They'll be able to see us from the café. And we can't dawdle about here outside Huber's apartment. She's another person we don't want to see."

"OK," said Büchner. "Let's make a dash for it. Why are we avoiding all these people?"

"No time to explain. Oh Lord!" Standing at Gruber's desk chatting were Herr Ritter and Michael. Seeing Pastor Pokorny, Herr Ritter stepped forward, quite delighted. "Why, there you are, Herr Pastor, so glad you are out and about. But you have been in the wars, I see."

"Michael," said Christa urgently. "We have to get him upstairs without Sister Agatha seeing him."

"Oh, excellent," said Michael. "Open rebellion!"

"The men's room. Fast," said Gruber.

"What?" said Büchner.

"Sister Agatha is in the shop. Out any minute."

As one man, Büchner, Herr Ritter, and Michael flanked the wheelchair and charged together into the men's room. "Well, she won't come in here," said Michael, and they all laughed.

Büchner opened the door a crack. "She's coming out of the shop," he said. "We can't all stay in here. I have my reputation as a police officer to think of." The burst of hilarity that greeted this remark must have reached her ears. Büchner could see her speaking to Christa and looking around with some perturbation. She said something to Gruber, who came out from behind his desk and walked with his usual stiff dignity toward the men's room.

"I have been sent to investigate," he announced and was greeted with more laughter.

"Look," said Michael. "We need to do something, or else she'll catch us all. Come on, Herr Ritter, we can be the sacrificial lambs. Distract her attention. You'd better be ready, Herr Inspektor, to make a dash for it."

Herr Gruber accompanied them to the desk. "Only these two gentlemen, Sister," he said, "having a little joke."

"Thank you, Herr Gruber," said Sister Agatha in her most piercing and peremptory voice, which could be heard in the men's room. "Aren't you supposed to be in the café at this time, Michael?"

"Yes, Sister," he said loudly, for the benefit of the listeners. "But occasionally, one does have to go to the men's room." A high-pitched giggle escaped Herr Ritter. Büchner pushed the door slightly more open, but closed it again quickly on a warning signal from Gruber.

"I do apologize," said Pastor Pokorny, "for dragging you into this."

"Well, at the moment, I am the one who appears to be dragging you. Are you sure you want to be doing this? What is going on?"

"I want to go home."

"Yes, but what were you doing over there in the first place, and what happened to your face?"

A frantic knocking at the door interrupted this exchange. Büchner opened it to Christa. "Hurry, Herr Inspektor, the coast is clear. She's gone." Gruber was standing at the elevator and had already pressed the button. Büchner got in and pulled in the wheelchair backward.

"Oh, Lord, let the door close," prayed Christa aloud. Just as the warning-for-the-blind signal to close sounded, the three faces looking out froze as they saw Frau Huber heaving into view around the corner of the café.

"Head her off at the pass, Gruber," said Büchner.

"Yes, sir," said Gruber as the door closed.

"So far, so good," said Christa. "If we can just get him into his room."

"You have your key, Herr Pokorny?" said Büchner.

"I never lock my door. I have nothing to hide, or to fear."

When they got off at the third floor, Sister Barbara was coming out of her apartment. "You're back, Herr Pokorny," she said. "That's good. Pressed into service, Georg? That's good too."

"Don't slow down," whispered Christa urgently. "We have to get him inside."

"I was hoping to have a word with you," said Büchner over his shoulder. That was, he thought, the whole point of his having gone over to Martin Luther. He really wasn't keeping his eye on the ball.

"I'm going down to the café, you can find me there if you like," she said and walked on.

"Well, she doesn't seem to mind any of this," Büchner said to Christa.

"She's not the problem. Come on, they'll be up here soon enough now that Frau Huber has seen us." She tried to open the door of Pastor Pokorny's apartment. It was locked. "Who did that?" she said. "What do we do now?"

"A good thing you have me on this expedition," said Büchner, taking out the master key he had just got back. He opened the door, rolled in the wheelchair, and Christa collapsed on the armchair in the sitting room.

"Well, what now?" said Büchner. "Perhaps you would explain this whole thing to me."

"I'm afraid," said the pastor, "that I have an urgent need to go to the bathroom."

"Ah, yes," said Büchner. "Can you walk?"

"Not easily," said the pastor, adding hastily, "not yet. Perhaps you could push me there for now, Herr Inspektor."

When they got to the bathroom, the wheelchair would not go through the door. Büchner helped the pastor to stand and supported him in the few steps to the toilet. "I'll have to sit down," said the pastor.

"Oh, quite," said Büchner. The process of turning him around was not easy. When he was sitting down, Büchner went out, leaving the door slightly ajar.

"So what now?" he said. "What *is* all this?"

Christa's former intense resolve seemed to have faded now that the immediate goal was reached. The apologetic note returned to her voice as she said, "Well, you see, Herr Büchner, he fell and hurt his face and, most of all, I think, his knees, and Sister Agatha insisted he be taken to Martin Luther and not back up here to his own place. And they gave him a sleeping pill and put him to bed, and when I went over to see him, he was so unhappy to wake up and find himself there, and he kept saying, 'It's all over. I'll never get out of here.' And I said, 'Nonsense, come on, let's go.'

And he suddenly got his old spark back, and I got him out of the bed and into the wheelchair, and that's where you came in."

"That was very daring of you," said Büchner. "But what's going to happen now? Who's going to get him in and out of the bathroom, for a start?"

"Yes, well, I hadn't thought of that. But I've seen it before, you see. People get taken to Martin Luther and don't ever come back. And in that room of Frau Winkler, where she died . . ." Her voice trailed away, and he could see she was beginning to lose her nerve, but a quavering voice from the bathroom called him, and he went in and helped the pastor up off the toilet and back onto the wheelchair.

"I think I'd better lie down for a minute," said the pastor. Büchner helped him into the bedroom and onto the bed. He was still wearing his hospital gown, and Büchner could see how badly bruised and swollen his knees were. Good God, he thought. I must be mad. I should never have done this.

"Thank you, Herr Inspektor," said the pastor, and a beatific smile spread across his face. "What bliss to be in my own bed!"

Chapter 13

The chapel in the Haus im Wald was usually empty. On Sunday mornings, a minister from one of the Lutheran parishes in Vienna would come to conduct morning service at ten thirty. Frau Winkler, widow of a Lutheran pastor, had almost always hobbled over to the service on her own two feet, but the sisters made it their business to go through Martin Luther to help wheel down as many residents as could manage it. The Melanchthon residents, quite capable of attending under their own steam, were usually less in evidence, though on the day that Hans Graf's body had been found, a number of them had been there, no doubt in honor of the Christmas holiday. The younger Herr Graf had found the body shortly after the last Christmas carol had been sung—the ancient and beautiful carol of a rose that sprang from a tender root in the midst of the cold winter, halfway through the night—a song to herald birth and not death. The minister had already left by the time of the ugly discovery, and it was Pastor Pokorny who, on hearing the news later that day, had gone into the chapel to pray. A member of what in Austria is regarded more or less as an odd sect, namely the Baptists, not officially recognized as a church but as a "religious confessional community, he was one of the few residents who used the chapel for private devotions. Frau Beck, a lapsed Roman Catholic, was another. Since short memorial services for all deceased residents were held there shortly after their death, it may well have been that the chapel—light, plain, and pleasant as it was—belonged more to death than to life. The only residents who wanted to spend time there seemed to be those who really believed that death was the door to a better world. The usually empty chapel in the Haus im Wald tended to suggest that such residents were in the minority.

1

Eleanor walked into the little hospital room and at once saw Franz quickly closing his eyes. She was kicking herself for her own stupidity. What on earth had prompted her to ask Hofer that idiotic question about Frau Hagen, just because she wanted to bring her name into the conversation and see how he reacted? Some sort of crazy jealousy on her part, and after all, Frau Hagen was an old woman. But such an elegant one. She sighed, looking down at her really quite awful fingernails.

Without opening his eyes, Franz said, "Gone, has he, the Indian snake charmer of the outer suburbs?"

"Franz," she said, "you are appalling. It was very kind of him to come."

"Yes, yes," said Franz. "Very kind. Maybe he's also afraid of lawsuits."

"Be that as it may," she said. How funny it was that men always assumed that other men were afraid of lawsuits. She would never have thought of that as a motive for Dr. Hofer's showing up. On the other hand, Hofer had immediately imputed it to the AKH doctors. "How do you feel now?"

"A little better," said Franz, and he managed a long-suffering smile. The back of his bed was raised, and he was resting his head on a large pillow. The bruises on his face were turning from a reddish blue to a deeper shade of blue. His pale blue hospital gown came up to his neck.

"Quite the symphony in blue," said Eleanor. He opened his pale blue eyes and looked reproachfully at her. "Sorry," she said. "I think you do look better resting there though. Better than earlier in the apartment, I mean."

"I'm glad you think so. We can only wait now and see what happens. At least they are now . . . keeping me under observation." He seemed to relish the phrase. He closed his eyes again.

Wait and see what happens? Surely he doesn't expect me to sit here and wait indefinitely while he snoozes on his pillow. His hands were neatly folded on top of the white sheets—he looked all set to contain his soul in patience for the duration. She had never really liked the look of his hands—short with rather stubby fingers and hair growing on the back of them—very different from Dr. Hofer's slender, smooth hands, his long well-manicured fingers. Well-manicured—she sighed again.

"Are you suffering?" said Franz without opening his eyes. "You seem to be sighing a lot."

"Am I? Well, there's a lot to worry about at the moment. We really do have to deal with the question of your mother's funeral, for example. Do you think we should have a small service in the chapel at the Haus im Wald? That seems to be the done thing."

A pained expression appeared on Franz's face. "Not now. I cannot deal with that at the moment. Couldn't you talk to Ingrid about it?"

"Yes, OK, perhaps I should get going and do that right now. You seem to be well taken care of here, and you probably need to sleep.

He opened his eyes and looked skeptically at her. "All right, will you be at the apartment later?"

"It's already half past four," she said, looking at her watch. "Yes, I'll go back there now, but I did tell Christa I would stay the night, remember?"

"Oh God," he said. "Isn't that overdoing it?"

"No, I don't think so. Some very weird things are happening there, and she's nervous. And now you're here. I'll come in and check on you in any case later."

"All right. Whatever you say. I think I need to rest now." The blue eyes closed again, and Eleanor took this as a sign of dismissal. She went over and kissed him on the forehead. He didn't say any more as she left the room.

She made her way down to the parking garage. Now she had committed herself to coming in the evening. Well, she certainly wouldn't go back to the apartment now. The only reason would have been to get sheets and stuff for the night. But surely

Christa would have something. She really should have stayed in the hospital longer when she was there, but her patience had quickly run out. Only her guilty conscience had made her suggest visiting again this evening. Why guilty? She was going to the Haus im Wald for the best of motives, after all: to give Christa some support. Was that true? Yes, it was, but she also wanted to go back there for her own reasons. Traffic was heavy on the Gürtel, and she had to concentrate. It took longer than usual to get to the Heiligenstädter Straße, and she began to look forward to the Haus im Wald. She was immensely curious about what was going on out there and couldn't wait to get back into Marple mode. Not that she had done very well as a sleuth in her recent encounter with Dr. Hofer. She cringed again at the thought of that silly question about Frau Hagen. He had looked quite taken aback, and she had made a fool of herself. Her earlier almost romantic feeling that she hoped to run into him again seemed to have disappeared. He was the last person she hoped to see at the moment. He must think she was a complete idiot, stumbling about getting out of chairs, displaying grime in her fingernails, and asking silly questions. His tête-à-tête with Frau Hagen did continue to fascinate her, however. So unlikely, somehow, right after the death of Herr Graf. Why couldn't she just have asked Dr. Hofer a direct question? I say, Doctor, what in the world were you doing there with Frau Hagen, of all people? No, impossible; she could never have said that. And in any case, why was she worrying about it? Did she really think that Dr. Hofer and Frau Hagen had anything to do with the crime? Her suspect was the man-hating Sister Agatha, she remembered. And Frau Hagen had loved this man. Think of her look of complete shock and disbelief when she first heard the news of his death, back in the café. That seemed like ages ago though it was only a couple of days. Two days ago about now, actually. She looked at her watch as she finally drove onto the expressway. She fairly whizzed along it and turned into the road through Feldberg into the woods. It wouldn't be inappropriate at this point, surely, for her to call on Frau Hagen and inquire how she was. Damn, if she'd only thought of it in the hospital, she could have bought flowers.

Pulling up yet again into a parking space—how familiar this was all getting to be—she sloshed through the dirty snow to the door. Wet feet again.

"Grüss Gott, Herr Gruber," she said, signed her name, and wrote in, *Visiting Frau Beck, apartment 35.*

"Is she expecting you, Frau Fabian?" asked Gruber.

"Oh yes."

"I see," he said, very uncertainly for Gruber. "Shall I call ahead to be sure she's there?"

"Not a bad idea. Come to think of it, the last time I saw her, she was visiting in the Martin Luther wing."

A ghost of a smile flitted across Herr Gruber's poker face. He was certainly softening toward her, she thought. He tried the number. "There's no answer," he said. "But I have an idea where she might be." He dialed another number, and this time got an answer.

"Frau Beck," he said. "Frau Fabian is here. What shall I say?" He listened to the answer and then said, "Very well," and hung up. Turning to Eleanor, he said, "You may go up, but Frau Beck is at the moment in the apartment of Pastor Pokorny."

"How very odd," said Eleanor. "But OK, what number is that?

"Number 36. Right next door to Frau Beck. I will make the correction in the register."

"Thank you, Herr Gruber. You are very kind."

"Not at all." Another half smile.

Coming toward her on the staircase was the detective, as usual in a hurry. "Frau Beck will be glad to see you," he said. "She needs reinforcements."

What is going on? wondered Eleanor, and she went on upstairs.

Christa opened door 36 immediately. Behind her stood Frau Huber, arms akimbo.

"What are you both doing here?" asked Eleanor. "Where is Pastor Pokorny?"

"In there," said Christa, "trying to rest."

"Here?" said Eleanor. "How wonderful!"

"It is not wonderful at all," said Frau Huber. "It is an outrage. I shall go and report the entire incident to Herr Direktor Schramm. Immediately." She stalked toward the door, turning only to say, "And how is your husband, Frau Fabian?"

"In the AKH," said Eleanor, "under observation. Your ministrations were perhaps too much for him." She did not know what had prompted her to say this, but a sort of apoplectic rage rippled up through Frau Huber's bosom into her face, which became a dull red. She went out and slammed the door behind her.

"Oh, Eleanor," said Christa. "That does it."

2

Büchner passed Gruber's desk and saluted him in comradely fashion. He had to forget the pastor and find the sisters, then drop in on the director as he had promised. Schramm would only be there till six. When he reached the door of the café, he saw Schramm standing at the table where the sisters were drinking their afternoon coffee. Sister Agatha was on her feet—she was almost as tall as Schramm himself—wagging the index finger of her right hand at the director and saying in her most piercing tones, "It will not do, Herr Direktor. We cannot have residents taking things into their own hands."

Büchner contemplated retreat, but Schramm had already seen him; and for once, his face showed relief at the appearance of the detective.

"Ah, Herr Inspektor," he said. "I gather you were somehow involved in the unfortunate incident of the removal of Pastor Pokorny from his bed in Martin Luther."

"Involved?" said Büchner, playing for time.

"Quite definitely involved," said Sister Agatha. "Barbara has told us she saw you pushing the wheelchair along our corridor."

Barbara shrugged apologetically at Büchner. "Sorry, Georg," she said.

"Helping a lady in distress," said Büchner. "You know what they say, a policeman, your friend and helper." Turning boldly to Schramm, he said, "I believe we have an appointment, Herr Direktor, shall we go to your office?'

"Certainly," said Schramm with alacrity, already backing away from the table. "I will take care of the other matter, Sister Agatha. Please leave it to me. Auf Wiedersehen."

"Will you ladies be here for a while?" said Büchner. "I'd like to have a word. In twenty minutes perhaps? Oh Lord." Frau Huber had appeared in the doorway, looking around. Büchner bowed to the sisters and stepped smartly behind the counter. "Through the back door, Michael, please," he said, and the two men scuttled out the back way through the kitchen and into the lobby.

Once in the director's office, Schramm motioned Büchner in a friendly, almost-conspiratorial way to the armchair by the window and sat down himself.

"Now, what is all this, Herr Inspektor? I do not need trouble at this point, neither from Sister Agatha nor from Frau Huber."

"I think," said Büchner, "that we have bigger problems on our hands than an old man who just wants to sleep in his own bed." This was no time, he thought, to bring up the issue of the bathroom. Hardly police business. "Perhaps we can get down to business for a moment." Schramm looked almost relieved. "I would like to go back to the matter of the keys, and to another matter, which is at this point related to the key issue. You have not rediscovered your original master key, I take it."

"I have not."

"I can tell you now that when our men dusted your safe for fingerprints, they found it wiped completely clean, and only a recent print or two of yours were in evidence, no doubt from the time when you and I looked at it together, since it was dusted soon after that. So whoever took the key did it very carefully and, presumably, with aforethought."

"But how would anybody get into my office?"

"Herr Direktor, there are at least two people whom we know to have master keys: Frau Huber and Michael."

"Yes, but anyone who already has one hardly needs to steal another one."

"True, but someone might have temporarily appropriated one of their keys for the purpose of stealing the big one." Or, he thought, one of them might have wanted to direct suspicion elsewhere.

"But how would they know the combination code for the safe?"

"I don't know, but it is probably a simple enough system to crack, simple for someone who knows how, that is. Do you, in any case, keep it written down somewhere? Do you use it for other things?"

"I haven't got it written down anywhere because it's a number I can always remember, so, yes, I do use it for other things, for that reason."

"Such as?"

"Well," said Schramm with some embarrassment, "you know, suitcase locks, for example, bank automats, that sort of thing. Just a random number, 1750, not my birthday or anything, well, fifty is the year I was born."

"You'd better change it now," said Büchner. "In case I run off with all your money. Could anyone else know about it?"

"No, not really. Well, I suppose if anyone examined my briefcase when it wasn't locked—it has a small combination lock." He got it from behind his desk. Büchner looked at the little numbers, 1750, easy enough to read if you had good eyesight, or good glasses.

"So much for security in the Haus im Wald."

"But it never occurred to me . . ." Schramm looked genuinely dumbfounded.

"No, well, unfortunately, it often doesn't. But in any case, somebody has that key. And somebody," he said, "used a key to get into the locked room of the Graf apartment between the time when I personally locked it yesterday and the time when I went into it with the younger Herr Graf this morning."

"How do you know?"

"Because of this," he said, holding up the yellow sticker in a plastic bag. He handed it to Schramm and watched him carefully while he read it:

HERE LAY THE BODY OF AN AGING LECHER
DID HE LAY THE LADY? YOU BET YOU BETCHA

He gave it back to Büchner and shook his head. "Where did you find it?" he asked, visibly shaken but not exactly astonished.

"In the chalk silhouette on the carpet, approximately where the head had rested."

"Sickening," said Schramm. "Quite sickening."

"Yes. Did you know, Herr Direktor, that someone had been leaving yellow stickers about with unpleasant messages?"

"Gruber came to me with one that he had found on the notice board concerning him and"—Schramm gave a slight laugh—"and Frau Huber. It had a bit of a rhyme too—Gruber, Huber, you know. Struck me as a joke of some kind—not a nice one, of course. Gruber was quite upset and considered it his duty to bring it to me. No one else has come forward with any such thing, and I decided to ignore it. Have you come across others?"

"I have. They will go to our handwriting people. There's no way of telling superficially if they're all written by the same person—deliberately childlike printing. Do you have any idea who might be doing this?"

"No. If these two are anything to go by, the writer seems to be obsessed with sex. Leaving such a thing quasi on the corpse of poor Graf certainly seems beyond a joke." Schramm seemed on the verge of saying something else but did not.

"Are you sure you have not seen any others?"

"Well, as a matter of fact"—Schramm squirmed uncomfortably in his armchair—"I suppose I have to admit that I got one myself. Before the death of Graf, a few days before Christmas, that is. And not long after Gruber got his."

"And why didn't you mention this to me before?"

"I didn't think it had anything to do with the murder inquiry."

"Herr Direktor, virtually anything that goes on in the Haus im Wald at the moment is of interest to me."

"Well, to tell the truth, I was embarrassed by it. A piece of absolute nonsense, of course, but not something one wants to pass around, nevertheless."

"Did you keep it?"

"Yes, as a matter of fact, I did. I put it in a folder with the Gruber one."

"May I see this folder?"

"I suppose so, well, yes, of course. I had hoped to be able to ignore it. He got up and took a folder from the back of the middle drawer of his filing cabinet, a drawer marked Accounts Receivable and Accounts Payable.

"Thank you," said Büchner as Schramm handed him the folder. "Are you regarding it as receivable or payable?"

Schramm was not amused. "I wanted to put it in a safe and private place, just in case. I knew that if any more turned up, I would have to take action in some way."

Büchner opened the folder. The two yellow stickers were on one page. The second one read:

ARE YOU A FAG HERR DIREKTOR SCHRAMM

YES DEAR BOY I AM I AM

"Oh dear," said Büchner. "I see why you wouldn't want to show this to anybody."

"As I say, Inspektor, it's the most awful nonsense," said Schramm, looking intensely embarrassed. "But I wouldn't want it to be passed around. I mean, I have a wife and daughters. I am a religious man. The Haus im Wald is a religious foundation. I hope I can rely on your discretion."

"You may rest assured," said Büchner, "that I will not hand it over to a reporter from the *Kronen Zeitung*."

"God forbid," said Schramm.

"As you say," said Büchner. "But talking of religion and reverting to the domestic crisis on your hands, Herr Direktor, how does it happen that a Baptist minister is so happily ensconced in this particular religious foundation?"

"Pastor Pokorny," said Schramm, "has a complicated, let us say, peculiarly Austrian history."

"Yes, I've heard some of it from him. But I gather that some people, not least the indefatigable Sister Agatha, do not think that he belongs here."

"Sister Agatha," said Schramm haughtily, "is not an official spokesperson of the Lutheran church. There are those of us who believe that restitution for wrongs suffered under the Nazis is a Christian duty. Pastor Pokorny certainly suffered in his youth, and when he came back to Vienna as quite an old man, he lived in a small apartment in Grinzing for a few years on an Austrian pension. He attended a Lutheran church in Heiligenstadt—there are a few Baptists in Vienna, but not out in this neck of the woods. The Lutheran church has its own past to live down, you know, Herr Inspektor, and when Pastor Pokorny began to find it difficult to manage alone, the church offered to subsidize his residence here. I like to think that he has been quite happy with us. Not everyone, as it were, approves of him, but he has my full support." Good for you, thought Büchner. "He also has considerable personal resilience."

"I can imagine," said Büchner. "After a life like that."

"Well," said Schramm with a wry smile, "we'll have to see how he does when the combined forces of Sister Agatha and Frau Huber are arraigned against him, as I take it they are."

There was a stentorian knock at the door. "That sounds like Frau Huber," said Schramm, standing up and straightening up to his full height. "I shall be here in the office probably for an hour or two longer in case you need me again this evening."

"Thank you for all the information. I fear you will now have to decide whose side you are on, Herr Direktor."

"An easier proposition in theory than in fact," said Schramm glumly. He took a deep breath and opened the door to a red-faced Frau Huber and, right behind her, a poker-faced Sister Agatha.

"Good evening, ladies," said Büchner, and made his escape rapidly along the corridor to the café.

3

The two women collapsed in laughter on the couch. "I don't know what made me say that to Frau Huber," said Eleanor. "I find her just so pompous and awful. But what *is* going on? How come Pastor Pokorny is here?"

"I brought him here," said Christa with a mixture of pride and embarrassment on her face. "It was really a mad impulse to get him out of that room in Martin Luther. I couldn't bear to think of him incarcerated over there, and he was so upset about it himself. I just got him into the wheelchair and made a dash for it."

"Wow, Christa! Well done!" said Eleanor.

"I might not have got him over the threshold of the bedroom if the inspector hadn't come along and given me a hand."

"Wow," said Eleanor again. "Did he really?"

"Yes, it was quite an adventure, I can tell you. But the question is, what do we do now? The inspector had to get him onto the toilet awhile ago. I'd never thought of anything like that."

"Lord, you mean he can't walk?"

"Well, he has trouble walking at the moment. That's no doubt why Sister Agatha had him in Martin Luther. There's no actual care provided over here, you see. You're supposed to be able-bodied. If we're not careful, they'll cart him back."

"What was the dreadful Huber doing here?"

"She saw us in the elevator and came to investigate. The inspector was here too when she arrived, but he quickly skipped off and left her to me."

"What did you say?"

"I said that the pastor was a grown man and a paying resident and had a right to be where he wanted to be."

"Well done! But what then?"

"She said, 'Who's going to look after him over here?' And I said—I was so carried away with it all—I said, 'I am.' She was just expressing some choice opinions on my inability to do that when you arrived and gave her the coup de grâce with your remark about her 'ministrations.'"

Again the two of them collapsed in laughter. "But look here, Christa, it's actually not funny. I mean, how can you possibly look after him?"

"No, well, I'll have to think of something," said Christa vaguely. "It's not so simple though. I can't see taking him to the toilet."

"No, well, that's what looking after somebody that age is all about," said Eleanor. "So who's going to do it? And what about food? And getting into the bath?"

"Maybe he'll get his strength back now that he's here."

"Let's hope so. But look, can we, for example, now go off and leave him here by himself?"

"Well, no, I suppose not, at the moment. I know who might help us—Michael. He entered into the whole escape thing when they hid in the men's room and Agatha almost caught them."

"The men's room?"

"A long story. Anyway, Michael can't stand Sister Agatha."

"Why don't you go down and have a word with him then? See if he can at least snaffle a bit of supper out of the kitchen for the pastor and bring it up here. He can also help him with the bathroom, maybe."

"I'd better run then, or he'll have closed up the café and left for the day."

After she'd gone, Eleanor looked in on the pastor again. He seemed to be sleeping soundly. Perhaps she could pop out for a minute. If Christa could get up the courage to spirit the pastor away from Martin Luther, surely she could get up the courage herself to go up one flight and knock on Frau Hagen's door and just inquire politely how she was. Ever since that first meeting, she had wanted to see her again. Why? She wasn't quite sure. She just seemed to be a fascinating sort of woman. Old, yes, but with those wonderful expressive eyes and a way of moving, of wearing clothes, so that even in her seventies—she *must* be seventy—heads would surely turn as she walked by and people would think, haven't they seen her before? In a movie? On TV? That's what it was. She looked like a film star—and so slim still, none of that awful elderly thickening of the waist and protruding of the belly. So did she just want to see Frau Hagen because she was starstruck? Maybe there was a bit of that, and then she really was supercurious about what she'd been doing in that café with Hofer. This was, after all, something that she knew and, presumably, the inspector didn't. It might have some connection with the strange goings-on at the Haus im Wald, and those goings-on were her main excuse for spending the night here, not playing nursemaid to an elderly pastor. So what the hell; let's just knock on Frau Hagen's door.

She left the door on the latch so that she would be able to get back in again. I won't be long, she thought. And she saw nobody on her way upstairs. She stood for a moment outside Frau

Hagen's apartment, then plucked up her courage and knocked. After a few moments, the door was opened, but only a crack. Eleanor could see that the chain was on.

"Who is it?" said Frau Hagen.

"Eleanor Fabian," she said. "We met in the café two days ago. I just wanted to see how you were."

The chain came off, and Frau Hagen opened the door. "Come in," she said. "You must excuse me, I am not dressed for company."

"Oh, but you look lovely," said Eleanor involuntarily. Because she did. She was wearing a long slender black velvet robe with a straight zipper all the way up to a high neck where it was fastened with a silver-and-turquoise pin. It was, Eleanor presumed, a housecoat, not that it at all resembled what she herself wore in the house. Her face was carefully made up, and a strand of her pale blond hair fell across her forehead. She pushed it back and smiled.

"Thank you. It's kind of you to say so."

"I don't want to disturb you," said Eleanor. "It's just that I've thought of you a lot ever since our first meeting when you heard the dreadful news, and I kept wondering how you were, so I thought I would just knock and find out."

"Please come in and sit down. Can I get you anything?"

"No, no, I can't stay. It's very rude of me just to drop in." Now that she was here, she felt big and clumsy and foolish.

"Not at all. Time hangs heavily on my hands these days. I was sorry to hear that you have also suffered a loss in the meantime."

"Yes, my mother-in-law died suddenly. We were shocked, of course, and my husband seems quite to have gone to pieces in various ways, but she was ninety-four, and your own loss is a very different one. I am so sorry. When I heard about it the other day in the café, I had no idea . . ." She stopped.

"No idea . . . ?"

"Well, I mean, I didn't really have any idea of what a shock the news of his death must have been to you."

Frau Hagen smiled again. "You mean, you have since heard that we were lovers."

"Good heavens, no. I mean, no one has said that. Of course not."

"Why not, because we were so old?"

"Oh no, I didn't mean that, Frau Hagen. You are so lovely, I can well imagine . . . Well, that is to say . . . it does not seem at all surprising . . . Oh dear . . . I'm not at all sure what I mean. I just wanted to be sure you were all right, to see if I could help in any way." As if, she groaned inwardly, there could possibly be any way in which she could help this calm and collected lady.

"I am not all right," said Frau Hagen. "I cannot say that. I will never be all right again. But no one can help me, my dear."

"We have found Dr. Hofer very helpful to us in the last two days since the death of my mother-in-law. He even came to the hospital today to check on my husband, who's under observation. Do you know him? He's very well up on things like meditation, relaxation, and all that."

"And all that," said Frau Hagen, giving Eleanor a quizzical look. "I think you know, Frau Fabian, that I know Dr. Hofer, since you and your friend saw us together in the Sacher café in the Kärntnerstraße this morning, or so Dr. Hofer has told me."

"Yes, well yes, I had forgotten that for a moment," said Eleanor lamely.

"Ah. Short-term memory loss. Be careful. You will soon be one of us."

"I do feel old here, somehow," said Eleanor, now literally forgetting the café incident and feeling only the very beautiful eyes of Frau Hagen turned upon her with an expression almost of pity. "You do not seem old, Frau Hagen."

"But I am at the mercy of time, just like everybody else. '*Time is a strange thing*'. Do you remember that line? The Marschallin in the *Rosenkavalier*. I have thought about her often in the last couple of days. '*Time trickles in our faces, in that mirror there it trickles . . . Sometimes I hear it flowing, unstoppable . . . Sometimes I get up in the middle of the night and stop all the clocks, all of them . . .*'"

"Oh, but nothing can stop time," said Eleanor. "That's the trouble, nothing at all."

"Love," said Frau Hagen. "Love stops time."

"But it doesn't," said Eleanor. "That's only an illusion. Look at the Marschallin. Stopping the clocks doesn't help her in the end."

"Perhaps you do not understand her. Perhaps you have never loved enough." She stood up and walked slowly across the room to the window, throwing open the curtains with a grand gesture and looking out into the darkness.

Eleanor had the sensation of being in the theater. "How I would like to have heard you sing," she said. Frau Hagen continued to stand motionless at the window, and Eleanor thought, it's time for the audience to leave. "I must go now," she said.

Frau Hagen turned around, inclined her head, walked silently to the door, and opened it. "Thank you for coming, Frau Fabian. Take a lover, that would be my advice to you. While there is still time. Time is a strange thing, remember." She shook her by the hand and closed the door before Eleanor could think of a word to say.

4

Engulfed as he was in a wave of sympathy for Director Schramm at the sight of the two formidable ladies at his door, Büchner did not think for one second of staying for solidarity's sake. Schramm after all was the boss, and the present situation obviously called for a decision from the top. For all his appearance of authority, his way of swanning about the Haus im Wald, accepting the deferential greetings of everyone he met, Schramm—Büchner was beginning to realize—seemed to be afraid of these two ladies, or at all events, wary in their presence. That was the word, he thought; Schramm was wary, in other situations too, as if he were always slightly nervous that some axe might fall. Büchner thought back to the conversation he had had the other day with Dr. Lessing about well-integrated personalities and of how she had hesitated to apply this epithet to Director Schramm. Büchner certainly liked him better now that he had begun to exhibit his frailties, but liking people was neither here nor there in solving a crime. The most likable people could do the most dastardly things, as he had more than once discovered.

He had thought earlier of talking to the two sisters, but Agatha was now obviously otherwise engaged. In any case, it might be just as well to have a word with Barbara alone. He looked into the café, and although it was already five thirty, she was still sitting at the same table staring into space, the coffee cups already removed. Michael was nowhere to be seen. Büchner went in.

"Hallo, Georg, I thought you might come, so I waited," she said. "We have just had an earful from Frau Huber on the abduction of Pastor Pokorny." She laughed.

"It doesn't seem to bother you much," said Büchner.

"No, it doesn't bother me at all. That sort of thing doesn't. I have other things to worry about. Agatha gets frightfully upset when the residents step out of line. So does Frau Huber. But they are rarely on the same wavelength. This time poor Pastor Pokorny has managed to run afoul of the two of them equally. So now they've gone off to tackle the boss."

"I know. I was there when he opened the door and saw the two of them standing there like avenging angels. What do you think he'll do?"

"Well, if I know Schramm, he'll agree completely with both of them—that'll be easy this time because for once they are both on the same side. But he'll try to avoid actually saying that Pokorny must be taken back. He'll suggest waiting till tomorrow to see what happens—Schramm is a great one for waiting to see what happens—and he'll try to think up some diversionary tactic to get their minds onto something else. Nothing will be resolved, but he'll have time to think, for what that's worth."

"That's worth quite a lot. I need time to think myself, but so far, the goings-on in the Haus im Wald do not seem to have provided much time for meditation—a funny thing since this is supposed to be, as Director Schramm just reminded me, a religious foundation."

"Since my involvement with religious foundations, Georg, I have discovered that in the busy life of a committed do-gooder, meditation often gets pretty short shrift."

"Is that how you see yourself, a committed do-gooder?"

"Nothing new in that. Isn't that what we all thought we were, back in the days of the student movement? What's the difference?

What one needs in life is a cause to live for, it doesn't really matter what it is. Perhaps I should say *I*—not *one*. What *I* need is a cause to live for."

"Yes, but presumably if you live for a religious cause, then you believe in God. That's surely a considerable difference. The student movement as we knew it was a fairly godless business. Was it your belief in God that got you into the life of a religious do-gooder?"

Barbara laughed. "God? No, to be honest, it was my belief in Agatha."

"I see," said Büchner.

"No, you probably don't. You probably can't begin to imagine the depths to which I sank when the student movement began to peter out and the commune I was living in at the time fell apart, and I was smoking pot and other things and drinking too much. Agatha rescued me. She found me in a women's hostel and literally saved my life. She held out a hand, dramatically speaking, and pulled me out of the gutter. She does believe in God, you see, and she got me involved in the work of her sisterhood, and I stopped drinking and started to live again and do good for others, but really, for Agatha. I couldn't live without her now. And I would do anything for her."

"Is Agatha a lesbian?"

Barbara laughed again. "Good God, no—if you'll pardon the expression. It would be completely against her religion. We are"—she paused and smiled—"sisters, Georg, that's what it amounts to. Sisters in Christ, the church calls it. Agatha does good in the name of Christ, and I do good in the name of Agatha. A fair amount of good gets done in the process, isn't that what counts?"

"It seems fair enough to me," said Büchner. "Don't forget I'm only asking a policeman's questions, trying to understand the suspects in the case, not to pass moral judgments on their contributions to society."

"You do see us as suspects then?" she smiled wryly. "Well, of course, you have to."

"Yes. Until clearer lines begin to emerge in this case, you are all suspects. There are lots of unclear lines. Why, for example, Barbara, did you not get yourself fingerprinted?"

"That was silly of me," she said. "I was afraid, and like our director, I wanted time to think."

"And have you had time to think now?"

"Yes, I'll go to the police station first thing in the morning and do it."

"Wouldn't it be simpler if you told me now why you needed time to think?"

"No, Georg, I'm sorry, but it wouldn't be very simple at all. I promise you, I will answer this question in the morning. Here's Agatha now. Could we just drop the subject for the moment?"

As Sister Agatha came in from the lobby, Michael appeared from the kitchen. "Evening all," he said cheerfully. "Time to close up."

"It certainly is," said Sister Agatha, "well past time to close up. Barbara, we need to do some preparation for the service for Frau Winkler in the morning, since I hardly think that Mr. Pokorny is going to be taking it."

Barbara looked questioningly at Büchner.

"We can finish our conversation later then," he said. "Good evening, Sister Agatha. Everything sorted out with the director?"

"If you mean in regard to the business of Mr. Pokorny, the director is quite shocked at what he sees as a breach of house discipline, but he wants to think about it until tomorrow, because in the meantime he has heard that Professor Fabian is in the AKH, under observation, and he suggested to Frau Huber that they should probably visit him this evening since his accident took place on our premises. She seemed to think this was a good idea, and I agreed to make some preparations in the meantime for the service tomorrow. I think we had better get on with that now. Come along, Barbara. Auf Wiedersehen, Herr Inspektor." She turned and went toward the door.

"You see?" said Barbara. "As I thought. The successful side step is Schramm's specialty." Michael laughed. "Until the next time then, Georg," she said and followed Agatha out of the room.

"And so," said Michael, "while Schramm sidesteps, the rescue party tries to figure out how to get the pastor onto the toilet."

"Have you been up to his apartment?"

"Yes, Frau Beck pressed me into room service. I took up a tray with his supper while Sister Agatha and Frau Huber were safely out of the way in Schramm's office."

"So what happens now?"

"Well, the two ladies are trying to figure out what to do about the night. I think they would have liked me to stay and help them, but I can't do that. I have other obligations, as it happens. I've said I'll check early in the morning though and take up some breakfast."

"That's something anyway. I'll go up there myself now and talk to them. You're locking up here, I take it."

They went out to the lobby. Gruber had already left, and Michael left by the side door. Büchner walked up the two flights of stairs and knocked on the door of number 36. He heard a timid voice say, "Who's there?"

"Büchner, Kripo Wien," he replied automatically.

The door opened quickly, and Christa said, "Oh, Herr Büchner, do come in. We're just being careful. Now that it's evening and dark and so on. You never know."

"No, quite right, you never know," he said. "Guten Abend, Frau Beck, Frau Fabian. How is the patient?"

Eleanor got up off the couch. "He seems to be much better," she said. "Quite cheerful. And he's eaten all the supper that Michael brought. He's even started talking about the service for Frau Winkler tomorrow."

"And what about . . ." Büchner paused.

"The bathroom?" said Christa. "Well, Michael took care of that for now. Pastor Pokorny is still unsteady on his feet. We were just talking about tonight and what to do."

Eleanor said, "Yes, not only the pastor problem, but last night, there was all that weird business with Christa's door and the door of Graf's room and so on. That's why I'm here really, so that Christa isn't alone tonight."

"Look," said Büchner. "I would like to keep an eye myself on what goes on in this corridor tonight. If I sleep on the couch in here in the pastor's living room, I can do that and also take care of bathroom duty if necessary."

"Oh, Herr Inspektor, would you do that?" said Christa. "That would be wonderful."

"Sort of kill two birds with one stone," said Eleanor. "Oh dear, not a tactful image. But a terrific idea. Terrific."

"I'll go down right now then and see if I can grab a sandwich in the dining room, and I'll be back around eight. Best not to mention this night plan to anybody else, by the way."

"No, of course not," said Eleanor. "I'll come down with you. I have to make a quick dash to the hospital to check on my husband. I'll try to be back around nine myself. That OK, Christa?"

Christa, beaming, saw them both out. "Oh, thank you, thank you," she said. "You have no idea how grateful I am."

"And how is the investigation going, Herr Inspektor?" said Eleanor as they walked toward the staircase.

"Coming along, Frau Fabian, coming along. Any helpful hints for me?"

"Well, I did go to see Frau Hagen this evening," said Eleanor.

"Did you really? And how is the lovely lady?"

"I don't know quite what to make of her. I was with her, you know, by chance, when she first heard the news of Herr Graf's death, and she was utterly shattered—went literally white with shock. But then this morning, Christa and I saw her in the Sacher café, the new smart one, not the old musty one, and there she was, beautiful in black and drinking a glass of prosecco with Dr. Hofer. How do you figure that?"

Büchner was considerably surprised but did not show it. "Interesting," he said. "And how was she this evening?"

"She was, as it were, in deepest mourning—all in black velvet with only a silver pin at the neck—looking very beautiful."

"What sort of a pin?"

"Oh, you know, a short straight band of silver with a turquoise stone in the middle, sort of like a tiepin. She is still a beautiful woman, is she not?"

"Yes." He did not add that he had been quite bowled over by her himself.

"I can imagine her on the stage," said Eleanor. "She quoted a passage from the Marschallin in the *Rosenkavalier* to me. I never heard her sing, did you?"

"No, but I wish I had."

"So do I. But anyway, I didn't get any idea from her of why she had met Hofer in the café, though I did try actually."

"Ah, doing a bit of sleuthing yourself."

"Oh no, not really. Just female curiosity."

"Well, thanks for telling me about it anyway. All information is welcome."

"Oh, good," said Eleanor. "Lord, snowing again, I'll be off. See you later."

"Yes, see you later," said Büchner. Well, well, he thought. So the lovely Frau Hagen and the handsome Dr. Hofer met today, not only in the lawyer's office, but also in the Café Sacher. And she seems to have acquired the disappearing tiepin. And Frau Hagen pulled out the role of the Marschallin for Frau Fabian as well as for him. He wished he could remember the plot of the *Rosenkavalier* more clearly. He opened the door of the dining room and was happy to see Frau Dr. Lessing sitting alone at a table. "Guten Abend, Frau Doktor," he said. "May I?"

"A pleasure," said Dr. Lessing.

"I have a question for you," he said, helping himself to the bread and various kinds of wurst that lay on a large plate in the middle of the table. "It is a question of literature."

"Oh, that's nice," said Dr. Lessing. "The plot thickens."

5

When Eleanor had left the hospital room, Franz fell into a deep sleep for a while. When he awoke, he was not sorry to find himself alone. Eleanor couldn't wait to leave, he thought and felt slightly annoyed about this, but nevertheless glad to keep his eyes closed and not feel her nervous, impatient presence in the room. Why is she bothering to come back this evening? She would much rather be out there, chattering with her friend Christa and playing detective in the Haus im Wald. Better she thought a bit about the death of his mother and what to do about burying her, instead of wasting her time fussing about the murder of someone she didn't even know. He couldn't take this whole murder thing seriously, hadn't really allowed himself to think much about it. Still an old man had apparently been battered and left to die. Intracranial hematoma, from what he had read, would suggest that he had lain there, alive but internally bleeding, for who knows how long. An ugly picture. Well, that was what it was to be old and alone, nobody really knowing if you lived or died. At least if you were married, somebody was looking out for you. Eleanor was looking out for him, more or less, though he had increasingly the feeling that she really wasn't thinking that much about him at all. He didn't exactly find it an unadulterated pleasure to think about her. Right now, he was quite happy to be alone.

He opened his eyes, and in the dim light of the room, he found he could now shift his gaze from one thing to another without pain. They had put him in a single room on a quiet corridor, thank God, away from the nurses' station. He remembered those nurses' stations from other hospital visits—all you heard all night were women's voices, nattering on endlessly, phones ringing, and people bashing things about. Here there were few sounds, even though his door, as always in hospitals, was open. Franz did not like open doors, but he found the austere, anonymous look of the room restful. His bed in the Zehenthofgasse was in a room full of memories of his father, of himself when young, of excruciating stays with his mother in her old age; he didn't want to think of any of this. He especially didn't want to think of his mother, still presumably in an ice-cold room in a police morgue in one of those drawers that they pull out on TV detective shows for some shocked family member to identify the body. It was altogether too bad that she had ended up there. For all his bluster about Hofer's prescriptions, he didn't really think she had been murdered, unless he himself had hastened her death. He didn't want to think about that either. Too many places where his mind couldn't rest. And what about that odd incident on Frau Huber's couch? This time he let his mind rest for a moment. Perhaps he had only imagined it—the softly, strongly exploring fingers. The thought was still pleasurable. He had so little sex in his life anymore, only the occasional act of masturbation, which in fact he still quite enjoyed. I suppose, he thought, if I'm even contemplating that, I probably do not have an intracranial hematoma after all. Certainly, the impulse to masturbate had not been included in the list of symptoms. He laughed to himself. Well, he did seem to feel less lethargic now, and his headache was certainly better. He had no great desire to get out of bed, however. A night in this anonymous bed, away from everything, would probably do him good.

He was less than pleased when there was a knock at the open door. Eleanor, no doubt, back already. "Come in," he said in a weak voice and closed his eyes. He was aware of someone approaching the bed, and a slight shock ran through him as he detected a presence that was not Eleanor. The little crocheted blanket came disturbingly into his head, and he opened his eyes to see Frau Huber leaning over him, smiling.

"Herr Professor," she was saying. "We do not want to disturb you. We just wanted to be sure that you were being well treated here."

We? thought Franz, and behind Frau Huber, the tall frame of Herr Direktor Schramm loomed up. What in the world? "Ah, good evening," he said, collecting his wits. "This is very kind."

Frau Huber stepped back, and Herr Schramm came forward and shook his hand.

"We," said Schramm, in his usual pompous way, as if he were talking on behalf of the United Nations, "we in the Haus im Wald are concerned about you, Herr Professor." A bit different, thought Franz, from his attitude this morning when he could hardly wait to get me out of his office.

"Thank you," he said. "But I am being well taken care of. They are only observing me overnight to make sure there are no further ill effects from the blow to my head. I fully intend to be out of here in the morning." In fact he hadn't fully intended any such thing, but he disliked the feeling of Schramm looking down at him from a great height and seeing him as a poor old thing in a hospital bed. "I don't want to keep you," he said, "but do sit down for a moment," looking around the room and seeing only one rather small chair.

"I'll see if I can rustle up another chair," said Schramm, and when he had gone, Frau Huber came conspiratorially closer and laid her hand briefly on his head.

"Head any better, you poor dear?" she said softly.

"Oh, yes, yes, definitely better," said Franz, feeling an onset of weakness at the knees even though he was lying down. What was it with this woman? he thought desperately, looking directly at her and trying to focus on her distinctly unattractive appearance. With a big green loden overcoat and a loden hat with a small feather, she looked like a caricature of a fat alpine housewife; but with that hand on his head, that look in her narrowed eyes, he had an insane fantasy of pulling her onto the bed, stripping off all that loden, and finally getting his hands on the rolling flesh. Madness, madness.

"Here we are," said Schramm, coming back, puffing somewhat, with a large chair on which Frau Huber settled herself, unpinning the little hat from her head and opening the coat to reveal the ever-confining uniform.

"So what do they say about you?" asked Schramm.

"Well, you know, after a blow on the head, there is always the danger of a slow-acting intracranial hematoma, blood under the skull, you know, and they just want to be careful."

"I gather," said Frau Huber, "that this was what killed Herr Graf."

"Where," said Schramm sharply, "did you gather that from?"

"Oh, I have no idea now," she replied. "You know how people talk. At all events, in his case, it couldn't have been so slow-acting, could it? I mean he was alive on Christmas Day and very much dead the day after. Dreadful to think," she said, with a look in her eyes that somehow did not seem to Franz to be dread, "that while we were all merrily singing Christmas carols that Sunday morning in the chapel, he was lying up there with blood seeping into his brain."

"I don't think this is a very good topic of conversation for this visit," said Schramm. "I didn't think, in any case, that you attended the chapel services, Frau Huber."

"Oh, at Christmas and Easter, I usually do, Herr Direktor, and of course I go to the memorial services of which there will be one tomorrow morning. The lilies are already on the altar, I have seen to that."

"You have?" said a voice behind them. "That's good." Eleanor had come in unobserved, clutching a bunch of rather bedraggled daisies. "Hi, Franz," she said. "These were all I could find. Sorry. Quite a full house, I see."

Schramm jumped to his feet. "Do sit down, Frau Fabian. We will not stay any longer. We just came to check up on the professor and to bring good wishes from the Haus im Wald for his recovery."

"Oh, do sit down, Herr Direktor," Eleanor said. "I can sit here." And she bounced down proprietarily and heavily onto the bed near Franz's feet, giving him a jolt at which he winced more with annoyance than with pain.

"So the lilies are on the altar?" she said to Frau Huber.

"We were just talking," said Schramm, "about the service tomorrow morning for poor Frau Winkler.

"Oh yes," said Eleanor, fixing Frau Huber with a provocative look. "I know all about that. Pastor Pokorny is going to be conducting it."

"I don't think so," said Frau Huber. "Sister Agatha has the arrangements in hand."

"But as I understand it," said Eleanor, "Frau Winkler always said she wanted Pastor Pokorny to conduct the last service for her when her time came. He was her friend."

"There is no way," said Frau Huber, "in his present condition that he will be able to do that."

"And how do *you* know?" said Eleanor rudely.

Franz sighed and closed his eyes. "Ladies," said Schramm, "the professor needs to rest. We shall think about all this in the morning." He stood up. "We'll leave you in peace, Herr Professor. I trust you'll have a good night and feel better in the morning."

"Thank you," said Franz. "Thank you both for coming."

Frau Huber stood up, pinning on her little hat with an angry jab of her hatpin and drawing her coat around her.

"Good night, Herr Professor," she said and walked out of the door, held open for her by the director.

"Amazing she can do up her coat at all, that fat lady," said Eleanor.

"Don't be childish," said Franz. "What's all this nonsense about the service in the morning? Why should you care one way or the other who conducts it? You never knew this Frau Winkler, and it's years since you darkened the door of a church yourself."

"Look," she said. "The thing is, if Pokorny can't get up the strength to do it, he'll really feel his life is over."

"His life *is* over," said Franz. "He's ninety-three years old. He believes in God. He'll go to heaven. Why should he worry?"

"It doesn't work like that, Franz, you know it doesn't. Nobody wants to die."

"OK, you may be right." He didn't have the stomach for an argument, still less for nonsensical chitchat about life and death. "You don't have to stay," he said. "I'm all right. I just need to rest. I think I'll get out of here in the morning."

"Are you sure?"

"No, I'm not sure. But I think so. I'll let you know. I'll give you a call or something. Leave me your friend's phone number, perhaps. Thanks for coming." He closed his eyes.

"OK," said Eleanor. "I'll find a jar for the daisies." He heard her filling something with water from the washbasin. "Maybe they'll pick up," she said. She kissed him on the forehead, stood there for a moment, then walked out of the door. He felt nothing. Nothing at all. He opened his eyes and looked at the drooping daisies on the night table. So nobody wants to die? he thought skeptically. But for what? For what, at my age, does anybody want to live?

Chapter 14

There is a nervousness in the old. It breaks out at different ages and in different ways. It can develop into sharp attacks of real fear, such as that observed in the senior Frau Fabian, of whom the casual expression 'she was scared to death' might be held to have had a less-than-casual meaning. Some residents, such as Pastor Pokorny, determinedly work at keeping up their physical strength with the conviction that mental, spiritual, and bodily powers go hand in hand, but almost all the residents keep a nervous eye on their own faculties. Are they more forgetful than they were? When they cross a room to water a plant and are distracted by a half-empty coffee cup and carry it into the kitchen and then stand there in the kitchen with a cup in one hand and a watering can in the other wondering why they wanted to pour water into the half-empty cup . . . oh dear, they think, is it beginning? The descent into confusion? Quite a few of the present residents of Melanchthon have already begun to be appalled by mounting stacks of paper—bills, bank statements, letters—that they do not seem to want to tackle anymore. Concentrate, says the enterprising seventy-five-year-old Frau Zimmermann to herself, when she sits down to work at her computer. Tackling the complicated tax returns of a rich gentleman like Herr Graf, she is happily conscious of pushing back the tides of distraction, because distraction is the first step on the frightening road to confusion. Visitors in the Haus im Wald who have never before thought of themselves as old reach a defining moment such as the death of a parent and are suddenly afraid. For years they have been irritated and constrained by an older, decrepit generation; and now with its passing, decrepitude looms up larger than life on their own horizons. It was, of course, their birthright all along. It's just that they were never frightened by it before.

1

"Yes, Frau Doktor, as you say, the plot thickens," said Büchner at the supper table. "But I still haven't filled in all the blank spaces. Perhaps I am beginning to see a picture in the bits and blobs and details, but no closure as yet."

"So why the question of literature?"

"I can't really tell you why—it is a question of what—a plot question. Do you remember the plot of the *Rosenkavalier*?

"I certainly do. I have seen it many times. It is a favorite of mine, and I have read the text many times too—not the usual third-rate text of an opera libretto, but a major poetic work. Don't you think?"

"I'm afraid I haven't read Hofmannsthal for many years. I really don't know that I ever read the *Rosenkavalier*. I saw the opera years ago, and I remember the opening scene where two very large ladies sang and embraced each other and were somewhat unconvincingly in love—one of them was supposed to be a young man."

Dr. Lessing laughed. "You should read the text—a wonderfully convincing meditation on the passing of time and the sadness of losing one's youth and finding oneself an older woman, relegated to the sidelines, a bystander who must watch the young fall in love."

"Is that the plot?"

"That certainly underlies the plot. You should go to a modern production, Herr Inspektor. You may find those early scenes convincing after all. Opera singers are more or less obliged nowadays to keep their weight down if they want to be hired to sing on the great stages of the world. You'll find that when the curtain goes up on the modern Marschallin, soprano, a good-looking older woman, in bed with her lover Oktavian, a young count, mezzo-soprano, slim and boyish-looking, the passion between them in the words and the music is also quite convincing in the flesh."

"I'll be sure to try and get a ticket to the next performance at the State Opera. But what actually happens in the plot? I remember a funny oldish man with a paunch who's convinced he's God's gift to the female sex. The only actual song I remember in the opera is his 'With me, with me, no night is too long.'"

"That's certainly the song in the opera that everybody knows—the famous comic song of Baron Ochs. Well, comic if you find massive self-delusion comic. He comes to the Marschallin to ask her if she will find a wellborn young man to take a rose from him to the rich young lady he wants to marry for her money. This *Rosenkavalier*, after an old custom, is to propose on his behalf. The Marschallin suggests Oktavian, and so the plot moves on, and the handsome young count and the rich young lady—a pretty young second soprano—promptly fall in love, and the Marschallin has to bow to the inevitable, namely the victory of youth over age."

"So that's the plot. A sad story with a sad end, then."

"Well, the one comfort that older women today can derive from all this is that the *older woman* in Hofmannsthal's text is perhaps thirty-five years old, and the count and the victorious young heroine are about seventeen. Nowadays, it takes a lot longer to become the vanquished older woman."

"Well, that's one small victory against time."

"Yes, but today or tomorrow or the next day, as the Marschallin says, it happens to every woman. And there are still women who can't accept it and certainly do not do so with the grace and the poetry of the Marschallin."

"It happens to every man too, Frau Doktor. Look at Baron Ochs. He is a more ridiculous figure than any of the women, and he also loses the lady of his dreams."

"Yes, but we know his greatest loss is the young lady's money—he is desperately in debt—so his loss doesn't affect us in the same way. The Marschallin breaks our hearts because she loses her lover and sees her own youth disappear with him—or with her, depending on how you are looking at it. We feel with her the inexorable passage of time, the frightening onset of old age."

"Yes, but I suppose Baron Ochs is only the comic side of the same coin—the male being inherently a more ridiculous figure than the female."

Dr. Lessing laughed. "I hope, Herr Inspektor, you are not just fishing for compliments. It's true that Baron Ochs has to be a man. No woman who looked and behaved as he does could convincingly persuade an audience that she thought herself attractive. The Marschallin is still a beautiful woman and has to be portrayed as such. The fear that fuels her role is the fear of losing her beauty, and with her beauty, love. The end of love is a terrifying thing, Herr Inspektor—for many people. But what does all this add up to in the developing picture at the Haus im Wald?"

"Picture or pictures," said Büchner thoughtfully. "Since our conversation at lunchtime, I've had in my mind some collections of lines that could create two different pictures. I remember in my brief encounter with psychotherapy, I was shown another of those ambiguous pictures. In this one, first you see an elegantly coiffed young woman in a feathered hat, looking backward, a three-quarter view to the left. Look again, and you have a side view of an ugly old woman also facing left but forward. Some people see the one first, and some the other. Some can only ever see one. Do you know that one?"

"Oh yes, another old chestnut. But an interesting one. In my experience, once you see the old ugly woman, you have to make quite an effort to refocus on the young one. There is a malevolence about the old woman that seems to crowd out the pert prettiness of the young one."

"Yes, but of course that doesn't mean that the old woman is the right one."

"Neither is right, Herr Inspektor. In the picture, they both simply *are.*"

"Yes, but my job, Frau Doktor, is to decide on the right picture. And to do that, I have to eliminate one of them. Ultimately, they cannot coexist, as in the picture."

Packing her table napkin carefully into its plastic container, Dr. Lessing stood up and shook Büchner's hand. "Make sure that is really so, Herr Inspektor. Before you consider your job done, that is. I wish you a good night."

"Good night, Frau Doktor. Thank you."

2

So what now? thought Büchner. He had eaten far too much bread and wurst while talking to Frau Lessing. He really ought to go for a walk before setting himself up for the night in Melanchthon. At least take a turn around the house and think a bit. It was well after six—he'd have to go out by the side door to follow the rules of the house. He did not want to advertise the fact that he had a master key any more than anyone else did. He would ring the bell when he came back as the regulations stipulated and see what actually happened when you did that. He picked up his coat from his office, put on his galoshes, and stepped out into the snow, which had accumulated, unswept, on the path. *Can't go too far in this,* he thought, but the cold air was refreshing. He walked along the path through the front gardens toward the woods, looking up at the windows of Melanchthon as he passed. The Graf apartment on the third floor was dark, but on either side, there was light in Dr. Lessing's apartment and in the sisters' corner apartment. On the next floor down, only the Hagen apartment was dark, the curtains were open; and for a moment, he thought he saw a face at the window, but then it was gone. The Ritters and Zimmermanns had their lights on and their curtains drawn. If only, he thought, he could hear some of the conversations going on behind the closed curtains. Especially the sisters. Something very odd about them. He realized that he didn't want to think about Barbara having anything to do with the crime, but their last conversation had been, to say the least, inconclusive.

He turned the corner of the building and paused, looking down the path into the wood where Herr Zimmermann claimed to have seen one of the sisters late on Christmas Day, identified by Gruber as Barbara. Well, there was no reason why she shouldn't have taken a walk after her Christmas dinner. But why hadn't she mentioned it? It must have been getting dark, and he would hesitate himself before plunging into the wood on a dark and snowy evening. He certainly wasn't going to do it now. He continued on the path around the house, past the chapel on the ground floor of Melanchthon. The only light on the third floor in the back of the house was in Pokorny's apartment. The ladies must still be there, since Frau Beck's apartment was dark. Going on past the back of the house, he thought he saw a light in the café, but maybe the light was from the lobby through the glass doors. Apart from the dark block that must be 24 and 12, one above the other, the two rooms permanently vacated by the old ladies Winkler and Fabian, all the lights on the two upper floors were on, but dim behind uniformly closed curtains. No doubt, someone went around drawing the curtains and later turning off the lights in the rooms of the residents of Martin Luther at a specific time. He thought of Frau Beck, opening the curtains for her friend on the last night of her life. He stepped back into the snow of the field behind the house and surveyed the length of the house from one end to the other. The regimentation of lights in Martin Luther was another sign, he thought, of how the older and weaker are essentially in the hands of other people, unless they happened to have a friend or significant other with the strength and devotion to come and open their curtains or their windows when they wanted them open. A small shiver went through him, not a shiver of cold but of apprehension. He had clung to his freedom through all the years when others were allowing themselves, as he had often seen it, to be chained in family life. Would this freedom of his in the end only lead to solitary confinement in an institution? He turned and looked the other way across the open fields to the trees, where against the sky, lit by a pale and intermittent moonlight as the clouds moved across it, you could see the dark blobs of the rooks' nests in the branches. Were those big black birds asleep up there now, waiting to swoop out at the crack of dawn? Just keep walking through the snow, Georg, he said to himself. You've got a few years left. He saw a light go on in Frau Huber's apartment on the ground floor of Martin Luther, and turning the corner to walk past the front of the building, he saw that there was a light on in Schramm's office. So they are back from their errand of mercy, he thought, and strode purposefully up to the entrance to ring the doorbell.

A voice promptly answered through the intercom. "Who is it?"

"Büchner, Kripo Wien."

A pause. "One moment. I'll be there."

Not prepared to buzz me in, he thought, I see.

The large shape of Frau Huber loomed up on the other side of the glass panes set into the front door. The door opened on the chain, and Frau Huber peered through the gap. She opened the door.

"I always check after dark," she said, "if I am not immediately sure of the voice."

"Quite right," said Büchner. "You can't be too careful. I was just taking a constitutional after your excellent evening meal—excellent, but tempting the middle-aged eater with too much good black bread."

"It does not seem," said Frau Huber, looking him up and down, "as if you need to worry about middle-aged spread."

"Eternal vigilance, Frau Huber, that's my motto."

"In everything?'

"In everything."

"And how long do you think you will be practicing your vigilance in the Haus im Wald? I ask only because there is a request from a relative for the guest room over the New Year holiday."

"I think you can rest assured that I will not be here then. In fact, I have every intention of leaving tomorrow."

Frau Huber stood still. They were outside the café, where their ways were about to part. "Tomorrow?" she said, clearly surprised. "Do you mean your investigation will be over by tomorrow?"

"I believe so," said Büchner. "I cannot promise. But I believe so. Do you, by the way, have any more news for me about the yellow stickers? Any more turned up?"

This time, her face did not turn red. "I didn't know what you were talking about the first time you mentioned them, Herr Inspektor, but now one has turned up on my own apartment door. I found it when I got back from the hospital this evening."

"Indeed. And were you not going to tell me about it?"

"I thought it could wait until tomorrow, but since you say you are near a conclusion of your work here—well, I'd better give it to you now. Do you think the stickers have anything to do with the murder?"

"As I never tire of saying, Frau Huber, everything that happens here at the moment is potentially connected with the murder, and I need to know about it."

"Come with me then."

They went into her apartment, and Büchner was motioned to take a seat on a flowery-looking couch.

"Here it is," she said, retrieving a sticker from a drawer in her little escritoire. "It's in rhyme, of all things." Büchner read:

OH FRAU HUBER WHATS WITH THE PROF

LYING ON THE SOFA AND HAVING IT OFF

"Oh my word," said Büchner, standing up rapidly, wanting to laugh, but also feeling a distinct need to remove himself from the flowery couch.

"I can't imagine," said Frau Huber, "what this disgusting person is thinking of. Were the other stickers anything like this?"

"Well, yes, as a matter of fact, though I don't know that they were left so blatantly on people's front doors. All a bit prurient, and all a bit childish."

"Childish?" said Frau Huber. "What sort of child would write this?"

"A grown-up one," said Büchner, and could not but notice that a dull red flush began creeping up Frau Huber's neck.

"Well, anyway, Herr Inspektor, there it is. I think I need to rest now."

"Yes, well, thank you for letting me in, and thanks for this!" He put the yellow sticker into one of the evidence bags that he carried in his pocket. "I'll be off then. I have a lot to think of before tomorrow. Good night, Frau Huber, sleep well."

A red-faced Frau Huber let him out of her apartment. He walked up the two flights of stairs to his room. What he really wanted to do at this point was to step back a bit and quietly look at the Graf will. This had been vaguely in his mind all afternoon, but he had allowed himself continually to be distracted by other things. Now with his master key already in the lock of his own room, he looked down the corridor. He really would like one last look at the two rooms where the old ladies had died, before Schramm put in new occupants. He took the key out of his lock, walked along to the empty room 24. It was dark inside, and he did not want to put a light on. As his eyes accustomed themselves to the darkness, he walked to the window and opened the curtains. The clouds had cleared for the moment. Moonlight on the snow. His heart almost stopped as he saw two points of light, tiny beady eyes looking straight at him from the railing. An enormous black bird slowly spread its wings, and stood high on its clawed feet. Büchner involuntarily stepped back. The bird wheeled and flew out across the field.

You are really losing it, he said to himself, sitting for a moment on the bed where Frau Winkler had died and from which Pastor Pokorny had so recently escaped. Suppose you were lying in this bed, he thought, and suddenly saw such a creature on the rail, a huge silhouette against the moon—it might well give you a heart attack, especially if you were a fragile old woman. Not there yet myself, he thought, but it's high time to get out of here. He locked the door behind him, walked back along the corridorent down to the next floor, and this time, purposefully opened the door of his own room.

3

This is positively the last time I'm going to drive through these woods today, thought Eleanor. She had been propelled this far by a feeling of extreme irritation. Frau Huber provoked this in her, though why she should care one way or the other about this silly woman she didn't know. Franz also provoked her—the way he lay there, almost enjoying his privileged state of illness, expecting her to make arrangements for his mother's funeral, and quite obviously disapproving of her involvement with the goings-on in the Haus im Wald. Why should she care whether he approved or disapproved? She seemed to have spent her whole life worrying about whether or not she was approved of—what the hell did it matter really? The Haus im Wald was presenting her with a graphic picture of what might lie ahead as her life closed down on her. She really needed to spend however many years she had left doing what she wanted to do and not what she thought, probably wrongly, other people wanted her to do. Why had she gone all the way to see Franz again this evening, only to find him happily conversing with Horrible Huber and Showman Schramm—and to take him those pathetic daisies? He probably hadn't much wanted to see her. But a wife doesn't *not* visit her husband in the hospital. Oh no? In any case, she'd wait now until he called her to say how he was doing. It had been rather gratifying that the inspector had clearly been interested in her story about Frau Hagen and Dr. Hofer in the café. This evening might be quite amusing with the inspector up on their floor too. Amusing? That really wasn't the way to look at it. But anyway, it would be a lot less boring than recent evenings in the Zehenthofgasse worrying about rolling up carpets and giving away furniture and trying to put Franz in a good mood and looking for stashes of banknotes—come to think of it, that seven hundred euros had never surfaced. She'd better mention that to the inspector. She drove up to a parking place in front of the Haus im Wald, and looking up at the lighted windows, she felt a pleasurable thrill at the thought of walking back out of her own life into what seemed like somebody else's story.

She rang Christa's bell, but there was no answer, so she tried Pastor Pokorny's. Christa promptly answered and buzzed her in. A small intelligent-looking woman with short gray hair and a slight limp got into the elevator with her. They greeted one another politely, each looking somewhat curiously at the other.

"Eleanor Fabian, just visiting," she said.

"Gerda Lessing, not, I'm afraid, just visiting," said the woman.

"Oh, pleased to meet you," said Eleanor. "You're the psychiatrist, aren't you?"

Dr. Lessing smiled. "Was," she said. "I was."

"Oh, but I don't suppose that's something you give up as you get older."

"Gradually," said Dr. Lessing, "you give everything up as you get older. Ah, we are going to the same floor."

"Yes." They got out of the elevator. "I'm going to see my friend Christa, but at the moment she is looking after Pastor Pokorny."

"Looking after?"

"Well, yes, it's a long story. He fell, you see, and they tried to put him into Martin Luther, but we brought him back here."

"You did?" Dr. Lessing smiled. "Well, if I can do anything to help. I am in apartment 31."

"Thank you, we'll probably need all the help we can get."

"Just ring my bell then. Good night."

That was a stroke of luck, thought Eleanor. She seems nice and looks very much on top of things still, though she seems to have a bit of a limp. But bright. I bet she's very bright. She rang the bell of Pastor Pokorny's apartment.

Christa opened the door, beaming, and said, "Look!" Eleanor looked and saw Pastor Pokorny sitting on the couch, also beaming. Eleanor went forward, shook him by the hand, and said, "Oh, well done, Herr Pastor. How did you manage that?"

Christa pointed to the wheelchair, and the pastor said, "I managed to get into that thing and out of it again, and Frau Beck did the rest. So that's a start."

"How are your knees?" asked Eleanor.

"Well, they just about hold me up, but I am still a bit unsteady."

"Herr Pokorny," said Christa, "didn't you tell me once that your daughter had sent you a walker of some kind? That might help."

"I never thought I'd need it," said the pastor. "It's at the back of the large closet between the bedroom and the kitchen."

"Shall I get it out?" said Eleanor.

"I suppose it's worth a try," said the pastor doubtfully.

Eleanor went and pulled out a folded three-wheeled object. She and Christa struggled a bit to get it open. "It's been there so long," said the pastor. "She sent it for my ninetieth birthday."

Finally they got the handlebars to open out; they could be adjusted up or down to the height of the user, and they had brakes.

"We'll have to check the height," said Eleanor, and promptly tried it herself, running it easily along the carpet, then locking the brakes, and leaning on the handlebars. "Oh, it's splendid," she said and rolled it briskly from one end of the room to the other, several times. "I love it," she said. "You try it, Christa."

At that moment, the doorbell rang. The three looked guiltily at each other. "Who could that be?" said Christa. "It's a bit too early for the inspector."

"Well, we'll have to open it," said Eleanor, striding up to the door and calling loudly. "Who's there?"

A little voice replied, "Ritter. Wondering about Pastor Pokorny."

An audible threefold sigh of relief filled the room, and Eleanor opened the door to the little man. "Do come in, Herr Ritter, how kind of you to come," she said.

"I just wondered, you know, after the events of this afternoon . . . Ah, Grüß Gott, Herr Pastor. I'm glad to see you safe in your own living room." The two men shook hands.

"I'm happy to see that you have two ladies to help you, Herr Pastor. I had wondered how you would be managing your supper."

"Michael gave us a hand with that," said Christa. "He brought something up from downstairs."

"A good boy, Michael," said Herr Ritter. "And how about the night . . . ?"

"So kind of you to ask," said Eleanor, "but Herr—" A loud cough from Christa stopped her, and Christa interrupted, "We will be able to manage." She had quite forgotten that they weren't supposed to mention the plan for the night. Though surely Herr Ritter . . . Still, better obey orders. "Yes, thank you, Herr Ritter, we can manage."

"It has been a terrible few days, Herr Pastor, has it not? I do not remember a time like this in the Haus im Wald."

At a signal from Eleanor, the two women withdrew into the kitchen, leaving the two old men together. "Let's try to find ourselves something to eat," Eleanor said, but she did not close the door.

"Yes, a terrible few days," said the pastor. "You and I know enough about horrors from our earlier years, but one thought all that was over, and all we needed to do now was to make peace with our Maker and then go quietly. Violent death here? I do not quite believe it."

"And Hans, of all people . . . I cannot think that he could have done anything to provoke violence. Not in these years, in this place. As a younger man, he might have done things that could have created great anger and resentment, but he has made up for that . . ."

"He was too young, surely," said the pastor, "to have been involved . . ."

"Oh, yes, yes, he was only sixteen when the war ended and Austria was liberated—well, that's how you and I saw it."

The pastor smiled. "I suppose at his age, Herr Graf might well have been among those who chose to regard themselves as being occupied by foreigners in '45 rather than liberated by them."

"I don't know the details of his background," said Herr Ritter. "But I do know—and probably you have heard it too—that his family had acquired property and paintings in the usual way in the thirties and forties, by Aryanization as it was called. I also know, however, that Hans came round much later to seeing the gross injustice of all that. I know this because I pursued my profession as an art dealer in the decades after the war, and so came to know him slightly at that time. He became very rich in his own right, and he made large contributions to the restitution funds, though I must say there are those who still think he has certain debts."

"Restitution," said the pastor. "A fine word and a fine idea, but they cannot restore to us the days of our youth. I am grateful, however, for my old age. Many of our generation are not here to enjoy it."

"Or to suffer through it," said Herr Ritter wryly. "But you are right, of course. You know, Hans Graf has left me his paintings, the ones he still has. I am touched by this. He must have known I would take care of any of his remaining, shall we say, obligations. I no longer have walls to hang them on myself. But I would prefer to have had the company of Hans until my own death. We used to talk about paintings, you know, we both loved them, and this blotted out other memories."

"Yes," said the pastor. "At least we can choose our memories."

"More or less," said Herr Ritter. "More or less. But, Herr Pastor, you must rest. You have only to call me if you need help of any kind. Good night, ladies," he called.

"So many things," whispered Eleanor to Christa in the kitchen, "that we know nothing about . . ." Coming out into the living room, she said, "Good night, Herr Ritter. It was kind of you to come."

4

Could he really have been frightened by the beady eye of a bird? Well, apparently, yes. A sad thought that poor Frau Beck might have opened the way to a quick death for Frau Winkler when she opened the sleeping lady's curtains to the night sky. A lot to be said for a quick death, but Frau Beck was hardly one to believe in euthanasia, and it did not sound as if Frau Winkler wanted to die any more than Herr Graf did. Büchner took the will of Johannes Erich Graf out from his underwear drawer. He sat at the little table in his bedroom and opened his own curtains to see the sky. The wind on the moon. That had been the name of a book he had read as a child, and he had wondered then what it meant. Tonight he could see the clouds racing across the moon with the wind at their back. There was no balcony here like the ones in the back, so no railings for birds to perch menacingly on. OK, Georg, read the will again now. Concentrate. He opened it up and read the personal message, father to son, several times:

> *My dear son, for you are my dear son though I have never known how to show this to you, I remember as if it were yesterday the day you were born and I held you in my arms and thought with overwhelming happiness, "A boy, a boy all my own." I wanted to give you the world. You never wanted the world I had to give. Now it is too late for us to know each other. In leaving you a large part of the material residue of the life that I led and you despised, I hope you will not reject it as you*

have rejected me, but see it as a gift of love to the boy who was, on that happiest day of my life, all my own.

He realized as he read it that it was impossible for him to think objectively about it because the imagined voice of his own father constantly interposed itself. Not that it was language he could imagine his father using. *Love* was not a word he had ever heard from the lips of his own father, and he could not imagine his ever using such hyperbolic phrases as *I wanted to give you the world*. But that was the trouble: with every sentence he read, he wondered, Did my father think that about me? This was not the question he was being paid to answer. The question in the head of Chefinspektor Büchner, as distinct from son Georg, was, Does this message ring true? It was important, he was sure, to have a clearer understanding of the character of Graf if he were to see clearly who had killed him. A dim picture of the murderer was forming in his mind, but whom had this person killed? A charming generous man who had wanted the best for his son but had failed to get across his love to the boy himself, perhaps because the mother had created a distance between them, or because the boy himself was simply not lovable? This seemed quite possible. Büchner could see well enough how he had made himself very unlovable to his own father in his teens and early twenties. But why the sentence, *Now it is too late for us to know each other.* Well, yes, it was too late by the time his son read it, but surely not too late when Graf wrote it. Graf was only seventy-six when he died, and his son fifty-four—why was it too late? Or did Graf actually have no desire to get to know his son, who lived in such a different world from his own, so unattractive, so uncharming, so unappetizingly poor, that it was easier to write him generously into his will and basically ignore him in his life? Quite probably the day of the boy's birth really was, nonetheless, a supremely happy day. It usually is for a father. I suppose so, anyway, thought Büchner. It is not something I will experience. Nor, most probably, will Erich Graf. Well, apparently Graf had, through his dying, and particularly through his will, given his son the chance to move on and perhaps become a happier man, late in the day though it was, and—thought the skeptical son Georg—at no cost to Graf in his lifetime. The notion of being his father's own boy probably did give Erich a huge lift despite everything. And of course, the half of his father's fortune didn't hurt either. Though Büchner did not think for one minute that Erich Graf had killed for that. In such things, he trusted his own intuition.

But what did his intuition tell him about the three other main beneficiaries of the will? Logically speaking, the only one who would benefit in a major way from Graf's actual death was Dr. Hofer, since Frau Hagen and Director Schramm, on behalf of the Haus, would presumably have gone on benefiting from Graf's largesse if he had stayed alive. The Hofer role in all this was mysterious. Why did Graf leave him such a large chunk of money? And what had he been doing in the Café Sacher with Frau Hagen? Of course, the simple explanation for that was that he accompanied her there after the reading of the will and bought her a glass of champagne because she was overcome with the emotion of it all. But why, for example, wasn't Schramm with them? The smaller bequests were straightforward enough on the face of it, though Frau Huber was markedly missing in the service area. A further word with all these beneficiaries might be instructive, and in particular with Hofer. If Schramm happened to be still in the office, it might be a good idea to talk to him before going over to take up night duty in Pastor Pokorny's apartment.

Büchner picked up his briefcase and nothing more—this was a night in which he did not propose to get undressed and go to bed. Eternal vigilance, he thought and laughed to himself at the thought of Frau Huber's face when she heard that his vigilance at the Haus im Wald might soon be ended. But, he thought, Frau Huber is not really a laughing matter. On the contrary. He put a few documents in his briefcase to take with him, locked his door with the usual skepticism about the point of doing so, intending to go straight to Schramm's office. Then he remembered that he had meant to look into the cordoned-off room downstairs, Frau Fabian's old room. He walked down to the next floor and was surprised to see light under the door of room 12. He stood outside for one long minute, listening to sounds inside that seemed like furniture being moved around. At this time of the evening, it was unlikely that this could be legitimate activity, even though

Schramm had been given the go-ahead to begin turning over the furniture to its owners, namely the Fabian family. He put his master key quietly into the lock, turned it, and slowly opened the door. At first he saw no one, though the scuffling noises had ceased the minute he put his key in the lock. He put his hand inside his jacket as if about to draw a weapon, feeling rather melodramatic as he did so—Büchner rarely carried a gun, and it had not crossed his mind to do so in the Haus im Wald. He moved quickly around the door to see Michael, standing stock still with acute embarrassment on his handsome face, holding onto the bookcase, which he had obviously been pushing back against the wall.

"Well, well, Michael," said Büchner. "And what is going on here?"

"Oh God, Herr Inspektor," said Michael, throwing his hands in the air, in a gesture not of surrender, but of despairing helplessness. "What are you doing here? I never expected that."

"Apparently not. May I ask what you are doing here?"

"Oh, all right, I might as well tell you." He pulled the bookcase back out from the wall, bent down, and picked up a wad of banknotes. "Seven hundred euros," he said. "I was putting it back."

"Putting it back?"

"Yes. I might as well give it directly to you now." He handed it over.

"Are you going to tell me you were taking an evening stroll through the cordoned-off rooms and happened to find seven hundred euros behind the bookcase?"

Michael laughed. "I don't know why I'm laughing," he said. "That would have been a good line. Would you have believed it?"

"No."

"No, of course not. Well, look here, Herr Inspektor, the fact is that I took it from the professor, borrowed it, as it were, because I was pretty desperate and was sure I would be able to put it back without anyone knowing."

"Ah, yes. Many people have come a cropper with that sort of modus operandi."

"But you see, Herr Inspektor, I was putting it back."

"Sticking it behind a bookcase? And carefully wearing gloves, I see, just in case."

"Your chaps are dusting all over the place, you can't blame me for that. Of course, I didn't want anyone to know I put it there. But I knew the family would have to move the furniture out. I was hoping they would think the money had fallen behind there and they'd be glad to get it back."

"Are you going to tell me how you came by it, or"—Büchner put on his TV-detective voice—"do I have to take you down to the station for questioning?"

"It's not admirable on my part—I know that—but when the professor was sitting in the wheelchair, semiconscious after his fall, I saw it sticking out of his inside pocket, and quick as a flash, without even stopping to think, I just took it out and stuck it in my own pocket. No one saw me. He had his eyes closed, and everybody else was in a flap because his mother had died. And I desperately needed money at that point."

"OK. Out with it. Why?"

"I've been paying for night nurses for my grandmother lately, because she's been getting up at night, taking her clothes off, and wandering about with nothing on—that sort of thing. It happens, you know, Herr Inspektor. I'd got in over my head paying for extra help for her. It costs seventy euros a night, and she's got no insurance that will cover that. I've been taking extra jobs, but I owed a lot of back payments, and I must admit, I told Herr Graf about this when he gave me my Christmas tip, and he promised to top this up right after the Christmas holiday, but of course, he didn't come down to the café the day after Christmas. So that was my last hope gone. I had to pay up at least a week's back payments at the nursing home or they wouldn't have provided any more extra help."

"Not a bad story, Michael, but tell me, when did Herr Graf actually give you the normal Christmas tip?"

"He had asked me to pop up there in the late morning, when I was helping Frau Huber in the dining room. The tip was, of course, nowhere near the thousand euros that I needed, which was why I told him the whole story. He told me not to worry, he would help me out. He wished me a Merry Christmas, and I left much more cheerily than I arrived."

"I can imagine," said Büchner, thinking, *Ciao Papa*—a cheery farewell to a sugar daddy. "Did you ever call him Papa?" he asked.

"Once in while, just for fun."

"Why didn't you tell me before that you had visited him on Christmas Day?"

"You never actually asked," said Michael.

"Did I not? Well, it all sounds plausible enough, Michael. And where did you get this seven hundred from? Another kind Papa?"

There was a long pause. Finally, Michael said, "I threw myself on the mercy of Direktor Schramm. He gave it to me, and we thought of this idea, to save face."

There was another long pause. "What will you do?" asked Michael nervously.

"I expect," said Büchner slowly, looking straight at Michael, "I shall talk to the director." Michael groaned. "And then I shall talk to the Fabians. It will be a question of whether they press charges . . . and against whom."

"Against whom?"

"Well, it looks as if the Herr Direktor is an accessory after the fact."

"But, Herr Inspektor, he was only an accessory to the returning of the money, not the taking of it."

"Returning it somewhat deviously, Michael, I suppose you will admit, with intent to cover up the actual stealing of the money. Is that the act of a totally innocent man?" Or, he thought, of a well-integrated one.

"He's a very decent man, Herr Inspektor. He's always been good to me."

"And am I now to take the word of a thief?"

"I don't like these words *thief* and *stealing*, Herr Inspektor. The professor really didn't need the cash at that moment, and I needed it for a good cause—and I fully intended to give it back."

"Ah yes, Robin Hood himself. Unfortunately, we are in the Vienna Woods, not in Sherwood Forest. And I am a policeman.

We shall have to see what transpires, Michael. We'd better lock up here, and I'll have a word with the director, if he's still there."

"Oh yes, he is."

They walked down the stairs, and Büchner knocked at the door of the director's office. Schramm opened the door, saying, "About time, Michael—" He stopped short at the sight of Büchner.

"Herr Inspektor!" he said.

"Good night, Michael," said Büchner. "See you in the morning, no doubt. May I come in, Herr Direktor?"

5

Closing the door behind Herr Ritter, Eleanor said to Christa, "Since he offered to help, we should have asked him for a couple of eggs. I could have made an omelet at least."

"I'm afraid, like old Mother Hubbard," said the pastor, "as we used to say in England, my cupboard is bare. I'm sorry. I take my meals largely in the dining room or go down to the Goldene Glocke in the mornings on my electric scooter. Will I ever do that again?"

"Of course, you will," said Eleanor heartily.

"Yes," said the pastor. "That is the tone I always take with the elderly who are on the verge of giving up. 'Come along, come along,' we say heartily. 'You can manage.' But there comes a point, my dear, where one simply cannot. Manage, that is."

"Oh, Pastor Pokorny," said Christa. "Don't say that. There's the service in the morning, remember? Frau Winkler always used to say that she liked to think of you in the little chapel saying a prayer for her when she'd gone."

The pastor smiled sadly. "She was a good person, and amazingly cheerful considering what she had lived through. All her life, you know, she accepted the silent veil drawn even by her coreligionists over the fact that her husband, as a young Lutheran minister, near the end of the war, was one of those beheaded in the notorious Morzinplatz prison for his work in the resistance. Were these men heroes for opposing the Nazis, or were they traitors for passing information to the invading allies? You will not find the Reverend Winkler's name signposted in the Grinzinger Graveyard on the list of honored Viennese citizens. You have to hunt for the grave. And no one will put flowers on it now that Frau Winkler has gone."

"Oh, Pastor Pokorny," said Christa again. "You and she never talked about this."

"What was there to say? Silence on certain topics has been a way of life. I really don't know why I'm saying it now." He paused. "I do not want to let her down. I will try to conduct the service."

"Oh, wonderful," said Eleanor.

"Not so wonderful," he said. "First, I have to be able to walk. And then I will have to find in my head the right words to say. I have been running words through my head, but they get very mixed up." He closed his eyes. "Perhaps in the morning . . ."

"Let's try the walker," said Eleanor brightly.

"Oh, not now," said Christa. "The pastor is tired."

He opened his eyes. "Well, maybe a few steps. I could try the bathroom."

"Well, OK," said Christa nervously.

"Don't worry," whispered Eleanor as the pastor got himself into a position to stand up. "I can manage in there. I've done it with my father." And if things don't improve, she thought glumly, I'll soon be doing it with Franz.

They put the walker in front of him, and each put an arm under the pastor's arms. He got to his feet and stood, his hands on the handlebars.

"Ready, steady," he said, "go!" and he loosened the brakes with his hands and took off at an unexpectedly fast rate toward the bathroom.

"Oh, Pastor Pokorny," said Christa. "Not too fast! Please!"

But the walker rolled easily through the bathroom door, and before they could do anything about it, the pastor was inside and had slammed the door shut.

"Please, please do not lock it!" called Eleanor. "Oh God," she said to Christa. "If he falls again in there against the door, we'll be absolutely stuck. Insane in a place like this that the doors open inward. Christa, couldn't you run down and see if the inspector is anywhere about, just in case? I'll hold the fort here and hope for the best."

Christa ran, and Eleanor waited, thinking of the many times she had waited thus, nervously, outside the bathroom for her own aged parents. She heard the toilet flush inside, then there was a long pause, then the pastor's voice. "Could you open the door? I can't seem to manage that and hold on to the walker." She pushed it open with great relief, and he stood there holding onto the handlebars with a look of triumph on his face.

"Well done, Herr Pokorny," she said.

"Ah yes," he said. "The triumphs of old age. We go back to the congratulatory phase of infant toilet training." But he laughed, a loud cheery laugh, quite like his old self, and began pushing the walker back to the couch. "I will take the service tomorrow," he said. "I will give it a go."

"Oh, well done, Herr Pokorny," she said again. "Christa will be so pleased. She went to see if she could find the inspector"

"While she has gone, I think I should show you something. It would upset Frau Beck greatly, I know, but it may be that you could just give it quietly to the inspector. I think I need to go to bed if I am to be in shape in the morning."

"What do you want me to give him?"

"Well, when I went into the bathroom, the cover of the toilet seat was up, and this was stuck on it in the inside." He held out to her a yellow sticker. "It is not the first time I have found one of these—one was once in my napkin case in the dining room. I threw that away. I have heard rumors of others in the house, but until now, I thought it best not to report it in any official way. But now I think the inspector should be informed."

"What is it?" said Eleanor, consumed with curiosity.

She took it from the pastor and read:

PASTOR POKORNY
KNOWN TO BE HORNY
CHRISTA LOVES IT
WHEN HE SHOVES IT

"I don't believe this!" said Eleanor. "How absolutely sickening! Who could possibly have written this?"

"I have an idea," he said. "There is only one person in the Haus im Wald who might be both coarse and cruel enough to write such things to people, but I do not want to point the finger without a shred of evidence. How could this have got into the apartment in the last couple of hours when we were all here?"

Eleanor thought guiltily of how she had left him alone to go and see Frau Hagen. "I can't imagine," she said. "Well, I did step outside briefly."

"In any case, give it to the inspector and suggest that he talk to Frau Dr. Lessing about it. She and I once discussed the rumors, and we both had the same suspicion. She is a professional observer of, shall we say, the human personality. So am I, of course, in my way, but I have to be more committed to looking for the best in people rather than uncovering the worst."

"Well," said Eleanor, looking indignantly at the yellow sticker, "there's not much good to be found in the person who wrote this horrible stuff."

"That's not for us to judge," said the pastor. "But I think it is time for the person to be identified and stopped, since there may be people of a more delicate psyche than mine who could be deeply hurt by this sort of thing. In fact, you should perhaps mention one more thing to the inspector. Herr Ritter confided in me that he had a particularly nasty one in which *Mike* rhymed with *kike*. He did not mention it to anyone else, and I can hardly bear to repeat it myself, but since, in my view, racial innuendo is even more dangerous than the sexual variety, I think the inspector ought to know about it, if all this is investigated. After all, who knows where it might lead?"

"Or have led! We have already had a murder here, after all."

"We cannot say there is any connection, but as I say, it's high time to identify this particular culprit. But now I think I must sleep. If you would just stand by, my dear, I think I can get myself up onto my new chariot."

He put his hands on the handlebars and, taking a deep breath, pulled himself up.

"What strong arms you have," said Eleanor.

The pastor gave another of his big laughs. "Yes, they saved my life in my youth, and I have made sure to keep them going in my old age. I have a set of weights in my closet too, you know."

"Oh, well done, Herr Pokorny," said Eleanor.

"Good night, Frau Fabian," said the pastor, wheeling himself into his bedroom and closing the door. She didn't feel nervous about him this time, but hearing Christa coming back through the front door, she put the yellow sticker in her pocket. Christa came panting in.

"I can't find the inspector," she said. "I think I can hear his voice in Schramm's office, but I didn't dare go bursting in there."

"It's OK. Everything's under control," said Eleanor. More or less, she thought. More or less.

Chapter 15

High on the list of taboo topics of conversation in the Haus im Wald is sex. How much it figures as a topic in the minds of residents is difficult to assess. Visitors of a younger generation would generally prefer not even to imagine sexual thoughts, still less such activities, in their very elderly elders, but are shocked when it dawns on them that they have themselves perhaps already slipped into a generation that can scarcely imagine such activities for itself. But why should these activities become unimaginable? Sex after all is an expression of passion, and passion certainly survives the ebbing of sexual opportunity. The Haus im Wald, as the visiting chief inspector has realized, still hums with passion of all kinds, from the obvious, not to say operatic, passion of Frau Hagen for the dead man, to the passion for absolute order burning away in such people as Sister Agatha, and the passion for living itself and surely for God in a fiery old man like Pokorny. What happens to passion in the old when it is thwarted and finds no outlet? Crimes of passion, it is said, are not usually committed by criminals but by so-called ordinary people, pushed by unbearably strong emotions to find release in what would normally be for them an unthinkable act. The passions of the old are held in check in the meeting places of the Haus im Wald, such as the dining room, where extreme irritation and certain kinds of nasty repartee are the only expression of undercover bubbling emotion. If more were said, if more discussion were acceptable, if less emotion were suppressed . . . if, if, if . . . if only they had more sex. But what then? Betrayal, jealousy, envy, revenge, injured pride, broken hearts—none of these classic motives for crimes of passion are obviated by sex, on the contrary. The fact is that the residents of the Haus im Wald are still alive, and so by definition, whether they have sex or not, their passions run high.

1

"Please come in, Herr Inspektor," said Schramm with none of his usual condescension. "Do sit down." They both sat at the small table by the window. The curtains were drawn. Schramm had on his overcoat.

"On your way out, Herr Direktor?"

"Yes, actually, I am. My wife is expecting me, I am already late for dinner, but I was waiting—"

"For Michael?"

"Well, yes. Did he tell you—?"

"Why don't you tell me your side of the story?"

"The story?"

"Yes, the story. Or are there more than one?"

Schramm remained silent and looked tormented. Büchner waited. Finally he said, "You have a bit of a habit, Herr Direktor, it seems to me, of telling me pieces of stories and letting me hunt around elsewhere for the other pieces. For example, the key story and the yellow-sticker story. Now, how about saving me a lot of trouble and telling me the Michael story. All of it. At once."

More silence, then, twisting his fingers together, Schramm said, "There is nothing like that between me and Michael."

"Oh," said Büchner and waited again.

"I like the boy. I have no son of my own. When he first came here and I gave him a job, he was like a breath of fresh air. Everybody likes him, well, almost everybody. He's very good with old people. He's devoted to his own grandmother." He fell silent again.

"Yes, that's very nice," said Büchner, and waited.

Schramm stood up and began pacing around the room. "It was Hofer, you see," he said finally, "who put me in a difficult position about all this."

"All this?" said Büchner patiently.

"Yes, you see, I occasionally go to a bar with Hofer after work. He's always been good company, and a day here can sometimes be on the depressing side."

"You don't say."

"Well, one night we had a few drinks too many. It doesn't take many to be too many for me. I'm not a drinking man, you know, in my position it would hardly be appropriate."

"No, of course not, a religious foundation and all that."

"Quite. Well, somehow or other, in the course of the conversation, I found myself saying to him that I had sometimes felt"—there was a long embarrassed pause—"a certain attraction to men. I never acted on it, nor did I want to, nor do I ever intend to, but there it was. I cannot imagine why I said it to him, but Hofer has a way of putting you at your ease and drawing things out of you, and so I said to him things I had never said previously to anyone."

"Do you feel attracted to him?"

"Good heavens, no, he's far too old," said Schramm quickly. "Well, what I mean is . . ."

"You mean you are attracted to younger men, such as Michael."

"Now look, Herr Inspektor, you have to believe me. It is a purely aesthetic thing. You know, sort of the Thomas Mann syndrome. We talked about that on that fateful evening, the way Thomas Mann used to sit in cafés looking at waiters and so on, but never did anything about it, of course. He was a married man with six children."

"Yes," said Büchner, "and he created the pathetic figure of Gustav Aschenbach, lusting in his old age in disease-ridden Venice after a beautiful boy and dying on the beach, without ever touching the boy or even speaking to him, if I remember rightly. A bit different from Michael, whom you speak to every day and"—he paused for emphasis—"who is in your employ!"

"Herr Inspektor. There is nothing like that between me and Michael. Yes, he is a handsome boy, but I have nothing but a fatherly relationship with him. I have always tried to help him. He is good for the Haus im Wald. He creates an atmosphere, for example, in the café, that is hard to find in residences for the elderly, an atmosphere of the outside world, to put it in a word, of youth."

"So why was the evening with Hofer so fateful if it's all so innocent and aesthetic and . . . well . . . literary?"

"Because"—Schramm stopped his pacing and clenched his fists, raising his shoulders in an angry shrug—"Hofer is so . . . smooth. He hasn't really done anything to me, and as far as I know, he didn't spread the information around the Haus, but he did say something about it to Graf, I know that. He and Graf were very thick in the last six months or so—all that acupuncture and massage and so on. You will have seen for yourself that Graf changed his will. A third of his estate was originally to go to the Haus im Wald, but then suddenly, Hofer was to benefit—as well as Frau Hagen, but that was understandable, given the relationship that those two had."

"But surely you do not think that Graf changed his will, as it were, against the Haus im Wald because Hofer told him that you, well, have certain unfulfilled fantasies."

"I know. That sounds absurd. But it was after that evening, at any rate, that Graf treated me with less cordiality and that I started to get the yellow stickers."

"Ah, you got more than you showed me.

"Yes, I threw the others away. They were all implying the same thing, one or two of them actually mentioning Michael. I began to think seriously of looking for another position."

"But why didn't you report them to the police?"

"Herr Inspektor, do you really need to ask that question? I did tell Michael about them, and he said not to worry, other people had got similar things. 'About him?' I asked, and he just laughed and said it came of his being so handsome. None of it seemed to bother him." Schramm smiled. "This made it easier for me to make light of them. He is a charming boy, you know, and I found his reassurances calming. So when he came to me with the confession of taking the seven hundred euros from the professor—I suppose you know about that—well, I just didn't want to see him in trouble, so I gave him the cash and said, 'Just hide it in the room, I'll make sure the Fabians find it.'"

"Herr Direktor, that amounts to covering up a robbery."

"Yes, I suppose it does. Well, now that you know about it, it does."

"You must surely see how it must look to an outsider: as if you were giving him the money as a way of preventing his talking about you. One might well, to say the least of it, suspect blackmail."

"Oh no, that's absurd."

"Is it? Do you suppose Michael could be the writer of the yellow stickers, using the nervousness of the recipients then to drum up a little cash from them?"

"Oh no, Herr Inspektor. Michael is not like that. He is sometimes foolish. It was very foolish of him to take the money, but I believe what he says, that it was an impulse at a time when he was quite desperate. He's not a blackmailer nor a thief."

"One hopes not, since he has a key to all the rooms in the house. And that, I believe, was authorized by you."

Schramm sat down wearily. "Yes, it was."

"You say the yellow stickers started appearing after the fateful evening—do you think Hofer could be the culprit?"

"No, they are much too crude for him. That's not his style. He gets under my skin in different ways, with small remarks and innuendoes to show that he has not forgotten what I said that evening. For example, one day when he noticed the combination number on my briefcase—1750—he said, 'Ah, one hundred and seventy-five. The notorious paragraph.' Well, of course, Paragraph 175 is the well-known one about homosexuals in the old German law book, but of course, I hadn't chosen it because of that. The number just came into my head the first time I had to choose a pin code, and after all, '50 is the year I was born. When I said that to Hofer, he just laughed. You see, that's the problem. Ever since that evening, I've felt he was laughing at me."

Büchner could feel his sympathy for Schramm growing as he pictured the oh-so—smooth Dr. Hofer taking oh-so-subtle advantage of an incautious confidence divulged in a bar. Schramm's distinctly naive stupidity was, however, hard to swallow. "Well, Herr Schramm, I'd better think about all this overnight. We shall no doubt see each other in the morning."

"Yes," said Schramm, visibly relieved that the end of the conversation seemed to be in sight. "But you do believe me, Herr Inspektor, that there is nothing between—"

Büchner interrupted him. "I am here to investigate a murder, not to pass moral judgments. I have to take all this under consideration. Thank you for what I hope is now, as they say, a full and frank disclosure. I will not appreciate new disclosures at some later point."

"Oh no, Herr Inspektor, believe me, that is all I have to disclose. It is, in some ways, a relief to have done so."

"Good night then, Herr Direktor."

Büchner went next door into his office. He had no wish to advertise the fact that he was on his way to Melanchthon. Very soon, he heard Schramm lock up his office, and drawing back his curtains, he saw him drive away. No, Dr. Lessing, he thought. Really not a well-integrated man, but probably not a criminal either. More a case for a psychiatrist than for a policeman. He sighed, picked up his briefcase, and set off in the direction of Melanchthon.

2

"Well, not quite everything is under control," said Eleanor. "For example, it's almost nine o'clock, and neither you nor I have eaten anything all evening. Do you have anything at all in your apartment?"

"I could make some toast," said Christa. "I think there's some bread left, and there's some of that wurst from a day or so ago."

"Ugh. I'd like something hot. I quite fancy an omelet, which wouldn't take a minute if we could rustle up a few eggs."

"People here don't usually borrow food," said Christa doubtfully.

"This isn't usually. Ritter offered to help us, and I also met that nice psychiatrist in the elevator. She did too. Why don't I try one of them?"

"Not the Ritters. I wouldn't want to face Frau Ritter asking for eggs at this time of night."

"You don't have to face any of them. I'm just a crazy foreigner, I'll do it. I'll try Lessing first. She's just along the corridor. Back in a minute."

A good way to broach the fact that the inspector needs to speak to her, she thought, feeling rather clever as she rang Dr. Lessing's bell. The door opened. "Heavens, Dr. Lessing, don't you check who's there?"

"No, I do not choose to do that sort of thing."

"Even after . . ." Eleanor gestured vaguely in the direction of Graf's apartment.

"Do just come in," said Dr. Lessing. "What can I do for you?"

"I'm sorry to bother you, but I'm taking up your offer of help. There are two things. The first one is that Christa and I have been racing about all evening, dealing with Pastor Pokorny and all that, and we haven't had a thing to eat, and I wondered if you could lend us a couple of eggs so that I can make an omelet."

"Yes, of course, I can give you three to be precise. That's all I have left."

"Well, and then there's something else. The eggs were partly my excuse for coming, though in fact I really would like to make an omelet."

Dr. Lessing laughed, went into the kitchen, and came out with the eggs. "And what is the other thing?"

"Pastor Pokorny asked me to ask the inspector to talk to you about . . . a certain topic. The inspector was supposed to come up here to check on things around nine." She looked at her watch. "About now, actually, so I wanted to be able to tell him to come and see you, and I want to be able to tell Christa that *you* asked him to come, because I didn't want her to know that the pastor had suggested this, you see . . ."

"I don't really see," said Dr. Lessing. "But certainly you may tell the inspector that up to ten o'clock, he may come. After that, except in the direst emergency, I would prefer not to answer my door!"

"Well, of course, Dr. Lessing, thank you."

"You'd better go and make that omelet. You seem to be so nervous about what to tell people and how, I'm almost tempted to come out with that old chestnut about how you can't make an omelet without breaking eggs."

"Oh dear, I don't mean to be nervous. I'm trying very hard these days to be direct."

"It doesn't work, does it? If you keep having to think of devious ways to tell one person one thing and another person the same thing in a different way and another person something else that actually *is* different. However, you came here for eggs, not for advice, so off you go, and make your omelet. Good night, Frau Fabian."

"Thank you so much," said Eleanor, and left. Oh Lord, she thought. All these clever old ladies seem to be way ahead of me. She jumped slightly and almost dropped the eggs on hearing someone coming off the staircase and into the third floor. "Oh, Herr Inspektor, good. Before you go in there, can I give you something? I don't really want to tell Christa about it, and Pastor Pokorny said I should give it to you and you should go and talk to Dr. Lessing about it because he and she had the same suspicion, and I have just got these eggs from Dr. Lessing, and she's expecting you."

"Take a deep breath, Frau Fabian. What is it you are supposed to give me?"

"Oh yes. Could you just hold the eggs for me for a moment? They are our supper." She fished around in various pockets and finally found the yellow sticker, which she handed to Büchner. "The pastor found it just awhile ago, it's quite disgusting. He's had them before, he said. He found it on the toilet seat."

"On the toilet seat? So he made it to the toilet?"

"Oh yes. We found him a walker, and he's quite keen on it. Well, that's another story, but perhaps you could go right now to Dr. Lessing, and I'll go and make our omelet."

"OK," he said, reading what was on the sticker.

"Oh, and Herr Inspektor, Pastor Pokorny also said to be sure to tell you"—she dropped her voice to a whisper—"that Herr Ritter had also got one in which the rhyme was *Mike* and *kike*. The pastor was particularly shocked by this."

"As well he might be. Thank you, Frau Fabian," he said and walked toward Dr. Lessing's door.

Eleanor, ringing the Pokorny bell, turned around quickly and said, "Oh, Herr Inspektor, the eggs."

"Ah, yes," he said. He brought them back to her. "Were none of us getting any younger," he said and retreated.

Christa opened the door. "Was that the inspector?" she said.

"Yes, he has to go and talk to Dr. Lessing. I told him we were fine and making omelets. The pastor's surely got a bit of bread and butter." They looked in the kitchen. Butter, but no bread. "Why don't you go and get yours," said Eleanor, "and I'll go on with the omelets."

She started to break the three eggs into a bowl. A simple enough image, she thought, but not bad. Why *was* she always so reluctant to take a direct route to where she wanted to go? Why not simply break the eggs and make the omelet, not try to arrive at the omelet in some indirect way and keep the eggs intact, if cracked. She took deliberate pleasure in cracking the third egg with a knife and dropping the yolk from a great height so that it smashed into the bowl. She beat the three eggs viciously with a fork, laughing at herself and yet enjoying the feeling of destruction. Good God, Eleanor, she thought. What is it that you want to destroy? She could suddenly picture how the murderer of Graf might actually have enjoyed bashing him on the head, if, that is, he'd been angry enough at the time. Why was she so angry? And where was Christa? It didn't take that long to fetch a bit of bread from next door. She found a frying pan, beat the eggs for another pleasurable minute, then thought, I'd better look and see where she is.

At that moment, the phone rang. Eleanor picked it up. "Christa? Why on earth are you calling on the phone?"

Christa's voice was nervous in her ear. "Eleanor, I'm sure there's someone in Graf's room. I got the bread and was just coming back when the door opened and then quickly shut again, just like last night. I shot back in here, and now I'm afraid to come out."

"Oh Lord, and the inspector is with Lessing."

"We can't just wait. Call Lessing. Look in that directory by the phone for her number."

"By then, the person might be gone, and again we won't know who it was. I'm going to look myself."

"For goodness sake, be careful!"

"You can't make an omelet without breaking eggs," Eleanor said.

"What?"

"Never mind. Speak to you in a minute."

She boldly flung open the door of Pokorny's apartment to find herself face to face with Dr. Hofer.

"Why, Dr. Hofer, what are you doing here?"

"I might ask you the same question, Frau Fabian," said Hofer calmly. "I was wondering about Pastor Pokorny, and since I was called in to see a patient in Martin Luther, I thought I would check."

"But it's very late," said Eleanor, looking beyond him to the door of Graf's apartment, which seemed now to be tight shut. "I thought I heard noises in there, and I was going to check," she said.

"Perhaps you should be more careful," said Hofer, very slowly and emphatically. "Anything might happen, you know, and you are a woman alone."

"Well, not quite alone," she said. "I mean, Christa is here."

"Which makes my point," he said.

Slightly annoyed, she could not resist adding, "And the inspector is about."

"Oh, is he?"

"Yes," said Eleanor. "Somewhere about. And you're here now too, in any case. Perhaps we could just both check as to whether Graf's door is locked or not." And she firmly crossed the corridor and tried the handle. "Locked," she said and listened at the door. "No sounds in there now, I must have been mistaken. Unless perhaps you were in there?" That was pretty good, Miss Marple, she thought. And very direct, Dr. Lessing.

"What would I have been doing in there?"

"I have no idea. I'm not even altogether sure what you're doing out here." Even better!

Dr. Hofer's smile stiffened slightly. "Do you need any help with the pastor?"

"No, no, he's asleep. He's much better. He'll be taking the service in the morning."

"In that case, I will take my leave."

What could she say to keep him until the inspector came out? There was something so odd about his being here; the inspector ought to talk to him.

"Perhaps you could just wait," she said, "until I get Christa back into Pokorny's apartment. She's scared of walking the corridor these days."

"And you are not?" smiled Hofer. "An indefatigable Englishwoman."

"American, I'm afraid," said Eleanor. "I became a citizen."

"The stars and stripes forever," said Hofer in one of those appalling fake American accents that German speakers affect.

Why did I ever fancy this man? thought Eleanor. She went to Christa's door and rang the bell. "You can come out," she called. "Dr. Hofer is here."

Christa opened the door and came out into the corridor. Just then the door of the sisters' apartment opened. "What on earth is going on?" said Sister Agatha. "It's after nine o'clock! According to the house rules—"

She stopped as the door of Dr. Lessing's apartment opened and the inspector came out, the Frau Doktor standing in the doorway behind him.

"Having a party, are we?" he said. "Where shall we go? My place or yours?"

3

A moment of silence greeted Büchner's question. All four froze in their tracks, not quite certain how to proceed. Sister Agatha was the first to speak. "Herr Inspektor, this is hardly the time or place for jocular remarks. According to the house rules, silence is supposed to be preserved in the corridors after eight o'clock in the evening. A great deal of loud conversation has been going on out here, and I think it should stop."

"Quite right, Sister," said Büchner. "Let us all withdraw to our various quiet hideaways. Good night, Dr. Lessing, it has been a pleasure."

Dr. Lessing, clearly entertained by the tableau of bemused faces in front of her, smiled and said, "Likewise, Herr Inspektor, good night."

"Come along, Christa, omelet time, finally," said Eleanor, and began to retreat into the pastor's apartment.

Dr. Hofer began bowing polite farewells to the ladies, but Büchner said quickly, "I wonder if you would just give me a minute, Dr. Hofer."

"It's very late," said Hofer. "Couldn't it wait until tomorrow?"

"It could not," said Büchner. "We can go into the locked apartment where we won't disturb anybody. I have a key. I assume it is locked."

"Oh yes, it is," said Eleanor. "Christa thought she saw the door open awhile ago, but when I went out to check, I found Dr. Hofer here in the corridor and the door quite closed. And locked, I tried it."

"Oh, very good," said Büchner, and smiled broadly at her. Her eagerness to join in the sleuthing activities might call to mind a middle-aged girl guide, but it was somehow endearing. And even useful. What the hell was Hofer actually doing in this corridor? "Do go have your omelets," he said. "Perhaps you'd better stay inside though to be on the safe side."

"Exactly what I suggested," said Hofer.

"You did," said Eleanor. "Though I must say, your tone of voice was different."

"Was it really?" said Hofer. "Well, good night, Frau Fabian, Frau Beck."

Büchner unlocked the door to Graf's apartment and motioned Dr. Hofer to go in first. Hofer hesitated at the threshold. "Isn't this rather a macabre setting for a conversation?"

"My dear Dr. Hofer," said Büchner, "it is likely, under the circumstances, to be rather a macabre conversation. Do go in. We are still disturbing Sister Agatha out here." She had continued to stand at her open door. "Good night, Sister," he bowed politely.

Dr. Hofer went in slowly, and Büchner followed him, immediately turning on the bright ceiling light. "Ah, I see," he said at once. "Yet another missive from the dreaded yellow-sticker phantom." He walked over to the chair at the window, sat down, and said, "Well, now, Herr Doktor, why don't you pick that up and bring it over here to this other armchair and make yourself comfortable and read it aloud to me."

"Why should I do that?" said Hofer, his face puckering with disgust.

"Why shouldn't you? Do you know what it says?"

"Of course not. I really do not know what you are talking about."

"Oh, come now, Dr. Hofer, almost everyone in the Haus im Wald seems to know about the yellow stickers, slow though everyone was to bring them to my attention. Come now, pick it up from its place where the head of your friend, Hans Graf, lay, blood seeping into his brain and cerebrospinal fluid seeping from his ears into his carpet."

The always debonair Dr. Hofer looked as if he were going to be sick. He had to step inside the chalk marks to pick up the sticker. He did so and slowly brought it over to the chair, holding it out to Büchner without looking at it.

"No, no," said Büchner. "You read it to me."

"I can't," he said.

"Why not? You haven't looked at it yet."

"I can't do it," said Hofer. "I can't do it."

"A fastidious gentleman. It must be an especially bad one. Allow me."

Hofer closed his eyes. Büchner took the sticker from his hands and read aloud, enunciating each word slowly and clearly:

HOFER HOFER

KNEELING BY THE SOFA

SUCKING THE DICK

OF THE RICH OLD PRICK

"My, oh my, Dr. Hofer. That is really not a nice one. Where do you get this language from?"

"It is not my language," said Hofer through clenched teeth. "No one who knows me could think that. And why should I write such ugly rubbish about myself?"

"To make it look as if you didn't write it? That's an obvious old trick, is it not? You did put it here, didn't you, Herr Doktor?

You were here a short while ago, were you not? Why else would you be wandering this corridor at this time of night?"

"I was concerned about Pastor Pokorny," said Hofer.

"Oh yes, that's your story, no doubt, once discovered in the vicinity. It's not very plausible, however. And there's this little yellow verse, how did it get here?"

"How do I know? Anyone could have put it here."

"Only someone with a key to the door. What is the combination number of Herr Direktor Schramm's safe, Herr Dr. Hofer?"

"I have absolutely no idea."

"You have never noticed the combination number on his briefcase?"

"Why should I have? For heaven's sake, Herr Inspektor, various people in this house have master keys. For example, Frau Huber, as is well-known, and Michael in the café, as is not so well-known, and obviously Schramm himself. Anyone of them could have let themselves into this room."

"Not one of them, however, is wandering this corridor tonight, and you are. And not one of them is mentioned with such distinction on this latest sticker. Shall I read it again?"

"For God's sake, Herr Inspektor. What exactly do you want from me?"

"The truth," said Büchner. "That's all. Nothing but the truth. For example, what, truthfully, was your relationship with"—he gestured to the fading chalk marks—"the unfortunate Herr Graf?"

"You cannot imagine that I had anything to do with his death."

"I would like to stop imagining and simply hear from you, as I say, the truth. Does this charming missive have any truth in it? I mean, were the services you performed for, or shall we say on, the unfortunate Herr Graf more interesting than simply acupuncture and, as it were, chiropractic massage?"

"Of course not," said Hofer, again wrinkling his face into an expression of extreme distaste. "That wasn't my idea . . . That is to say, I didn't write this thing, for heaven's sake."

"It was someone else's idea?"

"I didn't say that. But of course, it must have been."

"And why would anyone write such a thing if there is no truth in it?"

"A sick mind can think of any number of things."

"Well, if it is only the invention of a sick mind, you can have no objection to telling me what your relationship with Herr Graf was."

"I was his doctor. As I have told you, he suffered from severe back pain. In the last few months, I helped him with acupuncture and with massage . . . massage of his head and neck."

"Ah, yes," said Büchner. "The same head that lay there—"

"Please, Herr Inspektor," interrupted Hofer. "I have a graphic enough picture of that terrible event without your constantly alluding to it."

"I am alluding," said Büchner, "to a very nasty, slow death of an old man, and my interest is simply and solely to find out who was responsible for it. I really do not care, personally, whether you"—he consulted the sticker—"sucked his dick or not."

Hofer stood up angrily. "Will you kindly drop the language of that monstrosity," he said. "It is not mine, and I had nothing to do with the death of Graf. I became quite friendly with him in recent months. But this"—he pointed to the sticker—"is sheer nonsense."

"And yet he left you a considerable sum of money, did he not? Rather a lot for someone who was only his friendly acupuncturist, don't you think? How do you explain that?"

There was a long pause. "You really will have to give some answer to that question," said Büchner. "The heir to any part of a fortune is an automatic suspect in the murder of the person who wrote the will. You've surely seen enough TV drama to know that."

"I am not a TV watcher," said Hofer. "Try that one on Frau Huber. She's the big TV watcher around here."

"I shall," said Büchner. "But she did not inherit from Graf, and you did, in quite a big way. How do you explain it without resorting to the notion of . . . services rendered?"

"Very well," said Hofer. "The truth of the matter is that neither Graf nor I were very happy about Director Schramm's management of this institution, and Graf thought that, well, I would make a better director. We had ideas of making a massage room here and even a gym of sorts. He wanted to use his influence with the board to help this come about, and he told me that he would make me a legacy in his will that would express his personal confidence in me."

Poor old Schramm, thought Büchner. No match for this guy. "Talking of services rendered," he said, "did you prescribe Viagra for Graf?"

"Not guilty. I happen to know that he, like many Austrians who do not want to discuss this sort of thing with their GP, ordered it off the Internet, in his case, courtesy of Frau Zimmermann. She is a very open-minded lady, you know."

"But he did discuss this with you?"

"He mentioned it, in a joking way, once or twice."

"People do seem to confide in you, Doctor, don't they? Oh, and that reminds me of one last question I have for you, then perhaps we can call it a day for now. You were seen this morning at about eleven thirty drinking champagne with Frau Hagen in the Café Sacher in the Kärntnerstraße. Isn't this a little odd under the circumstances?"

"Circumstances?"

"Well yes. She is grief-stricken, and you are also presumably sad at the passing of your friend, and—shall we say—benefactor. Is this a time to drink celebratory champagne in a *schickimicki* café?"

"It so happened," said Hofer, "that Frau Hagen and I found ourselves this morning at the reading of the will in Schönholz' office. When we came out, Frau Hagen did not feel well, so I suggested we go and sit somewhere for a minute. The café is nearby."

"One might be forgiven for thinking that, having just heard of the large bequests, you were celebrating something, champagne and all that."

"Actually, it was prosecco. And sparkling wine is good for the stomach and the nerves. It has a calming effect."

"Ah yes, well, you are the doctor. You would know. And what, by the way, is your relationship with Frau Hagen? Any acupuncture or massage"—he looked at the sticker—"or anything, there?"

"I find these innuendoes offensive. I did occasionally help Frau Hagen with acupuncture and massage. She is an older lady, and let me remind you, Herr Inspektor, it is my profession."

"Indeed, Dr. Hofer, it is, and one that seems to be much appreciated by . . . senior citizens. Well, perhaps we can leave it there for now. I trust you will be in the Haus im Wald tomorrow morning? Have to keep a close eye on the place, don't you, if you are hoping to be director?"

"I would appreciate it, Herr Inspektor, if you would not pass that information on to anyone."

"And I would appreciate it, Herr Doktor, if by the next time we meet, you will have decided to tell me all you know about"—he held up the sticker with the tips of his finger—"these ugly little things. Good night, Dr. Hofer. You can let yourself out. I shall sit here for a while and meditate." He looked down at the sticker and, in a low voice, began to recite: "Hofer, Hofer, kneeling by the . . ." Dr. Hofer hastened through the door and slammed it shut. Dear, dear, thought Büchner. Sister Agatha won't like that. He drew open the curtains of Herr Graf's window and sat back once again to look at the night sky.

4

When Büchner disappeared behind Hofer into Graf's apartment, Christa was about to follow Eleanor into the pastor's apartment, but Sister Agatha spoke unexpectedly from her doorway. "May I have a brief word with you, Frau Beck?"

"Ask her to come in here, for heaven's sake," whispered Eleanor loudly. "I must finally make those omelets."

"Would you like to come in here for a moment, Sister? We are still trying to get our supper together. It has been a busy evening," said Christa.

"Very well." Sister Agatha came across the corridor and hesitated for a moment at the door.

"Please do come in," said Eleanor impatiently. "I hope you will excuse me, but I have to make an omelet in the kitchen."

She noticed suddenly that Sister Agatha looked quite exhausted. Her fine eyes looked sunken in her high-cheekboned face, and there were dark patches under her eyes, as if she hadn't slept for a long time. Eleanor thought of how she had rather admired the way Sister Agatha looked when she first saw her in the café few days before Christmas. Tall, straight, and somehow aristocratic-looking—she looked absolutely right in the plain gray garb of the sisterhood. Her thick gray hair pulled back from her face in a chignon gave her a severe but very dignified look that Eleanor envied. For the first time now, Eleanor thought that she looked unsure of herself, old, almost frightened. "Do sit down, Sister," she said in a warmer voice. "You look tired."

"Tired?" said Agatha vaguely. "Yes, I suppose I feel tired."

"Would you like some coffee or tea?" asked Eleanor, not having the foggiest idea of whether such were to be found in the pastor's kitchen.

"No, thank you. It's far too late for such stimulants. I wouldn't sleep a wink all night. You seem to have quite settled in here."

"Oh no," said Eleanor without thinking. "We're only staying here till the inspector comes back."

"Eleanor!" said Christa.

"The inspector?" said Agatha, standing up. "What is he doing here?"

"Oh well, he just said he'd be checking," said Eleanor lamely. "Do sit down."

"I have to be going in any case. Do please go and make your omelets, Frau Fabian. I just wanted a word with Frau Beck."

Eleanor retreated into the kitchen, leaving the door open, and put some butter in the frying pan.

"I only wanted to check with you, Frau Beck, about the service in the morning for Frau Winkler. Sister Barbara and I have chosen hymns and some readings, and we thought you might like to take a reading, since you were friendly with Frau Winkler."

"But, Sister Agatha, Pastor Pokorny is all prepared to take the service. I have agreed to do one reading and he another, and one hymn Frau Winkler always wanted was "A Safe Stronghold Our God Is Still." I can play that myself on the chapel piano.

Frau Winkler always said, you see, she wanted Pastor Pokorny to take the service if she died first."

"But Mr. Pokorny is ill."

"He is doing much better at the moment, Sister Agatha. He has a walker, and he can manage very well with that."

"'A Safe Stronghold,'" said Agatha, "does not seem to me very appropriate for what amounts to a funeral service. It is so warlike."

From the kitchen, Eleanor suddenly heard a strong male voice as Pastor Pokorny emerged slowly from his bedroom in his pajamas, pushing the walker past the kitchen into the living room, reciting slowly:

And though they take our life
Goods, honor, children, wife,
Yet is their profit small;
These things shall vanish all,
The city of God remaineth.

"A fine old Lutheran hymn, Sister. Why would it not be appropriate for the widow of the martyred Reverend Theodor Winkler? More than appropriate, I suggest."

Eleanor turned off the gas under the butter and followed the pastor to the door of the living room. There was absolute silence as the two old Christian antagonists stared at each other. Perhaps it's time for a non-Christian intervention, thought Eleanor. "Couldn't you both take part in the service?" she said brightly.

Sister Agatha flushed and said stiffly, "Please conduct the service as you see fit, Herr Pokorny. Good night." And she walked out.

"I need to go to the toilet," said the pastor, and he headed to the bathroom.

"What," said Eleanor, "was all that about?"

"Oh dear, Eleanor, you have no idea. You see, the Protestants in Austria, that is, largely the Lutherans, were very nationalistically minded, way before the Nazi period, Pan-German nationalists, that is, and a lot of them therefore supported the annexation of Austria by the Nazis. They had no objection to the Germans taking over

Catholic Austria, and many Catholics therefore saw the Protestants as a Nazi church. I mean, I'm using a lot of shorthand here, and I'm no judge of what went on. It was all hushed up after the war in any case, and for years, the Lutherans avoided politics altogether, until a lot of them came out for the Greens in the nineties, a big switch, and that's really when I fell in with them. They are very vociferous now, you know, against racism and hostility to foreigners and all that, and they have loads of women pastors. But Agatha is older, and I know she tended to avoid Frau Winkler, as all the good Lutherans of the older generation did, because of what happened to her husband. Either they disapproved of what he did or they had a bad conscience about what happened to him, either way, they couldn't deal with her. But Frau Winkler was a wonderfully happy woman. She loved life, the way Pastor Pokorny does. I wish she hadn't died."

"Oh Lord," said Eleanor. "It's all so complicated."

"Yes, that generation has a lot of skeletons in its cupboard. Where are the omelets?"

"And where is the inspector? I hope the pastor is all right in there."

They heard the toilet flush. The pastor came out and waved to them from the door. "Back to bed," he said cheerfully.

"I think he feels he won that round against the Lutherans," said Eleanor. "So do I. Great the way he recited that verse. Quite took the wind out of Agatha's sails."

"Yes," said Christa doubtfully. "But it's not a good idea to antagonize Sister Agatha around here."

Eleanor threw the beaten eggs into the butter. "Well, I don't know. I thought she looked exhausted tonight, didn't you? I wonder what's going on. There was that funny business of Barbara crying today in the toilet. The two of them seem to be going through something. Funny she's still fussing about Frau Winkler's memorial service."

"Oh well, that's Agatha. She takes these things very seriously and wants them to be all in order, in her order, that is," said Christa. "But you know, I've thought again about Christmas Day. I really did see her coming out of Graf's apartment. I let myself get in a muddle when the inspector asked me about it because I was afraid of pointing the finger—and I suppose I am a bit afraid of Sister Agatha—but I've been trying to recall the details of that day, and I've realized that it wasn't at three when I was coming back from dinner, but more like five when I went down to the chapel, just to have a half hour there by myself—an old Catholic habit, you know. And from the end of the corridor—it was pretty dark—I saw her come out through the door and close it behind her. I went on downstairs and paid no attention. I mean, we weren't all focused on Graf's door then."

"Here, Christa, for God's sake, eat this omelet finally." They sat down at the kitchen table. "Are you positive it was Agatha?"

"Well, you know, I'm very nearsighted, but I'm positive it was a woman in the gray cloak those two always wear to go out. I thought at the time it was Agatha. She cast a long shadow on the wall, and Agatha is so tall."

"Could it have been Barbara? I mean, shadows are deceptive. And they both wear those cloaks."

"I suppose so. But in any case, it was one of them, I'm sure of that, and that *was* the day of the . . . murder. I still can't bear to use that word."

"Christa, this time, you must tell this to the inspector."

"Yes, I suppose I must. Wherever is he, by the way? It's getting on for ten o'clock. Do you think we should go and check?"

"Go into Graf's place? Now? Certainly not. He told us to stay here."

There was a knock at the door. "There he is," said Eleanor, and flung open the door enthusiastically.

Outside was Sister Agatha. "Where is the inspector?" she said. "When I got back to the apartment, Barbara wasn't there. And now I can't find her anywhere."

"Oh Lord," said Eleanor. "We think he's still in there." The three women stood and looked as the door to Graf's apartment opened.

5

Sitting in Graf's armchair after Hofer's departure, looking out at the stormy sky, Büchner wondered if the dead man had sometimes sat here, waiting for the moon to appear on this side of the house. What did Graf think about in his last weeks in the Haus im Wald? He had been very happy, so the good Dr. Hofer had reported in their more amicable discussion a day or so ago. The happiest man in the world, he had supposedly said. Happy because of Frau Hagen? Because of the Viagra? No doubt that had helped his senior sex life, and why not? Good old Frau Zimmermann, thought Büchner. Tax returns *and* discreet orders on the Internet. Well, Graf had not forgotten her in his will, the will he made three months ago. Chances are the Viagra had been helping him for some time. Was Frau Hagen the only love of his senior life? Büchner looked down at the yellow sticker and laughed at the picture of discomfort on Hofer's face. No, he didn't really believe that Hofer indulged in that sort of activity. He would hardly want to ruin his good suits kneeling by the sofa. A guffaw escaped Büchner at the thought. He wasn't sure, however, that he would put it past the charming boy, Michael. But what did any of this have to do with the actual murder? Hofer stood to gain less in the long run from Graf's death than from his continued life and patronage, if his ambition really was to take over the Haus im Wald from Schramm, and certainly this move would put him in a very good position from which to expand some of his lucrative activities—massage, acupuncture, physiotherapy—for the elderly. He would be able to employ others to do much of the actual hands-on work and develop his own reputation for the organization of geriatric care. Büchner was sure that he would be good at this sort of thing, and why not? It could help many old people. And yet the way Hofer apparently wormed his way into people's confidences only to use these against them was, to say the least of it, unsavory. It did not make him a murderer, however. Absent the calculated gain of a premeditated crime, Hofer faded from the scene as an actual suspect, since a crime of passion could hardly be imagined from him. Smooth and suave as he was, passionate, he surely was not. Nor could he have written the yellow stickers. There Büchner agreed with Schramm. They were not Hofer's style; the look of disgust on his handsome face earlier had been genuine enough. But he was mixed up with them in some way, of that Büchner was equally sure.

Who had actually written them? Büchner had already narrowed the possible culprits in his own mind to one, but he had been questioning himself as to whether this was just a prejudice on his part because he instinctively disliked the woman. She, that is, Frau Huber, seemed to him capable of personal cruelty; and there was a coarseness about her, covered up as it was by her neat uniform and her manifest competence. The suspicions of Dr. Lessing and Pastor Pokorny had apparently gone in the same direction. "She is," Dr. Lessing had said, "not really liked in a warm way by anybody, and the isolation of the unloved and perhaps unlovable can lead to strange excrescences of behavior." Pastor Pokorny had apparently commented to her that at the center of Frau Huber's bustling bonhomie was a cold heart. They had both thought her capable of inflicting pain, Lessing had told him, but emphasized that this was a judgment based only on intuition, not on any actual evidence. Why, he had asked her, hadn't she told him about the yellow stickers before? No one, she had said, had actually given her one. She had thought it best to let them come to his attention, if they did, directly out of his investigation of the murder, so that the lines connecting them with the murder, if there were any, would be drawn by those actually involved. "I am only an observer in all this," she had said. "And though my observations are at your service should you ask for them, you will arrive at a solution, I am sure, viscerally, and not through the observations of others." This was indeed the way he usually arrived at solutions, but being sure viscerally that Frau Huber sat in her decorated apartment writing obscene rhymes did not bring him much closer to knowing, viscerally, who killed Graf.

The lines of the picture involving Huber, Hofer, and Schramm were now clearer. Quite likely, Hofer had 'discovered' in his subtle way that Frau Huber indulged a certain nastiness by writing dirty little rhymes to people; and he had seen in this a chance to undermine Schramm's confidence in himself, as well as loosen his hold on the reins of the house. If more and more residents began to be harassed by yellow stickers, the reputation of the house, under Schramm's guidance, would falter. This all seemed plausible. But what about Graf? He had been a recipient of yellow stickers; Büchner knew this from Frau Hagen. But the cowardly writer of anonymous rhymes was probably not in the business of knocking people on the head, frontally at that. Maybe some lines of this particular picture were missing, or maybe, if he could only see it, the picture of the murder was made of completely different lines. Passionate anger striking a fatal blow—from whom could one imagine this? Somehow it did not sit well on naughty, charming Michael. Frau Hagen? Yes, possibly. But to what extent was her passion the passion of a lifelong actress? Practiced and under control? And then the sisters? There seemed to be little to connect them to Graf—the old story of Agatha, the youthful jilted fiancée—but that was so long ago. And yet Barbara was keeping something back. Passion, Büchner felt, was not lacking in any of these three ladies, though he had yet to see how or why it might have degenerated into murder. The faces of the three of them came and went before his eyes, one replacing the other in the ambiguous lines, one blotting out the other, and then being blotted out.

Feeling his eyes closing, he forced himself to stand up. It was almost ten o'clock. He was neglecting his duties as night watchman for Pastor Pokorny. He leaned forward to close the curtains and was astonished to see one of the sisters' motor scooters careering rather wildly over the new snow in the driveway. He hurried to the door and opened it.

"Oh, Herr Inspektor, thank goodness," said Eleanor.

"What is happening?" he said, looking at Agatha, who looked distraught.

"It's Barbara," she said. "She's gone. I've looked everywhere."

"I know she's gone," said Büchner. "I just saw her riding away on her scooter."

"Driving away?" Agatha clutched at the doorpost. "But where could she be going at this time of night?"

"You ladies just stay here by the telephone. I'm going after her," said Büchner. He ushered them quickly back into the apartment, jotted down the phone number on his way past the phone, ran along the corridor and down the stairs, and used the master key to let himself out quickly through the front door. He cursed his car, which didn't start right away; and then when the motor started up, he skidded down the driveway himself and followed the tracks of the scooter into the road through the forest. Someway along this road, he saw exactly what he had feared. The scooter tracks veered off into the woods, and the scooter lay under a tree, its front wheel and handlebars buckled. Some distance away, he could see Barbara lying facedown in the snow, her gray hood covering her head. He got out of the car and ran toward her. Without moving her, he carefully felt for her pulse. He pulled out his cell phone and dialed the station, identified himself, and asked for immediate help. He then dialed the number of Porkorny's apartment. "I've found her," he said. "She's had an accident. She is still alive. No, please don't come. The ambulance will be here any minute, and they will take her away." He could hear Sister Agatha's voice in the background, "Where are they taking her? Where are they taking her?"

"Please, Frau Fabian," he said, "try to keep everyone calm. I will be in touch as soon as I can." He stood over the motionless body of Barbara and cursed himself. I should have prevented this, he thought as the sirens of the ambulance screamed through the woods.

Chapter 16

"O, call back yesterday, bid time return"—poetic words often pressed into service in meditations on old age and recently heard on radio Ö1 in a broadcast on the slowing down of the aging clock in modern times. Were older people, the commentator asked, really physiologically younger now than in earlier times? Or did they simply make great efforts to appear younger? Some residents of the Haus im Wald might have recognized their own efforts in this broadcast. Frau Hagen, for example, seemed to slow down the clock quite successfully with elegant clothes, diet watching, and no doubt, cosmetics. Frau Zimmermann employed deliberate mental exercise on the computer, and the late Herr Graf backed up the artistry of his excellent tailor with physical training and, it must be said, Viagra. But the most determined efforts at calling back yesterday must ultimately fail—they do not make time return. And, as Herr Graf, "the happiest man in the world," has demonstrated, one violent act on one ill-fated day can render null and void all efforts to slow down the aging clock. One stumble on the carpet has almost done the same for Pastor Pokorny. In any case, Shakespeare's cry for the return of yesterday is not really an expression of the nostalgic longing of the aged for lost youth and beauty. It is the admission of a lost cause, bad news broken by Lord Salisbury to King Richard II telling him that he is one day too late to save his kingdom. "O, call back yesterday, bid time return / And thou shalt have twelve thousand fighting men." The twelve thousand Welshmen who would have fought for him waited ten days and dispersed when

he did not come. That was yesterday. Then the king came, one day too late. And so it is sometimes. If you had known yesterday what you know today, you might at least have had a fighting chance. Perhaps the most enviable residents of the Haus im Wald are the ones who grasp in time that looking their present reality in the eye may give them a better chance to fight another day than calling back any of their yesterdays.

1

Eleanor closed the door behind the departing inspector. "Do sit down, Sister Agatha. I'll make a cup of tea, shall I?"

"The English and their tea," said Christa.

"Well, it can't hurt, can it? Not much chance of sleep now, in any case."

"I cannot bear to sit here drinking tea," said Agatha, "while . . ." she stopped.

"Do please sit down. Put the kettle on anyway, Christa," said Eleanor. "There's nothing we can do except wait to hear from the inspector. Have you any idea what possessed your friend to take off like that?"

Agatha sat down on a straight-backed chair and folded her hands in her lap, looking not at Eleanor but straight ahead. There was a long silence, and Eleanor made an almighty effort not to fill it with verbiage.

Still without looking at her, Agatha said, "She hasn't been herself lately." She gave a short laugh. "That's the sort of thing one is supposed to say, isn't it?"

"Is there something you really want to say now and are not saying?"

"I am frightened," said Agatha, and Eleanor saw that she was twisting her hands together tightly—still very beautiful hands, long fingers, the blue veins standing out on the back of them, as they do in the old, but in what seemed to be not a disfigurement but a delicate filigree. "I am frightened," she said again. Her unexpected vulnerability created for Eleanor a picture of a very different woman from Sister Agatha, martinet of the Haus im Wald, a quite lovely woman, thought Eleanor with surprise.

"Oh, Sister Agatha," she said foolishly. "Please don't be frightened. I'm sure the inspector will find Sister Barbara and everything will be all right."

"He will find her," said Agatha. "But everything will not be all right."

"Here is the tea," said Christa. "I've found sugar, but no milk."

She was putting down a tray with three cups on the little coffee table when the phone rang. Startled, she slopped the tea into the saucers. Eleanor ran to the phone. "They've found her. She's had an accident," she repeated the inspector's words to the other two as he spoke. "Ambulance on the way."

"Where are they taking her?" said Agatha, who had jumped to her feet and was holding out her hand wanting to take the receiver herself. "Where are they taking her?"

Eleanor hung up. "He says stay calm. We have to wait by the phone."

"But where are they?" said Agatha. "I must go after them."

"No," said Eleanor firmly. "The ambulance will be picking them up any minute, he said. We need to stay here until we know where they are."

"But what's happened? How is she?"

"She is alive, Sister Agatha, he said that."

"Alive!" Agatha almost wailed. "You mean she might be close to death? I must go." She started toward the door.

"Please, dear Sister Agatha," said Eleanor, putting a hand on her arm, which Sister Agatha impatiently shook off. "We all need to stay here, keep calm, wait till we know exactly where they are taking her."

"Have some tea," said Christa, who was vainly trying to mop up the tea out of the saucers with a paper towel.

"Yes," said Eleanor. "Let's all sit down and have a cup of tea."

Agatha waved an impatient hand, and Eleanor, hoping again to detain her, asked, "Is this what you were frightened of, that there would be . . . an accident?"

"Frau Fabian, Barbara has ridden her motor scooter through the forest on snowy roads many times and has never had an accident."

"Yes, but if she were very agitated about something . . ."

"I have known for days that she was, as you put it, agitated about something. And I did nothing about it. If she has crashed her motor scooter, it is my fault."

"Oh no, surely not," said Eleanor.

"Eleanor," said Christa uncharacteristically loudly. "If Sister Agatha thinks it is her fault, she probably knows what she is talking about. You can't go around telling people what they are supposed to think and feel."

Eleanor felt instantly upset, as if she had been slapped in the face. "I'm sorry, no, I didn't mean to do that," she said.

"It's all right," said Agatha. "It really doesn't matter. You are both trying to be kind. But I think I need to be alone. Please knock on my door as soon as you hear from the inspector. I'll get dressed for the outdoors. I can go on the scooter once I know where."

"Oh no," said Eleanor. "I have the car outside. I'll take you wherever you have to go. We don't want any more scooter accidents on these bad roads."

Agatha hesitated. "Very well. Perhaps that is more sensible under the circumstances. I hope we do not have to wait for long." She stood up, straightening her shoulders and back with deliberate effort, and left.

"I don't know if we ought to let her be by herself," said Eleanor.

"If that's what she wants . . ." said Christa.

"You seem to think I am so dreadfully bossy," said Eleanor. "And yet I rarely seem to manage to do what I want."

"I'm sorry. I didn't mean to snap at you. But people who spend a lot of time alone, like me, tend to take other people at their word. I mean, all the social chitchat tends to drop away from you over the years, and you go back to the biblical 'let your yea be yea and your nay be nay' type of communication. If Agatha says she feels guilty, then OK, she's probably got something to feel guilty about."

There was a lot in that, thought Eleanor. Good Lord, now even Christa was getting the better of her. "What do you think she's guilty of?"

"Haven't got a clue. I'm not a detective. And I don't want to be one. She's very upset, obviously. I've never seen her look so vulnerable before."

"Probably that's why she wants to be alone. Doesn't want to show that side of herself."

"Eleanor, the woman is devastated. I doubt if she's thinking of the impression she's making."

"No, of course, you're right. Oh, thank God, there's the phone."

"Herr Inspektor? Yes, thank you for calling. Yes. Yes, I'll be bringing her in the car. May be half an hour before we get there. OK. Yes, I'll drive carefully."

"She's going into the emergency surgery unit, AKH," she said to Christa. "She might pull through. That's all he'll say. Agatha had better come, he said." She was already putting on her coat. "Oh Lord, Pastor Pokorny. What will you do, Christa, if he . . ."

"The least of our worries at the moment. I'm sure he'll be able to manage. But I have to stay here obviously. Please drive carefully."

"Yes, OK, bye, Christa." She gave her a big hug. "You're very good for me, you know," she said, wondering as she said it if it were really true, but noting with pleasure that Christa looked pleased. "Oh," she said, "if I come back alone, will you let me in?"

"Of course, I'll just rest a bit on this couch."

"Yes, try to get some sleep. You've also got that service in the morning to think about. Put the chain on the door though, to be on the safe side."

Christa saw her out, and Eleanor went across the corridor to knock on Sister Agatha's door. They all seemed to have forgotten last night's funny business of the doors. She tried the Graf door handle—tight shut. She knocked at the next door, and Agatha came out promptly in her outdoor clothes.

"We're to go to the AKH," Eleanor said. "Sister Barbara is in emergency surgery." Agatha nodded, and the two women went quickly down the two flights of stairs into the lobby. Midnight past, the house was very quiet. It was ice-cold outside, and the snow crunched under their feet. She started up the car and set off yet again in the direction of the AKH. Precisely what she had said she wouldn't be doing again that day. Well, in any case, it wasn't that day anymore. That day was already yesterday. Should she try to talk to Sister Agatha, who was sitting beside her in the car with her hood still on her head, partially hiding her face? This reminded Eleanor of the odd business of the hooded sister whom Christa had seen coming out of Graf's apartment at about five o'clock on Christmas Day. This was hardly a time for interrogation. Still, nothing ventured, nothing gained. The headlights of the car fell upon a whole lot of tire tracks into and out of the wood. Maybe that was where Barbara . . . Best then to distract Sister Agatha's attention in any case. "Please say, Sister Agatha, if you'd rather not talk, but there's something perhaps you ought to know. Christa thought she saw you coming out of Graf's apartment on the afternoon of Christmas Day."

"Oh," said Agatha wearily. "So it was Frau Beck who said that. Well, it wasn't me. I mean, I didn't."

"No, but the person she saw—and I really don't think she imagines things, she's certainly nearsighted—but the person she saw was definitely wearing a gray cloak and hood. She assumed it was you because it seemed to her to be a tall person—it cast a long shadow, she said. But shadows can be deceptive, and maybe it was a short person. I mean, to put it bluntly, perhaps it was Sister Barbara."

A sharp intake of breath greeted this remark and then silence. Looking sideways, Eleanor saw Agatha's hands, now elegantly clad in long silver gray leather gloves, clench and unclench on her lap.

"That's hardly possible," she said. "We were together all day on Christmas Day."

There was a long silence as Eleanor drove from the expressway into the Heiligenstädter Straße. Then Agatha said in a low voice, barely audible above the sound of the car, "She did go for a walk. She wanted some fresh air. We were going down to the chapel at five thirty, so she went out beforehand at about a quarter to five." Eleanor said nothing. "What time did Frau Beck say she saw this person?"

"Well, she thought it was about five."

The silence in the car was beginning to be unendurable, and Eleanor eventually said, "I'm sorry I brought it up at a time like this. There's surely a simple explanation. All that matters now is that we get to the hospital in time."

"In time?" repeated Agatha. "We can't really get there in time, can we? The accident has happened. And I did nothing to prevent it. Nothing."

"Until we're there, we won't know how bad it is. You mustn't blame yourself."

"Oh, don't talk nonsense," said Agatha. "You don't know what you're talking about." She pulled herself up short. "I'm sorry. I am grateful to you for driving me into the hospital. But I need to think now."

She closed her eyes, and Eleanor thought, It's true, I don't know what I'm talking about. But if Barbara really had come out of Graf's apartment at five o'clock, it seemed as if she might have murdered him. She'd have to tell the inspector about this. If only she and Christa had been clearer about this earlier, they might have prevented the accident too. Though if Barbara had really murdered Graf, then maybe a fatal accident would be better for her than being arrested. Why hadn't she talked to Barbara earlier when she found her crying in the ladies' room? Why all this reserve and silence when terrible things were happening? Why not tackle people's misery head on and try to help instead of always looking the other way and pretending one hadn't noticed anything? That's what she was doing now, of course. Agatha seemed to be in a state of tense agony. And she couldn't think of a thing to say. She drove in silence to the Gürtel and then around it to the AKH. "We'll soon be there, Sister Agatha," said Eleanor, turning into the now-familiar emergency room entrance. She heard Agatha take a deep breath. "You hurry on in," said Eleanor, stopping the car at the door. "I'll park the car and follow you."

"Thank you," said Agatha, and got out, pushed back the hood from her head, and straightened her shoulders, almost gulping in the cold air. Eleanor saw her in the rearview mirror pausing at the entrance and bowing her head for a moment. In prayer? thought Eleanor. Well, at least she's got that, which is more than I have.

2

Büchner followed the ambulance in his car. It was almost midnight. He drove fast, but not as fast as the ambulance, screaming its way intimidatingly through traffic lights onto the autobahn ahead. He rarely drove a police car with sirens of its own. Usually, he was satisfied with his own way of policing, merging into whatever landscape the scene of the crime presented him with and trying to understand it from the inside. If this didn't work in a short space of time, he would be satisfied to turn to more orthodox police methods, but he bitterly berated himself now for his slowness on the day just ending, particularly in the matter of the little woman whose body had surely been badly broken in its collision with that huge snow-covered tree, which was still standing there, showing scarcely a mark, while the ambulance carried her away. He had taken off his coat and put it over her in a vain attempt to keep in some of her body heat while he stood waiting for long minutes for the ambulance. Just about four hours earlier, there had been a moment when he could perhaps have prevented this from happening at all. He had asked her about the fingerprinting, and she had evaded the question, saying she would go to the police station in the morning and do it. He had known at the time that he shouldn't let it go at that. She needed time to think, she'd said. The ambulance was now out of sight and out of earshot as he turned into the Billrothstraße. His mistake had been to equate her need for time to think with his own. He'd wanted to think it all through himself before taking any definitive steps. He had welcomed the prolongation of ambiguity for just a bit longer, or so it seemed to him now, looking back on it. He really did not think that his old comrade, Barbara, had actually murdered a man, so it did not seem desperately urgent to push her into an explanation. What he had not seen was her own desperation. When he had talked to her, his head had been occupied with two things, the subplot of the yellow stickers, and what seemed to him then to be a crucial line in the main plot, namely the role of Frau Hagen, of beauty and the loss of beauty, the time-is-a-strange-thing theme of the *Rosenkavalier*. The face of the lovely aging Frau Hagen had blotted out in those crucial investigating hours the not-so-lovely, earnest face of the small gray-clad Sister Barbara, not made for a tragic fate, but now perhaps forever still in an ugly accident that he should have prevented. He would not have a chance to finish the conversation as he had planned to do early in the morning. It was too late. Looking at his watch as he drew into the AKH parking lot, he saw that the new day had begun.

He identified himself at the entrance desk and was directed to the waiting room of the emergency surgery unit. An orderly at the entrance told him that Barbara was already on the operating table. He sat down, not grateful as he usually was, for time to think. He wanted now to act, not to think. His old enemy, procrastination, fostered by his early literary studies and, he had often hoped, overcome in his successful career as a detective, still hovered about him, and sometimes won the battle, as in the latest instance. Some lines rolled through his head that he had written years ago:

Procrastination is a vice
Why is it then so very nice
To sit and think
And bide your time
And watch the birds
And see the sky
The sun, the clouds,
The days go by
And put off till tomorrow
What others in their sorrow
Want you to do today at any price?

Maybe Barbara had wanted him to push her on the fingerprinting question. And if he had, maybe he would not be sitting here and she lying in there. But think forward, the detective in him admonished the interloping man of letters. The door of the waiting room opened, and Schmidt stood there, holding a bag containing Sister Barbara's belongings. "This was in her pocket, addressed to you, Herr Inspektor." Büchner opened the sealed envelope and read:

Dear Georg,

This is the best way out of my impossible life. I am responsible for Graf's death. I thought I could live with it, but I cannot. You will find the cane that killed him if you walk along the path in front of the building beyond Melanchthon. Look on the right hand side of the path. I wiped it clean of fingerprints. Tell Agatha this is what I want. She must go on with her work. I love her. Please do this for an old comrade.

Barbara

He put it in his pocket as the door of the waiting room opened again, and Agatha came in, white-faced but resolute. "Herr Inspektor," she said, drawing off a long gray glove and giving him her hand, cold despite its glove. "Please tell me what is happening."

"Barbara drove her motor scooter into a tree," he said. "She was thrown some distance and is very badly hurt. I don't think it was an accident."

There was silence while Agatha stared at the door to the operating room. "I know that this is a bad time to be asking questions," said Büchner.

"An impossible time," said Agatha very tensely.

"But I have no choice," he said. "If I had asked Barbara some more questions yesterday, perhaps she would not be in there now."

"Or if I had," said Agatha. She stood up and started to pace the room. Eleanor appeared at the door of the room, and Büchner held up a warning hand so that she disappeared again before Agatha could see her. The sister stopped pacing, took off her cloak, and sat bolt upright in a straight-backed chair facing him. In her severe long gray dress, she looked like an old-fashioned schoolmarm about to address the class on its lack of manners. To his surprise, her face softened, and she smiled. "Barbara," she said, "is very dear to me. I have never had a husband or a child. No one has been as close to me as Sister Barbara. She *is* my sister, and I love her as a sister. I have tried to look after her.

She is vulnerable because of her past, and just lately, I had begun to fear . . . But never mind that now . . . You know something of her past, I believe. She took on the vows and the garb of the sisterhood, but I knew that she could not find the faith in God that should go with these. She had faith in me, and I in her, and I do not believe that she is dying in there." She gestured toward the closed door. "God could not be so cruel."

"I'm afraid he can," said Büchner deliberately harshly. "There is only a slight chance that she will recover." Agatha flinched. "Please tell me anything you may know about why she is in there now, in all probability, dying."

There was another silence. "Very well," said Büchner. "Let me show you this. It is a note found in Barbara's pocket after the accident." He handed it to her.

Agatha gasped as she read the first sentence, and tears appeared in her eyes as she read on.

"This cannot be true," she said. "Do you believe it?"

"I don't know," said Büchner. "If it's not true, why did she write it?"

"She had no reason to strike a blow at Hans Graf. Why should she? She has been in a disturbed state of late. And it is true that I was angry with him—" She stopped.

"Why were you angry with him?"

"It started several weeks ago with yellow stickers that someone started leaving in our apartment."

"You also received stickers?"

"We did. Did other people?"

"A lot of trouble might have been avoided if these stickers had been promptly reported and collected in the first instance."

"Herr Inspektor, the ones we received, I would never have shown to anyone."

"Have you destroyed them?"

"Of course."

"Please tell me what they contained."

"They were very nasty rhymes, referring to me and Barbara and our friendship, using ugly words like, well, *dike* and *butch*—horrible alliterative stuff like *Butch Barbara*. Oh, I don't want to be talking about this at a time like this."

"You say," said Büchner calmly, "that it all started with this. But how did it go on? And what did it have to do with Graf."

"For one thing—this had nothing to do with Graf, well, only indirectly—it set off real depression in Barbara because of the way it seemed to play on her own past. We had some . . . very difficult discussions about all that, I can't talk about it at this moment, Herr Inspektor, it was highly personal. But then Hans Graf entered the picture in a nasty way. As I told you at one point, he and I had our own past, unimportant as it had become over the years, but someone, perhaps knowing of that, gave one of these stickers to him, about me and Barbara, and he apparently told Dr. Hofer about it. Hofer told Barbara this and quoted the actual wording, ostensibly to warn her of what was going on, but in fact, she said, she had the distinct feeling that he was laughing at her. I was extremely angry about this. She told me about it on the morning of Christmas Day. I was angry, not so much with Hofer or even with the writer of the stickers, whoever that was, but with Hans. I don't know. I suppose I expected some sort of decency from him. Hofer is not really a gentleman, but Hans is, or was. And I suppose I have always been angry with him in any case, at some level, since that early episode in our lives. I had every intention of giving him a piece of my mind, and I told Barbara this. But of course, I knew that on Christmas Day he would be with Frau Hagen, and then the following day . . . well, it all became irrelevant. He was dead."

"You realize, Sister Agatha, that if either you or Sister Barbara were actually in Graf's room that day—Barbara, you may know, absented herself from the fingerprinting, and your fingerprints were found there—then one or the other of you might be open to a murder charge?"

"Oh, but wasn't Hans struck much later in the day?"

"He died much later in the day, but it turns out that the blow was struck earlier. He died of slow intracranial hemorrhaging."

"Well, then Barbara couldn't have done it at five when Frau Beck saw her coming out of the room."

"Is that what Frau Beck saw?"

"That's what Frau Fabian just told me."

"No, if that was the time when Barbara was in the room, it is unlikely that she could have struck the blow."

"Thank God," said Agatha.

"But you could have struck it earlier. That might have been what Barbara thought. She then tried to protect you by claiming responsibility."

"But I didn't!"

"So you say," said Büchner.

The door to the operating room opened, and the surgeon came out. "We have done all we can," he said. "It's a matter of waiting now."

"You will want to stay here," said Büchner to Agatha. "I must go back to the Haus im Wald." He turned to the surgeon. "Thank you," he said. "Please keep the sergeant informed." Then turning again to Agatha, he said, "Herr Schmidt will stay here with you and bring you back to the Haus im Wald when you are ready."

"Am I under guard, Herr Inspektor?"

Büchner smiled. "Take it as you will, Sister. You have more to tell me, I think. If you had been more forthright earlier, we might not be here now."

"Yes, I'm sorry," she caught her breath as the stretcher was wheeled out of the operating room. All that was to be seen was the bandaged head of Barbara with tubes attached to various wheeled stands that were rolled alongside the stretcher. "Follow them then," said Büchner. "And good luck."

"Luck?" she said. "I would prefer you to wish us Godspeed."

"Prefer as you will, Sister, I wish you what I can." Even in extremis, he thought, this woman has to teach a lesson. He realized that he felt desperately tired.

3

Franz tossed and turned in his hospital bed. After Eleanor had put her daisies in the vase and left, he had fallen into blissful oblivion for a few hours. He wasn't sure for how long. He turned on the light switch and looked at his watch. Two o'clock. Well, at least it was after midnight and he was into a new day. At the moment of waking, he hadn't been sure where he was. Then the whole nightmare had crept back—his fall, the awful mess he'd got into in the apartment, the dreadful Dr. Hofer, oh God, Frau Huber and the couch, and then, after all these things had slithered through his head, the one solid, stunning, inescapable fact, his mother was dead. Had all these other things really happened, or were they part of some lunatic nightmare? Well, he was here in a hospital bed, wasn't he, presumably in the head-trauma division or some such. He was "under observation," though nobody much had been observing him as far as he knew. Of course, he'd been asleep. He needed to go to the toilet, so he got out of bed and opened the door in the corner of the room. Yes, there it was. The toilet had a frame on it with a high seat and arms on either side. OK, a thing like this had been fitted onto one of the toilets in the apartment too for his mother. Maybe all the hospital toilets were like this. He sat down. He was slightly chagrined to discover that the frame actually did help him in standing up again. He looked at himself in the mirror over the little sink. His hair looked thin and wispy around his bruised face, and there was stubble on his chin and upper lip. What a sight. And this silly pale blue hospital gown didn't help either. But his head felt distinctly better. I haven't got an intracranial hematoma, he said to himself. There's no downward trajectory. I definitely feel much better after that sleep than I did before it. It had all been a lot of fuss about nothing. He wondered now why he had felt almost pleased when they decided to keep him here overnight. Just to prove to Eleanor that it was *not* a fuss about nothing? Might as well clamber back into bed and try to sleep.

He bent over the bed to straighten the pillows, and hearing someone come into the room, he clutched quickly at the back of the hospital gown, which was, he realized, wide open, revealing his buttocks. Nothing but humiliation these days. A young male voice behind him said cheerfully, "Do you need help, Herr Professor?" The voice was vaguely familiar, and for some reason, a silly pop song went through Franz's head:

I want to be forgiven,
I want to hold you in my arms again.

The café, he thought. "Do I know you?" he said, straightening up and holding the two pieces of gown firmly together in the back with his right hand while fumbling about on the night table for his glasses with his left hand.

"Why, yes, Herr Professor. Michael from the café."

Continuing to fumble, Franz said nervously, "Can't find my glasses."

"Here they are," said the young man, reaching around Franz in the narrow space between the wall and the bed and thus encircling him with his arm. "They were behind the lamp."

It must be a dream, thought Franz. Some new sort of sexual temptation in a dream. He sat down on the bed, and the young man gently placed the glasses on his nose. "You see?" he said. "Michael from the café."

Franz saw. It really was Michael, in the deep green overall of a hospital orderly. "What in the world are you doing here?" he asked, trying to pull back the sheets on his bed and swing his legs into it from a sitting position in as unobtrusive a movement as possible, keeping his hospital gown firmly around his lower body.

"Let me help you," said Michael, grasping for his ankles.

"Good heavens, no," said Franz, jerking his legs away. "I'm not completely decrepit."

"Of course not," said Michael soothingly.

Not for the first time in the last twenty-four hours, Franz felt that he was being humored, placated as people placate those who are too far gone in senility to be worth arguing with. But it was, for some reason, quite difficult to get his legs up onto the bed and safely stowed away under the sheets, which were tightly tucked in. Michael stood quietly by until Franz managed it and could put his head back on the pillow.

"That's better," said Michael encouragingly.

"What are you doing here?" Franz asked again sharply.

"I sometimes moonlight as an orderly a couple of nights a week in the AKH," said Michael. "Brings in a little extra money, and in any case, I have sometimes thought of getting into the nursing profession myself. I've taken some courses."

"Bit of a coincidence that you should turn up here tonight."

"Not really," said Michael with a charmingly apologetic look. "I wanted to talk to you about something actually, and when I heard you were here for the night, I called in to offer my services on the geriatric floor for the night."

"On the *what?*"

"The geriatric floor."

"But what does that have to do with me," said Franz, genuinely perplexed.

"That's what this floor is, didn't you know? The geriatric floor."

"What?" Franz felt a kind of helpless outrage.

"They put you on the geriatric floor for the night."

"But . . . but . . . why?"

Michael, who had clearly thought nothing of it until that moment, now seemed to be floundering himself. "Well, I mean, they had to put you somewhere to keep an eye on you, and they probably thought—"

"All right, all right," Franz broke in. "I can imagine what they thought. Only too well. I thought I was here under serious observation for a head injury. They no doubt thought they would keep this old man quiet for a night." Hence the toilet, he thought, with the frame. Oh God, he had to get out of here.

"Look," he said. "There's really nothing wrong with me. I want to get out."

"But, Professor, it's two thirty in the morning. You can't just walk out. You have to be discharged."

"I shall discharge myself," said Franz, struggling to kick the tightly tucked-in sheets off the bed.

"Please, wait till tomorrow at least."

"It is tomorrow. I don't want to be here a minute longer."

"If you disappear," said Michael, "I'll get the blame." He opened his eyes wide and looked appealingly at Franz.

He is a very handsome young man, thought Franz, and remembered what Michael had said before he dropped his geriatric bombshell. "Whatever, in any case, did you want to speak to me about?"

"It's a long story. Wouldn't you prefer to wait till I bring you your coffee at six o'clock before I go off duty?"

"Give me the short version now. I may have done a moonlight flit before then."

"Oh, please don't," said Michael, and Franz, putting his head back on the pillow, thought, Well, perhaps I won't.

"Let's hear what you have to say, young man," he said, lying still and trying to retrieve some sort of dignity.

"I have a confession to make. The day you hit your head in Martin Luther, I . . . borrowed . . . seven hundred euros from your pocket."

"You did what?"

Michael lowered his head and held out his arms in a gesture of penitence. The silly song from the café went through Franz's head again: *I want to be forgiven.*

"I was desperate for money to pay the night nurses at my grandmother's home," he said. "I needed it badly that very day, and I was sure I could rustle it up to give it back to you as soon as you were back on your feet. So I took it. I've never done anything like that before. And I have given the money back."

"To whom? I haven't seen it."

"To the inspector. He knows the whole story. But I was hoping to get to you to tell you before he did."

"You want to be forgiven?"

"You might put it like that."

"You probably don't remember that when I first saw you working in the café in the Haus im Wald, you were humming a pop song with those very words."

Michael flushed. "No, I don't remember that exactly. But I know the song."

"Yes, the next line is 'I want to hold you in my arms again.'" He laughed, feeling in a peculiar and somehow perverse way, some of his old strength returning. "Don't worry. I'm not going to ask you to sing it for me. What do you want me to do?"

"I hoped," said Michael, "that you might tell the inspector you didn't want to press charges."

"And how did you hope to achieve this?" For the first time in days, Franz felt he had the upper hand with somebody.

"I thought if I explained to you how sorry I was, how I had acted on impulse and was under great pressure, you might see your way—"

"Yes, yes, I'll see my way, fine, but if you really want to be forgiven, you'll have to help me in return." Franz sat on the edge of the bed and waited.

Michael took a step closer to him. "Well?" he said, and he waited too.

Good Lord, thought Franz. He probably really would. Amazing all the kinky sexual opportunities that seemed to be cropping up in his path lately—and all since he had entered geriatric country. But it was a country he wanted quite desperately to get out of. "You will have to help me to get out of here," he said, "with no one noticing, and give me a way to get into the Haus im Wald. I want to find my wife."

"Herr Professor, it's worth my job."

"My dear young man, you will lose all your jobs if you are convicted of theft."

Michael took a deep breath. "OK. I'll do my best. But if they catch you, will you please say you walked out by yourself."

"They'd better not catch me."

Michael pulled a cell phone out of his pocket. "I'll have a taxi waiting for you at the main entrance," he said. "You get dressed, and I'll tell you when the coast is clear. By the way, your wife was here in the hospital a couple of hours ago."

"Here? Why? Not to see me?"

"No, I saw them arriving when I came for the midnight shift—she and Sister Agatha. I ducked out of sight because I didn't want Sister Agatha to see me here. But she's got other problems. I asked at the emergency desk, and they told me that Sister Barbara crashed her motor scooter and your wife drove Sister Agatha in here to the emergency room."

"Good Lord."

"Yes, well, I happen to know," he said conspiratorially, "that Sister Barbara consumes certain substances. Not altogether surprising that she would ultimately crash. Your wife left later with the inspector."

Oh, she did, did she? Franz was pulling on his trousers. "Just get me out of here."

"OK. You wait here until I call the cab, check the coast is clear, and get the elevator. Stand by the door, you'll see when the elevator lights go on."

Franz put on his coat and went to the door, going back only to grab the bedraggled daisies and throw them with a lordly gesture into the wastepaper basket. When the lights went on, he scuttled along the corridor. Michael was already in the elevator and pressed the button for the ground floor.

"Good-bye, geriatrics," said Franz.

"You'll be saying hello to them again soon enough when you get out there," said Michael. "Here's my key. This'll get you into the Haus im Wald and essentially into any room in the house. Don't tell anybody about it though. And I really want it back."

Franz was distinctly enjoying the feeling of conspiring with this handsome and clearly wicked young man. They stepped out of the elevator, and Michael said, "I'll chat with the porter, and you just go boldly and quickly through the front door into the taxi. It should work. See you tomorrow in the Haus im Wald."

"Today," said Franz. "It is already today."

And this, he thought, settling into the backseat of the taxi and strapping on his seat belt, is a day that I finally intend to seize. It was three o'clock in the morning, and he didn't even feel tired.

4

Eleanor was getting tired of pacing the corridor outside the emergency surgical unit. She had already spent more time in this hospital in the last couple of days than she cared to remember, and now she'd been kicking her heels outside this room for a good twenty minutes. The inspector had given her a clear sign to stay out of the waiting room where he was talking to Sister Agatha. Interrogating her, perhaps. Eleanor would have loved to hear what they were saying, but she didn't want to be seen openly eavesdropping. It was a strange business, this visit to Graf by one of the gray-clad sisters. But what motive could either of them have had to hit Graf over the head? It must have been done in anger and have taken Graf completely by surprise. Nothing else could account for the severity of the blow—and its strength—enough to knock an able-bodied man down. Graf certainly hadn't looked frail to her on those days when he had sat in the café, happily drinking his schnapps with the lovely Frau Hagen. What could have made a woman that angry? A kind of puritan disapproval of a loose lifestyle surely wouldn't do it, which was all she could think of in Agatha's case, unless Agatha cherished a secret love for Graf and did it out of jealousy. If this seemed unlikely in Agatha's case, then it was even more unlikely in Barbara's. Unless Agatha was secretly having a love affair with Graf and Barbara had found out. These were silly speculations, Eleanor knew that. She just didn't have the facts. Still, she did know that one of them had come out of his apartment at five or so on Christmas Day. Did the inspector know that by now? she wondered. She'd better stick around and tell him. Otherwise, she might as well have gone straight back to the Haus im Wald. I'm getting very tired, she thought, and nowhere even to sit down. What she really wanted to do right now was go to bed. She paced up and down the corridor several more times, and then the door opened. She flattened herself against the wall as a stretcher was wheeled past. She could see little of Barbara's face as her head was swathed in bandages. Agatha was following the stretcher, with her usual straight back and dignified walk—appropriate for a funeral. She was looking straight ahead and did not even seem to see Eleanor. Wachtmeister Schmidt took up the rear position in the procession and gave Eleanor a small salute. Then Büchner came out of the room. "Ah, you're still here, Frau Fabian." He did not look delighted, but why should he? He looked dead tired too.

"Yes, I thought I'd better wait in case I was needed, to take Sister Agatha back or something."

"Kind of you. No. She'll be staying here. We'd better get to the car park and back to the Haus im Wald."

He began to stride quickly along the corridor, not seeming very inclined to talk, and Eleanor had to make an effort to keep up with him.

"What's the news of Barbara?" she asked.

"Bad news," he said. "Doesn't look hopeful. Even if she survives the night, there's a question of when or whether she will come out of the coma."

"Oh God," said Eleanor.

"Yes, God. That's about the only hope. Maybe Sister Agatha has a direct line."

They were in the elevator going down to the basement, and Eleanor was getting her breath back. "Herr Inspektor, there is one thing. Christa is now really sure that she saw a gray-cloaked woman coming out of Graf's apartment at five or so on Christmas Day. She thought it was Agatha, but this was mainly on the basis of height, that is, she saw a long shadow, and I thought it might just as well have been Sister Barbara. Christa is nearsighted, even with her glasses on. And she wasn't paying close attention. She's not an inquisitive type, watching her neighbors go in and out and all that." Büchner did not say anything. "I just thought you ought to know," Eleanor added lamely.

"Yes, thank you, it is useful corroborating information. Let's hop into our cars now and go back. Is Frau Beck still with the pastor?"

"Yes, she said she'd buzz me in when I got back."

"Then I'll go in with you. Thank you. Please drive carefully."

She started up the car and drove first out of the parking lot, seeing his lights go on in her rearview mirror as she drove out on to the Gürtel. He certainly hadn't been very forthcoming. A long wait for nothing. But he was staying behind her now, and he had a more powerful car than she did—decent of him. Keeping an eye on her perhaps. Somehow nice to think of a man like that looking out for you. Quite different from the rather fussy concern of Franz, which always seemed to contain a hefty dose of criticism for whatever it was you were doing or trying to do. Of course, she didn't really know this man, the inspector. Not exactly good-looking, certainly not in the manner of the handsome Hofer, but she had always liked the lean and hungry look. So why, she wondered, had she married a rather stubby man like Franz, who was tending more and more to rotundity as he got older? Of course, the inspector was younger. How much younger? she wondered. Surely people retired from the police force at about fifty-five at the latest. He couldn't be over sixty. He didn't have that over-sixty look. She sighed. He was probably holding back in his car not out of any masculine sense of chivalry but because he thought she was too old to be allowed out in a car late at night. Defiantly, she put her foot on the gas and skidded slightly as she turned the corner into the Heiligenstädter Straße. A warning honk came from behind. So he was still there. She slowed down a bit. Mustn't be silly, she thought. We've got enough trouble tonight. Soon they would be back in the Haus im Wald. She really did need a couple of hours sleep. Surely so did the inspector. Perhaps the conversation with Agatha had solved all his problems and he now knew who did it. In which case, he could sleep the sleep of the just and forget the whole thing. Somehow he hadn't looked like a man whose troubles were over. She liked his face. The quizzical lines around his eyes. The way he looked straight at you and made his mock-serious, detective-type remarks, as if he were playing a game that he really enjoyed. Did he take all this detection business seriously? He would hardly be a chief inspector if he didn't. She could still see his car some distance behind her as she drove the short stretch along the expressway and turned into the road to Feldberg and into the woods. It was very dark on this road now. There was no moonlight. It occurred to her that if the inspector hadn't happened to see Barbara riding off like that, she might still be there, lying in the dark words, slowly being covered with snow. Eleanor shivered. How much, she wondered, in real detection, actually depends on pure coincidence? Soon she was leaving the dark forest road behind her and pulling into the dark driveway to the Haus im Wald. Only the dim night-lights from the corridors of the Martin Luther wing and the lobby of the house were to be seen—and then the one bright light edging the curtains of Frau Hagen's window. Doesn't she ever turn off the lights and go to bed? Oh well, she had no intention of looking into that tonight. Frau Hagen had not been exactly ecstatic to see her earlier that evening, and she would hardly appreciate a visit in the wee small hours of the morning. As she got out of her car and locked it and stood waiting for the inspector to do the same, the words of that old Frank Sinatra song ran through her head:

In the wee small hours of the morning,
While the whole wide world is fast asleep,
You lie awake and think about the girl
And never ever think of counting sheep.

Romance, thought Eleanor. Whatever happened to it?

"Thank you, Herr Inspektor, for keeping an eye on me on the way back." She whispered—it was all so quiet.

"You're welcome," he whispered back. They stood for a moment looking at the house.

"Once more into the breach," she whispered, ringing Pokorny's bell. "Odd isn't it that Frau Hagen never seems to turn out her lights and go to sleep, not even in the wee small hours of the morning."

He didn't pick up on Sinatra—well, that was too much to hope. "It's me, Christa," she said in a loud whisper into the intercom. "*And* the inspector."

They were immediately buzzed in and tiptoed through the quiet lobby, Eleanor with a feeling of implausible lightheartedness. Büchner seemed so tall as he stood beside her in the elevator. Glancing sideways at him, she thought, Maybe he is over sixty, that would be nice. Somehow. You're just tired, she told herself. Don't be silly.

Christa let them in. She looked very tired too. "What happened?" she asked.

Eleanor told her briefly. "Anything go on here?"

"No," said Christa. "Not a sound, not even from Pastor Pokorny."

"You ladies had better go and get some sleep," Büchner said. "I'll just doss down here for a couple of hours. If anything happens, just call."

"Good night, Herr Inspektor. Count a few sheep," said Eleanor.

Büchner bowed formally, escorted them to the door, and watched while they let themselves into Christa's apartment.

"Such a nice man," said Eleanor, and sighed.

"Do you think so? Yes, he does seem to be kind."

"Yes. Now let's try to sleep a bit. Do you have a blanket for me or something?"

Christa brought out a double sheet, folded it over on the couch, then fetched a pair of pajamas and a blanket and pillow. "Will that do?"

"Christa, I could sleep on a clothesline," Eleanor said.

But when they finally settled down, she found that her head seemed to be wide awake. The house was quiet, very quiet. The whole wide world is fast asleep, she thought. Except perhaps Frau Hagen, and maybe the inspector. Was he sleeping peacefully on his couch? she wondered. She thought about him and held that nice face of his in her mind and dropped off into a restless half sleep.

Suddenly she was wide awake and sitting bolt upright as she heard what sounded like somebody at the door. The same thing Christa heard last night, she thought. Only she had forgotten to put the chain on. A key turned in the lock, and the door opened slightly and closed again. She crept off the couch, looking around for something to defend herself with. Nothing. She pulled the sheet off the bed and stood behind the door, her heart beating loudly as the door opened wider this time. Someone was coming into the room. Blindly she held the sheet high in both arms and flung it over the head of the person, pulling the ends of it tight as the person staggered, fell to his knees, gave a loud yelp, and in a muffled shout said, "What the hell is going on? Let me go!"

"For heaven's sake," said Eleanor, "Franz." She tried to remove the sheet, but he was struggling with it from the inside. Finally, after seconds of pulling one way and another, his head emerged, and they stared angrily at each other.

"What do you think you are trying to do?" he said, breathless and still kneeling on the floor.

"What the hell are you doing here?" she said. "You're supposed to be in the hospital."

"Is that any reason to suffocate me?" he said.

Christa came out of her room. "What is going on?" she said, bleary-eyed. "I had just fallen asleep."

"Oh, go back to bed," said Eleanor. "It's only Franz."

Christa looked at him, kneeling, half covered in her sheet. "I give up," she said helplessly and retreated into her bedroom.

Franz struggled to his feet.

"I can't deal with this," said Eleanor. "I'm dead tired. I've got to get some sleep. How dare you turn up here in the middle of the night and terrify the daylights out of me? How do you think either of us is going to get any sleep now with only this little couch between us? The whole thing is absolutely ludicrous."

"Hush!" said Franz. They both listened. There seemed to be somebody walking along the corridor and stopping outside their door.

"What now?" said Eleanor. "You have a look. I'm not going near the door."

Franz stepped out from the tangled sheet and, first putting the chain across, peered out. "A little man seems to be trying the door handle of the door opposite," he said.

"Oh God, Graf's room," said Eleanor. "I'll call the inspector. Let me see first."

As she looked, the little man turned around. He caught sight of her peering through the cracked-open door and came toward her. "Oh, Frau Fabian," he said. "There seemed to be so much coming and going overhead, quite unusual at this time of night. I am a light sleeper, you know. And then I thought I heard bumps on the floor as if someone might be in trouble. I thought I'd better check in view of what's been going on."

Eleanor took the chain off the door and pulled the door open. "Herr Ritter," she said, trying to recover herself and project some sort of dignity, standing there as she was in Christa's baggy and ill-fitting pajamas. "It's very kind of you."

"Not at all," said Herr Ritter. "There were odd sounds up here last night too, you know. I came and looked around and even checked the door of Hans' apartment. It was open, oddly enough, but no one was there. And I couldn't hear anything going on here either, though I listened quietly at the door for a while, just in case."

"You're not afraid to wander about in the night, Herr Ritter?"

"Afraid? No, my dear, I haven't been afraid of anything very much for many years."

Franz coughed impatiently.

"Do you know my husband? No, everything's OK here. It was all a misunderstanding."

"Dear me," said Herr Ritter, stepping into the room and seeing the sheet lying there. "Are you trying to sleep on the floor, Herr Professor?"

"No, well, that is to say . . ."

"My *husband*," said Eleanor, investing the word with as much scorn as she could muster, "has at the moment nowhere to sleep."

"Then do come with me," said Herr Ritter. "We have a couch in the living room if that will do."

"That will do fine, thank you, Herr Ritter. Good night, Franz," said Eleanor. "You can send him back up here in the morning, which will soon be upon us in any case."

Before Franz could open his mouth, she thrust the sheet into his arms, bundled the two men out of the door, put the chain firmly across it, lay down on the couch under the blanket, and fell into a deep sleep.

5

Franz's mood of bravado after his escape from the hospital had dissipated rather quickly after being trapped in a sheet by Eleanor. Letting himself into the silent house and walking quietly up to the third floor of Melanchthon, he had still felt distinctly clever, daring, and, well, young. He was not sure what he expected to find when he quietly used what seemed like a magic key to let himself into her friend's apartment. Did he think he would find Eleanor in bed with the detective? Or, even more laughable, did he think she would leap up with delight to greet him and applaud his tale of derring-do? Of course not. But he did not expect to be felled by a sheet either and then pushed out through the door with an elderly little inmate. He had thought to escape the geriatric scene, but as that young Michael had pointed out, here he was, back in it with a vengeance. The little man was nice enough, and when he offered him a peppermint schnapps, to settle the stomach, as he said, Franz accepted it with pleasure; and they sat together drinking schnapps and chatting—quietly, so as not to wake Frau Ritter, though according to Herr Ritter, she heard very little when her hearing aids were out. Franz, after emptying one glass and accepting another, told the story of his hospital escape, at which Herr Ritter laughed merrily.

"Well done," he said. "Never give in to them!" This was heartening, though Franz was uncomfortably aware that Ritter was expressing the solidarity of the old "us" against the younger controlling "them." He did not tell the story of the seven hundred euros, and Ritter thought it a great and happy coincidence that Michael had chanced upon the professor in his moonlighting job.

"I know he sometimes works nights at the hospital," he said. "He needs money badly, you know. He takes care of his grandmother. I help him out now and then—not with money," he added hastily, "my wife wouldn't care for that. But for example, when he gets in straight from the hospital, he sometimes comes up here and takes a shower in the apartment. I'm always up with the lark, well, with the rook, I should say, in this house, and Hildegard hears nothing in the mornings. No one else knows that he does this, by the way."

Franz could well imagine that Herr Ritter would enjoy the feeling of conspiracy with the handsome young Michael, just as he had done himself. Oh God, he thought. The meager emotional kicks of the elderly.

"What is it like living here?" he asked, leaning back comfortably on the couch and enjoying the feeling of the third glass of schnapps slipping smoothly down his throat, heating his belly, and distinctly lightening his head.

"Oh, Herr Professor, what can I say? As these places go, I'm sure this is one of the most comfortable. The tales I hear from Michael about life in other kinds of homes would make me thank God for my good fortune, if I really felt it was absolutely necessary for me to live in what they call sheltered accommodation. But I don't really feel that. Not necessary for me, that is. Hildegard, my wife, she needs it, and so I need it because I cannot cope with looking after her needs by myself. But believe me, Professor, if I were alone, I would fly away, far, far away."

Franz was overcome with a feeling of great sympathy. This really quite delightful little man weighed down with that awful wife. Well, he'd only seen her once or twice; this wasn't quite fair, but still—

"Why don't you just run away?" he said foolishly, buoyed up by the schnapps, but waving away the offer of a fourth glass. "Like me from the hospital."

Herr Ritter laughed. "It's not so simple. When I was younger, the solitary life used to beckon—with its uncertainties and possibilities—but I always owed a great deal to Hildegard and her family. Her family rescued me from the worst, you see, in the bad old days. Without them, I, as a "half-Jew," would not have survived. Ritter, in fact, is *their* name, you see. And later, her father set me up in the art-dealing business, which I loved. It was always expected that I would marry Hildegard. I never used to talk about these things, but maybe the time has come for people to stop hiding from each other in these woods of ours."

Franz was not sure that he wanted to know this much about the Ritter family. He reached for the bottle himself and poured himself a fourth glass.

"I suppose," he said, "we should catch an hour of sleep."

"Yes, of course. I do not mean to keep you awake with these old stories. I'm sorry."

"No, no, don't apologize. Flying away quite often appeals to me too. I know only too well the seductiveness of the dream of the single life—a silent study, books, paper and pen, quiet music—none of the wearisome negotiations of married life, the endless explanations, prevarications, dissemblings. Vivaldi and veritas," he said, knowing that he was already a bit drunk and enjoying it.

"Well, you still have time, Herr Professor. You must be ten years younger than I am." More than that, surely, thought Franz. "You can still strike out on your own before you find yourself one of a trapped couple in sheltered living. Oh, just not to be sheltered! Oh, for just a little more free life before the last curtain falls! To Vivaldi and veritas!" He raised his glass. Then his face clouded. "The last music I heard coming from Hans Graf's apartment was Vivaldi."

Both men sat for a while in silence. "You have a charming wife," said Herr Ritter. "We shouldn't be talking like this."

"Yes, well, I am getting a bit sleepy," said Franz.

“Of course. I’ll get you a blanket and a pillow. You have a sheet, I see.”

“Yes, I didn’t tell you that my wife almost suffocated me with it when I came in, thought I was the house murderer, I suppose.”

Herr Ritter let out a short laugh, then winced. “The house murderer,” he repeated. “Oh dear.”

“Sorry. Too much peppermint schnapps.”

Herr Ritter showed him on tiptoe to the bathroom and wished him a good night, what was left of it. Franz stripped to his underwear and lay down on the couch, his head spinning. Into his head came the seven hundred euros. I wonder where it is, he thought. I’ll get it, take it to the airport, buy a new ticket with cash, nobody will know, fly south somewhere, and disappear. Siracusa. When he was younger, he used to fantasize about disappearing into lovely, decaying, rococo Siracusa. Maybe it wasn’t too late, he thought, sinking into a restless sleep.

Chapter 17

In the Haus im Wald, seven residents had now died in the month of December, a number beginning to tip over from the usual into the shocking. When Direktor Schramm heard early on Wednesday morning that Sister Barbara had died in the night, he must have begun to fear that his days as director were numbered. He might argue that the elderly tended to succumb to the ravages of age in the bleak midwinter, but two of the most recent deaths had been sudden, and two others had been not only sudden but violent. How could you explain that to prospective new residents? Yes, people came to the Haus im Wald prepared ultimately to die there. They did, however, hope for a quiet death, a good death, as it is sometimes called. At least 70 percent of the citizenry claim, in surveys, that they would like to die at home, many of them no doubt having seen people dying in hospital beds, unconscious or semiconscious, attached to respirators, feeding tubes, catheters, and the like. Happy the man who dies at home, quietly, his family and friends around him. Happy—and rare. Almost 80 percent of the citizenry die in hospitals. We may dream of dying at home, but apparently most of us are not quite prepared to care at home for the dying. The Haus im Wald is a halfway house between home and hospital, and although the residents undoubtedly hope to die there, rather than in a hospital, their more immediate intention is to live there. Even hospices, as listeners to Radio Ö1 have recently been told, no longer claim to specialize in death and the dying but describe their specialty as the "end of life." The December deaths are sending a tremor through the residents.

They know they are in the Haus im Wald for the end of life. But most of them would surely like to keep body and soul together for just a while longer.

1

Büchner awoke to find himself fully clothed on a couch in a strange apartment. Pastor Pokorny. Of course. He had vaguely thought once in a waking moment that he heard the pastor going to the bathroom, but there was no cry for help, so he had gratefully stayed asleep. Something had woken him up now. He looked at his watch—7:00 a.m., Thursday, December 29—his third morning in the Haus im Wald. The cawing of the birds seemed more distant from this inner room than from his room in Martin Luther, which looked directly onto the driveway and the woods. Nonetheless, it had probably woken him up, and just as well. He got up and stretched. The bedroom door was open, and as he walked to the bathroom, he heard the pastor's voice from his bed. "Herr Inspektor, is that you?"

He stuck his head around the door. "Yes, sir. Good morning. How are you?"

"Stiff knees, but otherwise fine, I think. I've been awake for an hour." Beside him on the pillow was a small very worn leather-covered bible. "When my friends, the big black birds, wake me in the mornings, I read this old book," he said. "It has accompanied me throughout my long life."

"You see the birds as friends? To me there is something threatening about them. That cawing of theirs is somehow dark and ominous."

"Plenty of other people in the house think that. Frau Winkler, to whom we make our last farewells today, was always quite frightened of them. To me they are strong and free. They are here for a few months in the winter, and then in their own time, they spread their mighty wings and fly away. They are not caught in the snare. Do you know the verse in this book: *as the birds are caught in the snare, so are the sons of men snared in an evil time, when it falleth suddenly upon them*? I have known what it is, Herr Inspektor, to lose my freedom, caught suddenly in a snare in an evil time. The cawing of the big, free birds of the forest in the early morning gives me new heart every time to launch into a new day. I feel, alas, that an evil time has lately fallen on the Haus im Wald. And most of us here cannot fly away from the snare, as the big black birds can. Forgive this old preacher, Herr Inspektor, for pouncing on you so early in the morning with a sermon."

"It's a pleasure, Herr Pastor," said Büchner, sitting down on a chair at the end of the bed. "And I am relieved to find you feeling so well. Perhaps you will forgive this dyed-in-the-wool detective for asking you a question or two about this 'evil time.'"

"Go ahead."

"I have talked with Dr. Lessing—at your suggestion, I gather—about the infamous yellow stickers that have lately been visited upon residents of the house. Do you regard them as signs and symbols of the 'evil time'?"

"Yes, I do. When I first heard about them, I found the idea of them most unpleasant. There is a nastiness about the whole concept of anonymous notes. And when in addition they are, well, dirty, one might say, and even xenophobic in their content, then one has to think that there is a spirit abroad in the house that far exceeds the occasional crossness and pettiness that is bound to arise among people involved in communal living."

"When did you first hear of them?"

"It was Herr Ritter who first mentioned them to me. He and I, you know, share a common past of a kind. We both knew persecution under the Nazis, for different reasons, but we were both 'fortunate,' as people say, in surviving that time—a fortune that is in itself riddled with complications. We are not, I would say, close friends, since we have otherwise little in common, but we have a healthy respect for each other, and Herr Ritter admitted to me that he was bothered by these stickers. He did not show me any, though he told me some of their content. You will have heard about that from Frau Fabian, at my request. My advice at the time was to ignore them as the handiwork of a nasty small mind. Perhaps I was wrong. When I received one yesterday and saw for myself the extent of their crudeness, I changed my mind and so suggested that you talk to Dr. Lessing. Did she divulge our suspicions?"

"She did. And I shall be following up on this first thing this morning. Another question though, Herr Pastor. Do you think these stickers are connected with the death of Herr Graf?"

"Well, they fall into the same evil time and may be in some way connected. I would not go so far as to suggest that the person who wrote the stickers also struck the blow. But after talking to Herr Ritter the other day and after thinking about the life and death of Frau Winkler for the upcoming service, I did wonder whether this small-scale evil time here has anything to do with the massively evil time that befell Europe in the thirties and robbed me and Herr Ritter of our youth, and Frau Winkler of her young husband. He was, you know, a Lutheran pastor, executed, that is, murdered, by the Nazis."

"No, I didn't know that. But Graf is surely too young to have been involved himself in the guilt of the perpetrators of that period."

"He would have been about sixteen years old at the end of the war, and so, as you say, too young for that. But as you have undoubtedly heard, his family made great financial gains from the so-called Aryanization of property in Vienna in the thirties and forties. Whatever restitution he made later, one never knows what resentment there might be against him and what form this resentment might take. Of course, this might equally well have played no part at all in the murder. But one cannot ignore the possibility."

"No," said Büchner, "one should not." He had thought about Graf's past in the new postwar Austria, but his vision, he realized, had been limited by his picturing Graf as a member of his own father's generation. His father, however, had come from a family very different from Herr Graf's. He had to get moving. "Do you need any help?" he asked the pastor. "I should get on with the business of the day. There was, I regret to have to tell you, another very bad event late last night. Sister Barbara crashed her motor scooter into a tree in the forest and is now near death in the AKH."

The Pastor drew in his breath sharply and closed his eyes. "That nice Sister Barbara," he said. "What in the world is going on here? An evil time, you see, Herr Inspektor." He opened his eyes again and said urgently, "Yes, please do get on with your work. You seem to be a good man, and the house needs the help of a good man." He turned his head away to the window. "Oh that poor, nice Sister Barbara."

There was a ring at the doorbell, and Büchner opened it to find Michael there with a tray of coffee, a boiled egg, and some toast. "Oh, Herr Inspektor, you're here!" he said. "I promised the ladies I would bring up breakfast for Pastor Pokorny. I'm afraid I didn't think of you." Michael looked neat and spruced up as usual, but very tired around the eyes, Büchner thought.

"Don't worry about me," he said. "I'll come and grab a coffee in the café later if you're there. But go ahead and take in the breakfast for the pastor. He's upset at the news of Sister Barbara. I take it you know about that already."

"Well, yes, I heard that she died in the night."

"She died?" said Büchner, sickened by this news.

"Yes, I thought that was what you meant. Didn't you know?"

"No," said Büchner, not even thinking to ask how Michael knew. "No, I didn't know." So I was too late, he thought. Too slow and too late by far.

He went out into the corridor and looked at the closed doors, behind two of which some drama he still did not understand had played itself out to end in death. This was a day in which he dared put nothing off until tomorrow.

2

Eleanor woke with cramp in her right leg. She forced this leg onto the floor, wincing with the pain, still half asleep and with no idea in the first few seconds where she was. Christa's apartment. OK, should she try to sleep some more? What a night! She thought of Barbara. God, let her still be alive. Funny how one went on saying these things in one's head long after one had ceased to believe in any god. Somebody ought to check on Pastor Pokorny. But the inspector was still there. How nice he had seemed last night. Well, she'd better spruce up a bit and go over there. The bathtub didn't look too inviting. Better just stand under the shower. She got under the warm jet of water and deliberately held her painful shoulder under it. That was nice. How annoying that she had no clean clothes to put on. At least she felt a bit more awake. She could hear Christa moving about, and then the phone rang.

When she went into the living room; Christa was sitting on the rumpled blanket on the couch, tears again running down her face.

"She died," she said.

"Who did? Oh no!"

"Yes, Sister Barbara, in the night."

Eleanor sat down beside her, and they both looked straight ahead, not wanting to meet each other's eyes.

"It's too much," said Christa, and surprisingly reached out and took her hand. "Oh, Eleanor, what is going on here in the Haus im Wald?"

"Look, we just have to pull ourselves together. Get up, shower, get dressed—there must be some way we can help, something we can do. Who called you?"

"Michael."

"Michael? What does he have to do with it?"

"I don't know. He called to say he was in Pastor Pokorny's apartment. He'd brought him breakfast. The inspector had left, he said, as soon as he'd told him about Barbara. So one of us had better check on the pastor, he said, because he had to get down to the café."

"Michael told him? How did he know?"

"Haven't the faintest idea. All he said was that Barbara had died in the night. I was too upset to ask anything else."

"Of course. Well, you'd better get under the shower. It does help, you know. I've just thrown these same clothes on. I'll go round to the pastor's apartment."

"Michael said he'd leave the door on the latch for us. By the way, whatever was going on with Franz last night? Where is he now?"

"He went off with Herr Ritter."

"Herr Ritter!"

"Yes, I'm not really sure about it all myself, and there's no time to think about that now. If you hear anything from Franz, tell him where I am. I wonder where Agatha is."

"Oh, Sister Agatha, how dreadful for her!" Christa's tears began to fall again.

"Into the shower, my dear girl. I'm off."

Eleanor grabbed her purse and left. She knocked on the pastor's door. Hearing no answer, she opened it and called, "Grüß Gott, Herr Pastor. It's only me, Eleanor Fabian."

"Come in, Frau Fabian," came a strong voice from the bedroom. "I am slowly getting dressed."

Eleanor sat down on the couch. If everything was all right here, she would go down to the café and look for Michael to see if he could tell her any more about Sister Barbara. Maybe the inspector was there. The pastor emerged slowly from his bedroom, using the walker but standing straight. He was not a tall man, but he stood square in the doorway, very upright, his head held high, inviting inspection, looking much younger than his years. He was wearing a black suit, a white shirt, and a black tie. His shock of white hair was brushed and combed. His blue eyes were positively shining this morning, and the small cuts and bruises on his face seemed suddenly insignificant. Eleanor, quite overcome by this presentation of his public persona, said, "Oh, Pastor Pokorny, you look absolutely splendid."

He laughed. "You are flattering a vain old man." Well, yes, she thought. He is clearly vain about his appearance. Vanity is probably a huge factor in keeping oneself really alive in old age, she thought. Look at Frau Hagen—clearly vain and still living in a world where people attract each other. "It's not flattery," she said. "It's a statement of fact."

He laughed again and made his way to one of the hard-backed chairs. "I need to be strong this morning," he said. "The service for Frau Winkler will be doubly sad—you have heard, I suppose, about Sister Barbara."

"Yes, terrible. What did the inspector say?"

"He seemed shocked, and he dashed off. He is a good man, I think, and I hope he can put a stop to what is going on here."

"What *is* going on, Herr Pokorny?"

"It's no good asking me, my dear. I am an old man with one foot in another world. I know that something ugly is happening to us. As Luther's great hymn has it, *The ancient prince of hell / Has risen with purpose fell.* We'll all be singing that shortly. I can only put my faith in the trusty shield of my God to protect us. But perhaps our good inspector is also wielding a sword on our behalf."

"Well, I certainly hope so. But if you are OK for now, Pastor, I'll go down and see what's going on. My husband is also somewhere about. Christa will be in to see you shortly."

"Just be careful, Frau Fabian. Auf Wiedersehen."

She went along the corridor to the staircase and walked down. She should be careful, she supposed, if the ancient prince of hell were on the prowl. The only Mephistophelian character she had yet encountered in this place was the handsome Dr. Hofer. Maybe he had a cloven foot. She should look more closely. She had thought him attractive a couple of days ago. Well, that was what Mephistopheles was supposed to be—a seductive devil. She was shocked as she turned the corner into the lobby almost to collide with the devil himself, who seemed on the verge of making his nefarious way upstairs to the Melanchthon apartments.

"Good morning, Frau Fabian," said Dr. Hofer brusquely, and turned on his heel to go back toward Gruber's desk. Herr Gruber was nowhere to be seen.

"Good morning, Herr Dr. Hofer," said Eleanor, and walked on through the lobby to the café. Hofer somehow did not look his usual suave self. What if he were the murderer? Maybe she should warn the inspector that he was going up into Melanchthon. She went around the corner and waited for a moment. She peered back into the lobby to see him disappearing into the elevator. So he *was* going up there. Should she perhaps warn Christa to keep the door locked? But surely the ancient prince of hell would not want to tangle with Pokorny, man of God. Well, to hell with it, to coin a phrase—she would try to see where he was going. She went back to the staircase and hurried up the stairs, panting as she got to the second floor. The Ritters were on this floor. If Hofer saw her, she could always say that she was looking for her husband. She stepped boldly, if breathlessly, into the corridor just in time to see the door of Frau Hagen's apartment closing. So he had gone in there. Well, that was a turn up for the books. She'd better go and tell the inspector promptly, just in case.

At that moment, the door of the Ritters' apartment opened, and out hopped Herr Ritter, looking, as usual, neat and spruce as a sparrow. "Oh, Frau Fabian! Good timing. I was just coming to find you. I've made some breakfast for your husband and thought you might like to join us. I'm sure you want to see him."

No, thought Eleanor. I don't want to see him. Not at the moment. Not at all, really. "Why, yes, Herr Ritter, how kind of you," she said and allowed herself to be ushered into the apartment.

3

As soon as Büchner got to his room, he threw off his clothes as if they were contaminated and got under a strong jet of hot water. I don't believe in evil times, he said firmly to himself, scrubbing his hair with soap and feeling better by the second. He had always rejected explanations of the Nazi period in Germany and Austria that used the image of evil descending on a society. It was altogether too easy an abstraction. It shifted the responsibility of the individual and the body politic onto some evil force that came from who knows where and took over the minds and bodies of the people. Rubbish, thought Büchner, forcing himself to turn the water onto cold and to stand under it without flinching. The Nazi period came about through the criminal actions of unscrupulous and perverted men and the total political failure of decent men to stop them. Women too, he reminded himself, stepping out of the cold water and glowing with new energy. And so it is in the Haus im Wald, he thought. The time is not evil—some individuals may be evil, if you want to use the word. In any case, they have been doing some pretty nasty things. Pokorny had called him a good man. Well, it was time for this good man to take some action. Goodness alone didn't hack it when you were facing the truly criminal. He preferred the word criminal—evil was a word for the pulpit. He put on clean underwear and a clean shirt, and, thinking of the service for Frau Winkler, he pulled out the one tie he had with him and put that on too. He looked at his watch. Eight o'clock. Time to start knocking on doors.

He walked down the stairs slowly this time, building up within himself the sensation of being a man of action, moving resolutely in on his target, John Wayne walking down the main street and pushing open the swinging doors of the saloon. He laughed. No time to laugh, he said to himself and sternly approached Frau Huber's apartment. Not exactly saloon doors, but still . . . He knocked loudly and also rang the bell. A voice from the other side said, "Who's there?"

"Büchner, Kripo Wien."

"I'm not dressed. Please come back later." The voice was also loud and authoritative.

"I must see you now. Please open the door."

There was a long pause. Finally, the door opened, and Frau Huber stood there, wearing a pink chenille bathrobe, no makeup, and a hairnet on her head. Her face was red.

"Herr Inspektor," she said, "what is the meaning of this?"

Saloon doors, he thought and simply strode across the threshold, closing the door behind him and forcing her to retreat backward.

"I have some questions for you," he said. "Would you like to call a witness?"

"A witness? What is all this about?"

"Shall we go in and sit down?"

She walked ahead of him into her sitting room.

"Please sit down," he said, motioning her toward the flowered couch. He sat down on a straight-backed chair immediately opposite her. Without her uniform, her considerable girth flopped about, barely contained by the pink chenille and making her look like easy prey rather than a formidable adversary. Büchner allowed a full minute of silence to elapse during which the red of Frau Huber's face deepened. Then he said quietly, "How long have you known Dr. Hofer?"

"Why do you ask me that?" she said, a slight tremble in her voice.

"I need to know how long you have known him and what he knows about you."

"What he knows about me?" she repeated faintly.

"Yes. I cannot believe, you see, Frau Huber, that a sensible competent woman like you would have done the things you have done unless some sort of pressure had been exerted on you."

"The things I have done?"

"Yes," said Büchner kindly, almost gently. "I think we both know that you have been writing nasty little verses on yellow stickers and using your master key and your knowledge of residents' routines to place these stickers unobserved where you knew who would find them and when they would be found. I think we both know that, don't we? My question is, who put you up to it? I cannot believe that it was your idea, no matter what others may suggest." He paused, not taking away his eyes from hers and wondering whether she would fall for this or whether she would bluff her way out of it and deny the whole thing. There was no reason why she should not do the latter—he had no actual proof that she had written the stickers.

"The only two," he said, "as far as I know, that were put in public places where anyone could see them, were ones in which your name played a part—a rather clumsy way of suggesting publicly, perhaps, that you were also a victim of these nasty things?"

Again he paused, and into the silence came a ring at the doorbell. "Please don't answer that," said Büchner as she half stood up. But then they heard a key turn in the lock. "Ah," said Büchner," another master key."

Frau Huber looked nervously at the door. It opened, and in walked Dr. Hofer. He stopped at the threshold, seeing Büchner.

"Do come in, Herr Doktor. Frau Huber is telling me about your joint activities."

"Joint activities?" said Hofer. "What is this nonsense, Frau Huber?"

"Nothing," she said. "I told him nothing."

"Of course not," said Hofer quickly. "There is nothing to tell."

"Let me go back to my original question," said Büchner. "How long have you known each other?"

"I met Frau Huber some years ago," said Dr. Hofer, "when she was working as the assistant housekeeper in a large nursing home outside Vienna. I was impressed by her capabilities and recommended her here when the position of housekeeper became vacant."

"And what, Herr Dr. Hofer, did you know about her that helped you induce her to work with you on the yellow-sticker project?"

"There was no yellow-sticker project," said Hofer irritably. "This is all an absurd conjecture on your part."

Büchner turned to Frau Huber, whose round red face was now quivering with what might have been fear. "Is that the case, Frau Huber? Let me remind you that I am investigating a murder here. I already know that the yellow stickers mark a trail leading to one death. Do you want to be arrested for murder? No, don't look at him. You are the one who will be held responsible. You wrote the stickers. We will be able to prove this with the help of a handwriting specialist. You had better tell me the truth."

"Yes," she said, her face red enough to suggest apoplexy. "I wrote the stickers. But that's all. I had nothing to do with anything else. And most of it was his idea."

"Herr Inspektor," said Hofer. "We are dealing here with a rather sick and hysterical woman. When I discovered that she was writing unpleasant verses on stickers, I tried to stop her."

"What?" shouted Frau Huber. "You did what? I was foolish enough to tell you about the one that I had written, just a little joke to bring Sister Agatha down a peg, and then you used those old stories to get me to write some more."

"Old stories?" interjected Büchner.

"You might as well know, Herr Inspektor, that in her previous job, Frau Huber had acquired a bit of a reputation for, shall we say, helping various elderly gentlemen in . . . various ways."

"And so you recommended her for the position here?"

"Well, yes," Hofer hesitated. "I really only discovered her reputation later."

"None of it was true," said Frau Huber shrilly, getting up off the couch and drawing her robe around her. "I have never . . . helped anyone who did not want to be helped."

Hofer laughed. "Well, that's one way of putting it. Some stories you have told me—"

"I do not know why I ever told you anything . . ."

"Nor do I," said Büchner. "It seems to be a mistake many people have made. But you can fight that out between you." He stood up. "One way or another, you have managed to wreak havoc in this house. Direct lines connect these yellow stickers with death. If either of you wishes individually to tell me more, you may find me either immediately before or after the service for Frau Winkler." He left the room and the apartment and closed the door firmly behind him. He could well imagine how Hofer, in confidential little sessions, had charmed Frau Huber into admitting various things to him and had then been able to manipulate her. Let them stew in their own juice for a while, he thought. Very nasty people doing very nasty things. Neither of them, he was sure, had struck the blow that had killed Hans Graf; but they had, he was equally sure, set in motion with their poison pen the chain of events that had led Sister Barbara to her death in the forest. Somewhere along that chain of events lay the death of Hans Graf. And despite the note she had left him, he was viscerally sure that Barbara had not struck the fatal blow either. There must be no more incidental deaths. Time was running out.

4

A quick word with Gruber, thought Büchner, but he was not at his desk. Odd. Gruber would only leave his post off schedule at the request of his boss. He knocked at Schramm's door, and hardly waiting for an answer, he walked in. As he had expected, Gruber was there, standing almost at attention in front of Schramm's desk, both men in dark suits and black tie. Schramm sat on his imposing director's chair behind his large desk, looking anything but imposing. When Büchner burst in on them, he was rubbing his forehead like a man with a sinus headache. He didn't even stand up.

"Do sit down, Herr Inspektor," he said, gesturing wearily to a high-backed chair. Gruber turned as if to leave, but Büchner said, "You sit down too, Herr Gruber, if you please. I need to speak to both of you."

Gruber looked at Schramm, who said, "Take a seat, Manfred."

Büchner, surprised at the familiar form of address, raised an eyebrow at Schramm, who made a throwaway gesture with his right hand and said with the same weary air, "No point in discretion anymore. Everything seems to be on the table now. Yes, Gruber and I knew each other when we were children. Both our fathers belonged to the Austrian Communist Party in the days after the war. They were friends. Mine resigned from the party in 1956 when the Soviets moved in on Hungary. I was eleven. His committed suicide when Manfred was twelve. My father did pretty well in business himself, and he looked out for Manfred as best he could, but as a former Communist, he had no influence on certain things. For example, he was no use when Manfred was turned down for the police force in 1965. We lost touch when I went to the university, but when he turned up here and applied for the job at the Haus im Wald, I was glad to give it to him."

During this narrative, Gruber sat stiffly on the second high-backed chair and registered nothing.

"So you might have been a policeman," said Büchner.

"Water under the bridge," said Gruber. "I am what I am."

"Oh, quite," said Büchner. "And what are you two old comrades up to at the moment? Why have you left your post, Herr Gruber?"

"We are not old comrades," said Schramm crossly. "This could at best be said of our fathers, long since dead. I asked him to come and see me because I wanted to tell him myself about the death of Sister Barbara—though as it turned out, Michael had got there before me. How does that young man come to be so well-informed?"

"And how were you informed?"

"I had a call from the hospital when I came in half an hour ago. I am extremely upset about it. I wanted to get Gruber's opinion—I trust him completely, you see. Sometimes it seems as if he is the only one I *can* trust in this place." Schramm's voice took on the pathetic note that was beginning to sound very familiar to Büchner.

"His opinion about what?"

"Why she died," said Schramm, "what's going on here, why she rode off in that crazy way in the middle of the night."

"And what is his opinion?" Büchner turned to Gruber.

"I am not paid," said Gruber, "to have opinions."

"You are, however, paid to keep an eye on the comings and goings in this house, and I happen to think you have a very sharp eye and would have made a very good policeman. It would help me a great deal now if you would waive all other scruples in view of the violent deaths that have occurred, as it were, on your boss's watch and for his sake, if for nothing else, give us some of your thoughts on what you have seen and heard in recent weeks. You told me, for example, that you saw Sister Barbara leave the house close to sundown on Christmas Day to walk in the woods. Was there anything unusual about her at that moment? Remember that she has died. And we need to find out exactly why. Every detail is important."

Gruber had relaxed his demeanor during this speech. "Her death is a loss to this house," he said. "She was kind to everyone. I was disturbed that she would go out so late on a cold day, and I said so. She was as white as the snow on the ground. If she had not returned in ten minutes, I would have gone to look for her. I went to the door and watched the path she took. But she came back. She still had a blank look in her eyes. She said only, 'Good night, Herr Gruber, I am going to the chapel.' It wasn't the first time I have seen her with that blank look, however, so I did not think anything new was happening."

"A blank look?"

"Yes," said Gruber. "I am not unfamiliar with that look. I have worked many years in hospitals and nursing homes, where it is sometimes held to be better to maintain people in a blank state than to allow them to be in full touch with their own miserable feelings."

"That's a bit strong, Manfred," said Schramm.

"I am not referring to the Haus im Wald. It was a look that I had observed in Sister Barbara only in recent weeks."

"You didn't mention it to anybody?" said Büchner.

"It's not my job—" began Gruber.

Büchner interrupted him. "Is there easy access to various kinds of drugs in the Haus im Wald, Herr Direktor?"

"Certainly not. Drugs are prescribed by individual physicians for individual patients and have to be obtained from the pharmacy in Feldberg. We do not keep supplies here of anything but over-the-counter medications, such as aspirin. That is our policy. We are not a hospital, and we have no licensed pharmacist on the staff."

"You might talk," said Gruber slowly, volunteering for once a comment of his own, "to Frau Zimmermann. She has a computer. And she is very friendly."

"My thought precisely," said Büchner, and Gruber almost smiled. "I shall do that right away." He looked at his watch. It was now nine o'clock. "A bit early to visit the unmarried married couple," he said to Gruber as they walked to the lobby together. "But that's where I shall go now. If anything noteworthy happens here, I hope I can rely on you to contact me immediately."

"Yes, sir," said Gruber. Büchner rode up in the elevator to the Zimmermanns' floor and rang their bell.

"Who's there?" responded a voice immediately.

"Büchner, Kripo Wien."

"Why, Herr Inspektor," said Frau Zimmermann brightly, opening the door with alacrity. She was already fully dressed in a neat black jacket and skirt and a white silk blouse. Another one ready for the funeral, thought Büchner.

"What can we do for you so early in the morning?"

"It is you I wanted to speak to, Frau Zimmermann. Something has happened in which you may, more or less unwittingly, have been involved."

"Whatever do you mean?"

"Sit down for a moment. First, I have bad news. Sister Barbara is dead. She died in the night."

The habitually cheerful look vanished from Frau Zimmermann's face. "Oh no, that cannot be."

"I'm afraid it can and is. Do you have anything to tell me about her?"

"Oh God, oh God," she said.

Büchner said, "It is not illegal to order medications on the Internet. It may be unwise, but it is not illegal. I happen to know that you did Herr Graf a favor by discreetly ordering Viagra for him. I am not in the least interested in the rights and wrongs of this kind of thing, but I do have to know now if you did the same favor for anyone else, such as Sister Barbara. Please tell me the truth, Frau Zimmermann. We can find out of course in any case, but you will save time and perhaps lives if you tell me the truth."

"Valium," she said, in little more than a whisper. "I did order Valium for Sister Barbara. It is frequently advertised on the Internet and easy to obtain—you know the sort of thing. 'Valium. On sale. Buy now.' That sort of thing. I ordered it in the lower doses appropriate for the elderly—only 2 mg pills—and I printed out all the information that came with it, side effects, etc. Herr Inspektor"—her voice trembled—"you are not telling me that she died of an overdose?"

"No, I am not telling you that."

"Thank God."

"Perhaps you should hold off thanking the deity for a while until we know more. She died after her scooter had run into a tree."

"Oh, dear God."

"Yes, quite. All I need to know from you at this moment are two things. First of all, did Sister Barbara talk to you at all about why she wanted the Valium, and—this is very important—have you ever ordered drugs for anyone else in this house?"

"She told me she was under a lot of strain at the moment and just needed some temporary relief."

"Why did she come to you?"

"It seems that Michael had told her you could order such things on the Internet. It didn't seem so bad to me—I have known women all my life whose doctors prescribed Valium from time to time."

"No doubt. Have you ever taken it yourself?"

"Heavens, no. I believe in positive thinking, not drug-taking. I said this to Sister Barbara at the time, and she laughed and said she didn't have much to think positively about at the moment and just wanted to sleep better at nights. So I ordered it—about a month ago. She asked me to have it sent in my name. She obviously didn't want Sister Agatha to know about it. Of course, I told nobody."

"Nobody?"

"Well, in a weak moment, I once mentioned it to Dr. Hofer. But he is very discreet, you know."

"Oh yes, I know that."

"I told nobody else."

"You would have done well to tell me, as it turns out. And in view of what has happened, I think you should now tell me whether you have ever ordered anything for anyone else."

"No, I haven't. But . . ." she hesitated.

"Well?"

"About three weeks ago, Frau Hagen asked me if anything like Viagra existed for women. I asked her why she thought I would know, and she said she knew I had ordered it for Herr Graf. How did she know that? I asked. Had Herr Graf talked about it? No, she said, a friend of his had told her. She did not tell me who the friend was. I said I had no idea what there was in this line for women. She had better talk to her doctor. I was a bit upset about this conversation. I did not want to start gaining a reputation as some sort of drug dealer."

"I can imagine that," said Büchner drily.

"What's going on here?" Herr Zimmermann came into the room, wearing a bathrobe and looking distinctly annoyed.

"I am just leaving," said Büchner. "Thank you, Frau Zimmermann, you have been very helpful."

"Helpful?" said Herr Zimmermann loudly. "And what have you been helping *him* with?"

Büchner smiled. "I'll leave you to field that one," he said and left the room. And now Frau Hagen, he thought, looking at his watch again. Only half an hour to go before the service. He needed to hurry. He was about to ring the doorbell when he thought he heard raised voices from inside her apartment. He stood quietly outside the door, listening.

5

The table in the Ritters' charming sitting room was set for breakfast, and as the door opened, Eleanor saw Franz sitting on the couch in his underwear, swinging his legs out from under a blanket onto the carpet. They glared at each other, as Frau Ritter came lumbering in with her walker.

"Why, good morning, Frau Ritter," said Eleanor, averting her eyes from Franz's bare hairy legs, hoping he would have the grace to cover them before Frau Ritter made her way around to the front of the couch.

"I didn't mean to disturb you, my dear," said Herr Ritter to his wife. "I was just giving our guests breakfast. Before the service, you know. We will all, I presume, be going to the service."

"What does the service have to do with it?" said Frau Ritter crossly. "Have all these people been sleeping here?"

"I'll explain it all later," said Herr Ritter pleadingly. "Do sit down and have a cup of coffee, Frau Fabian."

"Well, thank you," she said, relieved that Franz had now covered his knees with a blanket. "Just a cup of coffee then. I can't stay long. I have to go and find the inspector."

"Oh, you do?" said Franz.

"Yes, I do," she said defiantly. "And then there is the service. You'll have to get dressed, Franz, if you're coming to that."

"I see no particular reason—" he began.

She interrupted him and completed his sentence, "—to discuss that here. Quite so, anyway, I'm going to the service."

"Of course, we are too," said Herr Ritter. He was already wearing a dark suit and tie.

"Well," said Frau Ritter, "I certainly intend to go. Perhaps you could leave your guests for a while and come and help me get ready." She began to maneuver her walker back into the bedroom.

Eleanor gulped down her coffee. "I'll be off then," she said before Herr Ritter could leave the room. "If you don't come to the service, Franz, I'll see you afterward. Thank you so much, Herr Ritter," she said, rushing to the door.

Glad to get out of there, she wondered now why she had thought it so urgent to tell the inspector that she thought Hofer was visiting Frau Hagen. She walked slowly past Frau Hagen's door and lingered outside it. She could hear nothing. She walked down to the lobby and stood for a moment, uncertain of what to do now, since the inspector was nowhere about. Well, she could look in at the chapel. She could at least sit and think there for minute and try to compose her mind for the farewell to Frau Winkler. As she turned the corner, she could smell the flowers—a rather heady, oppressive smell, as if they had already been there a bit too long. She went in and sat in the back pew. An area had been cleared in the front and a trestle set up, presumably to receive the coffin. So this would be an actual funeral service, not just a memorial service for the Haus im Wald residents. This was, after all, home for that bright old lady whom Eleanor had last seen choosing a piece of cake with great gusto in the café. How cheerful she had looked! She seemed to have been happy in the Haus im Wald, and she had died suddenly in her own bed there. In a week of sudden deaths, hers seemed to be almost enviable. Eleanor had witnessed the slow death over months and years of her own mother. How much better to be happy one day sitting in a café and gone the next. Of course, Frau Winkler had died alone, and no one would ever know what her last hours were like. Everyone dies alone—an expression that rolls easily off the tongue but is not so easy to imagine for oneself. Frau Winkler had had a happy evening before with her friends, Christa and the pastor. A few days ago, Eleanor would have thought it insane to consider moving into a retirement home, but thinking of that happy little band of friends, oddly assorted though they might be, seeing them through Christa's eyes, she could see that it was far better than eking out a solitary existence in increasing disorder and lonely confusion. And through her own eyes? She had never seriously contemplated what old age with Franz would be like. She hadn't seriously contemplated it without him either. But to spend their remaining years together, increasingly irascible, increasingly inflexible, less and less mobile, more and more cast upon each other's company—suddenly, taking a cozy little single apartment in the Haus im Wald seemed to be not a bad option at all.

Forget yourself, she told herself. Focus your mind on that place where the coffin will soon rest, and think of the departed soul of Frau Winkler. You don't believe in the soul. OK, picture the living Frau Winkler, and pay your respects to her memory. She could feel her head nodding forward. Too little sleep. Better go off again in search of the inspector, though she could barely remember what she had wanted to tell him. The café. That's where she would go. He might be there, and in any case, maybe she could get Michael to give her another cup of coffee.

Michael opened the café door. He looked tired, with dark rings under his eyes, but handsome nevertheless in his black suit.

"Oh," he said, "Frau Fabian. How's your husband?"

"My husband?"

"Yes, did he find you after I got him out of the hospital?"

"You got him out?" Eleanor was mystified.

"Oh, hasn't he told you?"

"I've hardly seen him actually. He's having breakfast with the Ritters."

"The Ritters?" Michael looked mystified.

"Yes."

"Oh, well, then I can find him and get my key back."

"It was your key? That's how he got in?"

"You'd better talk to him, Frau Fabian. He can tell you the whole story. Would you like a cup of coffee?"

"Oh, would I not! And if you have a bit of bread or something, I wouldn't mind nibbling on that either."

Michael laughed. "Sure. Have a seat. You look tired."

"I have to get myself together somehow to go to the funeral. I look awful, I know. I didn't sleep much."

"I know what you mean." Michael busied himself in the kitchen, and Eleanor sat on a stool at the bar where she could see him. She thought of those early days when she had sat in this cafe and idly observed the residents.

"Heavens, Michael," she said as he brought her coffee and a croissant with butter and jam. "How many people have died here since this last time last week? Oh, thanks, that looks delicious."

"Better not count. It's too depressing."

"It's pretty unusual, don't you think? What do you make of it all? You must know all these people pretty well. I mean, Sister Barbara, for example. What on earth was going on there?"

"Well, you know—or maybe you don't—there has been a rather weird business here in the last month or so of people getting anonymous notes, little verses, saying obscene things. And I know the sisters got a few because Sister Barbara asked me, in confidence, if I had any idea who was writing them."

"Yes," said Eleanor. "I had heard about them. But would something like that make her drive into a tree?"

"I didn't take those things very seriously, but for people like the sisters, well, it's pretty heavy stuff. Sister Barbara used to talk to me sometimes. She thought Agatha was a bit hard on me, and she would try to make up for it by being extra nice. She would ask me about my grandmother, and a few times, without telling Agatha, she went across town to the old folks' home to visit her. Nobody else from here did that. I appreciated it, I can tell you. When I noticed a few weeks ago how strung out she was, I gave her a tip about getting hold of some tranquilizers. Sister Barbara had a bit of a past with alcohol and drugs and all that, she'd told me about it—she wasn't ashamed of it. Why should she be? She had got over it."

"Is that what the notes were about?"

"No, they were mostly about her and Agatha. Laughable to anybody who knows Agatha. But not laughable to poor old Barbara—probably stirred up all her latent longings. In fact, the only one I actually saw involving Barbara was one Dr. Hofer showed me that Frau Hagen had got."

"Frau Hagen?"

"Yes, apparently she had given it to Hofer and asked him to try and find out who was writing these things. He thought it was pretty funny and showed it to me. It was something like this: 'Barbara the onetime lush / Seems to have a brand-new crush

/ Doesn't love the dried-up sister / Loves old Hagen since she kissed her.' Crazy stuff."

"Good Lord, Michael, are you serious? Hofer thought this was funny? Have you told the inspector?"

"No, I don't see what it's to do with him. I'm only telling you because you're a complete outsider and I'm so upset this morning, I feel like talking to somebody. It was such a piece of nonsense in any case, these old folks are always kissing somebody. I should know. They're always kissing me." He laughed, looking more like his usual mischievous self. "And that got into some of the stickers too." But his face clouded over. "I really liked Sister Barbara. She was one of the best people around here. I wish to God I had never told her about the tranquilizers on the Internet. That may be why she lost control of the bike." He sat down at the bar and put his head in his hands. "I'm so damned tired. I worked all night in the hospital. Your husband'll tell you all about that. It was a horrible shock to hear about Barbara there. And I'm sorry for Agatha. I don't like her, and she doesn't like me, but for all her straitlaced morals, she was devoted to Barbara—can't imagine how she'll be on her own."

"Should somebody go up and check on her, do you think?"

"Well, not me, she can't stand me. And in any case, there's only twenty minutes left till the service for Frau Winkler. In the midst of life, we are in death, as our venerable leader Schramm never tires of telling us. I have to go to the front door and wait for the coffin. Are you going to the service?"

"Yes, I intended to. But I have a mind to go up and at least offer condolences to Agatha. Surely she won't appear at the service."

"Never know with Agatha—the Spartan personality, you know."

"Well, thanks a lot for the coffee, Michael. See you later."

That latest yellow sticker, she thought, hurrying along the corridor, really is something the inspector ought to know about. She passed several residents from Martin Luther being wheeled along in the direction of the chapel. Direktor Schramm stood at the front door looking at his watch, Gruber at his side. Where was the inspector? Well, she'd go upstairs and look around; and if she got up the courage, she would knock at Agatha's door. She waited for the elevator. The heavy smell of the flowers made her feel slightly sick. Another small batch of wheelchairs passed her, the faces of the occupants registering nothing, as if bracing themselves to be unmoved by yet another last farewell. From the chapel came the unmistakable strains of Bach's cantata, "It Is Enough," no doubt a CD on Christa's boom box brought down for the occasion. As the elevator arrived and the doors slowly closed, she could make out the words of the solemn aria:

Sleep tired eyes
Softly close in bliss
World, I'm leaving you behind
My part in you is over.

Eleanor closed her eyes as the tones of the transcendent strings were cut short by the clamping shut of the elevator door. Death, she thought, is not the worst thing.

Chapter 18

It took a funeral to fill the chapel at the Haus im Wald—every pew taken, the aisles crowded with wheelchairs, members of staff and sometimes visitors standing at the back. There were no visitors to be expected at Frau Winkler's funeral. Her husband's death sixty years earlier had isolated her, the ambiguity of his dying, a hero and a criminal, a man who betrayed his country rather than betray himself and his God. Frau Winkler had faced life alone, an anomaly in the postwar Austrian landscape. Where did she belong? She could not forget, but she was, as we say, by nature, a happy woman; and she believed in God, in the glorious martyrdom of her husband, and in their literal reunion in the afterlife. She had found a home in the last ten years of her life in the Haus im Wald, where she was happy to live and quite possibly happy to die. There were other residents of the house whose grasp on the things of this world was a great deal more frenetic. Gathering in the chapel that morning, greeted by the soaring elegiac cantata of Johann Sebastian Bach, "Ich habe genug," how many of them could happily say, with the hymnist, "I have had enough, I rejoice in my death"? No matter how beautiful the plaintive strains of the farewell to the world, there were surely those who rebelliously shouted in their heads: I have not had enough. I am not ready to say "good night to the world." Herr Graf had surely not been ready. And someone in the community now gathering to pay its last respects to a little old lady must know why this rich, well-preserved, ebullient gentleman had died before his time. The sweet resignation of the Bach cantata filled the air, the soul of Frau Winkler might now depart in peace, but those residents of the Haus im Wald still bodily filling the pews surely sensed the angry ghost of Herr Graf, whose two feet had been planted firmly in the pleasures of this world when he was visited by a most unwelcome death.

1

Büchner stood quietly outside the door of Frau Hagen's apartment listening, well, eavesdropping. This was not a position he cared to be discovered in, and he would, he realized, either have to knock at the door again or move on. In any case, he could only intermittently hear what was going on. Frau Hagen's voice was loud and penetrating, sounding angry, but she seemed to be storming about the apartment, and so he could sometimes hear clearly what she was saying and sometimes she was quite out of earshot. The man's voice—she was clearly talking to a man—was low, his actual words largely inaudible, but Büchner thought he recognized the smooth modulations of the charming Dr. Hofer.

"You promised me," she was saying now. "You promised me, and you lied."

Hofer's murmuring did not seem to calm her down.

"Why did I ever trust you? Perhaps it was all lies."

And then, "My life is over. Nothing is left to me now." Frau Hagen had once said something like this to Büchner himself. Was all this a histrionic performance by the lovely aging diva? Her stage voice carried clearly into the quiet corridor: "I can destroy you too! I will not be silent!"

The voice of Hofer emerged suddenly, clearly. "Stop this at once. The entire house will hear you."

There was a long silence, and then footsteps came toward the door. Büchner withdrew into the shadows of the staircase. Hofer came out into the corridor and got quickly into the elevator. Odd. He was going up, not down. Why? Büchner made his way quietly up the stairs hoping to see where he was going. Stepping into the corridor on the third floor, however, he was faced with Pastor Pokorny and Christa, the pastor maneuvering his walker, and Christa beside him.

"I hope to be down for the service," Büchner said hastily. "Have to check a few things first." Pastor Pokorny looked amazingly good in his dark suit.

"I have to do my job," he said cheerfully, clearly relishing the prospect, "and you yours. We are relying on you, you know."

"Doing my best," said Büchner, annoyed that in those seconds he had lost Hofer. He walked along to Sister Agatha's apartment and again listened at the door. This is turning into a nasty habit, he thought. He could hear the quiet murmuring of women's voices—no Hofer there, by the sound of it. A door opened on the corridor, and Büchner turned around quickly.

"Well, well, Herr Inspektor. Can I be of any assistance?" Dr. Lessing stood at her door, looking quizzically at him.

Embarrassed, he said, "Perhaps so. May I step inside your apartment for a moment?"

"Certainly," she said. She was wearing a dark gray suit and leaning on her cane, no doubt on her way, like everyone else, to the chapel.

"I don't want to hold you up," he said. "But your doorway would be a useful vantage point for me at the moment. You may carry on down if you wish."

"I don't want to hold you up either," she said. "But I hope your line-drawing efforts are now producing a clearer picture."

"Two portraits are still bothering me, Frau Doktor. I concentrate on one, and I lose sight of the other."

"Ah yes, Herr Inspektor, but remember, the lines in the ambiguous portraits do in fact coexist. It is your eye that separates them into two portraits."

Büchner nodded, looking beyond her to the corridor.

"I will not waste your time," she said. "I'll go on down to the service for Frau Winkler. Like everyone else here, I have a superstitious fear of missing last farewells. Who knows which of us will be next? Good luck, Herr Inspektor. You are welcome to use this vantage point as long as you like. Auf Wiedersehen."

"Thank you, Frau Doktor." He watched her walk to the elevator with her little limp. What lines, he asked himself, might connect the two faces in his head, the round, earnest, seemingly transparent face of poor dead Barbara with her trusting eyes, and the fine-boned, expressive face of the elusive Ursula Hagen? He stood behind the half-closed door and watched the other doors on the corridor. After a minute or so, the door of the "sealed" Graf apartment opened, and out came Dr. Hofer. He waited until Hofer was passing Dr. Lessing's door and then threw it wide open.

"Would you step in here for a moment, Herr Doktor," he said.

Hofer looked unpleasantly surprised. "I would like to attend the service," he said. "It must have started already."

"No doubt, but just a word, if you please."

Hofer came into the apartment, and Büchner closed the door. "We won't be disturbed here," he said. "What were you doing in Graf's apartment? It is supposed to be locked."

"Frau Huber gave me the key," said Hofer smoothly. "She asked me to check on the situation. She thought she saw lights in the apartment last night."

"Not a very likely story, Herr Doktor. If that were really the case, she should have reported it to the police. Be that as it may, you seem to be the *confidant* of a number of people in this residence, not least Frau Huber, as we established earlier this morning."

"We established nothing," said Hofer quickly. "You voiced various suspicions, all of them unfounded."

"You will not deny, at any rate, that you have seen a great many of the famous yellow stickers shown to you, shall we say, by the recipients and others, all of whom seem to have trusted you."

"That is so. Quite a lot of people do trust me, it may surprise you to know."

"It does not really surprise me to know it. What does surprise me is that so many people seem to be so lacking in judgment."

"I see no reason why I should allow myself to be gratuitously insulted by you, Herr Inspektor. If you have any actual accusations of misbehavior on my part, please state these clearly. Otherwise, I suggest we go down to the service."

"I am the one making suggestions here, Herr Doktor, not you. I suggest that you tell me why Frau Hagen is so angry with you that her rage could be heard all over the building."

Hofer looked no more than slightly put out. "Just what, Herr Inspektor, did you hear? People who eavesdrop, you know, frequently mishear."

"Why, for example, does she think she can destroy you?"

Hofer laughed. "You must have misheard that one."

"Well, I can always ask her directly if you do not choose to answer. But tell me, Dr. Hofer, what do you know about the death of Sister Barbara?"

Hofer hesitated, then said, "Perhaps you should rather ask the question, Herr Inspektor, what did Sister Barbara know about the death of Hans Graf?"

"And why should I ask that, Herr Doktor?"

"Two women, whom Sister Barbara cared for, cared themselves for Hans Graf. That might constitute a motive for murder, you know. Jealousy is a powerful force."

"Are you suggesting that Sister Barbara cared for Frau Hagen as she cared for Sister Agatha?"

Hofer smiled in a superior way. "Everyone in this house has fallen for the charms of Ursula Hagen, in one way or another, and Barbara was, shall we say, particularly susceptible."

"So the meek Sister Barbara picked up a blunt instrument and struck Hans Graf a deathblow to remove him from the scene so that she would have free rein for her illicit passions?"

"You are making a ridiculous picture out of something that is entirely possible."

"Yes, and Sister Barbara is dead, so unable to defend herself."

"Why would I be making unfounded accusations?" said Hofer. "You surely do not believe that I killed Hans Graf?"

No, thought Büchner, I really do not. And I have probably got as much out of this gentleman as I am likely to get at the moment. He looked at his watch. He wanted to see who was and was not at the service for Frau Winkler. But first he would do a quick check in Graf's apartment to see if there were any suggestion of what Hofer had actually been doing there.

"No," he said. "I doubt if you are capable of anything as direct as actually killing a man. Why don't you go on down to the service, Herr Doktor, that's what you wanted to do, I believe."

Hofer inclined his head, turned around, and left the apartment without a word. After a minute or so, Büchner went along the corridor, took out his own master key, and let himself into the apartment of the dead man.

2

Eleanor got off the elevator at the third floor, knocked at Pastor Pokorny's door, and then Christa's, but got no answer at either. She lingered for a moment outside the door of Herr Graf's apartment; silence within, she did not dare try the door handle. Oh, come on, she said to herself. Just knock at Agatha's door. She did. She could hear someone moving inside. She waited. Finally, the door opened, and Agatha stood there, clad as usual in her long gray woolen dress with the little white collar, standing as tall as ever, her hair smoothly drawn back from her face, but strain in every line of her face, and in her eyes naked pain.

"I'm sorry," said Eleanor, feeling every inch an intruder. "I only wanted to know whether you were all right."

"All right?" said Agatha.

"Is there anything I can do?" said Eleanor.

"No." But she didn't close the door, so Eleanor just stood there.

"Well," said Agatha faintly. "Perhaps there is something. Please come in."

Eleanor went in. "Please sit down," Agatha said. Eleanor obeyed, but Agatha walked slowly to the window and looked out.

"The snow is dazzling this morning," she said.

"Yes," said Eleanor. "With the sun on it."

In the silence, she could hear the sound of a car coming into the driveway, its tires crunching on the crisp snow. "The hearse," said Agatha. "I must go down to the service."

"Oh heavens," said Eleanor. "You don't have to do that at a time like this."

"At a time like this?" Agatha turned around and fixed Eleanor with something more like her usual schoolmarm's look. "At a time like this, what else should I do?"

Iron discipline, thought Eleanor, is all very well. But why doesn't the woman just break down and cry? She'd be better off. Let her hair down, throw herself on the bed, and scream. "Of course," she said. "It's the best thing probably. I'll come down with you. I wanted to go to the service myself. But what was it you thought I might do for you."

"Speak to the inspector," said Agatha. "I need to tell him a couple of things that may be of use in his investigation, but I do not want to talk to him at the moment. It is easier for me to say these things to another woman, if you don't mind. They must be said. Though it is not easy for me, and I don't know how important they are."

"Well, of course, I'll do that."

"Thank you. You are an outsider to the community, and you will soon go away and forget all about us. Here is what the inspector perhaps needs to know. He was concerned about our movements on Christmas Day, especially since Barbara left a note for him suggesting that she was responsible for Hans Graf's death."

Eleanor gasped.

"Yes," said Agatha. "Of course, it's absurd. Barbara could not have struck a blow of the kind that killed Hans Graf. I saw the body soon after it was discovered, a brutal frontal blow to the forehead, which must have been struck in extreme anger, or else in extreme sadistic coldness—neither of which Barbara would have been capable of. However, she was also not a liar, so she must have thought herself in some way responsible."

"She left a note for the inspector? Nothing for . . . anyone else?"

"No, nothing. I have searched the apartment but have found nothing for me. You can tell the inspector that, and give him this. She did keep a diary. Of course, I never looked in it before, but now, well, it seemed important. It is not a record of personal thoughts or anything like that, just dates and times when she had appointments for this or that, and sometimes notes for events she perhaps wanted to remember. The notes for Christmas Day itself are cryptic: '16:45, did nothing.' You should tell the inspector that was when she left here to take a walk. And then for the next day: 'a.m. three calls.' I can make little of this. There is nothing at all after that."

"Yes, well, I'll give it to him. Of course, I know nothing about it all. But it seems very strange." She thought of the yellow sticker that Michael had mentioned to her, sick at the thought of the fastidious Agatha being faced with that kind of crudity. "Funny things have been going on here, Sister Agatha," she said. "I have heard about these yellow stickers."

"Oh yes," said Agatha, extreme repugnance appearing on her face. "All this was set in motion by them. Whoever wrote them has a lot to answer for. What I could not bring myself to address directly to the inspector was about them. Have you actually seen any of them, Frau Fabian?"

"Well, yes, I have. A couple."

"Then you will know how revolting they are. The ones that were clearly intended for us, placed here in our apartment by someone who must have had a key and have known when we were not here, had to do with . . . our friendship, Barbara's and mine. They implied in the nastiest possible language that our relationship was"—she paused and brought out the word as if it were in itself an obscenity—"a *lesbian* one."

"Oh dear," said Eleanor.

"Yes, well, I have told the inspector this. What I did not tell him was that Barbara herself had in the past had such a relationship. I knew about it, but of course, this kind of thing was no option for me, nor for her once she joined the sisterhood. She was my *sister* in every sense of the word," she said in a low voice. "And a part of my life." The pain burned in her eyes. Go ahead and cry, for God's sake, thought Eleanor.

As if she read her thoughts, Agatha said, "Do not think that my failure to cry for her means that I feel nothing. Some people do not cry. I never do." Eleanor felt tears in her own eyes.

"Please don't you cry," said Agatha sternly. "I just have to finish telling you this, and it's difficult enough as it is. The yellow stickers brought up all these old questions, Barbara's past and so on, and in the last few weeks, we had some . . . not very nice discussions of all of it. I suppose"—she turned away to the window again—"if the truth be told, Barbara would have liked . . .

such a relationship with me." She turned back to face Eleanor again. "A few weeks ago, I said to her, I will never discuss this again. And I knew"—she swallowed painfully—"that she was in some sort of agony in these last weeks, but I would not talk about it. You must tell the inspector that if anyone is responsible for Barbara's death, I am that person. And whatever connection she had with Hans Graf's death, it could only have been a tangential one, and I am responsible for that too. I let her down. Barbara did not murder Hans. Just tell the inspector all this, Frau Fabian."

"Very well, Sister Agatha, of course. But he will surely want to speak to you personally."

"Tomorrow, but not today. I want to go down now to the service and spend the rest of today here in silence and meditation. I am still a sister of the Lutheran church. It is more important for me to make peace with my God than to justify myself to the world."

"Oh yes, of course," said Eleanor. "Let's go down then. The service must have just started. Afterward I will talk immediately to the inspector."

"Thank you," said Agatha. And together they walked down the stairs to the chapel. The voices of the congregation were raised in the last verse of Luther's hymn as they entered, Christa accompanying valiantly on the piano.

And though they take our life
Goods, honor, children, wife

The nurses and other able-bodied people standing at the back parted to make way for Sister Agatha, who drew herself up to her full height and walked through the wheelchairs in the aisle to the front, where she took the last remaining place in the front pew, directly facing Pastor Pokorny. She stood with her head bowed while the last lines were sung.

These things shall vanish all
The city of God remaineth.

Eleanor stood at the back. There was no sign of the inspector. Surprised, she recognized, a few seats in front of her, the back of Franz's head. She hadn't expected that. He was sitting next to the Ritters. Schramm was getting up from his seat in the front row. At the lectern on the side, he began to read in his pompous way: *"Man that is born of woman has but a short time to live and is full of misery."* Irritated, Eleanor thought that not only was Frau Winkler a woman born of woman, but she was hardly full of misery, and she had lived a pretty long time. *"In the midst of life,"* Schramm read on, *"we are in death."* Eleanor inadvertently caught Michael's eye—he was also standing at the back, and he winked at her. She had an inappropriate desire to laugh. I'd better get out of here, she thought, and go and find the inspector. *"Thou knowest Lord the secrets of our heart,"* intoned Schramm as she edged out of the room.

Well yes, thought Eleanor. And the Lord is about the only one around here who does know them, unless the inspector is really making headway. Where might she find him now so that she could pass on to him the few secrets that she had managed to accumulate? No answer at his office door. It looked as if she would have to go back up into Melanchthon and see if he were there. Most people were in the chapel; it could be a bit eerie hunting around. Oh well, there wasn't much choice. She walked up the first flight of stairs, and her own footsteps seemed to echo loudly in the silence of the building.

3

Franz sat in the chapel, wedged between Frau Ritter and the wooden end of the pew. He felt exceedingly uncomfortable and regretted mightily not having resisted the expectation of Frau Ritter that he would accompany them to the service. He wasn't dressed for the occasion. The dark suits and black ties everywhere made him feel like some sort of street person who had stumbled in here by mistake. He hadn't taken a shower, he hadn't shaved, and he had never even set eyes on the old lady incarcerated in the coffin at the front. Meanwhile his own mother . . . No good thinking about that. He tried to concentrate. Oh Lord, now that Christa person was making her way to the lectern. He really didn't like listening to women reading in church. Well, of course, he hadn't heard anybody reading in church for some years, not since the last funeral he had gone to, probably. When was that? He couldn't remember. His head was aching. All that peppermint schnapps had probably done him no good. Still, it had made a pleasant interlude. But now he was stuck with sitting through this amateurish funeral service. That ass, Schramm, making like a clergyman—too much—and now what's-her-name reading. She bobbed her head about in an irritating way and put undue emphasis on certain words. But the words themselves caught his attention. Not the usual clichéd rubbish about rising from the dead and the Lord giving and taking away and so on. *"Who can find a virtuous woman? For her price is above rubies."* Who indeed? thought Franz. *"The heart of her husband can safely trust in her."* What's-her-name's voice had an unappealing quiver in it, but, oh yes, there was something appealing about the picture painted in this passage.

> *"She will do him good and not evil all the days of her life. She seeketh wool and flax, and worketh willingly with her hands."*

A lot to be said for that kind of woman, not that he'd ever really known one. Maybe the dead lady had been such a person. Obviously, someone had chosen this passage as a tribute, concentrating on her life and not on her death. Not a bad idea. Where was the passage from? He'd missed the beginning, thinking about something else.

> *"She looketh well to the ways of her household, and eateth not the bread of idleness."*

And doth not play around at being a detective while her husband languisheth in pain. Really, Eleanor had let him down in recent days. Where was she now? Here he was, wedged against this massively unattractive woman—suddenly a picture of the large Frau Huber came into his mind. She didn't seem to be here any more than Eleanor was.

"A woman that feareth the Lord, she shall be praised." Christa closed the Bible and her eyes. Bowing her head, she said, "May

the Lord add His blessing to the reading of His Word," just like some evangelical preacher. Franz was seized with an irresistible desire to get out of there. He muttered an excuse me to Frau Ritter and left, edging through the wheelchairs, aware that he was causing a bit of a commotion but wanting only to get out. The heady scent of flowers, combined with what seemed to him to be the faint odor of urine, made him feel quite sick.

As he left the room, he saw Michael standing near the door; and once outside, Michael popped up beside him. He said in a loud whisper, "Are you all right, Professor?"

"Yes, I'm all right now. Just couldn't take it in there any longer. You haven't seen my wife, have you?"

"Yes, she looked in here, but then she left too. By the way, did you get your money back?"

"I did not."

"Well, go and ask Gruber for an envelope with your name on it. Schramm told me he'd leave it there for you. He expected to get the original banknotes back from the inspector now that you'd decided to consider the matter closed."

"That is so," said Franz.

"I'd better get back in there then."

Franz went to Gruber's desk, asked him for the envelope, took it into the men's room, and counted the banknotes. They were all there—well, in fact he'd gained ten, because he had given one ten that day to the taxi driver. Schramm hadn't known that of course. This amused him. He thought of his fantasy last night of fleeing to Siracusa. Silly, the idea that because he had unexpected cash in his pocket he could just make a getaway. On the other hand, why shouldn't he? Nobody really needed him here, and the thought of sitting through a ghastly service like that for his own mother was too much. If there were mourning to be done for her, he'd prefer to do it alone.

Coming out of the men's room, he found himself going to the door of Frau Huber's apartment. He knocked on it and waited, with little idea of what he would say if she opened the door. First of all, there was no reaction to his knock, then he heard a voice, quite unlike the stentorian tones of Frau Huber. "Who's there?"

"Fabian," he said and waited.

The door opened slowly, and he found himself looking at a rather different Frau Huber. He had seen her before in outdoor clothes—in the hospital, wasn't it?—in these same outdoor clothes, the green loden coat and the hat with the little feather in the brim. But her face was different: the self-satisfied, confident look had gone, and in its place what looked to him like apprehension, even fear.

"Oh, it's you, Herr Professor," she said, and then, after a moment's hesitation, "Please come in."

She led him into her sitting room and took off her hat. He kept his eyes averted from the flowered couch and sat down quickly on a hard-backed chair. Two quite large suitcases stood by the door, strapped and seemingly ready to go.

"You are leaving?" he said. "I wondered why you were not at the service."

"Surely it isn't over yet?" She looked nervously at her watch.

"No, no, I left after a quarter of an hour. It was still in full swing, as it were. I was looking for my wife."

"Well"—a trace of her former acerbity returned—"you won't find her here."

"No, well, actually," he was surprised to hear himself say, "I believe I was looking for you."

"For me? Surely not. What have I done?"

"What have you done?" Franz was confused. "Nothing. I mean, you were kind to me. I wanted to see you, that's all."

At this, Frau Huber sat down herself on the flowered couch and burst into tears.

"Good heavens, Frau Huber, what is the matter?" He thought wildly of sitting beside her, putting his arm around her, trying to comfort her. But no, that was obviously a bad idea. "What is the matter? Are you leaving?"

She pulled out a handkerchief and blew her nose. Her face was blotchy now and, he supposed, objectively quite ugly, her eyes screwed up and her nose red, but somehow he felt a certain warmth for her. *A virtuous woman, her price is above rubies,* the line reverberated in his head.

"Yes," she said. "I'm leaving. And I want to be gone before the service is over. Perhaps you can help me. I don't want to see any of them ever again."

Franz felt great sympathy with this point of view.

"Yes, of course, I'll help you. Can I carry your suitcases?"

"Well, one of them anyway. That would be a help. There is supposed to be a car outside for me in five minutes. I want to leave when Gruber is on his toilet break and all the rest are in the chapel. Are they all there?"

"Well, of course, I can't really say. I don't know them all."

"Hofer," she said. "Dr. Hofer. Is he there?"

"I didn't see him."

"Well, you could help me by checking if the coast is clear in five minutes' time."

"Why are you leaving? Has Hofer upset you?"

"Upset me?" She gave a small bitter laugh. "Hofer is a snake."

"My feeling exactly," said Franz. "I never liked him when he attended my mother—he did so for years. But what has he done to you?"

"It's too long a story," said Frau Huber. "To put it in a nutshell, he leads people on to tell him things, and then he uses these against them. He has built up quite a lot of power in this place by that method."

"Oh dear," said Franz. "Why don't you tell the inspector this?"

"I don't want to be involved," she said. "That's why I'm leaving. The death of Sister Barbara was the last straw."

"Good heavens. Was he mixed up in that?"

"He's mixed up in everything. But he never actually dirties his hands. Other people do that. They'll never pin anything on him. That's why I'm leaving."

"But shouldn't you stay and be sure the truth is told?"

With a rather unpleasant laugh, Frau Huber put her hat back on her head, jabbed it with a hatpin, and said, "The truth, Herr Professor? That will never be told around here, and certainly not by me. I am in a vulnerable position here, you know. Whoever believes the"—she sniffed—"domestic staff?"

"Where are you going?"

"Taxi to the airport. And then away to somewhere no one will look for me, not that they will want to, of course."

"I would like to see you again," said Franz to his own surprise.

"You would?" she said, her eyes opening wide.

"Yes," he said, opening his jacket and taking the envelope with the seven hundred euros out of his inside pocket. "Take this. It will help you on your journey. But promise me that you'll let me know where you are." He handed her a card with his e-mail address on it. "You can track me down from any Internet café. And I won't divulge your whereabouts, if you don't divulge mine." He roared with laughter. "And now you'd better go or you'll miss Gruber's toilet break." He strode out of the room in a masterful way, feeling ridiculously pleased with himself.

In a half a minute, he was back. "Come along, Gruber just went in. Coast clear." He picked up the larger suitcase, trying to disguise the fact that he felt as if the weight were breaking his back. Frau Huber picked up the other with little effort, it seemed, and he hastened behind her to the entrance just as a taxi drew in. The taxi driver jumped out, put the suitcase in the trunk, and Frau Huber climbed into the backseat. Franz bowed politely as the taxi left, and she stared at him through the window, astonishment on her face.

Gruber was coming back to his post. "That taxi," said Franz," was for someone else. Would you be so kind as to call another one for me?"

He stood on the sidewalk outside the Haus im Wald. I don't want to go back in there, he thought. I am going to take a trip. My life will be over soon enough. He thought of little Herr Ritter's longing to fly away. Really, he said to himself, the only way to fly away is to fly away. He would take a flight to Milan that day—there were surely plenty of those from the airport in Vienna—and then just go south from there.

"Auf Wiedersehen, Herr Gruber," he said grandly, looking in through the front door. "If you see my wife, please tell her I've gone. She'll find a note in the apartment."

"First to the Zehenthofgassse in the nineteenth district," he said to the cabdriver. And then, "Auf Wiedersehen, Haus im Wald," he said aloud as the taxi pulled away.

"What was that, sir?" said the driver.

"Nothing," said Franz. "Just glad to get away."

"You're not a resident?" said the driver.

"I am not," said Franz firmly. "I most certainly am not."

4

Eleanor tried to tiptoe up the stairs, not liking the sound of her own footsteps. Then she heard the footsteps of someone else coming down the stairs toward her. Startled, she missed her own step and fell forward, saving herself from slithering down the staircase by clutching onto a stair with her hands and digging in her knees. Raising her head from this undignified kneeling position, she found herself looking into the mocking eyes of, inevitably, the Ancient Prince of Hell himself.

"And what are you doing there, Frau Fabian? Simulating the Stations of the Cross, perhaps, on your knees? There is an elevator, you know. You might be safer in there." Dr. Hofer held out a hand to her, and she scrambled up, mortified to see that she had torn her stockings and there was blood on her knees.

"You and your husband," he said, "do seem to get in the wars. Are you all right?"

"Perfectly," said Eleanor, feeling in fact quite shaken. "I only slipped." She had, of course, slipped because of a sudden fear at the oncoming footsteps. How stupid. Precisely a moment when one should stay cool. Trying to regain lost ground, she said, "You seem to be spending a lot of time going up and down these stairs yourself today, Dr. Hofer. Are you not going to the funeral?"

"I am. At this very moment. And you? You seem to be going in the wrong direction."

"I have to collect something in Christa's apartment," she said. "I'll be down."

"Do be careful on the stairs then," said Hofer and went on down. She stood for a while until she could hear his footsteps no longer. I'd better go and wipe this blood off my knees at least, she thought. Oh, how stupid. On the corridor of the third floor, however, she saw that the cord across the door of Graf's apartment had been moved. Could the inspector be in there? She listened at the door, pressing her ear against it. It opened suddenly, and she fell sideways into the room, almost losing her balance again, steadied by a man's hand under her elbow.

"Oh dear," she said. "I'm sorry. I was hoping you'd be in here."

"Listening at doors is a dangerous habit," said Büchner. "You'd better sit down."

She did and saw him looking her torn stockings, runs all the way down to the ankles, an ugly sight. "I slipped on the stairs, you see," she said breathlessly. "I was looking for you, and then Dr. Hofer appeared suddenly and gave me a shock."

"And why were you looking for me?"

"A few things cropped up that I thought you ought to know. I have to try to collect myself now and remember what they were. It's all been such a muddle this morning, and I've had hardly any sleep."

"Just keep calm and tell me." He smiled encouragingly. Such a nice man, she thought again.

"OK. Well, first of all, I had wanted to tell you that I saw Hofer going into Frau Hagen's apartment. He went in there when most people were going to the funeral. But now I've just seen him on the stairs, so he's not there now. 'Going to the funeral,' he said."

"Were you there?"

"Yes, briefly. I left to look for you."

"Was Frau Hagen there?"

"No, well, I didn't see her there. And there was another thing. You know the yellow-sticker business?"

"I do."

"Yes, of course, you do. Well, I was talking to Michael this morning, and he came out with a story of a yellow sticker given to Frau Hagen about Sister Barbara."

"Barbara?"

"Yes, I can't remember the exact rhyme—you know how they're all in rhyme. Well, this one had a rhyme on lush—that was Barbara, who used to drink, apparently—and crush, and it implied that Barbara had a crush on Frau Hagen ever since she kissed her. Well, 'kissed her' rhymed with 'sister,' so you never know how much this yellow-sticker person just makes up events that suit the rhyme. I suppose if you're working with 'sister,' then 'kissed her' is pretty well irresistible. Anyway, I thought I should tell you in case you hadn't heard of that one."

"No, I hadn't," said Büchner. "It does perhaps fill in a new line for me, Frau Fabian, and I thank you for your efforts. I'm sorry you were wounded in your efforts to find me." How nice he looked when he smiled, she thought.

"Oh, that's OK. The other odd thing was, Michael had actually seen this sticker because Dr. Hofer had showed it to him—ostensibly, according to Michael, because he thought it was funny. Well, I thought that was a bit much. I mean, first of all, it wasn't exactly funny in itself, as far as I was concerned, and spreading round this kind of rumor isn't funny at all. Michael himself said it was a piece of nonsense. These old people, he said—of course, we're all old people to him!—these old people are always kissing somebody, he said, very often him. He laughed. He's probably right about that."

"No doubt. Did he tell you anything else?"

"Yes, he was really upset about Barbara's death, I could tell that, she was always nice to him, apparently, visiting his grandma and so on, and he now felt very guilty because he'd told her about how you could get tranquilizers off the Internet, and he thought that might have contributed to the accident."

"Anything else?"

"Oh Lord, yes. I almost forgot about this. I also talked to Agatha this morning."

"You've had a busy morning."

"Yes, and she said she didn't want to talk to you today, she was going to the service and then needed to spend the day making peace with her God and all that. But I was to tell you—she was very adamant about this—that she and Barbara had had a very bad time lately because of these stickers accusing them of being lesbians, and maybe Barbara would actually have liked such a relationship with her, but she, Agatha, had refused to talk about it and had, if you like, emotionally deserted Barbara during these past weeks when she was clearly having a bad time, so she was, she claimed, herself responsible for Barbara's death, and insofar as Barbara had any responsibility for Graf's death, it was only tangential and she was responsible for that too." Eleanor came out with all this in a great rush, seeing that the inspector was beginning to pace the room. "And she gave me this for you. It is Barbara's diary, and there are two recent entries in it, one on Christmas Day and one on the day after."

Büchner stopped pacing and looked at them: "'16:45, did nothing.' That's odd."

"Yes, very odd, considering that this was when she went out for a walk. Agatha said be sure and tell you that four forty-five in the afternoon was the time she went out. So she did in fact do something then. She went out."

"And then 'a.m. three calls.' Did Agatha have a clue about what they were?"

"No."

"They ring a bell with me. Someone talked to me about three phone calls, but who? When? Must think about that."

"I don't want to hold you up," said Eleanor. "Is there anything I can do to help? Otherwise, I'll go and clean up my poor knees and so on."

"If you are not too badly hurt, the most useful thing you could do is go back down to the service and just see who's there and what happens."

"OK. I'm pretty much past caring what sort of impression I make. I look awful in any case." Büchner smiled absently, his mind no doubt on other things. "I'll go down there then. I should think the service must be more than half over."

"Thank you for your help," he said.

Eleanor felt absurdly pleased and went straight down to the service, holding the banister on the staircase going down. Her knees were still shaky; her shoulder was aching. All in all, she was a wreck. But she had a task, and Miss Eleanor Marple was going to do it.

The congregation, such as could get to their feet, were standing singing another hymn, another old familiar Lutheran hymn, and a joyous one at that. Pokorny, she could see, had avoided the traditional funeral hymns, and so here was the Haus im Wald, all thanking God *with hearts and hands and voices, who wondrous things hath done, in whom the world rejoices.* Christa was striking out the sturdy melody on the piano, and the pastor stood at the altar table, supporting himself only lightly with his hands on either side of the lectern, singing, his old tenor voice still strong enough to lead the congregation.

And keep us in his grace
And guide us when perplexed
And free us from all ills
In this world and the next.

Well, yes, thought Eleanor. A little guidance wouldn't come amiss. She was certainly mightily perplexed by all the bits of information she had accumulated just that day. Whoever had in fact killed Hans Graf? Surely Agatha was right, and Barbara could never have struck such a blow. And yet she had admitted responsibility, apparently. "Did nothing," she had written in her diary for four forty-five on that fateful day. Eleanor let her mind go blank and let the phrase sink in. *Did nothing* was at first sight by definition harmless. But suppose she had gone in there and found Graf still alive? Then *did nothing* would be a stupendous statement. A seeming sin of omission that instantly became a major sin of commission. That might well have driven someone like Barbara to drive into a tree. Eleanor almost ran out to express this thought to Büchner, but he had asked her to see who was here in the chapel and who was not here. She realized on looking around that Franz was no longer sitting with the Ritters. Where was he? Well, that was irrelevant. Hofer was there now. She looked across at him; Mephistopheles, singing heartily, *All praise and thanks to God / the Father now be given*—some nerve. Could he have done it? He did seem to her now to be the most villainous character in the Haus im Wald, with the possible exception of Frau Huber—whom she couldn't see at all. That was also extremely odd. You'd think her presence would be more or less required.

The congregation sat down at the end of the hymn. Pastor Pokorny looked quietly out at what must have been a sea of old lined faces and said, "Is there anyone among us who would like to speak a word in memory of our departed sister?" Eleanor could tell from the rather disturbed shuffle that went through the congregation that they were not used to this kind of request. Probably not done, she thought, in the services organized by Sister Agatha. There was quite a long silence, and then a collective gasp of surprise as Herr Ritter got to his feet, struggled past his wife, who seemed to try to dissuade him, and walked up to the front. Pastor Pokorny beamed at him, shook him by the hand, and said to the congregation, "Our sister, Frau Winkler, would rejoice in this moment."

Herr Ritter, his little voice gathering strength as he spoke, said, "My name is Samuel Finkelstein Ritter, born a Jew, baptized a Lutheran, believer in God. I am very, very sad at the passing of dear Frau Elfriede Winkler, who brought joy to all of us who knew her. She was not the only one in this congregation whose memory often went back some seventy years to that time when we, Austrians all, stayed alive, while great Lutherans like the Reverend Helmut Winkler gave their lives in an unequal struggle with an almighty evil. We do not now face such mighty challenges. But that does not mean that we should not face up to the smaller ones that surround us. Evil things are happening in the Haus im Wald today. We all know this. Let us stop whispering behind closed doors. If we open up to each other, we can surely combat the cruelty of gossip and innuendo that leads to great suffering and even to unnecessary death. The peaceful death of Frau Winkler stands in stark contrast to the tearing from life of our friend Hans Graf and our own much-loved Sister Barbara. May the open and generous and forgiving spirit of Frau Winkler prevail in this house. Today she finds her rest. We must pray also for the souls of the living and the dead who are not yet at peace."

He stood with bowed head, and a silence fell on the chapel. Eleanor saw that Dr. Hofer seemed to be trying to make his way to the exit, but two or three wheelchair occupants, their eyes fixed on the still figure of Herr Ritter, blocked his way. They did not budge as Herr Ritter went back to his seat, pausing as he went to shake hands with Sister Agatha.

Who would have thought it, she said exultantly to herself. That little sparrow of a man. Pastor Pokorny, still beaming, only said, "Amen." Then he opened his Bible and hardly even looking at the text, he began to recite the passage from Ecclesiastes that she had been waiting for—*"Remember now the Creator in the days of thy youth"*—a passage, Christa had said, more suitable for a man like Graf than for the little old woman, Frau Winkler. It seemed to be ringing out now for all the dead of the Haus im Wald. The poetry and the strong voice of the pastor held the congregation motionless in their seats—*"or ever the silver cord be loosed or the golden bowl broken, or the pitcher be broken at the fountain, or the wheel broken at the cistern. Then shall the dust return to the earth as it was: And the spirit shall return unto God who gave it."* Sister Agatha dropped her head into her hands, her proud shoulders stooping forward. Strange, thought Eleanor, that in this hour of collective mourning, the chief mourner for the violently dead Herr Graf simply wasn't there.

5

Of course, thought Büchner, standing as he often had at the window of the dead man's room. Of course, Frau Hagen had struck the blow that felled Hans Graf, that struck him down to die slowly, dripping bodily fluids onto his expensive carpet. Büchner looked down now at the silver-and-turquoise tiepin that he held in his hand. Why had Hofer, of all people, brought this pin and placed it on the carpet inside the fading silhouette of Graf's body? A last romantic request by Frau Hagen? She must have known that the game was up. Hardly an image suitable for Frau Hagen—say rather her drama was coming to an end, and he was the one who somehow had to bring down the curtain. If he had wanted to find Frau Hagen guilty, he could probably have done so sooner—at least two days ago when he had sat in this room quietly talking to her and she had played her Marschallin role. The Marschallin, she had said, had lost her young lover to youth; she had lost her old lover "to what, to whom?" she had cried, and then, "Are you going to find out, Herr Inspektor?" A theatrical plea, but surely there was real despair in it, the despair of someone who had destroyed her own happiness and could not explain it to herself. The fragments of conversation that he had heard half an hour ago had suggested that she blamed Hofer. But what had he promised her? What lies had he told her? Hofer was too clever to deal in direct lies. He passed on truths or half-truths in such a way that they could hurt, do damage, frighten, drive people to despair or worse. Was he, however, really to blame? Were not people themselves conniving in their own misery by allowing him to use their secrets instead of casting caution to the winds and letting their secrets come out? Hofer was perhaps, in Dr. Lessing's definition, a criminal who sees himself as stronger, cleverer than his fellow men, preying on society, manipulating it to his own ends; but, of this Büchner was sure, his was a crime that would not be prosecuted, and the one who struck the fatal blow would be the one in the dock. Ursula Hagen, once prima donna of the Vienna State Opera, pale, old, beautiful, accused of a crime of passion against a noted Viennese citizen in the Lutheran home for the elderly in the Vienna Woods—it would certainly appeal to the boulevard press. But what exactly had her motive been? He had essentially no proof that she had actually done it. And he did have a suicide note from Barbara claiming responsibility. Hofer, the sliding, slithering link between these various stories, would never tell the truth. He would have to talk to Frau Hagen. And that, he realized painfully, he simply did not want to do. How very much easier to accept Barbara's note, to take on board the easily described motive that Hofer had implied—an aging, frustrated lesbian, half in love with the lovely Frau Hagen, but locked in a domestic liaison with Sister Agatha, enraged at Graf for his involvement with both women, takes a swing at him with a cane and leaves him to die, then commits suicide with remorse. If he, Büchner, made nothing of the fact that the blow was struck some hours before Barbara went into his room, probably no one else would make anything of it either. Barbara was dead. Who would be the worse off for this simple closing of the case? Frau Hagen was hardly likely to make a career of murder in her fading life in the Haus im Wald. He could go home, leave behind this hotbed of jealousy and innuendo, and take a course in strength training to make sure he never landed in an old folks' home himself.

But he wasn't going to do that, was he? Pastor Pokorny was expecting him, the good man, to swing his sword on behalf of the true and the right. He laughed to himself. He had gone into this profession with some such picture of himself. He was still, even at his advanced age, prepared to swing his sword for the true and the right, if it was really clear what the true and the right was. Presenting a new nine-day sensation on a plate to the cheap newspapers did not seem to be a cause worth fighting for. And in any case, if the truth be told, he was half in love with the beautiful old Frau Hagen himself. This thought brought him to his senses. Get in there, Georg, he said aloud, and do your job. He took a last look at the tiepin, put it back down on the silhouette, and thought to himself, If I were a religious man, this gesture would be a prayer for mercy and for the soul of the departed Herr Graf. But I'm not. So good-bye, Graf, old man, the truth will out.

He locked the door behind him, smiling at the uselessness of this gesture too, and walked down the stairs to Frau Hagen's apartment. As he did so, the surprisingly sturdy voices of the congregation of old people wafted up through the stairwell:

Now thank we all our God
With hearts and hands and voices
Who wondrous things hath done.

Oh yes, thought Büchner, hasn't he just? Maybe he'll do one more and save me from what lies ahead. Fat chance! He knocked at the door.

It opened almost immediately. Frau Hagen stood there in a long black velvet robe, no jewelry, no rings on her hands, no makeup on her face. She held both hands out in a gesture of welcome and said, "I was expecting you, Herr Inspektor."

He walked in, and she put the chain across on the door. "I do not want us to be interrupted," she said. She gestured to the armchair in the living room. "Please sit down," she said and sat down herself on the chaise longue, putting her stockinged feet up on it and her head back on the pillow. Music was playing. This is, thought Büchner, basically too much. I should not let myself be hooked into this kind of atmosphere. But then again, how lovely she looks. She still knows how to drape herself charmingly on a chaise longue. A woman's voice was singing—of course, he thought, Ursula Hagen as the Marschallin. Too much.

"I still have an old-fashioned record player," she said, "so I can listen to my old recordings. Do you recognize that one, Herr Inspektor?"

"I can guess."

"Yes, of course." They listened in silence for a few moments, then she said, "Listen to this line, *I let him go and did not even kiss him*. That's the end of the first act, when the Marschallin realizes that her young lover has gone, gone forever from her." The needle began to scratch at the end of the record, a sound Büchner had not heard for years. "Could you, Herr Inspektor?" she asked.

He got up, put the arm back in its holder, and turned off the record player. He resisted saying, "The show's over," and sat down again in silence.

Frau Hagen, still with her eyes closed, said, "*I let him go and did not even kiss him*. This is what haunts me now. I did not think of saying good-bye. I had no idea it was the end, I was for the moment blind with rage, I snatched up the cane that always stood by the door, hit him with it, and swept out. I have, you see, Herr Inspektor, swept offstage in a rage many times in my life, and always the drama was back onstage the following evening. But not this time. It was all over. *I let him go and did not even kiss him.*"

There was a long silence. Finally Büchner said, "But why?"

Frau Hagen stood up. "I was jealous," she said and walked to the window. "I have stood here since, night after night, looking out at the snow and the cold moonlit sky. Sometimes a big black bird would fly across the face of the moon, or so it seemed. Have you watched the birds, Herr Inspektor? They haunt us here in the Haus im Wald. I would think of Hans and wish he could be at peace, not crisscrossing the moon in anger and sorrow."

"Frau Hagen," said Büchner coolly, "Hans Graf is dead, his body is lying in the police morgue. Are you telling me that you killed him?"

She drew in her breath sharply, turning from the window to face him. "I am telling you that I struck him in anger, in jealousy. Do you know jealousy, Herr Inspektor?"

Well, thought Büchner, no, not really. Oddly enough. "I think I can understand it," he said. "But no, I have never been madly jealous."

She laughed. "As I said recently to that American lady, perhaps you haven't loved enough. I loved Hans. And I knew it was my last love. It meant everything to me."

"So surely anything would have been better than losing him?"

"Oh, Herr Inspektor, that is a rational position. I adored Hans with all the passion of a last love, which—any poet who has lived long enough will tell you—is stronger by far than a first love. Compare the *Trilogy of Passion* that Goethe wrote in his seventies, for the young Ulrike von Levetzow, with the love songs he wrote as a young man."

She has a point, thought Büchner. But this is no time to be drawn into a literary discussion. "So what happened?" he asked firmly.

"It was a reciprocal love affair, a true romance that I had no right to expect anymore at my time of life. He felt very strongly about me too, I know that. I even know from our friend Hofer that he was taking Viagra to boost his sexual prowess. At first I took this as a sign of his feelings for me. But then Hofer implied to me that he had other things in mind too. He told me that he had once seen him kissing Michael. At first I didn't believe it, but I kept thinking of it; and then on Christmas Day, after we had drunk almost a whole bottle of wine, Hans mentioned, quite casually, that Michael had dropped in just before lunch and he had given him his Christmas tip. 'And did you kiss him?' I said. I just couldn't resist it. I expected him to deny it immediately, but he didn't. He said—I remember his words exactly and the way he looked at me—'There is something lovely about the young, of whatever sex.' He was looking at me in a certain way, almost mocking, I thought. I knew I looked old at that moment, you know, the way one does after drinking too much, and I was utterly enraged. I seized the cane from the stand by the door, hit him, and ran out."

"But, my dear Frau Hagen, why didn't you go back later when you calmed down and see what had happened?"

"I didn't calm down. I was too proud. I was still angry. I did not think I had hit him that hard, though I saw him stumble backward."

"And you just let the hours pass without even checking?

"First, I thought he would call me and say come back. Then I thought, well, his son will probably visit. Then I thought, perhaps I should take a look, and in the corridor, I saw Sister Barbara. She is—was—quite fond of me, and I thought she was a nice little woman, so I said I'd hit him in a rage and asked her not to say anything to anybody, but just to look in and see if he was all right. She said she would, and I didn't hear any more. I called Hofer in the evening, and he promised me he would check. As it turned out, though I didn't know it at the time, he didn't."

"So he knew you struck the fatal blow, and he protected you?"

"Protected?" Frau Hagen laughed. "Hofer thinks only of maximum protection for himself. Knowing such a thing about me gave him enormous power over me, and he could always find ways of using such power. This time, however, he chose the wrong victim. After we heard the reading of the will, he invited me for a glass of prosecco in the Café Sacher, as you undoubtedly know already, and I knew then that his picture of us as partners in crime was not going to suit me. I did not want his kind of protection."

"But, Frau Hagen, Hans Graf lived some hours after you hit him, you might have saved his life, rescued him."

"Barbara might have and didn't. I assumed he was all right. Why didn't she come and tell me? She didn't speak to me again. The next I heard of her, she was dead too. A nice little woman."

Perhaps it was the dismissive tone of this remark that hardened Büchner's heart. The nice little woman knew what Frau Hagen had done, and she "did nothing," as her diary stated, but took away the cane under her cloak and buried it in the snow. She let Graf die. To save this lovely lady? To avenge Agatha for past wrongs and present insults? Because her head was numbed and tranquilized? But not enough to save her from terrible remorse and an ugly death.

This whole thing, thought Büchner, will have to be blown wide open. Does Frau Hagen think I will save her?

"I am going to have to charge you with murder," he said.

She smiled. "Yes, I'm afraid you are. For a day or so, I thought we could avoid that. Hofer certainly thought so. Just keep a cool head, he said. No one can prove anything. But why should he avoid it all?"

"He will not be tried for murder."

"No, but the justice system is not too hard on crimes of passion, and surely not by an old lady tormented by suspicions of homoerotic behavior. This is Austria, after all. At my age, I have little to lose. He, on the other hand," she said with a steely vindictiveness that further hardened Büchner's heart, "has everything to lose."

Büchner took out his cell phone and called the local station. "Herr Wachtmeister," he said. "Please come to the Haus im Wald." Then he said, "I think you had better change your clothes, Frau Hagen, and call your lawyer."

"Thank you, Herr Inspektor," she said and, turning to go into the bedroom, "I do not need a lawyer."

No, thought Büchner, she probably does not. He would have liked to think she was taking this action to cut the Haus im Wald loose from the web of cruel innuendo in which it had been caught. But no. She had hit Graf in a fit of jealous rage, and she was about to strike Hofer in her naked desire for revenge. Pure emotions. He had often wished his own were purer. But then again . . .

After a few minutes, she came out in a long well-cut black cloth coat, her face beautifully made up, every hair in place, holding in her hands a pair of black kid gloves.

"You may tell Erich Graf, by the way," she said, "that there is no point in looking for the pair of gold cuff links that Hans left to Michael. I threw all the gold cuff links away." She flung out her right arm in a throwaway gesture and laughed quietly. Büchner saw that she was wearing her new silver-and-turquoise ring.

"Shall we go, Herr Inspektor?" she said and took his arm. Aware that he was blushing to the roots of his hair, he walked at her side out of the room, along the corridor, and down the stairs, thinking absurdly that he was glad he had put on a tie and a clean white shirt. Wheelchairs were emerging from the chapel, and the chorale from the end of Bach's "Kreuzstab" cantata was sounding through the lobby:

Come, Death, thou brother of sleep,
Come and lead me away.

"Not quite yet," said Frau Hagen, smiling and inclining her head regally toward the wheelchair occupants. "Not quite yet."

Epilogue

Eleanor sat in the late afternoon in the café of the Haus im Wald. She had a cup of coffee in front of her and was even thinking of having a piece of cake. How could she even think of cake on a day like this? Franz seemed to have disappeared into thin air. Frau Hagen had been escorted before her eyes to a police car and solemnly handed into it by a gallant Inspektor Büchner. Christa and the pastor had gone happily off to their respective apartments, seemingly triumphant at the fine farewell to Frau Winkler, and now here she was, obediently sitting in the café waiting for Franz's cousin Ingrid to come and talk about arrangements for Mother's funeral. Maybe after all she would get a piece of cake. What else could she do at this point? She walked up to the counter, thinking, could it really be only three days since she was eating chocolate cake when the then unknown Michael announced to the then-unknown Frau Hagen that a certain Herr Graf had passed away? Three days? Time was a strange thing.

"I'll have a piece of cake, please, Michael," she said.

"That's the way," said Michael, as cheerful as ever. "You deserve it."

"No doubt you say that to all the old ladies," she said. "But I do. I haven't had any lunch." And she hadn't. After the service had ended and she had finally extricated herself from the wheelchairs, the walkers, and the elderly souls walking with canes, she had heard Herr Gruber calling her name.

He had dropped his voice discreetly when she got through to him and said, "Your husband left in a taxi, Frau Fabian. He asked me to tell you he had left, and I should tell you, you would find a note in the apartment."

At first she hadn't taken this in. She had been more occupied with absorbing the stately departure of Frau Hagen under police escort. "What was going on there, Herr Gruber?" she asked.

"I cannot say," he said. "It is not my job."

"No, of course not," she interrupted and then asked him to repeat what her husband had said. The *he had left* now took on a more-than-casual tone. She had really wanted to talk to the inspector, but maybe that was now pointless if he had arrested Frau Hagen, unlikely though this seemed. Better check on what Franz was up to. She had got into her car and wearily stepped on the gas for the familiar road to the Zehenthofgasse. Looking down at her knees, she had been more appalled at the sight of her torn stockings and the congealed blood on her knees than at the thought of what might await her there. How was it that someone like Frau Hagen managed to make a stunning exit, in a police car no less, and she couldn't even cut a respectable figure at a funeral? The apartment in the Zehenthofgasse had looked much the same as always until she went into the little study and saw, first, that the portrait of Franz Joseph had been removed from the wall and, second, that Franz's suitcase was no longer there. On the desk was a short note to her (on a yellow sticker no less) saying that he was going to catch a plane, there was nothing much to say, she should go on back to New York, he would be in touch. Suddenly exhausted, she had lain down on the couch in the living room and fallen asleep, probably for a couple of hours, only to be awakened by the telephone. Franz, she had thought, and rushed to get it. But no, it was Ingrid, wanting to know what they were finally going to do about a funeral, the police wanted to return the body. I couldn't care less what you do with the body, she wanted to say, but she heard her voice saying, "I'm sorry you are having all this trouble, Ingrid. I'll be in the Haus im Wald in about an hour. I'll meet you in the café, and we can talk about it." She had got into the shower, changed her clothes—not that any of her clothes looked anything but rumpled at this stage, but who cared really, who was looking?

And now here she was, putting a forkful of chocolate cake into her mouth when a voice said, "Ah, Frau Fabian, I wanted to thank you for your help before I leave." And there was the lovely inspector. She struggled to swallow the chocolate cake in her mouth quickly and succeeded only in coughing and almost spluttering it all over the table.

"Oh, I'm sorry, Herr Inspektor. I didn't have any lunch, you know."

"That's all right," he said. "May I?" He pulled up a chair and sat down.

"I had a thought, you know," she said, "during the service, about the diary—but it's probably all too late by now."

"Never too late," he said. "What was it?"

"Well, it occurred to me that if Barbara had actually found Graf alive at four forty-five, then *doing nothing* would not be doing nothing, as it were, it would be doing something pretty terrible, namely, leaving him to die."

"That's a good piece of deduction," said Büchner. "And I think you're right."

Eleanor felt a great rush of joy. She smiled broadly, hoping that there was no chocolate cake stuck between her teeth. "I couldn't think of how to explain the phone calls the next day though."

"I think I can do that. I remembered afterward that the younger Herr Graf had had three phone calls on the morning after Christmas Day, and no one had answered when he picked up the phone. It may be that Barbara was somewhat desperately and belatedly trying to alert him to a problem with his father. And from what he said, this worked. He did make his way out to the Haus im Wald. But too late. His father was already dead."

"So," said Eleanor, "did then, in fact, Frau Hagen—" She stopped as Ingrid came up to the table. "Oh, Herr Inspektor, I believe you have met my husband's cousin."

"Indeed," said Büchner, standing up and bowing politely. "I am very sorry that the police have caused such a lot of trouble over the death of your aunt. Have you heard from the station?"

"Yes," said Ingrid coldly. "I am about to discuss funeral arrangements with my cousin-in-law."

Oh, you are, are you? thought Eleanor crossly.

The inspector held out his hand to her and said, in stiff school-English, "Good-bye then, Mrs. Fabian, and thank you.

I wish you and your husband a good trip back to the United States."

"Thank you," she said. "Auf Wiedersehen, Herr Inspektor."

So that's it, she thought blankly. It's over. She watched as he walked to the door, giving a wave to Michael on the way by.

"And now," said Ingrid, "perhaps we can finally sort out the matter of the funeral."

"Well, perhaps we can," said Eleanor, and then heard her voice add with the timbre of childish repartee, "and then again, perhaps we can't. Franz has gone, you see."

"Gone? What do you mean, gone?"

"Gone off. In a plane. What does this mean? I have no idea. About his mother, I suggest you check with Pastor Pokorny and my friend Christa—they seem to be the funeral experts around here. I have got other things to think about."

She picked up the plate with the chocolate cake and brushed the remnants into the garbage bin. Intending to sweep out of the room with some dignity, she found herself colliding with Herr Direktor Schramm.

"Ah, Frau Fabian," he said with a broad smile. "I'm just popping in to say good afternoon to the residents, as usual." He looked very pleased with himself. "Everything all right?"

"Just fine," she said. "Thank you."

As she left, she heard him saying cheerfully to Michael, "Everything under control?" and Michael replying equally cheerfully, "Oh yes, Herr Direktor, everything under control."

The last she heard before the café door slowly closed behind her was soft music from the radio and the clinking of coffee cups, the sounds that she had enjoyed so much at first in the Haus im Wald, several days and an eternity ago. She'd had about enough for now of the pleasures of old ladies.

"Auf Wiedersehen, Herr Gruber," she said on the way out of the front door. "Would you tell my friend, Frau Beck, that I had to leave? I'll be writing."

She turned the key in the gas, and the car jolted forward over the snow in the driveway, along the road, into the woods and away. She laughed as she drove too fast onto the autobahn, and then she started to sing.

Author's Note

If you take a walk through the Vienna Woods or the vineyards of Grinzing in winter, you will find the big black birds of this narrative, but you will not find the Haus im Wald, the House in the Woods. The characters and events described in the book are not based on real people or real happenings and the Haus im Wald is a purely fictional construct. Chief Inspector Georg Büchner of my equally fictional Viennese police force does bear the name of a historical figure, famous in nineteenth century German literature and politics. The inspector carries the legacy of his namesake with a tongue-in-cheek awareness of his own lesser place in history.

All translations from the German that crop up in this novel are my own.

Source materials for some of the concepts of Gestalt psychology discussed by Inspector Büchner and Dr. Lessing are to be found in:

Perls, Frederick, Ralph F.Hefferline, and Paul Goodman. *Gestalt Therapy*. New York: A Delta Book, 1951.
Perls, Fritz. *The Gestalt Approach & Eye Witness to Therapy*. Science and Behavior Books, Inc., 1973.

Friends, family members and professional colleagues have read and criticized drafts of this novel as it went along, and I am grateful to all of them for helping me launch the career of Inspector Büchner. Particular thanks for help in actively preparing the manuscript go to Gail Wiese and Jackie Ward for close reading and correcting of the early drafts. The final preparation and production of the book owe a lot to Janet Hulstrand, an editor of great talent and tact.

More and more people nowadays are living to a great age, some more successfully than others. This book salutes them all and is dedicated to the memory of two ninety-year-olds who lived and died in two very different places. They both faced up to that last daunting decade of life with great fortitude of mind and spirit. In their different ways, they gave me the idea for *A Place to Die*.

6882892R0

Made in the USA
Lexington, KY
29 September 2010